Nigel looked out a [barcode] n, calm and serene as an angel's heart. He glanced sideways at Mr. Perigord. "We should make landfall in the Cape within two days," he said.

Mr. Perigord nodded. "No small thanks to you. It takes a good flight magician to predict the weather so well, and to steer with it, not against it."

Nigel permitted himself a small smile at the praise, but whatever he was going to say got drowned in a shriek of magical sirens. At the same time, the ship faltered and trembled in a flutter of wood, a tinkle of glass, and a confusion of screams.

Nigel grabbed hold of the flight field as soon as his mage sense felt it falter, and threw all of his magical power into keeping the ship going, and keeping it steady.

"What the—" Mr. Perigord said, his pale lips forming the words that Nigel couldn't hear above the din.

At that moment, from either side of the glass wall that ran across the front of the flight room, dragons appeared— one blue, one red, one pale green, and yet another an indefinable shade of violet.

"Chinese dragons," Nigel said to himself—because he was not foolish enough to think anyone else could possibly hear him.

And yet Mr. Perigord's voice echoed behind him. "Man your stations! Grab your powersticks!" he bellowed with certainty and command, loud enough to pierce the noise of the alarms.

The dragons flew closer, seemingly heedless of the danger. Suddenly, as if on command, they all flamed. A curtain of fire covered the glassed-in front of the room, blazing red and orange and gold and obscuring everything else from sight. . . .

ALSO BY SARAH HOYT

Soul of Fire
Heart of Light

HEART
and
SOUL

Sarah A. Hoyt

BANTAM SPECTRA

HEART AND SOUL
A Bantam Spectra Book / November 2008

Published by
Bantam Dell
A Division of Random House, Inc.
New York, New York

ISBN 978-0-553-58968-9

Printed in the United States of America
Published simultaneously in Canada

www.bantamdell.com

OPM 10 9 8 7 6 5 4 3 2 1

To my husband, Dan Hoyt. Always.

DEATH IN THE
DRAGON BOATS

Red Jade held her breath as her brother prepared to set fire to the paper boats and the hordes of carefully detailed paper dragons. She wanted to close her eyes and shut out the scene, but her will alone kept them open. Through the screen of her eyelashes, she saw Wen approach the altar upon which the funerary gifts for their father had been set. Above that, another altar held the tablets of their ancestors.

Red Jade had supervised and arranged it all. She had made her father's women cut and glue and color and gild for days, so that on the lower jade table there stood a palace in paper—the palace her family hadn't possessed in millennia. To the right of it stood row upon row of paper boats, minutely detailed, like the barges upon which Red Jade had spent her whole life. In the middle stood representations of the court—men and women meant to be her father's servants in the after-life: a coterie of pretty paper dolls for a harem, and a group of broad-shouldered male dolls for the hard tasks her father's spirit might want done, and to protect him from whatever evil he might encounter. On the left, in massed confusion, were perfect, miniature paper dragons. Herself, in dark red. Red Jade. And Wen in blue. For some reason, seeing them there, before the palace that would never be theirs, made the tears she refused to let fall join in obscuring her sight.

Her brother, whom she must now think of as the True Emperor of All Under Heaven—though their family had been in exile for many centuries and she doubted the present usurpers even knew of their existence—held the burning joss stick in his hand and dropped slowly to his knees.

Let him not fall, Red Jade prayed. She wasn't sure to whom, though it might have been to her father's spirit. Only she didn't know if her father cared, and she wished there was someone else she could appeal to. *Let Wen not fall,* she told herself, sternly, and felt a little more confident. It was insane to think she could keep Wen upright and within the bounds of proper behavior through the sheer power of her mind, but then . . . She always had, hadn't she? And she had hidden his addiction from their father as well.

When had she ever had anyone else to ask for help? So when she saw Wen's head start to bob forward, like the head of one overcome with sleep, she willed him to stay up, on his knees, facing forward.

Wen straightened. The joss stick swept left and right, setting all the pretty paper images aflame. And Red Jade fought against the sob climbing into her throat even as the sound of her father's concubines erupting into ritualistic screams deafened her mind. She would miss her father. She was afraid for Wen and her own future. But, in this moment, all had been done well, and Wen was behaving as he should.

She finally allowed her eyes to shut as Wen's voice mechanically recited the prayers that should set their father's soul free and make it secure in the ever-after.

Their father was dead. He'd been the Dragon Emperor, the True Emperor of All Under Heaven, the latest descendant of the ancient kings of China. Wen, his only son, must inherit. Because Wen was the right and proper heir. And because only Wen could protect his half-sister, the daughter of the long-dead, foreign-devil concubine.

She followed him to his room after the ceremony. It was her father's old room, in the main barge of their flotilla. Servants and courtiers prostrated themselves as Wen passed by, knocking their foreheads against the dusty floor, but he didn't seem to notice. Wen was tired and anxious. His eyes kept darting here and there, as though he had trouble focusing both sight and mind.

The men surrounding him—his father's advisers—probably knew as well as she did that he longed for his fix of opium, but they gave no indication of it. It was all "Excellency" this and "Milord" that as each competed with the other, asking boons on this, his first day in power. Repairs to this barge and additions to that one, and a promotion in the precedence of yet another.

All of them Wen ignored, walking just ahead, his eyes blindly seeking. But as the entourage prepared to follow him into his quarters, he spun around and clapped his dismissal. At the back of the group of followers, Red Jade stood waiting, not quite daring enter her newly powerful brother's room without his permission. For years she'd protected and helped him, but now he was the emperor and her ascendancy over him was gone.

Yet seeing her at the back, he smiled and motioned for her to approach, which she did, closing the door behind her.

"We're done now, Red Jade," he told her, his man's tones distorted into a child's whine. It was a voice that had only developed after he started smoking opium. "I've done what you wanted, and now I'm tired."

Part of Red Jade felt sorry for him. They were of an age, she and Wen, though Wen was the son of the first lady, their father's official wife. Red Jade was only the daughter of a concubine with red hair and blue eyes who had been stolen off a foreign carpetship.

And though Red Jade looked Chinese, with her long, smooth dark hair and black eyes, she knew her eyes had a blue sheen, and there was something to her features that wasn't quite right. She was also too tall.

Her father had teased her about it, telling her they'd never get her a husband. No man would want to look up at his lady.

The recollection that Zhang would be out there, prowling and planning to make her his, sent a shiver of fear up her spine, and made her catch her breath. "Not yet, Older Brother," she said. "We must be able to lift and move the Dragon Boats. I—" Lifting the Dragon Boats for the first time after the emperor's death and the new emperor's ascension was something only the emperor could do. After that, everyone could lift them and fly them. But that first time was the confirmation that the new emperor had the mandate of heaven.

He gave her one of the startlingly cunning looks that he could give—a sudden expression of knowledge that belied the normal dreamlike tone of his days. "You mean *you* must lift them."

His look was so like their father's that she bowed deeply and whispered, "I do not mean to take over your—"

"No," Wen said, and shook his head. "No, of course not. But let's not play games, Younger Sister. Not with each other. We both know that the opium interferes with flying the boats. It interferes with all magic. I would not risk my people." He turned abruptly toward a table that was set at the foot of his bed. Bed and table both were gilded, and inlaid heavily with semi-precious stones. They were very old and had come—centuries ago—from their ancestors' palace. Now they stood in uneasy contrast with the rest of the furniture, which ranged from heavy, foreign, mahogany furniture scavenged from carpetships to improvised pieces put together from flotsam and tatters.

The boxes, like the table, were made of fragrant woods and covered in gold leaf and jewels. Jade had seen them open before, when her father had searched for something. So she knew what they contained—papers and jewels, most of them magical and bequeathed to them by long-lost generations. Wen rummaged through the boxes as if he knew what he was looking for, and Jade held her tongue while he did so.

"Ah," he said at last. He held aloft a heavy signet ring, with a bright red stone, upon which were chiseled the characters for Power and Following. Jade, who'd never seen that ring, blinked at Wen.

"Father showed me all these boxes before he died," Wen said. "And he told me what each jewel and paper did—magically, as well as symbolically. This ring was worn by our father when his own father was incapable of ruling the Dragon Boats, in his final years of life. So our father wore the ring, and with it could command the Dragon Boats with the magic of the emperor and keep the magic of the emperor active so people could keep flying the Dragon Boats—even if the emperor himself was too weak to do it. He could also command all of the Imperial power. And it's magical, so it will stay on through the change into dragon and back again."

"But..." Red Jade said, stricken. "I am only a woman. And my mother—"

"Was a foreign devil, yes," Wen said, with unaccustomed dryness. "But, Jade, you've been doing half of Father's work for years—everything that didn't require Imperial magic. And now..." He shrugged. "I can be the emperor, or I can dream." He gestured toward his opium pipe on the small, rickety pine table near the gilded bed. "I'd prefer to dream."

Their eyes met for a moment. Jade had never truly discussed his addiction with him, because Wen would get defensive and change the subject. So he'd never before admitted the power his dreams held over him, and never so bluntly confessed that he cared for nothing else.

What did he mean to do? Did he mean to leave her in charge of the Dragon Boats while he ignored them?

Did he think that the Dragon Boats would accept the rulings of a woman, and a woman with foreign blood in her veins at that?

Zhang would take over. Zhang would . . . She felt her throat close. She couldn't tell her brother the disgust she felt for his second-in-command—once their father's second-in-command. Though he was of an old dragon dynasty, and powerful in magic and might, she didn't trust him. And she did not wish to be his wife.

But Wen was reclining upon his cushions and looked at her, mildly surprised, as though she had stayed much longer than he expected. He waved his hand. "Go, Sister. I am tired. I've had too much reality."

Jade bowed and walked backward—as she'd once done in their father's presence—till she was at the doors. These she opened, without turning around, and left, still bowing—making sure that everyone saw her bow, so they knew she respected her brother and valued his authority.

While the guards at the entrance of her brother's chambers closed the doors, she turned and walked away, linking her hands together as she did so. Her right hand covered her left, and she felt the red jewel on her finger. It felt cold and hard and powerful. The jewel with the power to make the boats fly.

But the jewel only worked if the emperor had power. Had Wen's opium dreams grounded the boats forever?

THE STRANGE DESTINY OF ENOCH JONES

Nigel Oldhall walked along the carpetship port's narrow cobblestoned passageways, between the deeper indentations of the carpetship docks. Above those square indentations, the carpets floated, just inches off the ground, tethered with strong ropes. And above the carpets, buildings of various sizes and shapes—the carpetships themselves—rose.

Nigel counted the various exotic flags—Turkish and Armenian, Russian and French. And he hoped he looked the part of a carpetship magician who'd been doing this for a very long time, and had no other expectations in life.

He was a tall, spare man with such perfectly chiseled features that he might have posed for one of the portraits of the angel with a sword depicted in the old stained-glass windows scattered throughout Europe during the early Middle Ages, the one who was supposed to guard the faithful against invading armies. Except that his features were just a little too spare, a little too strong, to truly look unmanly. As it was, he merely looked refined—an appearance that betrayed his noble origins.

Anywhere else but in a carpetship port, someone would have noted the contrast between his features and his well-worn suit; his heavy, almost military boots and the scarred travel bag on his shoulder. But here, he merely looked like a carpetship magician—that strange breed of men who went from port to port and from ship to ship, rarely lingering more than a few days in one place. More often than not, they were renegade noblemen, fugitives from justice or other such shady characters.

Nigel felt shady enough to fit the part. The gleaming pale hair he'd once worn tight-clipped to his head had been allowed to grow unkempt, so that he looked as though he'd fallen on hard times. His once-pale skin now sported the reddish tan of someone who lived too much in the sun and wind. His clothes—which once had been carefully tailored and made of the best fabrics money could buy—had been lost in the wilds of Africa. In their place, he'd acquired serviceable, slightly worn, secondhand clothes made of good material. These, too, had once been tailored, but not for him. They molded uneasily to the body his errant life had given him. The coat stretched tight across shoulders that had grown more muscular in the past year. And coat and waistcoat and shirt all hung loosely over a waist that his frequent, intense use of magic had made far slimmer than it ever had been before.

The carpetship port in Venice was built just outside the city, and it was rumored that all of it was balanced on stilts. Until it had been constructed a century ago, there had been no houses around it. Now it seemed impossible to imagine the carpetport without the bustling, busy multinational beehive at its feet.

In assigned docking spaces, over carefully laid cobbles, carpetships from every country fluttered. Bright-fringed, new carpets supported multistory pleasure ships. Frayed carpets supported tramp vessels that carried cut-rate European goods abroad. And there was everything in between, too—merchant ships, troop transports—each of them bustling with activity. And near the docking ramp of almost all, a blackboard stood, listing when the ship would be departing and for where, and what kind of personnel it needed.

Almost all of them, at the very top, advertised their need for a flight magician, because of the very nature of the breed. To begin with, all but a few flight magicians had to be of pure noble blood; lesser men hadn't the power to make the heavy constructions of wood and glass and metal sail upon the currents of air. This requirement eliminated the half-magicians and quarter-magicians—those by-blows of noblemen—who made the textile factories and the trains of England hum, producing the goods with which England flooded the world and held her empire.

Flight magicians were thus generally poor second sons of noble families that had squandered their fortunes on amusements, or bastard sons whose parents were both noble. Or young men who had committed one of those crimes for which even noblemen got punished. And very few of them flew the same ship on two voyages. Rather, they moved from ship to ship and from continent to continent, crisscrossing the globe like nomads, forever barred from their birthright. Which they were. Which Nigel was, too—if not forever, at least until his mission was done.

His name and everything about him had been arranged to fit with the role he'd chosen—the only role that would allow him to travel haphazardly all over the globe and to not attract attention. For months now, always moving and attracting no attention had been the twin goals of his existence, the only way he knew to stay ahead of those who, doubtlessly, were trying to capture him.

But this time, it was different. This time he had to go as far down into Africa as he could manage.

He knew no carpetship flew where he wanted to go, to the secret village atop a sacred mountain where the first avatar of mankind hid. But if he could just take a ship to a larger African city, he could always rent a small flying rug to make it from there on his own.

Once, the idea would have terrified him. Once, he would not have dreamed of going into Africa without an entourage of carriers, and without the comforts of civilization. Such a time was long past, and it seemed to Nigel that he had been a wholly different man then.

He scanned the tablets with an intent eye, almost not seeing the ships to which they were attached. He read *Cape Town* and a departure date of that day, then he looked up to see that the ship was British and a pleasure ship. Though not quite so upscale as that in which Nigel had traveled on his honeymoon, it was nonetheless three stories tall and newly built, looking like a small palace in wood and glass. Which, he thought to himself with a sigh, was good, since it usually meant that better food could be obtained than on the cargo carpetships, or those that carried penniless immigrants. And because flying the carpetships consumed energy and flesh from the magician's own body, food had become very important to Nigel.

Nigel bounded up the plank used by personnel and hailed the man at the top—an employee in the blue-and-white uniform of the carpetship: the *Indian Star*, as proclaimed by the letters embroidered on his cap. "I see you are in need of a flight magician."

The man gave him a quick once-over that seemed to take in both his refinement of features and his shabby clothes, and came to the conclusion that he was typical of his breed. "The captain is this way," the man said. And, turning without seeing if Nigel followed, he led him up a flight of stairs and through the maze of utilitarian tunnels that defined the carpetship's flight deck. At the end of one such narrow corridor, faced in unpainted wood, he knocked on a door.

Someone answered from within, and the man opened the door. "It's a flight magician, sir. Or he says he is." The words seemed to denote not so much a doubt of Nigel's words as a suspicion of all flight magicians as a class.

"Ah. Send him in, send him in," said a hearty voice from within.

The man stepped aside and Nigel entered a surprisingly well-lit and well-appointed room. It was as large as the library at his parents' estate, back in England, and the furnishings were much the same—well-built bookshelves in dark wood, and vast armchairs in which one could lose onself for hours. Closer at hand, there was a massive desk covered with papers, and at the desk sat a portly man with salt-and-pepper hair and a kindly expression.

He half rose as Nigel came into the room, and extended his hand. "Captain Portsmouth, of the *Indian Star,* from the Blue Yonder line."

"Enoch Jones," Nigel said, clasping the hand with a firm grasp. He opened his bag and retrieved his papers, which detailed his last ten jobs and the recommendations from his captains.

"Jones, eh?" the captain said, with a hint of amusement in his voice. "Original, at least. Our last three magicians were Smith."

Nigel kept his face impassive. Captain Portsmouth scanned the papers in his hand quickly. "Served on the *Light of the Orient,* did you?"

"Yes, sir," Nigel confirmed, recalling an upscale cruise carpetship that he had flown to India. A pleasant transport, with unusually nice personnel accommodations.

"Not on its last voyage, I take it?" the captain said. And then, with another quick look at Nigel, added, "No, since no one survived."

"Sir?" Nigel asked, in genuine confusion. Had disaster befallen the *Light of the Orient?* Though disasters happened and carpetships plunged down from the sky, it was so rare that all the papers carried news of it, and Nigel would have heard or read of it, wherever he was.

His genuine surprise earned him a sharp look from the captain. "Good God, man, haven't you heard?" He glanced at Nigel's papers again. "Well, you flew in it almost six months ago, didn't you? And last month you were in . . . America? Well, perhaps the news hadn't reached there yet, or perhaps the colonials didn't think it important enough to talk about."

"Sir, I am quite at a loss to—"

"The *Light of the Orient* was taken by pirates," the captain said, drily. "Those Chinese pirates in what they call the Dragon Boats. All passengers and crew alike were either killed or taken into who knows how degrading a captivity."

"I . . . I'm sorry." Nigel said, feeling faint. His mind scanned the memories of faces to which he could no longer set names. His young assistant, the deckhands . . . "All dead?"

"Or as good as." The captain took a look at Nigel's face and, reaching for a bottle of brandy, poured some into a glass. "Here, man. You look as white as a ghost. Three more ships have been taken like that in the last two months, but that one was the biggest and best known. Those Chinese devils are getting more and more daring—not that we have anything to fear from them. We are flying quite a different route, straight over the Mediterranean to North Africa, and then across Africa herself, to Cape Town. Not the sort of route haunted by Chinese pirates."

"No," Nigel said. "I imagine not." But he recalled how Peter had told him some confused tale about being followed by a Chinese dragon for months. And Peter had been carrying only one of the magical jewels that Nigel now bore.

It was all Nigel could do to resist checking to be sure they still rested in a flannel pouch beneath his loose shirt and waistcoat and coat. Instead he threw back the brandy, its caustic sweetness calming some of his panic, and told himself he would get the jewels to Africa safely. No one would intercept them.

The quest for these jewels—and the mission of returning them to their proper place as the eyes of the oldest avatar known to mankind—had distorted Nigel's life, ruined his marriage, and sent him careening around the world. But this was the last leg of that voyage, and once the jewels were out of his hands he could return to England and to his parents' estate, and resume again his place in the world. He could dispel his aged parents' fear that he had died. He could start anew.

The captain had looked at the papers again. He folded them briskly and handed them back. "They look well enough. You are hired. We depart almost immediately. The passengers are boarding as we speak, and I was afraid that we would have to delay. Can you set your things in your quarters and be ready to operate the ship in half an hour?"

"Of course, sir," Nigel said, taking the papers and putting them back in his bag, amid three changes of underclothing, his two spare shirts, and a lion's tail, ears and pelt, which he kept as a powerful fetish, since he, himself, had killed the beast to which they'd once belonged.

The captain rang a bell on his desk, and presently a sharp-featured little man opened the door. Without looking up, the captain said, "Take Mr. Jones to the flight magician quarters, if you please, Joseph."

The man led Nigel down a bifurcating corridor to

what felt like the south end of the flight deck, then threw open a door to a small but tidy room, with bed, desk, armchair and a small bookcase outfitted with a few books that—if Nigel's experience from other carpetships counted—would be what his predecessors had left behind. The furniture would all be attached to the floor, and the bookcase had strips of leather that went across the spine of the books to keep them in place when the air around the carpetship became turbulent.

Nigel put his bag on the bed and turned, to see that Joseph hadn't left, but instead stood in the open door, looking intently at him. When Nigel's gaze met his, the man managed to look at once disgusted and disdainful. "The flight deck is that way," he said, pointing. "Down this corridor then down the fifth corridor to the left, and all the way up that, till you come to the flight deck, which I trust you'll recognize as such?"

Surprised by the barely veiled hostility in the man's voice, Nigel blinked. "Yes, I'm sure I will. Thank you so much."

"And don't go putting on airs," the man added. "All you flight magicians might be lords in disguise, but I know your kind, and I know you're no more trustworthy than a snake. And no more worthy of respect. All the Mr. Smiths and Joneses who've ever served on this ship are always trying to make off with something— pens or paper, or anything at all they can sell. Our last Mr. Smith even tried to steal from the passengers' decks. That might happen in other ships, but I am the steward in charge of the personnel on this ship, and I'm serving you notice that it won't happen on my watch."

And before Nigel had time to recover his breath, let

alone answer, the man slammed the door, leaving Nigel alone with his thoughts.

He didn't doubt that most flight magicians were no better than petty thieves. Or, in fact, that most of them *were* petty thieves. By their very nature as men who felt dispossessed of their true inheritance, they did tend to be shifty.

But Nigel was not one of them. Just over nine months ago, Nigel had been the scion of one of the oldest and most respected noble houses in England. And he'd been sent upon a mission by the queen herself.

Many years before, Charlemagne had established his kingship and his power by sending an envoy to Africa to steal the jewels that formed the eyes of the oldest avatar of mankind. Those jewels—it was said—held all the magical power of the world. The man who bound them could bind the magic of Earth to himself and his descendants forever.

But the mission had only half succeeded. Charlemagne's man had brought back only one jewel, but that alone had been enough to make Charlemagne the ruler over all of Europe.

Alas, the great king had failed to count on human frailty. His power, thus acquired, had indeed passed on to his descendants and to them alone, but noblemen weren't any better at holding to the sanctity of the marriage bed than was any other man. Bastardy and poverty had meant that many of Charlemagne's descendants had mingled with the common populace till, by the nineteenth century, almost every European held some magic, and enough of them held sufficient magic to create new industries and fortunes. These new fortunes, in turn, undermined the nobility, and turned the whole world upside down.

Queen Victoria, alarmed by this degeneracy and the revolutions it engendered, had sent Nigel to Africa to search for the other jewel so she could bind the power to herself alone.

On the voyage, Nigel had come to doubt the right of European noblemen to rule the world, and become aware of the dangers the destruction removing both jewels from the shrine would bring. And so, while Nigel's friend Peter Farewell had headed for India to look for Soul of Fire, the jewel that Charlemagne had almost destroyed, Nigel had taken the other ruby—Heart of Light—and crisscrossed the world with it, staying just one step ahead of any magical detection, and of all who would want to possess the ruby.

But yesterday, Peter had given Nigel Soul of Fire—restored to its former power—and now both jewels rested in the pouch beneath Nigel's clothes.

By returning them to the avatar, Nigel would restore order to the world. Once the jewels were together and in their proper place, they would hide themselves and their village from prying eyes and minds.

Until then, Nigel must remain an anonymous member of that curious breed of vagabonds—carpetship flight magicians.

THE WAITING ENEMY

Red Jade saw Zhang before she lifted her eyes. Or rather, she sensed him, his hulking, broad-shouldered presence barring her way. Amid the various milling courtiers, only he stood squarely in her path.

He was a tall man, and though he was close to her father's age, he could still be said to be handsome. His dark hair showed very few white threads, and though he wore his beard closely shaven—unlike most men in the Dragon Boats—he let his moustaches grow long, framing his broad, sensuous lips. Jade had heard her father's women talk and giggle about him, claiming his dark eyes glowed like banked fires, but Jade could not see anything attractive in him.

She could not remember a time when she had not been afraid of Zhang. She remembered being very small—maybe two or three—and coming out of her mother's quarters to find Zhang in the hallway. She had instantly run back to the safety of her mother's arms, though she couldn't say what she'd thought Zhang might do to her. Surely even Zhang, arrogant as he was, wouldn't have dared to hurt the daughter of the True Emperor.

Since adolescence, Jade had found other reasons to dread the man. He looked at her with a covetous sort of hunger—the type of look she imagined a ravening tiger might bestow upon a juicy buffalo. It made her shiver and blush and look away. And, more often than not, this caused him to chuckle drily.

This danger, she knew, was more real than any she might have imagined as a toddler. Zhang was her father's second-in-command because he was the most noble of the Dragon Boat leaders. His family was descended from Jade's own family, many generations back. As such, he had royal blood in his veins, and was entitled to almost as much respect as Wen—and Jade, herself. If Jade's brother were to marry her off, whom else would he choose for a husband? Few of the landbound nobility even knew that Jade was their equal, let alone their superior, and most of them were descended from the interlopers and not proper noblemen of China at all. Not dragons. Not any kind of shapeshifters.

But Jade didn't want to marry Zhang, and now she made sure the look she gave him was full of a haughty chill. "Ah, Prince of the High Mountain," she said, addressing him by the title that his family had worn many centuries before.

"My lady," he said, bowing in the most correct way possible. But he didn't get out of her way and he straightened almost immediately, his eyes challenging her.

"Is there something you require of me?"

"Only to know when His Majesty, the True Emperor, intends to make the Dragon Boats fly. By tradition, he won't be fully in power till he does. Until then, it leaves things . . . in dispute."

Did Zhang intend to challenge Wen? Steeling herself, she said briskly, "His Majesty is tired. He's given me the ring and the power to fly the boats myself."

"You?" Zhang looked at Jade as though she had suddenly grown a second head.

"As his nearest in blood, I will be able to channel his power whenever he doesn't feel like exerting it."

"But . . ." Zhang looked like a man who had just had a rug pulled out from under him.

"Yes?"

"But . . . I'd talked to His Majesty your father, and I've . . . I meant to talk to your brother, too, but . . . I don't know if you . . ."

Surprised that Zhang could be so discomposed—Jade had never seen him in less than perfect control—she lifted her left hand with the oversized ring on it. "I hold the power of the True Emperor," she said, simply, even as her heart thumped hard in her chest and she wondered if Wen was in fact the True Emperor. If his magic, damaged as it was from opium, would be able to lift the Dragon Boats, even when channeled through her.

Zhang looked . . . worried. Which was odd, because if she and Wen couldn't make the boats fly, then Zhang would kill them both, and the power would devolve, naturally, upon him.

So what was worrying Zhang?

Looking up, she signaled, wordlessly, that she was

willing to listen to his words in private. Then she turned and walked purposely to a corner of the room where no one else stood. She heard his steps following her.

"It is about the Jewels of Power," he said, as soon as they were isolated enough that no one else would hear them. "The twin jewels." He spoke the words with reverence and so close to her face that his hot breath tickled her cheek. He smelled of ginger and garlic.

"What twin jewels?"

He sighed. "This is why I'd prefer to speak to His Majesty. Women are not told these things, nor are they supposed to enmesh themselves in the affairs of men."

Jade thought of Wen, who, by now, would be well lost in his opium dreams. He might have heard of the jewels—or not, considering that their father had never been very fond of Wen. If he'd told anyone secrets of state, he was far more likely to tell them to Jade. So instead of speaking, she simply raised her hand, with the ring on it.

Zhang made a sound like a pricked balloon. "There are two rubies of great power, upon which the whole power of the world rests. The whole magical power."

"Impossible," Jade said. "For if that were true, then none of us would have magic or the ability to use it."

Zhang made a sound that might have been a cough or a hastily swallowed put-down on the mental power of women. Having heard him deliver such opinions before, Jade suspected it was the latter. "I mean," he said in the tone of a master who is barely holding back from caning a disobedient pupil, "that the jewels anchor the power of the world. That without them, no one in our world would be able to hold magic. Beyond that..." He shrugged. "Many centuries ago, it is said the king of the foreign devils stole one of them and made the magic in it his own, so that magic would pass only to him and his descendants. Which is why the most magic in Europe goes only to a few families, and why European mages are much stronger than those in other lands—the Dragon Boat people excepted, of course."

"Ah, *a legend*," Jade said, managing to convey in those few words the disdain she felt for Zhang.

He recoiled as though slapped. And for a moment, as he looked up at her, his dark eyes burned with unmistakable hatred so strong that it shocked even her. But almost immediately he smoothed his expression into the vague, deferential gaze he usually gave her. "It is a legend with a lot of truth," he snapped. "The queen of the foreign devils, Queen Victoria"—he pronounced the name as an imprecation—"thinks so, too. She has sent envoys of her own to find the remaining jewel. I found out about it, with the foreseeing magic I command, and I have followed their exploits ever since. Even though they found the other jewel, they didn't give it to the queen. Instead, one of them took the new jewel and the other went in search of the old, spent jewel... which he found and healed somehow. Now one of the envoys has both jewels, and I know where he is headed. I had a vision that told me which carpetship he will be traveling on." Zhang's eyes burned with light, as if he were feverish. "We can intercept the ship. We can take the jewels."

"Why should we?" Jade asked, taken aback by the naked lust in the man's voice.

Zhang looked at her as if she had taken leave of her senses. "They are the most powerful jewels in the world. They contain power over all the magic on Earth. Whoever holds them can deny magic to everyone else by means of a simple ritual. Whoever holds them could rule the world."

Jade couldn't think of anything that Wen would want less. And if the rule of the world were to devolve upon her shoulders by default, then it was more burden than she needed.

"Your brother would truly be True Emperor of All Under Heaven," Zhang said.

"He *is* True Emperor of All Under Heaven," Jade snapped.

"In name, at least. But with this . . ." Zhang's voice dropped and slid, caressing like velvet. "With this, he could rule like your distant ancestors. He could take over the palace, and eject the interlopers."

At this, Jade paused. Getting back their proper place was something altogether different. Since the invaders had taken over the land of her ancestors, they'd lived like pariahs aboard the Dragon Boats. Most people thought them pirates, vagabonds, people of no account. To be able to recover their position and power was something that Jade could not turn down. In fact, it would be a sin against her ancestors to refuse.

And, a secret, almost unheard thought whispered, if she were to recover the throne of her ancestors, then she could find someone else to take over looking after Wen and she, herself, could choose a husband from amid all the noblemen in the kingdom. Not many might aspire to marry the daughter of a Dragon Boat pirate, but how many would vie for the sister of the Dragon Emperor?

"Ah," he said. "I see that you know your duty."

"Perhaps," she said, unwilling to concede anything. "But how are we to accomplish this daring feat? Yes, we've attacked carpetships before, but surely if this carpetship is carrying such a treasure as you describe, then it will have an armed escort. Are you suggesting that our Dragon Boats are enough to face the wrath of the devil-queen's army?"

"No escort," he said, making a dismissive gesture with his hand. "No armed men. This man who carries the jewels is no longer working for his queen, nor is he traveling with her permission. He is attempting to return the jewels to Africa."

"To Africa?" Jade said, in dismay, thinking of the distances they would have to fly to intercept such a carpetship. Not only that, but they would fly over many peopled lands, places where others were bound to see them. And with her magic being bound to the kingdom, she wasn't sure at all if it would work over foreign lands.

"Are you afraid that you can't fly the boats that far?" Zhang asked. "Perhaps we should ask His Majesty—"

"No," Jade said. His Majesty would probably not be much more use than an infant now. She thought hard. Her mother had told her, far back in childhood, that a good part of her magic was from the foreign-devil side of Jade's ancestry. Surely that would be enough to allow her to fly the Dragon Boats wherever she needed.

"Very well, then. How do we go about this?"

"I have drawn a map from my vision." From his sleeve, Zhang pulled a scroll which he opened, showing Jade where they were and where the carpetship would be when they reached it.

Jade looked at the vast expanse of undulating lines which she supposed signified the ocean in between and bit her lip, but said nothing. Then again, she'd never heard that Zhang had the gift of foresight. It was a rare, near-untamable power, one that was as prized as it was feared. But to draw this map of a future event, Zhang would have had to employ it. Why had Jade's father never told her of Zhang's power?

"So, milady, do you think you can make the boats fly?"

"I'm sure I can. By the power of my brother, the emperor." She glared at Zhang and swept past him, to the place where the emperor stood while making the prayer that caused the boats to fly. It was a place on the deck, just outside the emperor's quarters, looking out over the entire flotilla. "If you're sure we can take the carpetship?"

"That I am sure of. This ship is no stronger than the *Light of the Orient*. And your father and I took that easily just last month."

Jade did not dignify that with an answer. Instead, she stepped out onto the flat, polished deck. She could feel the courtiers assemble in a rough circle behind her, as they waited for her to make the boats fly.

She heard the conversations diminish from normal voices to whispers, and finally from whispers to a heavy silence. The news must have spread that she was using her brother's power. She could sense the doubt and confusion in all their minds. Those who knew of Wen's problem would doubt Wen's ability to wield any power, and those who didn't know of it would, of course, question Jade's ability to borrow that power.

Their doubt pricked at Jade's consciousness like thorns. In her mind, she said the prayer she'd heard her father say hundreds of times before, but nothing happened.

She folded her hands, her right hand covering the ring. Was she imagining it, or was the stone warm to her touch? She took a deep breath. Her father always said the prayer aloud. Perhaps she must do the same. But what if the prayer failed?

Jade choked back a laugh. It didn't matter. If Wen's power failed her, then neither of them would last long enough to worry about anything ever again. And the Dragon Boats would be Zhang's problem.

Taking a deep breath, she started reciting the prayer to the gods of wind and air, and to her ancestors. She begged them to take the Dragon Boats and bear them aloft, bend them to her commands.

After she finished, there was a long, expectant silence, then the whispers started again, behind her, in various tones of worry. Then, suddenly, the jewel caught fire. Warmth and light shone from it, displaying the bones of her fingers through her skin. She made a sound of surprise and removed her hand, and the red light of the jewel shone over the Dragon Boats. And then the boat rocked beneath her feet, rising slowly, like a bird taking wing.

With her ringed left hand, she pointed above and to

the west, in the direction the boats were to take. And, as one, they rose, bright and tattered under the sun—Dragon Boats with their elaborately carved prows, their multicolored sails, their shabby decks, their multitudes of gaudily dressed dragon lords.

Jade cast a triumphant look at Zhang. Was she mistaken, or did he look a little disappointed?

But he also looked excited. And greedy. They would raid at his command, but if he thought Jade would be confined to the women's quarters as she normally was when everything started, he was out of his mind.

The twin jewels, with their power, were too rich a prize for the ambitious Zhang. No, this was one raid Jade herself would take part in. Her father had taught her to fight as well as most men her age. And though he hadn't encouraged her to go to battle, she was as capable as most. More capable than Wen. She would put men's clothes on and join the fray.

Zhang could not be trusted out of her sight. And she had no intention of letting the Dragon Throne be stolen.

THIRD LADY

龙

Jade turned from the flying. Once the boats had lifted and been set on their course, the other Dragon Lords could make the adjustments necessary to the flight. The emperor—or his representative—was no longer needed. Her presence on deck wasn't required. And on this, the last day of her mourning for her father, the first day of her brother's reign, she wished to be alone, to seek the comforting solitude and familiarity of her quarters.

They were not on this boat. This boat was Wen's, and the domain of the male members of the family, their counselors and eventually their sons—though her father had produced no other son than Wen. And no other daughter than Jade. And whether Wen would ever produce sons . . .

Jade shied away from the thought. Her father, conscious of the frailty of his succession, had arranged Wen's marriage very early, when he was just fifteen. And when no children from this marriage ensued, he had given his son two more wives—the second wife a beautiful noblewoman of the Tiger Clan; and the third, a singsong girl of the Fox Clan, the youngest daughter of a minor fox nobleman. And though he showed more affection for Third Lady than for his first two wives, Wen's true love was still his opium dreams, and no son had so far made an appearance.

Jade took the plank at the back of her brother's boat, and stretched it across to the boat following so close behind that perfect timing was needed for the flying. There were indentations on both vessels for the plank. It might have looked like an unsteady bridge, but Jade—who had been used to these since earliest childhood—half ran, half danced across it to the boat that was the women's quarters.

She was removing the plank linking the two boats—because any sudden shift, however minute, was likely to splinter it—when she heard soft steps behind her. Turning, she saw Third Lady bowing to her.

Third Lady was beautiful—smaller than Jade and of a lithe, graceful build that went well with the triangular shape of her face and her slightly too large eyes. The whole made one think of a cat or perhaps of a fox—which of course was what Third Lady, whose real name was Precious Lotus, turned into. This perhaps lent a naturally cunning look to her eyes, but that look now seemed far more haunted than Jade was used to.

"Third Lady," Jade said, inclining her head slightly, but not bowing, because within the family her rank was superior to Wen's third lady, though not to his first one.

Third Lady bowed rapidly, and far more deeply than Jade, with the confusion of one who was so deep in thought and worry as to have forgotten the niceties of everyday interaction. "Oh," she said. Then again,

"Oh." And then in a rush, "I was waiting for you to return. I was hoping you might return soon, for I have a great need to speak with you." As she talked, she wrung both her slim, delicate hands together.

"Come to my rooms with me," Jade said. "If you would," was added as an afterthought.

Third Lady nodded and meekly followed in Jade's wake as she walked rapidly down the steps to the living quarters, and then down a long hallway whose floor had been painted a bright red and whose wooden walls showed the traces of careful paintings done upon them very long ago. Now the paintings were so faded that children's faces and, at the end of the hallway, the face of a wondrously beautiful woman seemed to peek from the gloom of nonexistence.

Jade opened the door and led Third Lady into the antechamber to her room. Her quarters were the best on the boat, the ones she suspected were normally reserved for the emperor's principal wife. In fact, she had once heard her father's principal surviving wife—she who had once been Second Lady—remonstrate with her father about giving Jade greater prestige than he gave his wives. The late emperor's dry response had been that none of his remaining women had ever given him a child, and so he would give what honor he pleased to the one daughter he did have.

Third Lady—and indeed, even Wen's first lady, who was of a retiring disposition—made no such demands. Instead she walked timidly into Jade's antechamber, which normally served her as a place to read and write letters. Since Jade had inherited her mother's effects—as well as what she suspected had been goods stolen from carpetships and given by her father as gifts to her mother—the room looked like no other in the Dragon Boats. There was a small desk in the corner, appointed with the quills the foreigners used to write, as well as the brushes that Jade used more frequently. Pulled up to the desk was a spindly chair, of the sort she was given to understand was much prized in England. Against the wall was a small bookcase with her mother's favorite novels, bound in now somewhat lusterless leather worn by long use and much reading. Jade's mother had taught her to read and speak English, and now, many years after her mother's death, Jade turned to the novels as her only way to recall her. In those novels she heard her mother's voice speaking the syllables she remembered.

A sofa, also of English manufacture, sat against the wall, draped over with a wildly embroidered Chinese cloth, showing dragons in flight. Jade remembered her mother embroidering that piece and could name all the dragons shown in it—herself and Wen, most prominently.

Now she turned away from the sofa with a sudden jerk, to avoid showing emotion. After the last few days of mourning and fear for Wen—and her own life—Jade was not prepared to think of her mother, not without the sting of tears inside her eyelids.

"Lady Jade," Third Lady said. There were many names that could with more propriety be used for Jade by her brother's wives, but every one of them—and the population of the Dragon Boats—called her Lady Jade. As her father's favorite child, allowed to remain unmarried even at such a late age as her early twenties, she had a separate position in the Dragon Boats.

And as the child her father often entrusted with diplomatic business and to whom he often confided his more daring plans, she was treated as a power in her own right.

That status was obvious now, as Third Lady gave her a shy look and an even shyer smile. "Lady Jade," the woman repeated, the smile belied by a nervous twitching at her lips. "I've come to talk to you about my lord...and..." She hesitated. "And about Zhang."

Jade merely inclined her head. She could not talk, or not freely. If she told Third Lady that she herself didn't like Zhang or that she was worried about Wen's feeble grasp on power, given his addiction, it would be either betraying the internal divisions in the power of the rulers of the Dragon Boats, or else giving her own brother up. She would do neither.

The formal gesture seemed to inflame Third Lady's nervousness. She stepped away, her naturally tiny feet appearing to dance a fast step, even though she didn't go very far. Jade knew that her sister-in-law's feet were not bound. Jade's father, like all the other Dragon Boat lords, would neither admit the practice of binding female feet in his household nor contract a spouse who had bound feet. The deformities such practice caused in the dragon form was enough to deter them. But Third Lady's feet were so small they looked like they should have been twice as large to support her—admittedly slim and small—body. Only the ease with which she moved them, nervously shuffling on the English carpet that covered the floor, was enough to show Jade that they were indeed natural feet.

"I come from the Fox Clan," Third Lady said.

"Though not from a very important family, and as the fifth girl in my father's house, I was sold very young to become a singsong girl."

Jade nodded. "My father told me," she said. This earned her a quick, startled look from Third Lady. "He told me almost everything," Jade said. She did not add that her father had discussed with Jade his decision to purchase Third Lady's contract from an entertainers' troupe that often was called in for Dragon Boat celebrations. Jade's father had decided to buy her contract and to acquire her because he often saw Wen looking at Third Lady. And Jade had encouraged him because she had noticed something that often evaded her father's notice—that Third Lady was looking back.

To this day, she noticed that, unlike Wen's first two wives, Third Lady seemed to devote most of her time to either attracting Wen's attention or to making him happy. And for this reason alone, she was Jade's favorite of all her remaining relatives, after Wen.

"I see," Third Lady said, and lowered her eyes, and looked upon the embroidered covering of the sofa as though it were the main cause of her visit here. She spoke, matter-of-factly, as if her voice were divorced from her eyes. "I don't wish to speak ill of someone who has your confidence, and I do not wish for you to misinterpret my interest in the matter. I have only one interest in this, and it is to ensure that my lord is protected and . . . and in command of that which is his."

"There will be no misinterpretation, Third Lady," Jade said, somewhat wearily. She knew that she'd kept herself too closed into her own impassive facade to serve as a buffer between the emperor and his court, and for that reason, few people knew her likes and dislikes and her unswerving loyalties. She realized that Third Lady was venturing but very lightly onto the thin ice of the politics of the Dragon Boats, and decided to help her. "You mentioned Zhang?"

To her surprise, Third Lady blushed and gave the impression of suppressing a sigh. "I beg your pardon," she said, humbly. "I did not mean to say anything about your betrothed."

"Betrothed?" Jade said. And something of her shock must have shown in her voice.

Now Third Lady's look indicated relief. "You're not betrothed?" She seemed to become, suddenly, dizzy or weak, and sat on the sofa with a quick, collapsing movement that gave the impression her legs had lost all their strength. "Oh. I was so scared. Because the rumor in the women's quarters—" She stopped, a hand covering her mouth, as if afraid she'd gone too far.

"Yes?"

A small startled sigh, as if in resignation at having to repeat rumors, and Third Lady continued, "The rumor in the women's quarters is that you, milady, were betrothed to Zhang by your father's dying wishes. That he wanted to arrange for you to have some protection after he was gone."

Jade shook her head. "If it were so, he would have told me," she said. And then, in a lower voice from which she could not keep a vibration of dread, "And I would have obeyed, but not with joy."

Third Lady lifted her face. It was triangular, with broad cheekbones tapering to a small chin, and tiny, heart-shaped lips accentuated by something—probably oil of almonds. Third Lady's slightly too large eyes looked at Jade with every appearance of querying her motives. As though seeing something in Jade's eyes that reassured her, she nodded. "Good, because I... You see, I have heard from my father. I might have been an unimportant daughter, but when I... when your brother took me as his third wife, my father, of course, wanted our clan..." She seemed to get lost within her own words and looked up at Jade, as though expecting her to help.

"You were an unimportant daughter, being the fifth born," Jade said. "But having married into the True Emperor's household, you are, of course an asset to him, and one he wishes to protect and enhance."

Third Lady made an inarticulate sound, somewhere between a gasp and a sigh, and nodded. "Yes, yes, you understand."

Jade nodded. She understood, indeed. It was the lot of the daughter to never be valued by herself, but always for what she could bring the family in either recognition or credit, which must come through her marriage.

"Well, my father, through his contacts..." Third Lady hesitated again. Jade understood the habits of survival in the Dragon Boats. The barges always traveled together, and all across them stretched families and servants and friends, all kin and dependents of one another. Jade imagined it might be very much the same thing at an emperor's court, except that, presumably, there would be nobles arriving from the provinces and more movement amid the familiar faces. Here, in the Dragon Boats, it was just the same faces year after year, century after century.

Oh, sometimes the other were-clans sent notes or gifts, but because the Dragon Boats were as outlawed in China as in the rest of the world, they had to tread very carefully indeed, which meant their "presence" at court and their tribute was no more than the occasional letter or information sent by a secret and hassled messenger.

In these circumstances, it was all the more important for Third Lady, one of the few strangers in the Dragon Boats and a mere third wife, to be very careful of whom she might offend. And if the target of her words was the all-powerful Prince of the High Mountain...

Jade decided to bridge the chasm between her sister-in-law's misgivings and her speech. She said, forcefully, and daring to guess, "Your father has heard of some treason of Zhang's?"

Third Lady ducked her head, as though half in fear of these words, but also in assent. "My father..." she said, and paused. "You know, milady, do you not, that the Fox Clan has emissaries and representatives, relatives and spies all over the world?"

It was Jade's turn to duck her head in assent. Her father had viewed this ability of the Fox Clan to live in foreign-devil lands, and to mingle with these creatures so patently inferior to the Chinese as something to be lamented. For that reason alone, Jade's father had told her that the Fox Clan must be considered inferior to all other clans.

But Jade, whose mother had been a foreign devil,

and who had learned one of the foreign-devil languages from childhood and been beguiled into the worlds of Austen and Sir Walter Scott, had a different view. She'd kept her opinion from her father—as she should—but she had thought to herself that perhaps this was an advantage to the Fox Clan.

And the fact that the foxes were mostly tricksters, thieves and beggars and often considered outside the realm of normal society couldn't be held against them, either. After all, when you have to live secretly, you have to survive in whatever way you can, and your natural advantages of shape-changing can then become added spurs to your secrecy and cunning.

"My father has spies in India," Third Lady said, gesturing in the direction of that great land that few among the Dragon Boats would know by name. "And there, he has followed..." Again, she paused, as though not sure that her interlocutor knew the whole story. "I trust that Lord Zhang has told you of the jewels that hold the whole power of the world?"

Jade started at that. She'd assumed that part of it to be a secret of state and well kept. "Who else knows of them?"

"No one. I do only because my father told me of them. They come from Africa, the great land to the south, where it is said that the first humans who could work magic lived. There, they found these two rubies and bound to them all the power of the Earth. There are several legends about them, my father says, and one claims that the gods themselves gave humans this power so that they might bind magic to this world. In other worlds..." She shrugged, daintily, her gesture a reminder of her having learned dance in her early role as an entertainer. "In other worlds, men have no magic at all and must survive by their cunning alone. But here, because we had the jewels and the avatar in which they fitted, everyone was born with a little bit of magic, and some with a lot."

"I know," Jade said, impatiently. "Zhang told me that a king of the foreign-devil continent bound to himself and his descendants all the magic in Europe, using one of the rubies. And that recently, the Queen of England was looking for the other ruby to do likewise, because meanwhile, through inheritance alone, most of the population of Europe is descended from that one king."

"Yes," Third Lady said, with that slight recoil, as though of fear, that she showed when Jade—or anyone—seemed far more knowledgeable. "The men who searched for the ruby found it, but came face-to-face with the avatar, which told them that to use the ruby in such a way would split the world wide, to al-low...to allow many more worlds to be birthed from this one, each with yet less magic than the last, till we were no more than a memory, a passing breeze in time and space. They recoiled from this, as they should, and their mission changed.

"One of them took the jewel and vowed to keep it free and unencumbered, until such a time as the other found the spent jewel and restored it. Then could the two jewels be returned to the avatar and—with the strength of those jewels—the avatar and the village that protects it could make itself invisible to evildoers once more."

"And these are the jewels that Zhang wants?" Jade asked, feeling a cold drop of ice trickle down her spine. She had known Zhang was ambitious. Indeed, ambitious and jealous of herself and Wen for having been born in a position above himself. But she had not thought him madly reckless about his own safety or that of the world. "He wants jewels that, if used, will destroy all of the universe? Or . . . or re-create it in such a way that it amounts to destruction?"

"I don't know," Third Lady said miserably. "Prince Zhang . . ." She cleared her throat. "That is, I think he believes what he wants to and he . . . ignores the rest."

Jade laughed, her high laughter quite out of keeping with the demeanor of women in the Dragon Boats. Her mother's laughter, floating wildly in this alien atmosphere. "You mean that Prince Zhang would gladly damn the Earth and all on it, provided it allowed him to gratify his ambition and to obtain power."

Third Lady blushed becomingly, a peach-colored haze on her flawless skin. She inclined her head but couldn't bring herself to repeat what Jade had said. "I believe," she said, "that he thinks we should not believe the words of foreign devils. Or perhaps the foreign devils with whom he is dealing haven't told him the whole truth."

"The foreign devils with whom . . ." Jade repeated, in shock.

Third Lady bowed, quickly, and straightened again. "That is what my father says. That Zhang has had discourse with foreign devils. While your father lay dying, and everyone at court was distracted and . . . and filled with other concerns, he took his dragon form, journeyed to India and tried to steal the one jewel that had been spent. He had talked with foreign devils, emissaries of the queen who rules the islands they call Britain. He arranged to give them the jewel. In exchange—" She stopped abruptly, spread her hands wide on her silk robes and bobbed a hasty bow. "In exchange, I know not what he wanted," she said, quickly, contriving to make her loss of courage seem like a quick plunge into a still lake. "But I fear it was nothing good."

Again, Jade allowed her laughter to ring out. "What he wanted is what he has always wanted, and it could not have been anything but to become the True Emperor of All Under Heaven. For you must know that he has always wished that he were my father's son and heir."

"Yes," Third Lady said. "Yes, and that's what scares me, my lady Jade, that he should want to displace my lord upon the throne and . . . and do him mischief." She spoke the last softly.

"You mean kill him?" Jade said. "Doubt not that is what he intends." She fell into her thoughts then, as though she had been plunged headfirst into a dark cave.

On the one hand there were Zhang's words: that if they stole the jewels—or rather possessed themselves of them, since as lords of the Dragon Court they could be held to own the whole Earth—they would be able to reclaim the throne her ancestors had lost so long ago. Less important to Zhang, at least, but standing foremost in Jade's mind, who had heard how weres were despised throughout the length and breadth of foreign lands, was the thought that if they recovered the Dragon Throne, they could change the lot of weres throughout the world.

For they were not despised in China alone. Even Jane Austen—who seemed to have a little more empathy and understanding than her compatriots—had made a couple of were siblings, Mary and Henry Crawford, the villains in *Mansfield Park*.

On the other hand, here was Third Lady's information which, if true, would mean that the jewels were, in fact, like insidious and beautiful poison, and should not be acquired—could not long be kept from their avatar without destroying the world and all in it.

This was, she supposed, the type of decision her father had to make his whole life. And perhaps that explained his lack of warmth to his own son, and the way he held himself apart from everyone else in his court. She had no more on either side than the opinion of someone who should be a trusted member of the court. If she was inclined to prefer Third Lady's opinion over Zhang's it was only because she valued Third Lady over Zhang. It meant nothing. Particularly since Third Lady got her information from her father, whom Jade didn't know at all.

Jade drummed her fingers atop the bookcase while she thought, but thought alone wasn't going to solve this dilemma. On the one hand, if Zhang was right, it would be the one chance her dynasty had waited for over the millennia, to regain all their power and influence.

On the other hand, if Zhang was betraying his kind and his emperor and seeking only power for himself, and furthermore, if what Third Lady said about the jewels was right, then to let Zhang proceed could lead to the clan's destruction.

From deep memory an image of her father came— his graying hair falling in a soft curtain to his shoulders, as he said, "In every great opportunity there is a great danger. Don't turn down the opportunity because of the danger."

She made a sound of frustration at her memory of her father. Third Lady looked up, startled.

"I will," Jade said, "take it under advisement. I will think about what you've told me, and contrive a plan." And to Third Lady's fearful gaze, she added, "I will not ignore your worry. I . . . I, too, care a great deal for our lord, the True Emperor of All Under Heaven."

Third Lady searched Jade's face as if to determine the veracity of her words. At last she nodded, as though satisfied. "Very well," she said, and bowed deeply. "I trust you, milady, to do what's best for the Dragon Boats and their sovereign."

"Of course," Jade said, and watched her sister-in-law withdraw, closing the door behind her. Then Jade walked through her front room into her bedroom proper, where a big mahogany bed that had been her mother's—though probably first captured from a carpetship—occupied almost all of the small cabin. The cabin was one of the exterior walls, with windows, and light bathed the bed and the bedspread.

Jade wanted nothing more than to lie down and shed the day—the grief of losing her father, her fears for Wen's rule. But she knew if she lay down, she would not rest. Her maid, waiting by the bed, bowed deeply to her, and Jade nodded her approval of the woman's coming to assist her out of the elaborate gown she'd worn for her father's obsequies, as well as help her unroll her long black hair from the elaborate hairstyle that held it up and away from her face.

She sat down, to allow her maid to unroll her hair from the little pillow around which it had been wound, while she tried to determine what to do. She could not allow Zhang to betray them, if such was what he intended.

But neither could she allow this opportunity to be lost because she was timorous.

At long last, as her maid hung up the heavy ceremonial robes and brought Jade one of the simpler shifts she was used to wearing, Jade thought—if not of a solution—of a way to keep an eye on things until she knew better what to do.

She must take part in the attack on the carpetship that carried the man who held the jewels. If the jewels were to be captured, she must be the one to hold them. Only then could she be sure that they wouldn't be illused.

And once she held them, she would use her own magic to see how far they resonated with the world and whether it might be true that they held the universe. If not, then she would use them to restore her family fortunes. If so, then she would restore them to their shrine, and hope for a boon in return. In either case, she would do her best to keep them out of Zhang's hands.

AN UNLIKELY ATTACK

龙

"*Steady as she goes, Mr. Jones,*" Joseph Perigord, the first mate aboard the *Indian Star,* told Nigel. And unbent himself enough to smile dazzlingly at the carpet-ship flight magician.

Nigel nodded back, but didn't smile. He knew that in the two weeks he'd been flying the *Indian Star* he'd impressed the first mate and steward of the crew.

He knew it because he'd accidentally heard Mr. Perigord tell the captain so. *Sober, clean and honest. Not like other flight magicians we've taken aboard,* he had said, while Nigel, waiting outside the captain's office, clutching the day's flight plans for approval, heard it through the slightly open door.

The first mate had gone on to suggest that they should do whatever it took to entice Nigel to stay aboard and continue flying for them. He'd talked about being weary of the constantly changing flight magicians, and most of them probably wanted criminals, too.

And though Nigel understood the man's sentiments, he'd felt the slight warmth of the jewels in the flannel pouch at his midriff, beneath his clothing. Much as he hated to disappoint both captain and first mate, much as the *Indian Star* seemed like a proper ship and properly run, he would not be staying aboard. He must deliver the jewels to Africa, to the village that had, from time immemorial, protected the rubies.

A slight, reminiscent smile twisted his lips at the thought of again seeing Kitwana, the heir to the village's chief, and Emily, who had once been Nigel's wife and was now Kitwana's. Then he all but sighed at the idea that he might never again find a wife. As far as polite society in England was concerned, he was a free man. Emily, having remained behind in her African village, would prefer—she said—to be thought dead by the family who hadn't appreciated her, and the friends who would be shocked at her choice. As far as his conscience was concerned, he was a free man as well. His marriage to Emily had never been consummated, and what should have been conjugal love had turned out to be no more than his wish to protect her and her wish to escape her circumstances.

But to be free to marry and to marry again were two completely different things. He'd thought he loved Emily, but now he realized he'd never loved any woman at all. Developed fixations on them, surely. Admired them greatly, undoubtedly. But though he might turn to regard them as they passed, he didn't think that any woman—not one, not even the courtesans that his brother, Carew, had insisted on introducing to his notice in Cambridge—had ever been indispensable to him. He wanted . . . he wanted that feeling he saw shine in Emily's and Kitwana's gaze when they looked at each other. He wanted the feeling that made his friend Peter look soft and gentle as he spoke of some Anglo-Indian beauty named Sofie.

And that, at long last—having traveled half the world over in the last six months, and seen women of every race and description—he'd not found anyone who might make him feel that way.

No, he would go back home afterward, to his parents. He would like to imagine they would be happy to see him, but he knew better. No matter how much they loved him, he could never replace their firstborn, Carew, in their heart and soul. They would wait for him till the day they died, and it wasn't possible for Nigel to tell them that Carew had died—a deserved death—in a far off savannah of a land they would never visit.

So he would go back and establish his routine as his father's heir, but without ever openly telling his parents he was the heir. He would do accounts, and he would look after his parents' magical responsibilities, keeping storms from the Oldhall domains, healing the cattle and the tenants, and whatever else he could to protect the little parcel of the world with which he'd been entrusted. And he hoped, maybe at some point, he would achieve contentment, since he could not achieve the happiness of love.

With a shrug for that wild passion he would never experience, he turned his attention to his charts and maps. The flight deck was on the lower level of the carpetship—next to the crew quarters and the kitchens, and the various other appurtenances necessary to make the voyage as painless and seamless for the passengers

as possible. Unlike the well-appointed, fashionably furnished rooms above—at least in the top deck, where
the first-class passengers lodged—this floor had an almost spartan beauty. Not uncomfortable, but furnished
only with the bare minimum. And the rooms could resemble the cells of a particularly demanding monasti-
cal order.

But the flight deck, as Nigel had learned through his
several travels, was undoubtedly the most wonderful
room in any ship. It ran across the entire front of the
vessel, on the bottom level, and was entirely glassed in,
so that from it the flight crew commanded a complete
view of the sky all around, save for one side. That side
was covered by seeing spells, run by one of the more
experienced magicians on board, and the result projected—like a miniature landscape—on the center of
the work table, on which was piled—as well—various
maps, charts and navigation implements. On the *Indian
Star,* the table was warm honey oak, which shone like
polished gold in the early-morning sun.

There were chairs around that table, where the various crew members met to discuss the charts and the
flight plans drawn by the flight magician and approved
by the captain. The flight magician's chair was not
there, however. Instead, it sat apart, like a throne, with
its back to the table and its front to the glass and the
wide-open skies. This was because, despite carefully
filed flight plans, it was not unusual to meet with some
disturbance.

Sometimes, small, local carpetships or—the bane
of every carpetship magician—flying rugs, would dart
right across the path of the carpetship. And sometimes,

some magical event—battle or mass healing or even sometimes building-shoring-up spells—taking place beneath the flight path would cause the carpetship to tremble and falter. There were even natural magical zones—ancient places of worship or of some great working—that caused the carpetship to lose altitude. Most of those were marked, but when flying, as the *Indian Star* was now, over the coast of Africa, not all places were as carefully charted as the flight magician would hope them to be.

When faced with the unexpected in such a way, it was up to the flight magician to make sudden corrections and sudden improvements—to turn abruptly, or to use his magic to maintain level flight.

Nigel, early awakened, looked out at the bright pink sky of palest dawn, calm and serene as an angel's heart, and smiled. He took a sip of his morning hot chocolate—in a mug that fit into an indentation on the arm of his chair, so that it shouldn't tilt even in turbulence—and permitted himself to look sideways at Mr. Perigord, who stood beside his chair, looking out at the same landscape. "We should make landfall in the Cape within two days," he said. "Those tailwinds past Guinea surely helped."

Mr. Perigord nodded. "They did, but it takes a good flight magician to predict the weather as well, and to steer with it, not against it. Why, on our last voyage, from Africa to India, we were almost three days late because we were fighting the winds, and Mr. Smith, as he called himself, could do no more than bleat that he was no weather magician."

Nigel permitted himself a small smile and nod, but

he didn't enlighten Mr. Perigord. It was not up to him to tell the man that, of course, he knew how to predict the weather. It was a necessary ability in the son of a man with an estate to tend. Without predicting and controlling the weather, you could lose all the crops in the field before your tenants had the time to bring them in.

"I wonder, sir, if perhaps—" Mr. Perigord started.

Whatever he was going to say got drowned in a shriek of magical sirens. The alarm was so activated that it echoed in everyone's ears as though it were being sounded just beside them, a claxon of screaming fury. At the same time, or perhaps just before it, the ship faltered and trembled, in a flutter of wood, a tinkle of glass and a confusion of screams.

Nigel grabbed hold of the flight field as soon as his mage sense felt it falter, and before, even, the physical tremble communicated itself through the soles of his feet. He gritted his teeth and threw all of his—not inconsiderable, since he was a direct descendant of Charlemagne on both sides of his ancestry—magical power at keeping the ship going, and keeping it steady.

And yet, even though the carpetship stopped trembling, the sirens still sounded, screaming fury all around them. If it were a mere disturbance of the flight field, then stabilizing it would stop the alarms. If the alarms still went on, there was more to it.

Nigel looked at Mr. Perigord, to find the man drawn and white-faced, staring back at him in as much confusion as Nigel himself felt. Because the sirens made them all deaf, he pronounced, with exaggerated care so the man could read his lips, "I wonder what could be causing the alarm?"

Mr. Perigord shook his head—but whether he was unable to hear what Nigel was saying, or unable to answer, Nigel did not know. Nigel, in turn, thinking of all the confusion that could be caused by the approach of a magical flying creature—say, a dragon—and knowing that not all such creatures were friendly, reached into the box he kept beside his flight chair for the lion's tail and ears. The magic in the powerful fetishes, imbued with Masai incantations, allowed Nigel to envelop the whole ship in a protective field that would repel any magical interference. And yet, the alarms went on.

Now, joining the alarms, came screams. Unlike the first screams Nigel had heard when the ship fluttered—which came a bit from all over the carpetship—these came from the upper levels only. The levels in which the passengers lodged.

"What the—" Mr. Perigord said, his pale lips forming the words, which Nigel couldn't hear above the din. He turned, clearly with every intention of heading for the wrought-iron spiral staircase at the back of the room.

At that moment, from either side of the glass wall that ran across the front of the flight room, dragons appeared—one blue, one red, one pale green and yet another an indefinable shade of violet. It took Nigel a moment to recognize them as dragons because they were nothing like the dragon that his friend Peter turned into. Peter's dragon wouldn't have been out of place gracing the prow of a Viking ship, but these dragons were mere zigzags of color, like lightning bolts given animated form—flying serpents with no visible wings.

"Chinese dragons," Nigel said to himself—because he was not foolish enough to think anyone else could possibly hear him.

And yet Mr. Perigord's voice echoed behind him: "Man your stations. Grab your powersticks," he bellowed with certainty and command, loud enough to pierce the noise of the alarms.

The other men in the flight room—the minor magicians, the map experts, others who allowed Nigel to do his job, ran to the rack at the back. These were strapped with Smith-Henry powersticks, charged with enough loads to conquer most of a small country. They took positions on either side of Nigel's chair, in classic style, one knee on the floor, bracing the powerstick for a possible shot. Nigel wished that, as aboard the *Victoria Invicta* on his trip to Africa, there had been a group of Royal Were-Hunters aboard. But there weren't. And most powersticks aboard carpetships were not spelled against weres, the dangers of finding weres on most routes being vanishingly small—and from Europe to Africa, nonexistent.

The dragons flew closer, seemingly heedless of the danger. Suddenly, as if on command, they all flamed. A curtain of flame covered the glassed-in front of the room, blazing red and orange and gold and obscuring everything else from sight. Nigel sat, holding his fetishes and refusing to get up, while he gritted his teeth and kept the ship flying, despite all the disturbance.

He was fairly sure that the men on either side of him discharged their powersticks, but the magical charges got lost in the dragon flame. The glass pinged, turned red hot and melted. A blast of fiery air, as from an open furnace, burst in on Nigel and the others. For a moment, he felt as if he were breathing heat. Not air. Not oxygen. Just heat. His hair seemed to curl away from his face in the blistering heat. His eyes teared.

The flame ceased as soon as it had started. Blinking away the tears that the heated air had brought to his eyes, Nigel found himself staring at the blue sky and surrounded by howling winds. The dragons had moved to the side, and in front of the ship as far as the eye could see was a flotilla of Chinese ships. There were barges and junks and rafts, such as he'd seen only once, during a visit to Hong Kong a few months back. He'd seen whole multitudes of them, seemingly crowding every possible river, had been told that many families lived their entire lives on water that way.

But there was only one set of such barges that flew—those of the feared Chinese pirates. The very same who had destroyed the *Light of the Orient*. Until just a few years ago they'd been thought legends. But then Englishmen flying in China had started being assaulted and learned they'd long been a scourge on the locals. And then they'd started striking all along the Asian coast. And now here.

Nigel swallowed, and concentrated on flying the ship—a superhuman task now that the magic of his auxiliaries had been withdrawn.

"Steady, Mr. Jones," Mr. Perigord told him in that

tone that pierced through all ambient noise. "Do not try to be a hero. We need you to keep the ship flying."

Nigel had no intention of being a hero. Not only was he aware that the carpetship and every life on it was dependent on him, he was also aware that his mission—returning the jewels to their avatar and their guardians—was more important than saving the property of his employers, or even their passengers.

But it was hard to stay on course and to think only of flying the ship as more and more junks—painted with eyes in their front and outfitted with wildly multicolored sails—boarded the carpetship by throwing ropes that magically attached to the front of the ship. Across the ropes, Chinese pirates came dancing.

While Nigel maintained course and altitude, battles raged around him. Whatever these pirates had in the way of magic must be very powerful, indeed. He saw several men withstand discharges from magical powersticks, and at close range, too. Unless, of course, every one of these attackers was a were. For weres, it took specially charged powersticks to kill them. The idea of that many magical shape-changers was almost impossible, but it seemed to be the only explanation.

Nigel heard screams and smelled blood, and was dimly aware of the hollow sound that could only be a head hitting the polished wood floor, after being severed from its body by one of the vicious sabers in the hands of the boarders.

None of this made sense. It was like a dream, in which the impossible happens despite the sleeper's attempts to wake or to set the record straight. In carpetships that were attacked—though Nigel had never been in one, he'd read about them often enough—the pirates usually went for the top decks and made off with whatever they could get before the crew—which always had a certain number of men with military background—came after them.

They stole jewels and clothes, furniture and some-times women. They did not attack the flight-deck crew. And what were Chinese pirates doing this far from Chinese shores anyway?

As Nigel thought this, a man came running toward him, holding in his hand what looked like a vicious saber. The sight of a man running full tilt at the flight magician, without whom the entire carpetship would collapse, was incongruous enough. But the man was stark naked, his salt-and-pepper hair and his amaz-ingly thin and long moustaches his only covering.

Nigel half stood, preparing for the onslaught. With a desperate, almost instinctive wish for a weapon, he gestured with the lion tail. A saber came flying through the air, the handle toward his hand. Nigel grasped it in the same hand as the lion tail.

His would-be attacker stopped a step from Nigel, saber raised. He looked at Nigel as though Nigel was not at all what he expected. "The jewels," he screamed, in English spoken with the accent of some-one used to a tonal language. "Give me the Jewels of Power."

"Never," Nigel answered, before he quite knew what he was going to do. While part of his mind still firmly grasped the flight field, making sure the carpet-ship stayed in the air, he lifted the saber to parry the assault, just as his attacker's saber came descending upon his head. The blades met, echoing in a clash of metal.

Through Nigel's head, almost as if it were a story he had heard long ago, went the memory of his flight some months ago in which the only amusement to while away the time when he'd not been on duty on deck, had been to learn saber fighting from a colleague and underling of his, a magician from Morocco who plied his rounded scimitar with vicious ability.

Now Nigel was glad of that training as he parried and counterattacked and parried again. Not that he could fight like the Chinese pirate. But he fought like a man desperate not to dishonor himself, not to lose the most important objects in the world. He could see in the pirate's expression the bewildered look of the expert meeting a confused but determined opponent, who might do anything at all. *There is nothing as scary as the armed amateur,* he remembered his sword master in England saying.

He was conscious of a couple of slashes, one to his shoulder and one to the front of his body. He assumed that they had not touched his skin, as he felt no pain. He couldn't understand why the ground was growing slick under his feet, unless he was sweating so much that the sweat pouring out of him was making his footing unsteady. But it could not be that, he thought, as he stepped backwards to avoid a series of savage slashes from his opponent.

If he was sweating that much, surely his eyes would sting, and they did not. They felt only slightly unfocused, as though someone were projecting a vision, but not very well, so the edges faded and distance didn't seem to matter.

His opponent swept the saber from side to side, and only Nigel's quick reflexes prevented his being disemboweled. He heard something fall to the floor and frowned. His innards could not be hard. They could not make that sound as they hit the floor. And then he remembered the jewels and put a hand down. It met with soaked fabric. And he looked up again, realizing he'd lowered the saber and expecting to meet with a lethal strike from his enemy. But the man had stooped to pick something up and was running madly toward the violated glass front of the ship.

The jewels. He must have picked up a jewel. Had he picked up both jewels? Nigel could only remember the sound of one hard object hitting the floor. Nigel looked down and realized he was bleeding. He must have bled a lot, because the front of his clothes were soaked, as well as his legs. And he must be dying, because as he looked up, he saw an angel.

She was the most unlikely angel he'd ever beheld, insofar as she was definitely Chinese, with long blue-black hair and the heavy-lidded eyes of the kind. But her lips, her nose, the whole of her oval face were so beautiful that he couldn't think of her as anything but angelic. And her clothes, wild and colorful, might be Chinese in cut and design—a short jacket and loose pants—but suited her so exactly that they could only be celestial raiment.

Her gaze, turned to Nigel, was alarmed—panicked, perhaps—and she spoke in perfect, accentless English. "Did he get both jewels? Answer me!"

Nigel tried, but his tongue would not obey him. He felt the saber fall from his hands. He felt his knees hit the deck. He tried to mumble the prayer his nurse had taught him, when he had been a very young boy carefully watched in a nursery in the Oldhall estate in the England he would never again see.

"Now I lay me . . ." he said. His last thought was to cast renewed magical force at the flying spells, willing them to fly the carpetship where it needed to go, to not let it fall. It took what remained of his facing strength, but it must be done. Just because he was going to die didn't mean he was willing to let those he was responsible for perish.

". . . down to sleep." And darkness descended.

IN FLIGHT

Jade had followed Zhang down to the flight deck. Followed Zhang, because he had gone ahead of her, through the fighting raging on all levels. Thinking that wherever Zhang was, the jewels were sure to be, Jade hurried down a spiral staircase built of ornate wrought-iron, past a vast salon empty except for a gleaming white piano, onto a deck of small rooms and narrow corridors.

She avoided crew members that attacked her, but tried not to kill them. Her mother had been one of their people and Jade wondered, sometimes, if she might not meet one of her relatives unaware in these circumstances. It seemed unfilial to kill her mother's relatives.

Following the greatest noise, running and squeezing past presses of fighting men, she found the carpetship flight deck, where the glass had been melted away by some of the other dragons from the Dragon Boats.

She found Zhang screaming at a blond, slim man, demanding the Jewels of Power. The man refused and, possessing himself of a saber, began to fight Zhang.

Jade, holding her own saber, stared, not knowing on which side to intervene or how. If the jewels were as powerful as Zhang had said, and not essential to keep magic and the world together, then Jade should join in on his side. On the other hand, if Zhang was lying, and if what Third Lady had said was true—that he'd sold out to the English—then she should join in on the Englishman's side.

That the Englishman fought like a demon, holding his own against Zhang, before whom trained fighters crumpled, Jade could see. Oh, it was obvious that Zhang was superior. Yet though he wounded the Englishman, the Englishman kept on coming, a berserker, possessed of a lethal will to fight.

From a purely aesthetic perspective, she found herself admiring the dancerlike grace of the Englishman's movements, the quickness of his hand, the ability with which he struck a guard or feinted with what had to be—to him—a wholly alien weapon.

Trained to fight with saber and sword from early childhood—at the whim of an all-powerful father who delighted in her—Jade could admire ability when she saw it. Both of the men fighting, back and forth across the flight deck, amid other men struggling together, were clearly more able than the others. Even if one was a master and the other just possessed of single-minded determination.

So absorbed was Jade in their contest that, when one of the Englishmen attacked her, she whirled and dislodged the blade from his hand—further administering him a blow with the flat of her saber to the top of the head, knocking him out—almost by feel, without ever taking her eyes from the fight before her.

Twice, the Englishman wounded Zhang, at wrist and shoulder. Twice, Zhang struck the Englishman. It was clear that both of them were tiring and yet that the contest could go on a long time without either getting the advantage over the other.

And then, from a slash across the Englishman's chest and middle, which Jade would guess was no more than skin-deep, something fell. It rolled, shimmering red, across the blood-smeared floor.

Zhang hesitated. It was the tiniest of missteps, the smallest of hesitations. Seeing it, the Englishman rushed forward one step. Zhang came out of his momentary trance and swept the saber up and in an arc. It was clear he meant to behead the blond man. But the man stepped back and turned slightly. The saber cut deep into his shoulder.

The Englishman looked surprised, but not mortally wounded. Zhang made a sound of annoyance and dove for the jewel on the floor. Jade dove at the same time, thinking that whatever the jewel was, it would be safer with her. Zhang looked at her. For a moment their gazes met. Zhang smiled a feral smile.

And then . . . and then he ran to the edge of the ship, where the Dragon Boats were moored.

Jade didn't know what she expected. That he would run across one of the mooring ropes and into the Dragon Boat? That he would try to make his way across and take command?

But instead, he stood at the opening for a moment, poised. He looked over his shoulder at her, his eyes full of calculation. And then...and then he jumped, changing into his blue dragon form and flying away.

Jade ran after him by instinct. "Stop him," she screamed at no one in particular. "Stop him now!"

She was met with incredulous stares. Those who understood that she wanted Minister Zhang stopped were doubtless too smart to show it. Everyone knew Zhang was fearsome in both forms and, though they might not have the slightest idea what he'd done or why Jade wanted him stopped, they would surely not want to face him in combat.

"Stop him," she said, again, but despairingly, and then turned back to the Englishman, who was still standing where he'd been, looking blank, like a man who is about to lose consciousness. She felt him do something, magically, but she wasn't sure what it could be, as she surged over to him, demanding, "Did he get both jewels? Did he? Answer me." She'd only seen Zhang pick up one of the jewels, but she thought he might have taken the other one before she arrived. At least, she could not imagine why else he had left like that, in one swoop, declaring his lack of loyalty to his sovereign and to the people of the Dragon Boats, where he'd been born and raised.

But the man, looking at her, dropped his saber and took his hand to his heavily bleeding shoulder. "Now I lay me," he said, "down to sleep..."

The words were familiar to Jade, the words of a prayer her mother had taught her in distant childhood. Jade hesitated, then shook her head. "No, the jewels," she said. But the man fell to his knees and then onto his face. She could see him breathing, and she could see the sea of red pouring from his shoulder. She bent down to search him. He wouldn't be alive long and, besides, the Dragon Boat people lived by stealing things from the carpetships. If he still had the other jewel, it would do him no good, and it could save her people.

But as she turned him over, she felt his magic. He'd left it on, intent and focused, as people might leave a magelight burning long after they'd fallen asleep. His magic was powerful, strong, though utterly alien to her. It felt somewhat like her mother's magic. But her mother had been a lady of small magic, whose ability to do any useful work had been further impaired by what she ironically called a proper education. As Jade understood it, the exclusive academy her mother had attended made sure that the young ladies in their care learned how to keep house with magic, and how to help their children should they experience health difficulties. And little more. After all, as Miss Austen had ironically pointed out in the person of her odious character Mr. Collins in *Pride and Prejudice,* a young lady who was as proficient in magic as those gentlemen who might court her would undoubtedly strike everyone as unnatural and unfeminine.

This man's magic was neither unnatural nor feminine. It seemed to be as much a part of him as Jade's own dragon magic was a part of her, and yet he seemed powerful enough to keep it going even after he lost consciousness. And what the magic did—even as it ate away at his remaining strength—was keep the carpetship flying toward their destination in Africa. She could feel its currents, its determined force.

Jade took only a few seconds to realize that without

this magic the carpetship would have already fallen, careening down and killing everyone aboard, her people included, since this was the carpetship flight magician. There had been raids when this had happened and Dragon Boat people were lost. And if Zhang knew he'd attacked the carpetship magician, he didn't care what happened to the ship.

But he knew, of that she was sure. If he'd not gotten both jewels—and she had a sense he hadn't—only the fear of the crash to come had kept him from doing so. He had to know he'd mortally wounded the flight magician. But he could not know this man was possessed of a supernatural sense of duty.

Retreat, she screamed mentally, putting the force of Wen's ring—the force of Wen's power—behind her scream. *Retreat now. Flight magician wounded. The ship might crash any moment. Retreat now.*

Around her, her people jumped and ran toward the Dragon Boats, some of them pursued by the few Englishmen left alive on the deck, others pulling at one another while they ran.

She, too, should leave. Or else she should search the Englishman and then leave. But as she looked at him—he had gone so pale that he seemed almost transparent—and felt him using all his strength, all the vitality that remained in him, to keep the carpetship flying, she lost her mind.

One thing she'd been trained to do, besides fight, was to treat the wounds acquired on these raids. More often than not, Jade was not allowed to join in the raid. Not unless her father thought there was some advantage to taking her with them. This usually meant, if she joined, it was to keep an eye on Wen and keep him safe.

But her normal place during these raids was in the Dragon Boats, in the women's quarters. Every man who had been injured came there. And Jade had been trained from a very young age to treat saber cuts and power burns.

She wouldn't have time to carefully heal the man's cut and repair the muscles. But she could keep him alive long enough to land this ship without killing everyone aboard.

She waved a hand and threw her power at his bleeding wounds, willing the skin to reknit, the muscles to close, the blood vessels to stop spewing forth blood.

The flow staunched and—without pausing to make sure this was due to her spell and not to his death—she got up and ran toward the rope that linked this ship to the Dragon Boats. Because if indeed the man were dead, the carpetship could crash at any minute.

She danced across the magically taut rope with the ease of long practice, her wicker-soled slippers not faltering, and jumped onto the Dragon Boat, turning immediately to magically untie the end of the rope from the English ship and to collect it in her hand in a tight coil.

Unmoor, unmoor, unmoor, she yelled, mentally, using the Imperial voice of command. *Unmoor from the foreign devils.*

Without turning to make sure her commands were being followed, she saw through the corner of her eye that the nearest boats were collecting their ropes and that the few stragglers were dancing across the ropes still tied to the carpetship. She bent down, at the very prow of the boat, and picked up the barge pole kept there to steer the boat in shallow water or midair—since the magical gesture steered it as easily as if it were in shallow water—turning the Dragon Boat around and steering it speedily away from the carpetship.

There must still have been people alive in the carpetship—enough crew at least to command their defensive weaponry—because large powercannons took aim at the fleeing ships, firing volley after volley of magic after them. The magical fire could not hurt them, of course. They were were-dragons. Or at least, almost everyone on board was a were of some sort. Even the spouses brought aboard were often members of other were-clans.

But the magefire could burn the Dragon Boats around them and cause considerable damage. And also, though dragons could not be killed that easily, they could be hurt, and could take a long time to recover. *Evasive maneuvers,* Jade mentally screamed, as she joined action to words and set the boat she was steering on a zigzag course and increased its speed. And then, quickly, as a blast of fiery magic flew past the bright red sails of her boat, *Those still in dragon form, return fire.*

Some dragons—probably the youngest of the attack party, since those always insisted on staying as dragons the longest—blew a curtain of fire toward the carpetship. They were too far away to burn it, but their fire formed a curtain of brilliance between them and whoever was firing cannons, thus blocking the carpetship's view.

Jade could swear she heard English curses, though she knew, rationally, that she was too far away to hear any such thing. Not pausing to think about it, she steered on a more erratic course, north northeast, perpendicular to the carpetship's route, which she'd seen clearly in the flight magician's mind. For a moment, she was afraid they'd turn in pursuit. If there were enough of them alive. If those cannons were fully charged.

But then she realized she was being foolish. Their carpetship magician was, if not dead, then near it, and they could not pursue the Dragon Boats without his power and his conscious intention.

Presently, she became aware the carpetship was too far away for the cannons to reach, and that they were flying, at great speed, over the African continent. What a foolish expedition this had been. She should never have embarked on it, so far from the Chinese coast, the area where her family had always raided. If one of her boats fell here, and in the domain of an European nation, she couldn't trust the friendliness of the locals to get the dragons out of trouble—as they would in China, no matter what the laws said. No, it would be the execution squad and the full power of the foreign-devil laws.

Besides, Jade's father had always talked about what he called the balance of power. Jade remembered him, in her earliest childhood, his hand over a disk that floated in midair, a carved wooden disk designed to represent everything under heaven. "There are many people in our world," he said. "And our dynasty learned early that it wouldn't do to claim our right to rule—even if we have that right, and even if the life of China is knit to our flesh, our blood, and us to it. But whatever our right, and our magic, we do not have the manpower to resist. By the time our dynasty was overthrown, the usurpers had secured all the people and all the physical power. There was nothing for it but to go into exile. It was the Mandate of Heaven.

"In the same way, though we know we are superior to all the foreign devils, right now it is they who are the more powerful. They hold their strength over us like a sword poised to fall. In these circumstances, and having lost the Mandate of Heaven, it is necessary that we do as little as possible to force the events. Because, should we do the wrong thing, we'll find ourselves suffering from the foreign devils' vengeance. It is acceptable—it is how we've always lived—to attack carpetships now and then. But not too many of them, lest we bring on a raid designed to eliminate us. And never outside of our territory. For should we start attacking carpetships on the coast of Europe, the foreign devils' queen could well look up and say, *These sons of heaven grow too bothersome. Let's uproot them everywhere we find them.* And if they notice we are dragons, considering how they feel about weres, they will set out to destroy us."

What foolishness had led her to bring her people this far? What madness had prompted her to risk them this way? She must get back to their haunts as soon as she possibly could.

She looked up from steering the boat, to find a

young man about her age staring at her. He was naked, as were those who had been dragons to the last moment. His features were regular. His carefully shaven face showed only a slight flush, and his eyes, larger than average, were open very wide, as was his mouth, clearly in shock at finding her here.

Indeed, he bowed to her, awkwardly, and seemed to try to regain speech against the turmoil of a disordered mind. When he spoke, it was in a tone of shock, almost dismay. "Lady Jade," he said. And bowed again, his hands on his knees. "How come you are here? And where is my father?"

"Your father?" she asked, breathless, feeling all of a sudden all the sweat and strain of her exertions. "Your father?"

The young man bowed yet again. "I am Minister Zhang's firstborn son."

Jade took a deep breath. She recollected, though she'd never paid much attention to it, that though Zhang's first wife had long ago died, he had a multitude of sons and daughters by an equal multitude of concubines. What luck of hers that she should have landed on his boat. She almost let go of the barge pole in disgust, but training was stronger than reflexive annoyance. Instead, she pulled the barge pole in, slowly, and laid it at her feet. "Your father," she said, "has left the Dragon Boats, and disappeared—in dragon form—taking a valuable artifact."

"He . . ." the boy started. Though he was close to her age, if not older, Jade could not help but think of him as a boy. "He . . . what?"

"He took a valuable artifact, which should by right

belong to the emperor. And he has left the Dragon Boats."

The effect on the young man was immediate. Aware of the punishments visited on the families of traitors, he sank to his knees and hit his forehead on the floorboards of the boat: once, twice, three times. "Lady Jade, this despicable son of an unworthy father did not know. My traitorous father never took me into his confidence." He looked up, pale and drawn, and fixed her with a look of pure terror. "I beg you to be merciful with my family. My father's ten concubines and his twenty children are all innocent." He kowtowed again.

Jade was not sure he was as innocent as he seemed to be, though she was certain that Zhang had, in fact, failed to communicate to his eldest son—or to any of his family—what he was planning. An old hand at court intrigue, Zhang would long ago have learned that there was no secret so safe as that which was never spoken at all.

But she was also sure the boy might have noticed comings and goings and strange activity. Zhang, living here in this beehive of a boat, or its adjacent women's quarters, could not have kept any absences absolutely secret. If he'd been—as Third Lady said—going to India and there entering into secret negotiations with Englishmen, then surely his oldest son would have noticed it. If he'd been plotting and laying aside money or clothes or something else for an eventual desertion from the Dragon Boats, his eldest son might have caught wind of it. And if any strangers—from other clans, or from the usurping rulers—had come onto the boat, again Zhang's eldest son must perforce know it.

She touched him with the tip of her slipper as he started on yet another round of kowtowing. "Get up, Zhang," she said, addressing him by his family name. Regardless of what he knew or didn't, to threaten him now would be unwise. A frightened young man who thought he would be punished for his father's crime was more likely than not to take his boat away and his whole clan with him. While a young man recently promoted, who had reason to want to hold on to those honors, would be more likely to exert his utmost memory and thought to find out what his father had done and why, and where he might have gone. "Get up, Zhang, and assume your father's position on this boat, and in my court." She waved the ring in front of his eyes. "Do you see this ring? Do you know what it means?"

"It means your brother, the True Emperor of All Under Heaven, gave you his power and his magic and his command, to act in his stead." The terrified younger Zhang remained on his knees, looking up.

"Yes, and in his stead, I appoint you to all the honors and positions your father has abandoned."

He gaped at her. "Me? Me, minister and in the planning councils?"

That look alone told her he was about as ready for the planning councils as she was for an assembly of gods. But then again, what would the planning councils be? They had an opium-addicted emperor, a half-foreign princess acting in his stead and an assemblage of plotters and traitors who would come out of the woodwork as soon as they found out Zhang was gone. Might as well add to it a very green young man who hardly knew how to comport himself.

"Yes. I have no doubt of your ability to keep your people in order or lead your boat," Jade lied. "And your loyalty to your clan that prompted you to protect them at this juncture tells me you'll be a good minister to the emperor." And that part, she thought, might be true, once he gained his footing and his sense of protectiveness expanded to include everyone in the Dragon Boats. "Meanwhile, I ask of you only that you try to recollect any strange actions or absences your father might have indulged in, in the last few months."

The younger Zhang kowtowed again. He must enjoy knocking his head on the boards of the boat. Or else, he thought that she might still turn on him, suddenly, and demand his death and that of his relatives. Perhaps she shouldn't judge him too harshly for that belief. After all, her father had been a man of sudden rages.

"My father was absent a lot in the last month. From . . . from things he said, I thought he had gone to India," he blurted. "In pursuit of someone. I heard the word *ruby* mentioned a few times. I thought he meant no more than to steal some valuable jewel and thought maybe even your father, the former True Emperor of All Under Heaven, might have given him instructions from the Dragon Throne. I never thought that he might be doing it as treason."

"Of course not," Jade said. Knowing the penalties for treason, she couldn't imagine such a conscientious young man would want all his relatives slaughtered. And he would be well aware that his entire family, including concubines and young infants, couldn't get away from Imperial rage fast enough, even if his father could. Also, unlike his father, the younger Zhang clearly cared if his relatives lived or died.

"Also . . . when he came back . . ." He looked up, and bit his lower lip, as though in deep thought, or perhaps trying to slow down the words that finally came pouring out of him like water overpowering a weak dam. "When he came back, he was grievously wounded and he said something about fighting with a foreign-devil dragon."

Jade remembered, dimly, something about a foreign dragon from Third Lady's tale. Or at least thought she did. "Rise, Zhang," she said. "I'm satisfied. Now I wish you to steer this boat near the Imperial women's quarters, that I might regain my proper place."

Zhang bent down to pick up the barge pole, bowed, then hesitated. Though he didn't make a sound, she got the strong impression he wished to speak, and added, "You may say whatever you wish."

He bowed hastily, an overlong lock of hair falling in front of his eyes. "It's only, Lady Jade, though I know it's my name, and . . . and my father's name . . . in my own family I've never been called Zhang, and it would be a great honor if you consented to call me by the name my family gives me."

Uncomfortable with calling the young man the name of the minister she'd always hated, Jade said, "I will do as you ask. What is that name?"

He bowed, quickly, then threw his head back, flicking his hair away from his eyes. "Grasshopper, my lady, because of my nature."

She did not ask if it was his nature to be jumpy, or if perhaps he suffered from seasickness and turned green. It was of no consequence. Instead she spoke, in a polite tone. "Steer me toward the women's quarters, then, Grasshopper, that I may change my clothes and think on what to do next. I must find where your father has gone. And what his plan is."

LOOKING FOR ANSWERS

"*I do not hold it against you, Third Lady,*" Jade said, having called her sister-in-law to her quarters. "That you were right in the warning given me and which I chose to neglect. I do thank you for your accurate information, and regret only that I chose to give Zhang the benefit of doubt."

Third Lady bowed, politely. It was now three days since the battle with the carpetship. Three days in which Jade had spent collecting reports on Zhang and which direction he had flown—toward home, everyone thought—and of what might be on his mind. His papers, turned over by a zealous Grasshopper, had not enlightened her any further. They contained marks of treason, but those were not, after all, a novelty by that time. There were letters from a Captain Corridon, in Her Majesty's Secret Service, which Jade read with fascination. Her near-native command of English allowed her to detect in the captain's words a curious mix of disdain and hopefulness. Disdain toward Zhang, either because Zhang was Chinese—she very much doubted even Zhang had been brave enough to tell the

Englishman he was a were-dragon—or because he was simply what the Englishman would think of as a flying-boat pirate. The hopefulness was harder to explain, but Jade assumed that Zhang must have given the British some token of his earnest intent to follow through in this plot. And as such, Captian Corridon sounded eager and almost childlike in his hope that Zhang could get hold of the jewels *so long desired by our queen.*

Mention of the queen's failing health led Jade to think the aged sovereign was dying. Judging from her own father's final illness she knew how much those in power held on to that life and power, and how they often tried to reach, one final time, for something that would give them back youth or vigor. If the English queen was truly dying, she would reach her moribund hands out for the jewels and hope more than ever for them to restore her vigor, not to mention her original intention of holding power in her family.

Jade had also found other things—or rather, Grasshopper had found them, and had brought them to her, in earnest of his loyalty and devotion—such as a magical farseer, of foreign design; exquisitely figured cloth and a pair of black knee-length boots that seemed to Jade to be the sort of riding boots to which her mother's novels often alluded. There were other things, too—powersticks with countless charges, a well-balanced sword, a crystal imbued with magical power to be called at will.

Altogether that was worth considerably less than the papers, even from the point of view of proving Zhang's innocence or guilt. After all, these things could have been obtained in a carpetship raid, and it might mean nothing. She suspected, though, that Zhang had kept the truly incriminating papers, as well as anything that might give her an idea of where he'd gone and why. At least, she didn't find any of it in the papers she had.

"The question," she explained to Third Lady, "is whether or not he got both jewels. If he got them . . ." She hesitated.

Third Lady narrowed her eyes at her, not in menace, but seemingly in deep thought. When Third Lady did this, it was easy to imagine her in fox form, calculating and mischievous. "If he got them, my lady," she said, slowly, "then we must find him with all possible haste, for you must know that none of us will be safe until he is found and stopped from whatever foolhardy course he means to undertake."

Jade nodded back. "That goes without saying. But I feel there is a great difference, if he has acquired one jewel, or else if he . . ." She shrugged. "If he has both jewels, we can probably agree he is even now approaching the English. It's been three days, surely time enough for him to have found the English outpost at which this Captain Corridon resides, and to have disposed of the jewels. In which case . . ." She frowned. "I might have to discover a way to recapture the jewels before the English take them to their queen. And I confess that the idea of how to do such a thing simply will not form in my mind. Not when I must go against the most powerful nation in the world with my ragtag band of Dragon Boats. On the other hand, if he has not captured both jewels, then where the other jewel is would depend on where the carpetship pilot died and whether, in the confusion of cleaning the deck of dead, they bothered to search his clothes. I have read that on these carpetships, when faced with a lot of bodies of which to dispose, they will simply fly low over the ocean and give the dead burial at sea. So the jewel that, together with its twin, could bring about the destruction of the world or the elevation of a throne might very well now be at the bottom of the ocean."

"What if..." Third Lady started, then seemed to check herself upon a word, as though afraid of saying whatever must be on her mind.

"What if...?" Jade prompted.

"What if the foreign magician survived?"

Jade frowned. "Unlikely," she said. "Not only had he bled too much, but he was devoting the very last of his strength to keeping the carpetship flying. That type of magic, set as it was to go on after one is incapacitated, does not come cheap. It eats alive the person who sets it off."

"But if he is alive?" Third Lady asked, with seeming stubbornness, then added, quickly, "It seems to me we must be aware of that possibility and plan for it, even if it is unlikely. It is much easier to plan on such things in advance."

"Undoubtedly. Well... if that magician is alive, then I would say Zhang will home in on him, somehow, perhaps through information given by the Englishmen. And we, too, would do well to find him, fast. For if he is alive and still has this jewel, our best chance of capturing it is to get to him before Zhang can."

Third Lady nodded. "So that is what we'll do."

Jade laughed. She couldn't help it. When her sister-in-law spoke like this, it was easy to imagine it was all a matter of making up their minds and then doing it. The truth was, of course, somewhat more complicated. "The problem," she explained, sobering up immediately, "is that I don't know which of the three things is true. I imagine my father had spies. At least I hope he did, since I suspect the Dragon Boats are riddled with spies anyway, and each of them, as my nurse would have said, pulling the smoldering coal over to roast his own meat. But whether my father had spies or not is immaterial now. For the last few months, he's been too ill and too weak to pay much attention to such things. And he certainly never told Wen—or even me—of any such people. I do not know how to find out where Zhang has gone, or what he has done there. I don't know if he's been in touch with the English yet. I could, I suppose, find some English newspapers, but any that could be found in this area of the world would be at least two days old. And then, too, this is the sort of thing the queen will not publish abroad." She opened her hands at her sides, turning the palms toward Third Lady, in a show of absolute helplessness. "The truth is, I do not know where to turn to find out what happened to Zhang. I cannot know how to proceed till I know what has already happened."

Third Lady looked shy and mischievous both, like a kitten reaching for a table scrap. "Have you thought... have you thought to ask, my lady?"

"Ask whom? Wen? Surely you know that he—"

"No." Third Lady shook her head. "My Lord is too lost in his dreaming. No. What I meant, my lady, is— have you considered asking tortoiseshell and bone? And if not, may I suggest you do? I can take you to the place where it can be done."

ANGELS

龙

Nigel was dreaming. Or at least he thought he was, unless he was dead. In his present state, he couldn't say which it was for certain.

There had been what seemed to him an endless eternity of heat and cold, of light and oddly resounding voices and the sort of jarring movement that made his whole body ache and seem to vibrate through his teeth like someone dragging a knife across his bones. And then there had been dreams—confused dreams. The Dragon Boats, and the carpetship, and his need to keep the carpetship flying.

And now there was a moment of calm and a moment of lucidity, and he became aware that he was resting on sheets which seemed damnably crumpled under him, on a pillow which appeared to be soaked through with his sweat. His hands were clutched on another sheet, which lay atop his body, making his skin insufferably hot. And he smelled . . . ill.

The smell of fever—or at least of his own sweat when feverish—was well known to Nigel, who had been born sickly and premature and had spent most of his young life confined to bed, suffering from one stupid complaint or another and strictly forbidden from joining the other boys at play—or his brother, Carew, at riding and hunting and other sport.

With a clutch of sudden fear, he realized that while he unmistakably had a body and remained a corporeal being—else, how could he feel the sheet atop him?—it was possible he might still be a very young man, somewhere in his parents' estate. Oh, not too young, but old enough to know of the world and to have dreamed of being allowed to go to Cambridge, of being betrothed to a beautiful Anglo-Indian woman, of being sent to Africa on a mission from the Queen of . . . of everything he'd dreamed of. It would be like himself, at that time, to have delusions of importance and strength, to picture himself as the man chosen by the sovereign to save the world. Or to imagine Carew as a villain from whose dastardly deeds Nigel would need to save everyone. His parents' favorite son had always revealed a far crueler side to Nigel, and Nigel, doubtless, wished the world to realize it.

His stomach sinking, as though a very cold, leaden weight had been placed upon it, Nigel gnashed his teeth together. He would have preferred to be dead and about to face eternal punishment than to be back at home in his sickly young body, with no guarantee ever that he would be able to leave the estate and go as far as boarding school—or as far as Cambridge and London—much less as far as Africa and India or to travel half the world as a carpetship magician.

As if to confirm his suspicions, he felt a man lift him

up, and a woman's hands turn the pillows under his head, so that they felt cooler now. He struggled desperately to open his eyes, against which a great light seemed to shine, far greater than had ever come through the window of his childhood room.

His eyes wouldn't obey him, but his lips did, and one word escaped, made emphatic—despite his weakness—by his desperate need to convey his annoyance. "Mother!"

"Aye, the poor gentleman," a woman's voice said, as the cool female hands withdrew. "He calls for his mother, and no wonder, for he's come as close to meeting his maker as any man ever should." It was a voice he'd never heard, and while Nigel allowed his mouth to drop open in shock, he heard something much like a man's chuckle from the other side.

Following the chuckle came a man's voice that Nigel felt should be familiar. Or at least he felt he'd heard it often enough before—but it was not the voice of any of his family retainers when he'd been young, not the voice of his father, or his uncle, or even Carew, though it would be like Carew to chuckle at Nigel's illness. "I don't think he was calling for his mother, Hettie, so much as he thought you were her and was telling you to leave him be."

A female gasp and the voice again. "Why, the poor gentleman. For I'm sure I've never been old enough to be anyone's mother, and he could plainly see that."

"He's not been in his own mind, Hettie, and that's the truth," the man's voice said, and Nigel now placed it somewhere in the carpetship of which he'd just dreamed, on the flight deck. It was someone there, someone with whom he'd spoken just before the attack. Did this mean that the carpetship hadn't been a dream, after all? "But I think, from that frown on his face, that he hears us and understands us now. Do you, Mr. Jones?"

Mr. Jones? What could the man be about? Nigel was not and had never been Mr. Jones. "Not—" he managed to whisper, and then remembered that he'd called himself Enoch Jones as a carpetship flight magician. At least on some of the trips he had. On others he'd used other names, to try to make it as hard as possible for anyone to trace his movements.

And then he remembered the fight with the Chinese man—Chinese dragon—and his picking up the gem. The ruby!

Spurred by sudden panic, his eyes flew open, and Nigel sat bolt upright on the bed. "The ruby!" he cried, in extreme distress, before he realized that he was looking at a room he'd never seen and which was far smaller than his room at his parents' estate. In fact, at his parents' estate, it might very well have been a servant's room, one of the ones accessible only from the back stairs. Like a servant's room, it contained a plain, almost institutional bed; a very tall, very dark and somewhat dingy wardrobe with a spotted mirror hung upon it . . . and nothing else. No desk, no books, not even that modicum of luxury that he was used to seeing in carpetship flight-magicians' rooms.

He looked to his right and saw, standing very close to the bed, a girl of maybe fifteen, with pale blond hair and very round blue eyes. Though she was unremarkable, she was not ugly—though no one would call her pretty—and her simple muslin dress was just what one would expect from such a young girl not yet out.

She was staring at him in horror, and slowly raised a hand to cover her mouth, even as a delicate peach color suffused her features. Looking down, Nigel realized that he was wearing nothing save his underwear, and that his sheet had fallen to puddle in his lap.

"Nothing wrong, there, old chap," the man said, and gently pushed Nigel down, while pulling the sheet up to cover his bare chest. "Hettie, I think I hear your mum calling? Perhaps you should go. And tell her next time she should assist me."

Nigel, blinking, looked at the man, a weathered creature, probably forty or maybe fifty, with white hair threaded through a receding curly thatch. His eyes had that slightly squinting expression of someone who has lived in tropical climates and become used to half closing his lids against overpowering light—and around them was a network of lines that spoke of a long time in such harsh latitudes.

Nigel heard the door close, and the man smiled, reassuring him. "There, my lord," he said, softly. "Nothing to fear. The ruby is safe." And then, to Nigel's still-blank look, "It's Joseph Perigord, my lord. The first mate on the *Indian Star.*"

"Oh," Nigel said, embarrassed not to have recognized the man before. Once he imagined him in the uniform and cap of the first mate, it was easy enough. Now attired only in a loose linen shirt and what seemed to be breeches of some very pale cloth, he didn't look like the same man. "Oh, of course." And then rallying, he added, "The rubies are safe?"

Perigord sighed. "One of them is, my lord," he said, as he fumbled with a bottle on the bedside table and poured a measure of some evil-smelling dose onto a spoon. "At least, when you were brought in and undressed, I found it among your clothes, and I have kept it safe for you. The other . . ."

"The Chinese pirate took it," Nigel said, bitterly, remembering the fight, and then the angel demanding of him whether the dragon had taken one jewel or both.

Joseph Perigord nodded. "That was the strangest thing anyone has ever seen, and it will be much talked about in Africa. And indeed, all over the world, I imagine. Already the reporters for the *Cape Town News* have been by twice, with an artist, wanting to draw your likeness for their paper. There is even talk here in town that the queen herself should recognize you and give you a medal, for you saved everyone aboard that carpetship. With such heroism did you clutch on to the magic to keep the carpet flying, after you were brought here, it took two healing magicians to make you let go of it. You gave yourself a fever, of course." He approached the bed with the spoon in hand. "Which is why the doctor has prescribed this, which if you would be so obliging as to drink and not make me fight you over it, as you did while you were feverish . . ."

Nigel, less concerned with being feverish or, indeed, with his state of health at all, than with the horrible news of his misadventure being reported abroad, opened his mouth, only to find the spoon pushed into it. He resisted the urge to splutter and swallowed, hastily, as the bitter liquid made its way down his throat. "Good God!" he said. "You cannot have allowed reporters—"

"No, milord," Perigord said. "I can't say as I know what you are about, but I much suspect it is something that wouldn't be helped by publicity. And owing you my life and the life of most of our passengers....." He shrugged. "I told the newspaper gentlemen that you were too sick to permit strangers in your room, that it would disturb you and possibly cause you to relapse."

Nigel swallowed at the bitterness in his mouth, and made a face. "What is in that medicine? It tastes—"

"Like ground-up stink bugs? Leastwise, that is what it smells like, and so I told my wife, and Hettie, too." He poured something from a pitcher to the glass and brought the glass to Nigel's lips. "Nothing to fear, my lord. This is lemonade. As far as I am concerned, I'd rather be giving you brandy—because if it were me lying there, well near death, I'd rather have brandy—but the doctor said it was the last thing you needed."

Nigel swallowed the lemonade, very much wishing it was brandy as well. What a hash he'd made of things. He'd let one of the jewels be stolen. It would never have happened if he'd allowed the two jewels to be fully activated and their power to shine through. He had reason to suspect that, in such a case, the jewels had their own means of defense and a way of searing through the heart of the evildoers.

The problem was, of course, that if you left them fully activated and shining, they were also as a beacon calling out to the entire world. And, as he knew, sooner or later they would call someone so lost to all decency, restraint and remorse that their magic, which called forth the best in men and used it to punish their evil, would fail. He hadn't been able to risk holding them openly, and so he'd let them get stolen. Or one of them. And now he must recover it, so that he could complete his original mission.

A thought occurred to him and he looked to Perigord. "You called me *milord*. Is it because most carpetship magicians are, or . . ."

Perigord shrugged, replacing the glass on the bedside table. "It is the thing with fevers, my lord, that people often talk when they have them. Which can be fortunate. It was only your talking that caused me to lie to the trooper."

"The trooper?" Nigel said.

"Some soldier. A Red Coat. He came to the door, and speaking very fair and meek, he tells us that you would have a ruby about your person and says that if I'd found it, I should give it to him for safekeeping, as you were on a secret mission for Her Majesty the Queen."

"A mission?"

"Yes, indeed," Perigord said, calmly. "And I knew, from your ravings, begging your pardon, that you were indeed on a mission, but that you'd found it wicked, and that if I were to give that jewel to the trooper, there was a good chance that I'd be doing something wicked and evil myself. So I kept my council and told him no jewel was found. At which point he stormed off, no doubt to search for it elsewhere."

"But if they know of the jewel . . . then they must know who I really am!" Nigel exclaimed. "And that means . . ." A panoply of horrors opened up before him.

Public recognition was the least of it. There would be the queen demanding to know what had happened and why he'd abjured the notion of ever completing the mission she had given him. And there would be his parents, doubtless wanting to know what had happened to Emily, his bride, whom he had married the very morning he'd set off on his mission. And why his honeymoon in Cairo had somehow extended to a trample over all the continents. And what had happened to Carew.

Perigord shrugged. "That's as may be. He came yesterday, a day and a half after you were carried to my house, delirious out of your mind, and I told him as in your delirium you'd given a name, many times. He asked if your name was perhaps Nigel Oldhall. I told him as no, not at all, and I had reason to think your first name was Gervase and your family name Southerton."

"Gervase Southerton?" Nigel frowned slightly. The second son of the Duke of Ulston was a notorious rake, whose name had been bandied all over town. Then after murdering a man over a game of cards—or some said the love of a lightskirt—he had disappeared. Some said he had gone to Australia, and some to America, but Nigel imagined there would be no reason at all he might not have become a carpetship magician. And now Nigel thought about it, though the two of them were very different in features, there was nothing at all in a casual description to alert anyone that he might not be Ger Southerton. He squinted at Perigord. "You know your nobility very well, Mr. Perigord."

"As to that," Mr. Perigord said, "let's say it's not just

flight magicians who escape their past sometime." His accent became notably more cultured as he spoke.

Nigel raised his eyebrows at him, and Perigord smiled. "Oh, it was nothing like Ger Southerton. I was never in that set. I fell in love with the third undermaid and...well...my father wished to pay her off and marry her to the gardener. Instead, we eloped and jumped a carpetship to Africa. Best thing I've ever done, and it suits me more than being the second son of a family with more pretensions than money would have done." He smiled. "I took my new family name from a bottle of my favorite wine."

Nigel laughed, surprised to hear a wheezy, weak sound in his own voice. "I took my carpetship magician's first name from the family dog's."

"Enoch? You have an unusual family, milord."

He shrugged. "My mother is very fond of improving reading, and there was a book about Enoch she read about that time." He looked up at the man's face. "But you should not call me *milord*. First, because it will only call attention to me. And second, because you know and I know we are equals."

"Very well, then," Perigord said. "I shall call you the dog's name, and since you are in my home, and cared for by my family—just wait until you're well enough to taste my Charlotte's excellent cooking—you might as well call me Joe. We'll make like we're old acquaintances, which will further muddy the water."

"And the ruby is...?"

"Ah, there's a trick to this. Let me show you." Joe touched what looked like an ornamental metal rosette in the wood headboard, then carefully unscrewed a round finial. "See, in there, my lor—Enoch? As snug as a bug." His accent had reversed again to a broad, generic lower-class tone, as it had been when Nigel first met him. "And there it will stay, until you recover yourself and are on your feet again."

Nigel groaned, deep in his throat. "I should leave now. I am a danger to you while I'm here."

"As to that," Joe said, and shrugged, "we would none of us be here if it weren't for you—at least none of us who survived the sabers and the fire aboard that carpetship."

"How many are there?" Nigel asked, somewhat hesitant to hear it.

"Well over two hundred. Only twenty crew members perished and none at all in the upper decks, though much was stolen. So you saved all the passengers and most of the crew. Though the captain, poor man, died. At least he went out fighting, as he should, and as he was due to retire soon, I'd like to believe he'd have preferred to go out with his boots on. Not that it isn't a sad waste."

Nigel nodded, thinking of it. "Yes, but all the same, I shouldn't put you in further danger."

Joe shrugged. "I have some magic. Not a lot. My family is not nearly so high up on the tree as yours. But I have enough to disguise your magic markers and some of your appearance, and to keep your dampers on that beautiful jewel there."

"But why would you trust me over Her Majesty's servants?"

Joe grinned. "Her Majesty never saved my life. And

besides, I've never been one to care much what authority has to say to anything. If I'd listened to my father, my Charlotte would be married to some scrubby gardener, and I'd never have had the chance to watch my Hettie grow up." His face became grave. "So you'll lie there, Enoch, and take your ease until you're recovered enough to continue your mission. And then you will go with my blessing."

Nigel nodded, but one thought tortured him. "I dreamed of a Chinese angel. I guess I must truly have been feverish."

Joe, already at the door, turned back, a wrinkle of thought on his forehead. "Well ... I don't know. It is possible you dreamed of the pirate girl. You talked of her enough. Uncommonly pretty, if I may say so, and I've wondered all along if you knew her, for her to do what she did for you."

"What did she do for me?" Nigel asked.

"Why, she stopped the bleeding from your shoulder. Without it, you would have been dead in minutes. And I've never heard—though I don't fly that part of the world much—of Chinese pirates being charitable before."

TORTOISE AND BONE

Jade followed Third Lady along the edge of the women's quarters boat. The boats were now moored on the river, with the familiar plain around them, looking like nothing but regular barges, inhabited by tramps or subsistence crafters, but certainly not pirates.

Here, on familiar territory, the boats were moored end to end, their edges touching and the planks normally extended between the boats set across them, to allow people to walk across when they pleased.

Third Lady had brought dark cloaks and they were both enveloped in them. Now she pulled Jade aside, toward a thicket of woods. In the woods, cool shadows fell on one of the lifeboats that were normally inside the Dragon Boats. So small it would fit just the two of them, end on end, it was, like the Dragon Boats, charged with its own flying spell, activated by the emperor's magic.

Jade looked at Third Lady. "I don't understand," she said. "If we must go at night, can't I just fly? I could carry you—"

Third Lady shook her head. She put her finger to her lips, as though requesting that Jade speak softer, then spoke in a trickling whisper. "At night is safer because fewer people are awake. But if they should wake..." Third Lady smiled, a sparkling, naughty smile. "If they see a boat being rowed away with two cloaked figures in it, they'll think it's the men going off to the city for a tipple, as they're likely to do in the evening when we're moored."

"They are?" Jade said.

"Oh, yes. Didn't you know? They can't go as dragons, not without explaining exactly where they come from, but our little boats are not the only charmed ones about. Every were-clan has them. People see rowboats in the sky all the time. Besides, my lady, if you'll forgive me... they would recognize your dragon form, but no one will recognize your cloaked form on the boat."

Jade shook her head. Another thought had intruded. This time she whispered, as she said, "But what about flying the boats? As the test of the new emperor's power and the proof that he has the Mandate of Heaven to rule the Dragon Boats?"

Third Lady nodded. "Of course," she said. "But all the clans swear allegiance to the Dragon Throne, so if the new emperor doesn't make the boats fly again, they will be grounded, as they were at his father's death." She smiled. "But once he makes them fly—and I thank you for doing it for him, milady—then all the boats in all the clan holds will fly."

"Oh," Jade said, and stepped into the boat, picking up an oar. Third Lady had an oar, too, but she sat near the rudder of the boat, ready to steer. As with the barge poles, they had to work the oars hard at first, until they'd gained enough altitude over the trees and the lights beneath, which indicated peasant cook fires. But soon they were flying through a night of such a deep blue that it seemed like nothing so much as Wusih silk, spun very even and deep, and Jade could lay aside the oar.

Third Lady leaned on the rudder and steered with a practiced ease. Jade wanted to ask her if she often went out like this at night, but looking at the little triangular face in the moonlight, she thought that it wouldn't be surprising if she did. It must be very hard on Third Lady to be imprisoned, a minor wife in a very formal household, and without even a child to take her attention and to keep her company. All alone, and with no distractions, she would be isolated in many ways, since most of the Dragon Clan, and even the Bear Clan, the Panda Clan and the Tiger Clan thought themselves by far superior to the Fox Clan. The foxes had a reputation throughout China as thieves, intriguers and tricksters, and where the peasants would shield a were-dragon, or even one of the other weres, they would only try to kill a discovered were-fox.

Jade frowned slightly at Third Lady as it occurred to her that she was entrusting her life and her honor to a member of the Fox Clan. She was sure everyone in all of China would laugh at her if she came to misadventure thereby.

Third Lady looked up, as though surprised at being so regarded, and Jade sighed. Because the other part of this was that she had known Third Lady for years, and she knew for a fact that she was the only one of

Wen's wives to truly care for him. "I was wondering," she said to cover up her thoughts, "how difficult it was in the women's boat for you, when you have no child and no particular vocation."

Third Lady blushed a little. "Oh. Oh," she said, as if it had just occurred to her that anyone might pity her, and the idea struck her as odd. "But it is not difficult at all. I have your brother, my lord. Oh, I know," she said, catching the look in Jade's eye, "he is often lost in his dreams, but I sit by him and hold his hands or . . . or hold him. He permits me to do so. And I wonder, you know, with Zhang gone . . ." She was quiet again. "I would not wish to malign the minister . . ."

"You may malign him as you wish," Jade said, tartly. "He left the Dragon Boats against my will and went off to parts unknown. Probably to negotiate with the British, as you intimated earlier. It is perhaps not proof of treason, but it is close enough."

"Yes, but this I never had proof of . . ." Third Lady said. "But I always thought . . . well, you know, that perhaps he was the one supplying my lord with opium."

Jade sat up straighter. This connected with something in Zhang's papers, a note about his receiving something from the English, something that was referred to only as "the packet." Jade had imagined it to be one of the many trinkets that littered Zhang's quarters, or perhaps strings of cash. But it might have been opium instead.

"Why do you think that?" she asked, almost breathless with sudden suspicion. Her father had trusted

Zhang implicitly and Zhang could have done almost anything behind the emperor's back.

Third Lady ducked her head. "It's not that I think it," she said. "Or not so much. It's just that I've thought, you know, whom it might benefit to have your brother lost in a dream. And the only person I could think of was Zhang."

"Oh," Jade said. She would have liked to deny it, but it was so. Because as she had thought, if she—that is, if Wen's power had failed to make the boats fly, then the Dragon Throne would have devolved upon Zhang, the descendant of the younger line. "But if it was . . ."

"If my lord doesn't find another supplier, and I don't think he will . . . for he is, you see, in general, aware that what he does is a bad thing and a betrayal of his rank and birth . . . if he doesn't find another supplier, then he will surely end by recovering from . . . from his dreaming."

"That," Jade said, "would be a very good thing."

"Yes. Oh, yes," Third Lady said, and yet the eyes she turned to Jade looked haunted. "My only fear, my lady, is what that will do to the Dragon Boats."

"What do you mean?" Jade asked.

"Well, I have seen what happens to people who get so far in the dreaming as my lord, your brother. And it is very difficult for them, painful even, to cure themselves of their need for opium. What happens, then, when his magic is thrown into turmoil by his recovery? What happens to the Dragon Boats?"

Jade opened her eyes wide. "I don't know," she said meekly.

"No, and neither do I," Third Lady said. "And that's something I, myself, intend to ask the Oracle of Bone."

Jade squirmed. "I've heard . . . that is, I know what the Oracle of Bone is. Or at least, I am aware of its existence and have read about it, but . . ."

"But?"

"But I always thought it was something a little . . . shameful? Something that should not be done?"

Third Lady shrugged. "As to that," she said, leaning slightly on her rudder and causing them to execute a gentle arc toward mountains that looked like a dragon asleep under the hills, "how can the daughter of the dragons avoid consulting the sleeping dragon?" She grinned suddenly, irrepressible, a more natural expression than she'd ever shown before. And then, as though feeling it was a great faux pas, added, "Milady, truly, this is the oracle of our kind, the priesthood composed entirely of weres. We ask the will of heaven and the mind of the Jade Emperor. But we ask it by intercession of the tortoise and the white tiger, the red bird and the dragon. Our noblemen—or rather, the foreign noblemen that rule over our people—might think this shameful. But this is the religion of the people of China, the people who came out of the Earth, the nine sons of the first dragon—our people, milady. What remains of the belief in our dynasty."

And Jade, whose ideas on this were all confused—having learned from her father a lot of the more cultured beliefs of Chinese noblemen and from her mother that all Chinese belief was superstition—felt guilty for being out with a fox shape-shifter at all, much less out and searching for an ancient oracle that her people shouldn't even consult.

But Third Lady inclined her head at Jade's silence and steered the boat carefully toward a dark cave that seemed as though it were the mouth of the mountainous sleeping dragon. As they approached, Jade could see fires burning within the cave, and she frowned a little, but said nothing as Third Lady pulled out one of the oars and used it to row against the motion of the boat, thus bringing it down slowly, gently, onto what would be the tongue of the dragon, had the cave been its mouth.

There were fires burning around the edges of the cave, Jade perceived, though those looked more like braziers built in heavy dragon-shaped iron pots than open fires. Next to each of the braziers stood a person—Jade thought a young woman, but it was hard to tell, as the glowing coals cast more shadows than light.

Third Lady stepped out of the boat first, and threw her cowl back, extending her hand to help Jade climb from the boat. Jade pulled her own cowl back, feeling suddenly vulnerable and defenseless, as Third Lady announced in a ringing voice, "I am Precious Lotus, the third wife of the True Emperor of the Dragon Throne, the Right and Hereditary Ruler of All Under Heaven. And this is Red Jade, the daughter of the former Dragon Emperor, the sister of the current one. And we come to ask the decree of the Great Tortoise and to find the Mandate of Heaven."

For a while, as Third Lady's voice reverberated around the cave, no one moved. It seemed to Jade that she and Third Lady had mistakenly come to a cave where no human lived and where only some statues kept watch, from their niches in the walls, as incapable of movement and speech as the stones that surrounded them.

And then, from deep within the cave, from the dark shadow opposite the entrance, a woman emerged. She was middle-aged, and somewhat heavy, wearing a white robe of the simplest design and the heaviest silk. The long sleeves, the ends of which were cut in a deep V where the tips dragged on the floor of the cave, might have been more at home in a palace than in this raw cave. She emerged from the shadows as if they had birthed her, and knelt in a fluid movement, kowtowing once, twice, three times, and yet somehow managing to convey she was simply following a ritual and not, in any way, abasing herself.

"We are honored," she said, still on her knees, looking up, "that the ladies of the Dragon Emperor have come to consult us. The Great Tortoise, the Sleeping Dragon, the Bird of the South, the Tiger of the West have awaited your arrival." Without asking their permission, she rose. Her gown, somehow, remained immaculate—at least as much as Jade could see in the light of the braziers. "If you'll do me the honor of following me," she said, and walked into the shadows.

Jade and Third Lady followed, side by side. There was just the glimmer of white silk ahead of them, and everything around was the deepest gloom—so dark, so absolute, that Jade could not tell how near the stone walls were, or how constricted.

She had the impression that the walls were very

near, indeed, that the passage they penetrated was very narrow, very low, leaving no more space than for her and Third Lady to advance side by side.

The woman guiding them was barefoot. They could see her feet glimmering beneath her gown every time she stepped forward. Smells of incense surrounded them. For a moment, it seemed to Jade that she heard low chanting.

She thought, from the way Third Lady shuffled her feet and from the glimmer of her frightened eyes in the dark, that her sister-in-law was desperate to shift, desperate to be a fox, smaller and more agile, more capable of defending herself or escaping these surroundings.

Jade wondered if Third Lady had been here before, or if perhaps this was just a place she'd heard about. She didn't act like someone who was confident in these caves; but then again, Red Jade wondered how anyone could be confident in this shadow and gloom and this all-enveloping ritual.

Little by little, the passage widened, until they emerged into a chamber. Red and perfectly round, it was not just circular, for even the floor sloped gently to the center of the curve, where an immense brazier shone, brighter than any of its counterparts in the outside entrance hall. It illuminated the chamber sufficiently for them to see an old woman sitting by the brazier and, seemingly—Jade would swear to it— sipping from a cup of tea.

Third Lady sank to her knees and kowtowed, but Jade looked around her. On first entering, she'd thought the red glow from the walls was only the reflected color of the burning brazier. But now she realized the walls themselves were a deep, dark red, as though they'd been carved out of cinnabar.

And in niches, forming four points on the wall, were statues of giant animals: tortoise and bird, tiger and dragon.

The old lady set her teacup down on a little table next to her low stool and looked up. "You do not kowtow, Princess?" she asked, a cackle lurking just behind her high, defiant words.

Jade shook her head. Then, thinking the woman might not see her, she spoke. "No. I do not know where I am. And I do not kowtow to that which I do not know."

The crone cackled. "You are in the belly of the dragon, girl, in the womb of the Earth. No, don't try to show respect now. I know your kind. I was your kind once." She got up and walked around Jade, slowly. She, too, was wearing a white robe of the best silk. It susurated with her movements and formed a counterpoint to the slap of her bare feet on the cave floor. She smelled of coriander and ginger. "Um..." she said at last. "Pity the strand of foreign magic in your power," she said, at last. "Else you might have stayed here."

Jade, who could think of nothing worse than staying in this place of shadows and glowing red lights, simply bowed, feeling strangely grateful for her mother's magical inheritance.

The crone spared a look at Third Lady, still bowing, with her face resting on the floor. "Stand up, wife of the Dragon Throne," she said, casually, as her bare feet slapped their way back to her low stool. There she sat, picking up a fan and fanning the coals. "What do you want?" she asked, with no ritual at all.

"To ask the verdict of the Great Tortoise," Third Lady spoke, her voice trembling. "And the Mandate of Heaven."

The crone cackled, and Jade wondered if she was mad. But, indeed, how could anyone live here and not be mad? She thought of her mother telling her once that most mystics, in all cultures, were mad. It was living too close to the supernatural, to the divine. The human mind, the human body, were not designed for it.

"Very pretty words," the crone said. "And what did you want to ask the oracle, Princess?" Her eyes, black as carbuncles and suddenly very lucid, stared straight at Jade.

Jade found her hands clasping each other behind her back, and her voice answering exactly as though she were a little girl reciting her school lessons. "I want to know where Zhang has gone, and I want to know why. I want to make sure I'm not judging him unfairly, and that he has truly committed the offenses of which I suspect him. And I want to know how to steer around the intrigues about me and...and what I should do about the rubies and whether they are the salvation of my dynasty, or whether they hold the power of the world and must be returned to their shrine."

"And you, Lady Precious Lotus?" the crone asked, turning to Third Lady.

"I want to know..." She cleared her throat, whether because her throat had constricted from the solemnity and the smoke or because she had lost her courage and must find it, Jade did not know. "I want to know how to save my lord husband, how to keep his madness, if it should come, from destroying the Dragon Boats. And how..." She lowered her face to look toward the ground, and her voice, too, sank, lower and lower. "And how to win his love."

The crone nodded. She gestured toward the entrance from which Jade and Third Lady had emerged. A matron—either the same who had escorted Jade and Third Lady in, or another, Jade couldn't tell—walked in carrying a huge, dark green tortoiseshell. A younger woman walked behind her, carrying something that looked like a small, very sharp knife.

The old woman set the tortoiseshell on the floor and started, laboriously, cutting characters on its dark surface. While she worked, she spoke in a low but resonant voice.

"Oh, Tortoise of the North, whose color is black, whose element is water, whose season is winter, listen to the question of the Lady Red Jade, the dragon, daughter of the dragon. Answer her on whether Minister Zhang is guilty as she believes." The little wrinkled hand, which resembled nothing so much as a claw, moved rapidly, cutting characters that shone dully by the light of the brazier and looked to Jade oddly regular and beautiful, considering the circumstances of their carving.

"Oh, Tiger of the West," the crone intoned, "whose color is white, whose element is metal, whose season is autumn, listen to the daughter of the Dragon Throne. She wishes to know whether the rubies of power will be her dynasty's salvation or the world's undoing." The hand carved, and a sound like knife on bone echoed through the round red chamber.

"Oh, Bird of the South, who is born from your own ashes, whose color is red, whose element is fire, whose season is summer, listen to the Lady Red Jade, who would like to know, of your benevolence, which course to follow to stay clear of intrigues and conform with the Mandate of Heaven and the decrees of the Jade Emperor." She finished writing, and then her eyes looked at Third Lady, standing now beside Jade.

"Oh, Dragon of the East, father of the Chinese, whose color is green, whose element is wood, whose season is spring. The Lady Precious Lotus, daughter of the Fox Clan, third wife of the true occupant of the Dragon Throne, Wen, the son of dragons, the grandson of dragons, your own child—she wishes to know how to preserve her husband from the doom his love of the dreaming smoke has brought upon him. She wants to know how to conquer his heart and how to secure him in his rule."

Third Lady trembled, from head to toe, and her hands clutched at her gown. Red Jade asked herself if Wen was that important to his third wife, or if perhaps Third Lady needed the security and prestige of bearing the emperor's child. For if she didn't, what did she have? And if Wen died an early death, as such smoke-dreamers often did, what could she claim for herself? Her contract with the singsong troupe that had trained her had been bought out by Jade's father. But this didn't mean that she could now easily ply her trade as though she were a free woman. The skill they had given her, she had let become rusty; Jade was sure of it. How could it be otherwise, since she had spent no more time in plying her trade than now and then playing the lute for Wen when he felt a need for music? No, when Wen died, Third Lady would find herself sent back to her father's house, once more the surplus daughter, and this time widowed and with yet less resources.

Jade managed to clear her mind in time to see the crone, displaying strength that Jade did not expect of her, lift the shell of the tortoise and drop it atop the brazier. For a moment, the brazier flared up in a most unnatural way, the flames enveloping the shell, so that Jade wondered if it had been greased before being thrown in.

A loud crack sounded, echoing in the room, bouncing off the cinnabar red walls. The crone reached in and lifted the tortoiseshell—seemingly unable to feel what must be a great heat emanating from it—now in two pieces. "Behold," she said. "The verdict of the tortoise, the voice of the Jade Emperor. The decree of heaven."

She laid the shell on the floor, and Jade saw that the pieces were jagged, the crack tending now more this way and now more that.

"Yes, Minister Zhang is guilty," the crone said. "The Prince of the High Mountain is in a conspiracy against the Dragon Throne." She frowned at the next crack. "As for the jewels, the verdict of heaven is that you must acquire them and that they are..." For the first time her voice hesitated and lost force. "Both. The salvation and power for your dynasty and, at the same time, precious and belonging to the whole world. So you must use them to restore your dynasty, but you must also restore them to their shrine. As for what you must do, my assistant," she gestured toward the dark passage, "is signaling that she has received a communication from on high, and will tell you in a moment."

She turned to Third Lady. "As for you, wife of the True Dragon, it is possible for you to bring your husband through this unscathed and to prevent his sickness from affecting the Dragon Boats. Your husband could be the first one in many generations to sit on the restored throne of his ancestors and to rule over all of China, and protect it from the turmoil ahead. In fact, the Jade Emperor decrees that he will. But to achieve this result, and your husband's devotion, you must be braver than woman ever was, and you must take great risks. Are you willing, oh daughter of foxes, wife of the True Dragon?"

Third Lady nodded, once, her face so pale that even the red glow of the brazier could not lend it color.

"Well, then," the crone said, and gestured toward her assistant, the same middle-aged woman as before, who now walked all the way to the brazier. "Give the ladies the decrees of heaven."

The woman knelt and kowtowed, first to Jade, then to Third Lady. Facing Third Lady, she said, "Wife of the True Dragon. Third Lady of the Dragon Throne. Mother of future emperors. The Jade Emperor commands, and the Great Dragon speaks thus: The son of the dragon must be wakened, and only death shall waken him. The maiden who loves him shall take him where only the souls of those dead go. There you will free his soul from the underworld courts, where it is held captive by the capricious lawsuits of Minister

Zhang and his ancestors. Once the soul is freed and reenters his body, the son of the dragon shall reacquire his strength and power. Go you to the underworld, Feng Du that they also call hell or Diyu, with your husband, and see Judge Bao, in the Office of Speedy Retribution."

The woman bowed again, while Jade wondered what Third Lady made of all that. Only death could waken Wen? Were they truly suggesting she kill her husband? Jade hoped not, and she vowed to spend her way back to the Dragon Boats in persuading Third Lady this would not be a wise course at all.

But she had to stop thinking of this and turn instead to the middle-aged woman, who now rose on her knees and said, "As for you, daughter of dragons, find the man whose hair is like light on the ice, the man who made ships fly. He is in the tip of Africa, in the town they call Cape Town." She handed Jade a crudely drawn map. "Minister Zhang is coming to get the jewel from him. This jewel you must keep from his traitorous hands. The jewels have the power to renew the world. Take the one you can get and waken the rivers, so that each dragon of the main rivers of China shall waken and testify in the council of dragons. Then take the two together. They can waken the sleeping great dragon. They can evict the ursurpers and sit the son of the dragon upon the Dragon Throne. This you must do, oh daughter of dragons. This you must fulfill. It is your destiny for which you were born. This is the decree of heaven."

Having spoken, the matron fell forward, onto her

face, giving less the impression of kowtowing as of having lost all power.

"You have your answer, daughter of dragons," the crone said in a reedy voice. "You know what you must do. As do you," she said, her voice softer, "Milady Precious Lotus. Go and act in accordance to the decrees of the Jade Emperor."

A young woman had come out of the shadows. She led the sisters-in-law out of the deep cave, past the passage, at a much faster pace than they'd gone in.

In the outer cave, their boat lay waiting. They climbed in, and before they could touch the oars, the boat lifted off. It flew through the deep blue. And Jade found herself too stunned to speak.

THE FOREIGN-
DEVIL MIND

龙

Third Lady was deep in thought. She didn't know what her sister-in-law had understood of the dictates of the oracle, but she herself was stunned. When they'd said the maiden who loved Wen should take him to the underworld, her heart had stopped beating for a moment. Not that she thought they meant for her to kill Wen, but that they'd referred to her as a maiden. Which, indeed, she was.

She remembered meeting Wen. It had been at parties he attended with his father, in the village nearby where the Dragon Boats were normally moored, and sometimes at parties aboard the Dragon Boats themselves. The local people were no more than successful crafters and merchants, or perhaps successful bandits, which often came much to the same in locals' estimation.

Oh, she wasn't so foolish as to think that every farmer family nearby didn't know that the collection of oddly assorted barges and boats was the domain of the True Dragon Emperor. She wasn't a fool. The peasants knew or suspected, even if no one else did.

But a long time had passed since the Dragon Dynasty had ruled China. Millennia. Men uncounted had been born and lived and turned to dust. The peasants still knew that some people had the power to become animals, and to each animal they attributed certain qualities. Nobility to the dragon. Sly scheming to the fox. But that didn't mean they necessarily believed there had ever been a first Dragon Emperor, a first dynasty connected to the land like one of its limbs. No. They would think it nothing more than a pretty legend, a nice story. And in the privacy of their own homes, talking to their grandchildren, they might speak of the barges and boats as the domain of the True Emperor. But in the full light of day, in the crowded rooms of the tavern, while they might know that these neighbors of theirs could change their form and fly through the air, they'd never admit to one another that they believed in lost monarchies.

Third Lady—Precious Lotus, as she then was—the main singsong girl in this party of traveling entertainers, had known right away that she was performing for her emperor. Her father often got magical dispatches from the dragon capital in which the dragon spoke from a magical image in midair. She knew the emperor's look, that pinched expression about his eyes, and the way his mouth was set as though he suffered from a deep discontent. She did not know his son. Wen—broad of shoulder, very slim, his hair like black silk, spilling down his shoulders—had seemed to her quite the most beautiful young man of her acquaintance. His slightly detached, distant look only made him more interesting and unattainable. And the fact that his eyes lit up when he looked at her did not disconcert her at all.

One night, after many months of thinking about only him, she had performed as if just for Wen. That night, he had stolen her heart. And when the emperor had come, having noticed Wen's partiality, to purchase her contract from the master of the singsong troupe, the man, not knowing the true status of the one addressing him, had demurred. After all, someone of Third Lady's ability and beauty might become even the first wife of a minor nobleman or a well-to-do merchant. Certainly, she could do better than third wife of a member of a ragtag itinerant merchant or crafter band.

It had taken all her cunning to persuade him to sell her contract. And only part of it had been done because the man negotiating was the True Emperor. Precious Lotus had never had dreams of becoming royalty or even of mingling with it. No. It had been done because she dreamed of Wen and wanted to be by his side. He had captured her heart with a glance.

But the marriage had not gone well. Wen had taken opium before their wedding night, and slept on his side of the bed, all but ignoring her. And it had not changed since.

He still preferred her. And in his more lucid moments, she thought she saw his eyes appraise her figure, covetously. But he'd not done anything about it, and therefore a maiden she remained. She didn't know about his other wives, whom she decorously called Elder Sisters, but she suspected that they were much in the same state. And just like her, they would rather die than admit their virginal nature.

If the oracle was right, then Wen's soul was captive in the underworld, held on some contrived offense by Zhang and his dead ancestors. She might attract his body, she might attract his mind, she might attract his heart—but she could never make him love her as he should, not until his soul was freed.

If she understood it all correctly, getting Wen addicted to opium had been Zhang's means to make sure that Wen's soul could be detached from his body and detained indefinitely in the underworld. She bit her lower lip, in deep thought, trying to remember what she knew of the underworld and of how to rescue someone held prisoner there. Even if the oracle hadn't told her, she knew Judge Bao—a judge who'd lived many centuries before and who, upon moving to the underworld at death, had become the ruler of the Office of Speedy Retribution—would be the man to appeal to. His court required far fewer bribes than others, and he was known for taking fast and conclusive action. Hence the name of his office.

But while, like every maiden of the Fox Clan, Third Lady knew well enough how to arrange the travel to Feng Du and how to conduct herself there, she was not versed in legal matters. She must consult some of the scrolls on the records boat, scrolls that went back to when Wen's ancestors were seated on a physical throne and ruled over an immense area. They were magically preserved, kept from aging, and they were open to all, provided you neither removed them from the records boat nor damaged them, something the hovering archivists ensured.

Sitting opposite her, Lady Red Jade cleared her throat. "You do not set . . . too much store by the words of the oracle, do you, Third Lady?"

Third Lady looked at her with eyebrows raised, and tried to keep her shock from her face. "Of course I do," she answered at last. "For you must know it is the most ancient oracle in China, dating from the time when your ancestors ruled the land in deed and right. And never has it been known to be wrong."

Red Jade frowned, as though she were struggling with the impossible. For one moment of panic, Third Lady thought she would ask about her being called a maiden, and felt her cheeks heat at the thought. But when the Lady Red Jade spoke, it was about something completely different. "But . . . were they telling you to kill my brother?"

The question so startled Third Lady that she laughed, a high peel of a laugh. "Oh, no, my lady. No."

Jade raised eyebrows at her, as though demanding an explanation, and Third Lady gave it, in tumbling words. "It is only, you see, that they want me to take him to Feng Du. It is a spirit journey, and it doesn't necessitate death. Maybe people have visited the hells and come back to tell the story. Indeed, it is quite normal for the courts of the underworld to summon living people to come and testify on some case before them." She fixed the rudder, now that they were set on a straight course for a while. From the east, a pinkish light had started to glow, making her hope they would make it back to the Dragon Boats before daylight bathed all and revealed they'd even been absent at all.

This done, she folded her hands in her lap and looked at her sister-in-law, who was staring back at her in puzzled wonder. Third Lady smiled a little, remembering that Red Jade had been raised in a very odd way.

It wasn't that the Dragon Boats didn't have a clan of women, or even a group of elderly matriarchs ready to transmit ancient lore to the new generation. It was that Red Jade had been doubly isolated. First, because she was the emperor's only daughter and arguably his favorite child. This had set her apart and made her someone who could not be impunely disturbed or confined to the standards to which most other young women adhered.

For one, past twenty though she was, she had never had a marriage negotiated for her. This was because Wen was sickly. Everyone knew that, should he die, the throne would devolve upon Jade and whomever she married. And, failing that, upon Zhang. But the emperor, desirous of preserving his line, had many times turned down the offers of the widower Zhang for Jade's hand, in part because he knew that once Zhang married Jade he would waste no time at all in dethroning Wen.

But it went beyond that. In his fondness for his daughter, or his desire to ensure she was well protected, he had taught Jade how to fight and use weapons like any boy. Sometimes, when he thought the raid would be less dangerous than usual—such as when they raided a small vessel, carrying only a family party—he would allow her to join in.

These things made her as alien to the matrons and crones of the Dragon Boats as if she had come from the moon. It also meant no one had taught her the uniquely feminine magical arts, the commerce with the underworld, the sorcery of foreseeing, foretelling and changing the path of events.

If she'd learned any sorcery at all, it had been from her foreign-devil mother, whom the emperor, in fondness or madness, had allowed to rear her. And Third Lady, who had heard not very flattering things of the efficacy of foreign women's magic, gave her sister-in-law a look of profound pity.

"You must know," she said, "often when people seem to be dead for a time, and then come back to life and are as before, that was what happened to them. They were taken to testify in the courts of the underworld."

"Oh," Red Jade said, but she didn't look as though she had accepted—much less believed—what Third Lady said. "But . . . surely . . ." she said, and paused. "Surely you don't believe in all that." She made a gesture that seemed to encompass their own flying boat, the velvet sky, the stars, and the scraggly forest they were flying over.

"All that what, milady?" Third Lady asked, genuinely puzzled, wondering what her sister-in-law could be thinking.

"Well . . . the . . . You can't believe that the underworld, or whatever you wish to call the time after death, has the same rules and laws as our world. You can't really believe they have an emperor who issues decrees, or a court that judges them. You cannot believe that living people sue the dead, or vice versa."

"But they do, my lady," Third Lady said. "Feng Du, or Diyu, is . . . well, we call it the underworld, because you can enter it from some caves, but it is in fact a mountain in another . . . universe. In there all the laws of China meet, and it . . . it rewards and punishes everyone according to their beliefs. Buddhists and Daoists and all are accommodated in Feng Du, where there are courts and judges, punishments and purification for all. And then there is heaven, and the court of the Jade Emperor, where he is the perfect emperor and rules those whose feats have made them almost gods and caused them to ascend to the heavens. And all of it, heaven and Feng Du, is ruled according to rules administered by judges, who also have power over the living. Have you not read records of how the emperors themselves can be sued? How we must purchase the space under the Earth from the gods of the underworld, if we wish to bury our dead there? How tomb contracts must be drawn between the living and the gods of the underworld? Why would we do this, my lady, were it not necessary? Do you think most people, living from hand to mouth as they do, would bother with things that aren't necessary?"

Red Jade opened her mouth, closed it. When she opened it again, it was to speak in a weak, young voice that made her seem like a girl begging to be instructed. "My mother said there was nothing like it. That there were two places people went after death, and one only if they'd been very good, one if they'd been very bad.

She laughed at the underworld courts and . . . and all that. And her people seem to have as much proof of the existence of their afterlife as you claim we have of ours. And then . . . there are other people—the followers of Buddha—who believe we must return in an ever-ending cycle of lives, until we give up the joy in life and any interest in human affairs. How do you reconcile that with your idea of the underworld? How can an underworld occupy so many varied places and satisfy so many different beliefs?"

Third Lady shrugged. "One cannot account for what foreign devils believe," she said, in certainty, while reasoning that the emperor had been foolish indeed to let his redheaded concubine raise her daughter. But the crone in the oracle cave had said that Jade had foreign magic. A strand of it. And if so, that must mean her mind, too, had a strand of foreign-devil thought, the poor thing. "But I can tell you," and she found her hands weaving midair as they had learned to do when she'd been trained as a singsong girl, while she was telling stories, "that thought is a force, and a force that moves magic. Why should not the beliefs of each kind of people create their own underworld? And why should not the people who believe in that underworld go there, or get reborn, or whatever they believe they deserve? And in the case of China, why should we not submit to the laws of China in the underworld as we do in the world of the living? Why should we stoop to the ways of the foreign devils?"

"You are saying that we each judge ourselves," Jade said, her eyes wide, as though the thought were impossible.

"Of course. Who knows us better? But after a time, too, the force of these thoughts for millennia creates entities as solid and real as the people here. The Jade Emperor is real, and he's seen generations born and die. He knows more than we do about how the world operates and how justice can be obtained. And the underworld courts are real, too." She shrugged. "And they summon witnesses and claim verdicts. On living and dead alike. For if people go on living, in some form, after death, how else are we to process claims against them, or they against us? The Chinese have orderly minds. Or at least I do, and I like to believe the rule of laws extends after we leave our bodies."

She didn't know if she'd managed to persuade the foreign-devil mind within her sister-in-law. Lady Jade looked at her a moment, her eyebrows knit as though she was deep in thought. "I cannot do it," she said. "If the oracle was right about me, then I must fail."

"Why?" Third Lady asked, looking at her. "They said you were born to do this. How can you choose to fail before even trying?"

"Because I cannot leave the Dragon Boats now," Red Jade said, in a low, miserable tone. "I cannot leave if you're going to take Wen away to the underworld. I cannot leave them with no one in charge. What if the boats should need to fly? What if Zhang tries to come back and claim the allegiance of all aboard? What if—"

Third Lady grinned, despite herself. She was not used to seeing her composed and masterful sister-in-law act like the one who did not know how to proceed. "Ah, but it is not that way." Her hand went up in the air again, her fingers instinctively weaving thought and words and gesture together. "It is not that way at all. The underworld does not run on the same time as our world. In fact, there are many, many legends that speak of people who spend what they think are a few hours in the underworld, and who come back to find that everyone they knew has been dead for centuries."

"That doesn't help," Red Jade wailed. "What you're saying is that though you may save my brother, his cure will come in some future century which I cannot touch or know. And that the whole weight of the Dragon Throne now rests on my shoulders. I suppose you think I will marry Grasshopper and breed a line of regents, until Wen returns to claim the throne."

"I think no such thing," Third Lady said. "Besides, regents are notoriously self-interested and unstable, and not someone I would trust with the throne of an absent ruler." Realizing her humor was lost on her sister-in-law, who was groping for words, she dared to reach out a hand and touch the other woman's cool, delicate hand. "My lady, it is not like that. While the time may run that way, it may run the other way, too. I can arrange it so it will be as though only a few hours have passed since your brother retired before we return from the underworld. People will think nothing but that he slept a little longer and woke up...well, devoid of his affliction. They might wonder if I used some magic to heal him, but that will be all." She patted the cool hand with her own small one. "And meanwhile, you may go and seek the jewel that the oracle says shall waken the rivers. The Dragon Boats can do well without you for a few hours."

"But—" Red Jade started.

"Trust me, milady. Trust the oracle. What else can you do?"

The Lady Red Jade clenched her fists tight and rested them on her knees, managing to give the impression she wanted to pound her knees very hard, to vent her fury. "Oh, why am I brought to such a nonsensical pass? Why must I trust oracles, and bones and—"

"A member of the Fox Clan?" Third Lady asked, with ready wit.

Red Jade looked at her with such a startled expression that it showed she hadn't been thinking it. Or at least, that she would never consider saying so. And for this Third Lady was grateful. Gratitude made her voice softer as she said, "Because it is what you were born to do, milady. For many years now, you've been your father's counselor, and carried on your shoulders part of his responsibilities. For many years now, you've had to think and rethink your every step and to carefully follow every path of conduct in your mind before you did it in fact. But...my lady, the oracle is telling you to trust the dragon, the Jade Emperor and the Mandate of Heaven. For once," Third Lady added, almost drily, "you're being asked to obey."

"And you think it's high time I should try it?" Red Jade said, with a cocked head and a defiant expression.

Third Lady, who had never been very fond of obeying herself, though the circumstances of her life had often demanded it, smiled a little and shrugged. "Only because you've run out of other things to do."

FEVER AND GHOSTS

Late on the fifth day, and after Mrs. Perigord—who truly was an excellent cook and who seemed to be a good wife as well as an extraordinary manager—had employed some rather forceful, if purchased, magical healing, Nigel found himself well enough to stand and, enveloped in a voluminous dressing gown that he felt sure must belong to Joe Perigord, he installed himself on the balcony to take the air.

It was early in the morning, and a pinkish glow burnished the roofs of the working class neighborhood in which the Perigords' home was set. In fact, for the neighborhood, the Perigords' home was practically lordly, consisting of two floors, the top one containing, presumably, the bedrooms, and the bottom the apartments usually found in such—kitchens and parlors, Nigel supposed. As yet, he'd not been allowed to see them.

The straight streets, lined with—at least here—modest one-floor homes, reminded him of the cities in America where he'd stopped more than once in his peripatetic life as a flight magician. In fact, it reminded him of the American West. Save that here, the narrow gardens of the houses were enclosed not by picket fences but by high, smooth, whitewashed walls. Within the confine of these flourished domestic paradises, often startlingly European in kind—pears and apple trees, peaches and roses. Their fragrance washed up to Nigel's balcony on the wings of a soft breeze that brought with it also the smell of the sea, from the Cape of Good Hope, which gave the town its name.

Above the town and behind it stood the massive, dark bulk of Table Mountain, its flat top seeming as though a god's hand had clipped it short in its attempt to reach for the heavens. To the left of it rose Devil's Peak, more than three thousand feet high. And the mountain to the right was, Perigord had been kind enough to inform him, Lion's Head, about two thousand feet above the town. Table Mountain itself was a thousand feet higher than Devil's Peak—a sheer, dark rock against the morning-fired sky.

As Nigel looked, it seemed to him he saw something flutter and tremble at the edge of the mountain, but squinting his eyes against the brightness of the day didn't bring anything into focus. It would be a heat mirage and nothing more.

He leaned his elbows on the balcony and his chin upon his hands, gazing out. It seemed to him—though it was hard to see it past the Perigords' garden wall—that there were people on the street. He heard high, musical calls that he rather suspected were peddlers promoting their wares, in that worldwide chant where individual words became unintelligible, unless you were very sure what language they were speaking and had a good inkling what they were selling.

The breeze was growing warmer. Close at hand a dog barked, but it was not enough to keep Nigel's eyes from closing, as though his eyelids were weighted down with lead. The day would be a scorcher. Later on, he would need to close the curtains to keep the heated light from the room, and the only comfortable activity would be to sleep for two or three hours.

Weakened as he was by his recent illness, Nigel felt as though he could sleep now. With his eyes still closed, he indulged in that state between reality and dreaming. And out of that space—out of his tired, still-fever-fogged mind—a voice came, "Nigel! Nigel, wake up."

He opened his eyes, startled, because the voice was that of his long-dead brother, Carew. And on opening his eyes, he realized he was looking into the angry, teeth-bared muzzle of a blue dragon, the mouth opening, a smell like a hundred old furnaces emerging.

Nigel screamed and jumped into the room, taking refuge behind the bed. This was a stupid thing to do, since, had the dragon flamed, it could easily have reduced the room, the bed, Nigel and, eventually, the house to ashes.

But the dragon seemed to have other ideas. It perched on the edge of the balcony railing with ridiculous delicacy, its taloned feet clasping the edge of the stone. Its head, which in dragons of its kind was vaguely feline and also vaguely mischievous, poked through the balcony door, shredding the lace curtain that Mrs. Perigord had hung there and carrying it, on the protuberances and bumps of the reptilian head, like a wedding veil.

The mouth, not shaped for speech, spoke in a voice full of hissing. "The jewel. Give me the jewel."

From behind his bed, feeling like a coward, Nigel looked above the soft mattress and the mounded sheets and blankets, at this horror that he'd last seen melting an entire glass wall. He wanted his answer to be defiant. But what came out instead was a simple, matter-of-fact denial. "No."

"Give it to me!" the dragon insisted, imbuing even the consonants with hisses. "Give it to me. You don't need it. I do. And I have the other one."

Nigel's hand, groping frantically under the bed, had come up with the fine, silver-tipped, rosewood cane that Joe Perigord had left there earlier, for Nigel's use. Not that there was anything wrong with Nigel's legs, but because he was weak, and Perigord feared that Nigel would fall should he try to do too much, or go too far, too fast.

The cane was a paltry weapon against a magical creature. And Nigel was a paltry opponent, barely able to hold himself up. But just now, he felt too enraged to be weak. It had dared come here. It had dared follow him. It—

With the cane firmly grasped in his hand, he threw himself over the bed. It was meant to be a single leap, but it turned into a jump-and-roll on legs that felt far too rubbery. Still, it carried him across the room, within striking distance of the dragon's head.

"No," he cried again, his voice clear. "Never!" And

lifting the cane in both hands, he hit the dragon repeatedly about the nose with the heavy silver ball at the end of the cane. Then he thrust it hard at one of the dragon's wide-open, green eyes. "No."

The dragon looked not so much injured as surprised. He looked, a snickering voice at the back of Nigel's mind informed him in dispassionate tones, like a hunter who sees the fox turn and attempt to wrest the powerstick from his hands. But Nigel was not listening to the voice in his mind, nor to the reason that told him he could never defeat this creature.

Instead, he heard only the furious pounding of his heart, felt the dryness in his mouth, the maddening rush of blood through his veins. "Go away," he yelled as he pounded at the creature.

And suddenly, the dragon did. It yelped and dropped backwards—not so much as though it had flown or jumped back, but more as though it had been pulled or had fallen.

The room was suddenly a lot more spacious without the giant head in it—and a lot brighter, since the Perigords' lace curtain was still attached to the creature's head.

Sweating and trembling, Nigel felt his illness fall upon him again like a heavy weight, constricting his throat and robbing him of strength. He would have crawled to the window had he not had the cane in his hand, which enabled him to support himself better than his weakened legs allowed.

The sight that greeted him, out there in the blazing morning sky of Cape Town, ranging from quite near the house to the distant blackness of Table Mountain, was unbelievable.

There were two dragons—one blue and one red—engaged in a fierce battle. Part of the battle was easily visible: the bodies twisting, the teeth biting, the bright blood—or was it ichor?—sprinkling the trees in the orchards, the roses in the gardens, marring the whitewash on the walls. And part of it seemed to be invisible. The dragons separated and jumped in answer to nothing the naked eye could discern.

From the streets, cries and screams echoed, and Nigel was aware that people had gathered to watch. He knew that Cape Town abided by Commonwealth rules, so weres would be outlawed, under a sentence of death if discovered. He wondered if there would be a Gold Coat detachment about. If they would march in and fire their powersticks at the dragons. And he wished they would.

The dragons fought with fire, too, singeing the tops of trees, and setting off a howling from the streets below. And now the sound of a fire engine's bells was heard, and then the hooves of the horses, hastening—Nigel presumed—to put out any trees that caught fire. In the suffocating heat of the day, fires would be a real danger.

Nigel had enough magical power to suspect that the dragons were also fighting with magic. Oh, it wouldn't be magic like his—not English magic. No. It would be foreign-dragon magic. He could almost feel it, though not see it. He could sense the fields of power extending from the creatures as the red dragon surmounted the blue and dug silvery claws into its underbelly, sending a torrent of red blood onto the street below like unholy rain.

The blue dragon turned and tried to grab at the red, but there was something in its way, something invisible that prevented it from quite closing its teeth on the red neck. And the red dragon, shimmering gold with the suddenness of—her? Nigel was almost sure that dragon was a female—turning, grasped the blue by the neck and threw it . . .

The blue dragon tumbled, head over tail, leaving behind the impression of a purple aura, which might have been an aftereffect of magic, or simply the trail of its passage slashing through the paler blue of the sky.

And now there was the sound of feet in marching formation from the street below, and Nigel could just catch a glimpse of a golden uniform. Gold Coats. Her Majesty's Royal Were-Hunters. They were in Cape Town, after all. They were coming to put an end to this.

He looked up from the street to the sky. The red dragon was quite gone, and the blue dragon merely a streak of color and shimmer in the distance. Voices from the street called instructions. "It went that way." "No, that." "East." "West."

Nigel guessed that when everyone turned to look at the Gold Coats, the red dragon had disappeared. Which made sense. It could either have flown away very fast, or assumed—her?—human form, and vanished somewhere. Though where a naked woman, and a naked Chinese woman at that, could hide in this neighborhood was a mystery.

Nigel stepped back on trembling legs until he fell heavily on his mattress and hid his face in his hands.

He heard heavy steps on the stairs—Joe Perigord's steps, he would bet on it. Nigel had come to know them. And then the door opened, and Joe said, "Thank God, you are well."

Nigel uncovered his face briefly and looked at his host who, trembling and pale, leaned against the door frame. Nigel gave him a wan smile. "I attacked the dragon with the cane, I'm afraid."

"Afraid? No. Don't be. If you ... if it worked ..."

"I was more afraid he would set fire to the house," Nigel said. "He would have, if the red dragon hadn't come and battled him. Not that I'm sure the red dragon doesn't want the same thing and means to ..." He shook his head. "It is too dangerous for me to remain here, Joe. Your entire family could have been killed today because of me."

"Nonsense."

"Only because of the red dragon ..."

"Well, that and the silver-handled cane," Joe said, seeming to be repressing laughter with his last shred of willpower.

"I don't think—" Nigel started, and was about to confess he didn't trust the efficaciousness of such a weapon, when hurried steps outside made them pause, just in time to hear a light knock on the door.

Nigel checked his dressing gown, and Joe said, "Yes?"

The door opened to reveal Mrs. Perigord in the doorway. She was a middle-aged woman, whose dark hair and bright blue eyes still revealed a hint of the beauty she had, undeniably, possessed. Even if her mouth was set in a severe line and her hands were twisting at her apron, she managed to look more worried than angry. "Joe," she said, and swallowed. "Mr. Jones . . . There's a lady downstairs. She says she must speak to Mr. Jones."

"A lady?" Joe asked, and Nigel echoed him closely.

"Well, at least she's a Chinese woman and completely . . . without clothes . . . but she speaks like a lady. And she says she must speak to the man with the luminous hair."

"She speaks English, then?" Nigel asked, blinking, and suddenly he was absolutely convinced this was the girl from the carpetship, and that she'd also been the red dragon.

"Oh, yes. She speaks English like a lady."

Nigel thought of asking if she was armed, or else if she looked like she intended him harm, but he realized that would be churlish. He had been weak and at her mercy in the carpetship. And what had she done? She'd stopped his bleeding and saved his life.

He looked up at the excellent Charlotte Perigord. "Show her up, please, Mrs. Perigord."

She nodded. "She's putting on a gown. One of Hettie's." She seemed to expect them to argue, and when they didn't, she nodded once sagely, as though her wisdom had been confirmed. She left, and returned moments later. Or rather, two sets of steps sounded on the stairs, one soft, the other heavy.

And then Nigel's angel appeared in the doorway. Dressed in Hettie's gown, she managed to look as Hettie never did. Though the gown was modest muslin and cut in such a way that it befit a girl not yet out—hiding everything to the neck and down to the wrists, covering this woman—it seemed to have acquired a sensual quality of its own, as though its folds, and the way the simple fabric draped, were designed to show the voluptuousness of the body beneath. And it was voluptuous, as Hettie's would probably never be—full breasts, and a small waist, and the suggestion of long, slim legs. Her neck, too, was long and graceful, acting as a pedestal to display her oval face.

She curtseyed to him—not the polite curtsey of a maiden in a ballroom, but a full curtsey, dropping to one knee, her gown a froth around her, exactly like someone being presented to the queen, and Nigel blinked at her in confusion—a confusion that turned to awe as she tilted her face up to look at him.

In his fevered dreams, he'd thought that he'd imagined the slight blue shine in her eyes, but he had not. Those eyes, wholly Chinese, with their heavy lids, looked completely black until she tilted her face up. And then—Nigel had only seen this once before, in a crystalline rock whose name he'd never found out. He'd discovered it in a cave in the depths of his parents' garden, on one of the rare occasions in childhood when he'd been well enough to tramp about exploring. It had looked like coal, only hard and vitreous. And when he'd broken it to see what it contained—having been raised on stories of diamonds found in lumps of coal—and exposed it to the light, the broken surface had glowed such a deep blue as he'd never seen. He'd kept the rock for a long time before losing it, and when he closed his eyes, he could still see that intense, shimmering blue.

He realized he was gaping at the girl and closed his mouth, but she didn't seem to see anything amiss. In fact, she inclined her head, and spoke with her head lowered: "Oh, bearer of the jewels at the heart of the universe, I know you have reason to doubt me, but I beg you to hear me."

Her accent was completely British and—as Mrs. Perigord, who stood by twisting her apron like someone who is not absolutely sure she has done right, had said—upper class. But her words were so incredibly Chinese that for a moment Nigel was not at all sure what she'd said—much less what she'd meant—and so he waited for her to say something more. When nothing came, he realized she had been asking his permission to continue and said, almost curtly, "Speak. And call me Mr. Jones." He hesitated only a moment, because somehow it seemed wrong to lie to angels, but he could not think any good would come of telling her his real name. Either she already knew it and was avoiding saying it for her own reasons, or she didn't know it at all, in which case giving it to her would be a danger. "Enoch Jones is my name."

She looked up, as though to gauge how she should proceed, and swallowed, the movement visible in her elegant neck. "Mr. Jones," she said, "I don't know how to explain my errand to you. When you last saw me, if indeed you remember when you last saw me—"

"Of course," he said. "You were with the Chinese pirates." It was all he could do not to tell her that he'd thought her an angel, but even he was not so stupid as to imagine that would make sense.

"Yes," she said. "Only..." She couldn't seem to find her way to the next word.

"You also saved my life," he said, feeling sorry for her and wishing to rescue her from her difficulties. "For which I have wished to thank you."

Again the pretty blush, a delicate pink tone on her soft cheeks. "I..." She shrugged. "I saw you were holding on to the entire carpetship and keeping it from falling and I...How could I not save that many people?"

"If I understand—and please forgive me, I haven't spent much time with your people, only had that sort of glancing contact one has when piloting carpetships into the cities where foreigners are allowed—but if I understand, your people do not care much who dies, if those who die are foreign devils."

"My mother..." she said. And she lowered her head, effectively hiding her face from him as she spoke. "My mother was English. She was taken from a raided carpetship. Her name, she told me, was Miss Augusta Bentworth. She was on a trip to join her fiancé, who was a building magician in Macao, when—"

"Gussie?" Nigel said. He could no more have kept silent than he could have grown wings. "Mama's Gussie? But Mama still speaks of her!"

"I beg your pardon?" the girl said, looking up, suddenly all British and missish.

He felt himself blush as if he'd committed some impropriety. And he was aware of something that sounded very much like Joe hastily swallowing a

chuckle from where he stood in the doorway. The unspoken play between the two of them would not have
evaded any English lord, no matter how long removed
from proper society.

"It is only," Nigel said, with pained exactness, "that
Mama was a great friend of Miss Augusta Bentworth.
Her disappearance, as Mama thought, in a carpetship
crash blighted Mama's first year of marriage, and she
always meant to name a daughter Augusta, should . . .
should she have had a daughter."

"Oh," the girl said, looking up, and for just a moment let a smile peek through her too-grave expression. "I don't remember a Miss Jones amid those my
mother spoke of, but—" She stopped. "But that would
be her married name, would it not?"

Nigel nodded. "Indeed. Her maiden name was
Amelia Roston."

"Oh." She smiled. "But . . . but that makes us almost
relatives!"

Nigel grinned. As strange as it seemed coming from
this very unusual girl, the comment amused him as
much as it pleased him. And he couldn't even tell why
it pleased him, except for feeling that it was good that
Mama's Gussie was not wholly gone. "Is she well, your
mother?" he asked.

The girl shook her head. "Oh, no. Mama died ten
years ago. She . . . My little brother died with her."

Nigel felt a momentary pang, but all the same, he
thought that his mama would prefer that Gussie had
left a daughter than not at all. Even if the daughter was
a Chinese pirate. Though he was not sure he'd tell the

pirate part to his mama. He extended his hand to her. "Please get up, Miss...er..."

"Lung," she said. "My name is Red Jade Lung." She grasped his hand with hers which seemed very little and soft in his, and, standing up, smiled shyly at him before lowering her eyes. "I am called...Lady Jade."

"But you did not know our mothers knew each other," Nigel said. "So you could not have been intent on..."

"Helping you because of that?" Lady Jade said, and nodded, as if understanding his difficulty. "No. It was just that...I never knew when anyone on a ship might be my relative, so I thought, perhaps I should avoid killing, as much as possible."

"Why do you attack carpetships at all?" Nigel asked, confused.

"Oh, that's...That's not easy to explain," Lady Jade said.

From the doorway, Joe coughed, just enough to catch Nigel's attention. "If you could make your way downstairs, Enoch, we shall serve you and the lady some tea, and you can speak there."

Realizing that he'd been making his chaperones stand in order to continue chaperoning them, Nigel clutched his walking stick and nodded. "I can make my way downstairs."

DREAMS

Third Lady had watched her sister-in-law depart.
She'd not told anyone because these days everyone
knew Red Jade was the true power behind the throne,
and if it were known she was gone from the boats it
would only cause panic.

Third Lady didn't want panic. She was scared
enough herself. She had read how to conduct her husband to the underworld, and how to behave herself
there, so as to return with him. She had collected
several rolls of paper cash, of the sort used at funerals, because she knew they were the currency of the
underworld. They weren't real cash, of course, just paper, printed with a value. The traditional amount of
cash to purchase a tomb from the gods was 999,999
strings of cash, and that was the value she took.

And now she stood, fearful, outside her lord's room.
On either side of the door, guards watched her with a
jaundiced eye while she hesitated.

At last she advanced boldly toward them, and
bowed. "I would like to see my lord," she said, "if you
would announce me."

In almost any other household, this would be thought too bold, for a wife to come visiting her husband who had not requested her presence, much less for a third wife to go disturb a husband who had not requested her presence. But Third Lady often found herself coming to Wen's room. It was, after all, almost the only way for her to spend time with him, since he never visited her—or his other wives, in fact.

She would often come and play mah-jongg with him while he dreamed his opium dreams, or else recline next to him and touch him, and derive what comfort she could from that. How strange her fate, that she should have fallen so in love with a man who did not love her at all—who loved nothing but his dreams.

But she thought of what the oracle had said. That if she took him to the underworld and back, she could win his love. She hoped the oracle was right. Suddenly, the fact that it was reputed to be an infallible oracle was not enough, and she wished she had more concrete proof in her hands. Perhaps the foreign-devil mind was contagious.

She tried to look self-possessed and convinced of her right to enter her husband's chambers. The door guard gave her a narrow look, but probably credited her with no worse intentions than a wish to conceive the future emperor.

He opened the door and went in. She heard him kneel—a rattle of arms—and address Wen. She heard Wen reply, in a slow, dreamy voice. She was not sure what they said. Then the guard came back out and stood aside, leaving the door open to her.

She went in and caught a glimpse of Wen on his bed,

holding his pipe. And she knelt. Normally, when she came to visit him like this, she would simply lie down beside him and enjoy his company. But now he was the emperor, and that changed things. She knelt and rested her forehead on the floor. "My lord," she said, "I would like the pleasure of your company." And then she remained like that, her forehead on the floor.

"Precious Lotus?" Wen said, as if puzzled. Then softly, "You may approach," either in the tone of one who had just remembered the protocol, or in the tone of a man moved by her presence.

She didn't know which, so she rose slowly from her position and looked up at him. He lay on the sumptuous bed that had been his father's, with its gilded frame and its multicolored silk pillows. In his hand, he held his opium pipe, with its carved jade stem, and—at the moment—a dark metal bowl.

Kneeling by the spirit lamp used to cook the opium was one of the younger members of the Dragon Boat clan, a boy maybe fourteen or fifteen years old and, from the look of him, probably one of Zhang's by-blows. That didn't surprise Third Lady. It would make sense for the minister to want his own son amid those who administered opium to the emperor. How else to make sure that Wen was still smoking it, and in dosages sufficient for him to remain ineffective?

Now that Zhang was gone, the opium might no longer be coming in, but there would still be plenty of it—enough to ensure that Wen would stay in his dreams a while longer. And disaster loomed once he stopped. Third Lady wondered exactly how much he'd been smoking. She knew that sometimes opium withdrawal—particularly sudden—could be fatal.

She counted the balls of dark amber opium rolled on the tray, waiting their chance at being heated and inhaled. There were five, which seemed to be rather a lot to be ready for a single smoker. How addicted had Wen become? She remembered that she'd once heard the story of a great friend of her father's, who was an opium addict and who usually smoked in his library. When he'd given up the habit, for months afterward they kept finding mice dead behind the bookcases, from withdrawal.

Kneeling beside the bed, she looked into her lord's eyes. His pupils were small as a speck of dust, and they shouldn't be. Not for someone who had been an addict as long as he had been.

She felt the attendant's curious gaze on her as she bent her head toward where Wen's elbow, resting on his pillow, supported his head. She looked up a moment to see Wen, too, looking at her—not so much with curiosity as with soft compassion, as though he knew well how much she loved him and how useless it was.

As a fox shifter, she had the power to attract all men. That was why she had become a singsong girl, because it was easy to entice men and bend them to her will. But no one had told her she could lose her heart, too. And though her clan was known for various forms of sorcery and magic, from witchcraft to herbal potions, Precious Lotus had left her father's home long before she was learned enough to be able to deal with this.

But she had read the manuscripts in the records

boat. She knew where the entrance to the underworld was and how she could attain for herself and Wen the sort of unconsciousness that would allow their souls— or at least her soul and his mind, since his soul was already held in the underworld—to roam free while their bodies were unconscious and safe aboveground.

Also, she had studied all the legal cases that could be brought against Wen or his family. And she had memorized a long list of witnesses, including the various ancestors, whom she could call for help.

Third Lady should have felt as prepared as she could be, and as confident as anyone would when facing the world of the dead, and the perils of the supernatural. What she didn't know if she could do was convince Wen to follow her to the cave where she might then be able to put her plan into action.

And without his following her, without her taking him to the underworld, there was a good chance he would die of withdrawal or that the turmoil wrought on his magic by the withdrawal would do harm to the Dragon Boats.

"Milord," she said.

He fumbled at her hair with his hand and it felt as if he couldn't quite coordinate it.

"Milord, Lord of the Dragon Throne," she said.

"What is it, Precious Lotus? What do you need, my fox-fairy?"

Because of the magic inherent in her clan, Precious Lotus knew that her people often got called fox-spirits or fox-fairies, but she'd never heard those words from her husband's lips. And looking up, peeking like a child afraid to face an adult fully, she saw him looking down at her, a loose, sloppy smile on his well-shaped lips. He looked amused and loving, but then he usually did look loving, particularly when he'd been smoking.

"Has anyone frightened you?" he asked in sudden alarm, perhaps catching the fear behind her eyes. He set his jade pipe down slowly and frowned at it, as if he was trying to think of something. Probably, Third Lady thought, trying to remember how many pipes he'd smoked.

He looked past his wife's shoulder and spoke, clearly to the boy who was waiting to heat the opium. "You may go to your boat. Come back in half an hour."

And then, as Precious Lotus heard steps retreat toward the door, Wen said, "You may speak to me, you know that. You may always speak to me."

She rose a little, and kissed his cheek, and said, softly, "I want you to come with me."

"Come with you?" he asked, sounding a little alarmed, as he always did when anyone asked him to leave the boat, or his opium dreams.

"Only . . . only for a moment," she said.

"Why?" he asked.

She realized that if she told him the truth—if she told him he needed it and she was doing it on his behalf—she'd be spurned. But the concern in his eyes as he looked at her was quite obvious. And she thought, against all logic, that he always seemed concerned for her, even in his confused state. In fact, he'd been so attracted to her that his strict father had thought it worth it to secure her as Wen's wife. And even now, Wen seemed to care for her.

She was a fox-fairy. Men who fell in love with her were supposed to be malleable in her hands. It was only because she loved Wen so much that her charm had failed her. And because she loved Wen so much, she could not allow it to fail any longer.

Looking up at Wen, she made her eyes as pleading and full of sorrow as possible. "I have a great need of your protection, milord. You see, I have been threatened."

Even through the haze of opium, which confused his mind and clouded his senses, and normally made him utterly indifferent to anything outside himself, Wen reacted. He sat up with what was, given his state, remarkable quickness. "Threatened!"

"Yes, milord."

"Who dared?" This was spoken through clenched teeth, and it gave her great hope that wherever Wen's soul was, it was already attached to hers.

"Some members of the Fox Clan," she said, wildly improvising. "They . . . they have somehow caught wind of my . . . maiden state." She blushed prettily as she said it. "And they believe you mean to repudiate me and, therefore, they want to marry me to someone else in advance of your repudiation."

He looked stricken. And also guilty. "It is the opium," he said, and hesitated. "You see . . ."

She knew that the smoking of opium often robbed gentlemen of their virile powers. And she'd not meant to reproach her lord, only to make him come with her. "I know, milord," she said. "But there is this place, this sacred cave where . . . Well, it is said that there . . . you could remedy the situation." She blushed again, partly from speaking of these matters and partly from her guilt at deceiving him. "If you come with me for just one night, you can save me from being torn from your arms."

Wen frowned slightly. His long, sensitive fingers toyed with the jade stem of his opium pipe. "Are you sure you wish me to, Precious Lotus?" he asked, in the tone of an insecure child.

"Milord! How can you ask that?"

"Well . . . it is all to nothing, you know . . . I might not be able to sire an heir, in that one time, and . . . and if I die, as is likely to happen soon, what will you be left with? Perhaps it would be better for you to be married to someone else before that happens."

Third Lady felt as if her heart were being wrung within her. She felt the color flee her face. "Of course," she said, "if you don't wish to . . . If you'd rather I weren't your wife at all, if our marriage was all the doing of your illustrious father, and you, yourself, would rather not be linked to me—"

"No," Wen said. "Our marriage was the one thing— That is, my father purchased your contract at my earnest entreaty. I know you're only my third lady, but in my heart you always have been the first."

"Then, milord, let us not worry about the future or if you should die, or if you might not leave an heir. The future might come or not, but I don't think I can survive another day after being torn from your arms, and I beg you to prevent it."

He sat up slowly and put his feet down, hunting for

his slippers. She found them and gently put them on his feet. They were loose. He was much too thin, his dreams robbing him of substance, as though they were translating him to another reality.

"Now?" he asked her. "We'd better go now, then."

A MAN WITH HAIR
LIKE ICE

"And so," Jade said, *lowering her head, "you see,* Third Lady's oracle was proven right in telling me where to find you." She looked at her hands and at the dark, polished table. She held a teacup, though the tea didn't taste anything like what they drank on the boats. Indian tea, they'd told her. It wasn't unpleasant so much as completely different. The teacups themselves looked rather like the ones Mama had bequeathed her, only with rather more roses. "I don't know what to do about the rest. The . . . jewel and all."

She looked up and saw a circle of their faces staring at her. There was the man with hair like light on ice, as well as the couple to whom this house belonged. They had sent their daughter out of the room, though Jade wasn't sure why, and she'd seen the woman give the man a significant glance when Jade had explained that Third Lady was her brother's third wife.

But Mr. Jones just looked very seriously at her, and listened to her whole tale, and now sat with his hands held together on the table, just like Jade's mother had taught her to hold her hands when praying.

Jade didn't know what to think. That this man was the son of Mama's friend was very odd. Somehow, those people of whom Mama spoke had always seemed to Jade like fairy tale characters, people she would never meet. And though her mother had taught her English, as well as the manners of a young English woman, Jade had never thought she would get to use either.

Also, as far as Mr. Jones was concerned, she had always thought that people with almost colorless hair looked odd, but she didn't think he looked odd at all. Oh, he didn't look like the men she had grown up with. But he didn't look ugly, either. He looked, she thought, like something quite different.

When her mother spoke of her youth in England, Jade had always imagined the people as looking Chinese. She knew that this was wrong, since her mother looked nothing like the Chinese people. But she could only fill that dreamland with people she knew. Now, for the first time, her mother's stories became populated with different people—people with hair like light on ice, straight noses and angular faces.

He looked at her, very grave. His eyes were blue—pale blue like the mid-day sky. "And what if I say I will not accept your partnership in finding the other jewel?" he asked. "You are asking a great deal of me, to trust an almost unknown. When you say that wakening the rivers of China and restoring your dynasty to its throne will not destroy the rubies, how can I be sure you have not deceived me?"

Jade bobbed her head up and down, less of a bow and more of a gesture of sympathy. "I understand I am asking a lot," she said. "But I am . . . you see . . ." She shook her head in despair at her own clumsy words. How much the people in the Dragon Boats would laugh at finding Lady Jade so tongue-tied. "You see, my family lost the throne many generations ago. Or at least not the real throne, but dominion over the land. And I'm not going to pretend they might not have deserved it," she said. "I . . . My father never spoke of it, but I have gathered, from other legends, and from things that aren't said in those legends, that those people who could shape-shift and who were the users of magic often subjugated people who could not shape-shift to their whims. When we lost the dominion over the land to invaders—again this is not said, but I have always understood it—the general population rose up against us. We lost the Mandate of Heaven." And then it occurred to her that he probably did not know what she meant by that. "What I mean is that—"

"You lost your right to rule," he said slowly. "I gather some of what that means, from my voyages to China, and I . . . I have read a lot."

She nodded. "Yes. But now, after all these millennia, the Mandate of Heaven is changing. Those who occupy the Dragon Throne—the usurpers—aren't even Chinese, but a foreign dynasty that imposes its will upon us. And my people . . . You know how things stand. We have lost wars to the English. So many of us have taken to opium dreaming, and the country is in disarray and often falls into famines. I believe," she said, and meant it, though she'd never thought of it in such terms before, "that Wen would make a better emperor than the current rulers. I believe that there is a very good chance he'll rule well. And we are connected to the land itself, you know. The dragons are the spirits of the rivers." She spoke quickly, aware that she didn't make much logical sense, but hoping that Mr. Jones saw beyond the logic of her case.

He sighed heavily. "My instinct would be to say I simply want the jewel back, and that I will take it to Africa where it belongs. That I do not belong in the midst of Chinese dynastic politics, dragons or not. That I do not have anything to do with your Mandate of Heaven..."

He stopped, and she looked up at him, hopefully. "But?" she said, sensing something unpronounced in what he'd said.

He shrugged. "But how do I recover the jewel from a Chinese were-dragon without your help? There are a hundred places he could be in China where no white man will be allowed to go—which reminds me, I don't know how I would go there even with you, but that's something else—and there is the fact that he might very well be in league with the English queen and her army. I cannot alone prevent the ruby being taken and used. And it is quite possible that, despairing of getting the second, they might decide the first is enough for them, and that they will use it the way Charlemagne did. So we are in a race against time."

His eyes, fixed on her, were clear and cold and full of calculation. "You have told me all about your people, even about the piracy—"

"Your race against time," the man whom Mr. Jones called Joe said, "is actually dependent on what the English are willing to do to reward this man, Zhang. I would guess they have so far refused to pay him off and demand he find the other ruby as well. Hence..."

"Hence the visit of one Captain Corridon," Mr. Jones said. And then, to Jade, "Someone who demanded that Joe give him the ruby, without so much as the courtesy of explaining why." He paused, a frown creasing his brow and making him look very grave and severe. "The thing that I wonder about is whether there is some way we can disguise me..."

"There is," Jade said, dredging from her memory an almost forgotten legend, and hoping that it was correct. "There is a magical draft the Fox Clan has, which can make a man look like another man. It is possible it could make you look Chinese."

For a moment the frown increased, and the man looked absolutely thunderous. Jade remembered how the people among whom she had grown up regarded being compared to foreign devils as a grave insult. She wondered if it would go the other way. She had gathered, from things her mother had said, that the English, just like the Chinese, considered themselves the pinnacle of humanity, around whom all other races must cluster and bow, as younger siblings to an elder son. She wondered if the man felt it would be an insult to look Chinese. The idea filled her with equal parts dismay and anger.

But before she could say anything, he spoke. "Well, it would be a way of disguising me," he said. "And of my disappearing from where the English will look for me." He looked at her, and the frown increased, but she could tell now that it was a frown of thought, as though he was trying to do something deep within his mind and reality struck him as a bother. "Of course, how will we disguise you? I mean, I presume that Zhang knows what you look like, and that he has his own resources within China?"

Jade frowned. "My . . . power signature is the harder thing to disguise, as it ties in with all the rivers of China, through my dragon ancestors. It is possible to disguise it somewhat, to make me seem only like a Chinese noblewoman, but I have to use my foreign magic to do it." She looked up as an idea occurred to her. "Though you probably can help me with that."

This seemed to amuse him. "I probably can. But you still sound concerned, as though this would be a doubtful endeavor."

"Well, it would be," Red Jade said. "The oracle said I should go and wake the rivers and if that's the case . . ."

"Yes?"

"My power will not stay disguised for long. It is simply not in the nature of it to do so."

"You mean the rivers will remove the disguise?" he asked.

She nodded, relieved that he understood. "It would be," she said, "like . . . going to visit relatives while wearing a big hat that hid your features. Your relatives would pull it off to see your face. It is also possible," she admitted, "that I cannot wake the rivers, even with the power of your ruby, while my power signature is disguised and thus not allowed to resonate with the river dragons. My power might be needed to wake them . . ."

"Like seeing a familiar face, yes," Mr. Jones said, still in that tone of odd amusement. "But that would mean only that you're momentarily unmasked and that we could disguise you again afterward."

She considered this, then nodded. "Yes, but I don't know if there might be other difficulties. You must remember, I've never done anything like this."

This truly seemed to catch his sense of humor, because he chuckled deep in his throat, and said, "Then we are even, since I have never done anything like this, either." He gestured with his hand. "All of it. I have never flown carpetships, or . . . or gone about not making use of my parents' fortune or their connections. I have never carried rubies of power between continents. I've never . . ." He shrugged. "I never thought I would have any adventures, you see. Just that I would stay in England all my life and have some boring job."

"Would you rather have stayed in England with a boring job?" she asked, trying to understand what he was saying.

"Oh, I don't know. Sometimes I think so. But then I think not. And then, today, I would have died if you hadn't intervened."

She shrugged. "Zhang has less power than I. He only wants to be of the Imperial line, but he is not, actually. Still, the fact remains that I do not know if I can prevail," she said. "I'll have to ask you to trust me, but I can't promise victory."

He gave her a disturbing smile. "You're telling me you can't predict what will happen and that it will be a wild adventure?"

She tried to guess what the smile meant. "I don't mean . . . That is . . ."

He shrugged. "I don't expect guarantees. For the last six months my life has been unscripted and wild anyway. However, I wish I had some way of judging your intentions." He looked apologetic. "Not for myself, you see, but for the safety of the jewel that is... the last piece of power holding the world together. It's not my opinion only that should count."

They looked at each other a long while, locked in that dilemma. How could she prove to him what her intentions were? Truth be told, she wasn't even absolutely sure her intentions were what he would consider good or right. Most of all, she wanted to protect her people. Unlike Zhang, she would not risk the rest of the world for her ambitions, but if the choice were between making the other nations of the world happy or making her people happy and putting her dynasty in power again, then she might very well choose her people over the rest of the world.

She pushed the now-empty teacup away and set her hands on the table, folded. "I don't know how to show you proof of my intentions. I don't know what I can do to show you that I do not wish to steal the jewel and strip it of its power... or give it to the Queen of England."

He opened his mouth as if to say something, and from the expression on his face, what he meant to say was grim enough, but before he could speak, the gentleman to whom the house belonged spoke from across the table. "I believe, from what you said in your sleep, Enoch, that you have the remedy for this matter within your own hands."

"My hands?" Mr. Jones asked, startled.

"Well, not your hands exactly, but in your possession," Joe said. And to Mr. Jones's blank look, "I believe you'll find that, if you get the ruby, it will either react to the Lady Jade as friend or as foe. And since it seems to read the minds of men...If I understood what you told me correctly, the only reason it is in the possession of Mr. Zhang is because you had it shielded against revealing itself and, by being shielded, it is incapable of reading the mettle of those holding it. And you can't reveal it while it is so far from us, and where anyone may grasp it, so shielded it must remain."

"Yes, but..." Mr. Jones looked, for a moment, almost panicked. "But if it judges against her?" he said at last.

"Then we'll have rid ourselves of a foe," Joe said, though the look he bent upon Jade was not in the least threatening.

Jade kept her hands folded on the table by an effort of will. Was she willing to let herself and her intentions be judged by an ancient magical artifact of unknown provenance and perhaps with a different moral value structure than either her own or Mr. Jones's?

The alternative, she realized, was to leave the jewel in Zhang's possession, and risk the loss of her brother, any hope of regaining the throne and perhaps all hope for the world.

She inclined her head. "I am willing to be judged by your ruby," she said.

A WIFE'S DUTY

It shouldn't be so easy to take the emperor from the Dragon Boats, Third Lady thought. But then, this was only because everyone put their hope and trust in Lady Jade and not in Wen at all. Third Lady could resent Lady Jade for this, but she knew that even now she was trying to track down the jewel that would awaken the rivers and put Wen upon the restored throne of his ancestors. Yet Wen must be ready to take the throne.

She had led Wen around to the back of the Imperial barge, past the guards. The guards had, in fact, tried to follow, but Wen had made a gesture of dismissal and they'd left.

And now she and Wen were in the boat and headed for the secret cave, where Third Lady hoped everything was ready per custom. According to the scrolls, it was a narrow opening in the mountains to the southwest, not at all like the cave where she'd taken Lady Jade.

This one was secret, known only to the Fox Clan. In fact, as she pulled the boat up at the entrance, then deep enough into the cave that no one would see it, she wondered if the cave would reject Wen. She hoped not, since Wen was married to her, and therefore, in some way at least, no matter how remote, a member of the Fox Clan.

The slit in the rock was barely wide enough for her to row the boat into it, carefully, making sure that nothing scraped. Wen was still in his opium dream, though he'd left his pipe behind on the Imperial barge, and he looked at her with unfocused eyes as she hopped out of the boat.

She offered him her hand. "Come, milord."

He looked around, his eyes very large in the darkness. "Are you sure?" he said. "It's so dark."

She shook her head. "Do not worry." She had to admit that the entrance to the cave was indeed dark, and smelled dank, and that nothing would look less appetizing as a place in which to make love. "Once we are farther in, I will light the magelights," she said. "But we must first get out of sight of the entrance. Remember, this belongs to the Fox Clan, and if they see the lights shining, they might know what I'm about to do and come to thwart it."

She extended her hand to him. His hand slid into hers and she pulled him gently out of the boat and onto the narrow tunnel ledge of the cave. Then she guided him into the cave, his steps hesitant and faltering.

"Are you sure?" he asked, once, as they navigated a particularly narrow part of the tunnel.

"Am I sure of what, milord?" she asked gently. "That I can light the magelights? Yes, my lord, I can.

They're in the walls already, waiting only to be activated, and they—"

He shook his head. She couldn't see the movement, but she could hear it in the dark. "No," he said, his voice an urgent whisper. "Are you sure you wish to stay with me?"

"Oh, my lord, always!" *Beyond this world and the underworld,* her mind added. *Beyond the will of gods or the decrees of heaven.*

She pulled him farther inside, his hand moist and cold in hers, until she judged they were far enough from the entrance. Under her breath she said a disguising spell, so that to anyone else, even to her relatives of the Fox Clan, the cave entrance would seem to be utterly closed by rock.

Wen must have caught the spell, because he said, "Wha—"

"Just disguising where we are, to make sure we are not interrupted," she said, and wondered that her husband was not—by now—frantic. After all, the Fox Clan had a reputation as tricksters and liars, deceivers and traitors.

But Wen gave no hint of doubting her word, and when she whispered under her breath the words that would cause the magelights embedded on the walls to ignite, all he did was look about with wonder and curiosity.

The truth was that the look of the lights surprised even her. She'd expected the normal white lights, embedded in niches, at regular intervals. What she got instead was a profusion of flickering colored lights, like captive fireworks, all over the rough stone walls. The lights picked at some veins in the wall that looked like mica and pyrite and made them sparkle, giving the whole cave the look of an enchanted land.

"Fox-*fairies,*" Wen said, in a low tone of appreciation, and smiled at her. She let go of his hand. If what she understood of her clan's history was true—per the instructions she'd received long ago in her girlhood—this tunnel would lead to an inner room, where the preparations could be made for travel to the underworld. And if things were as they were supposed to be there, then it would also look much like a bridal chamber, and perhaps Wen would have no reason for alarm.

He followed her willingly, so she didn't need to hold his hand or pull him. He touched the wall once and said, "I can almost feel the magic, but it is very ancient."

"It is an ancient lair of my clan," she said, "established by the Duchess Eterna."

"Oh," he said, because the duchess—sometimes called Queen Eterna—was a villainess of children's stories.

Third Lady looked over her shoulder and smiled at him, trying to appear reassuring. "She was not," she said, "everything she is claimed to be, you know. Though I daresay none of our ancestors were as good or as bad as it's claimed."

"No," Wen said, softly, and then in a slightly louder tone, "I am not afraid of you."

"I know, my lord," Third Lady said, feeling tears sting her eyes, but not letting them fall. Because though she'd fallen foolishly in love, and in love with an opium addict at that, she had also fallen in love with a man not of her clan who had never suspected her of double-dealing. And that alone would be worth traveling to the underwörld to keep.

As she thought this, the corridor opened into a vast circular chamber. Unlike the room of the oracle, it wasn't a vast sphere—merely a circular space, with flat floor and roof. Here the rock seemed to be all gold, except it couldn't be so, Third Lady thought, so it had to be pyrite. But it sparkled like gold in the light of the multicolored flares, which here covered and circled the ceiling, seeming to dance.

She almost breathed a sigh of relief—except she didn't want Wen to suspect that she had any reason to be particularly relieved—because it was, indeed, set up as a bridal chamber, with a broad bed in the center, a hearth all set up for lighting and cooking, with a teapot and jars that, according to Third Lady's information, contained herbs and tea.

With a gesture she bid the fire lit, and casually she told Wen, "If you'd lie on the bed, milord, there is a healing potion I must cook. Before we can . . ."

He smiled at her, shyly, and she felt herself blush at the tenderness in his eyes. There had been such tenderness and shyness on their wedding night, but then nothing had happened.

She set a pot of water—which had been kept under spells so that it was still fresh—on the fire, then came over to the bed and removed Wen's slippers and arranged his pillows. Her hands were shaking. Even now, if he should suspect that not everything was as she had told him, he could turn into a dragon and confound all her plans.

Dragons were the most powerful of all the were-clans, and though Wen might be addled by opium, his magic weakened because his soul was kept in the place of the dead, he was still the True Emperor of All Under Heaven, and there was a magic that attached to the Dragon Throne—a magic that Wen could call if he felt himself threatened, if he suspected his fox-fairy wife of double-dealing.

Before she could get away, he reached for her hands and held them both in his. She startled, but he only took them to his lips and kissed the open palms. It was an odd gesture. She'd never heard of it being done. But there was infinite tenderness in the touch of his lips.

"Thank you, Third Lady," he said soberly. "For choosing to stay with me. I hope you'll never regret it."

"Oh, never, milord," she said, feeling herself blush down to the soles of her feet and up to the roots of her hair. She heard the water boiling and returned to the fire. Into the teapot that sat next to the fire—an ancient porcelain work of art in the shape of a fox—she crammed the leaves that would cause them to leave their bodies and be able to enter the underworld. She had to be careful with the dosage since, if she were not careful, their souls might leave their bodies forever. And that was not what she intended. Besides which, Lady Jade would be most seriously displeased.

Atop the leaves of the various plants that made you sleep or dream, she added as much tea as she could, to disguise the taste. She packed the teapot as though she were making old-man tea, where people crammed the teapots full of leaves, then poured in only as much water as it took to soak them, and thus made a tea strong enough to get old blood pumping.

She waited, counting under her breath to two hundred. And then she poured the tea into two matching cups, painted with a fox that sat and grinned at them, as it must have sat and grinned at generations uncounted.

How many of her ancestors had come through here? How many had engaged in this ritual? How many had gone to the underworld? More importantly, how many of them had come back?

For the only thing the scroll said about finding their way back without going through the wheel of reincarnation was that they must—they absolutely must—insist on coming back. Precious Lotus wondered to whom they would have to insist, and how much they would be believed. She knew having jade disks—those safe conducts dispensed by the Jade Emperor—would help, but though Wen's family legends spoke of them, there were none in the records room. And so she must go into the underworld unarmed, save for her slim cache of documents and her roll of paper cash and the nine-colored silk—the nine-colored silk again being paper, but symbolizing a vast roll of precious fabric.

She walked to the bed with a cup in each hand. And this was a tricky point, for Wen must fall asleep, but she must stay awake long enough to be able to burn the paper cash, the documents, the nine-colored silk and the other provisions she'd brought for their journey. She must, in fact, not drink as much of the tea nor as fast as he did. But he also must not suspect anything.

Handing him a cup, she knelt by the bed. He looked

at her quizzically. "Why must you drink it, too?" he asked. "You do not need to be healed."

And she realized that the excuse she'd given him in fact provided her with what she needed. So she set the tea aside and said, "Very true."

She would drink it later. She'd never thought that anyone would drink anything given to him by a fox shifter, even one married to him, and not think that she might be poisoning him. But the thought was very far from Wen's eyes as he drank the tea in one gulp, then said, "Will it take very long to act? Oh." The *Oh* came as a surprised exclamation.

He extended his hand to her. "Third—Precious—" But he couldn't seem to hold the thought in his mind, nor the words upon his tongue. His hand found one of hers, and closed on it with a hard, convulsive grip. He collapsed on the bed and shuddered, once.

And then a great pallor settled upon him, making him look like a statue carved out of ivory. And he stopped breathing.

Her heart hammering, her hand hurting from his grip upon it, Precious Lotus madly ran through her mind the mix she'd put in the teapot. Had she used too much of one leaf, too little of the other? But the formula in her head held true. She'd used the exact amount.

And then a thought like a cold ice-shower formed in her mind. What if the opium that Wen had taken interacted with something in the tea and had, in fact, killed him?

"No," she said, as much to herself as to Wen's still,

silent body. "No!" And then at a faster pace, "No, no, no, no!"

She tore his fingers away from her hand—his grip still so strong that she was afraid she would have to do violence to his hand to wrench herself free. On her knees, blindly, she crawled away from him, not caring what happened to her fine silk gown.

By the fire were many pots, copper and scrubbed. She took a small copper pan back over to the bed and held it in front of Wen's lips, willing, wishing, praying that it would become dewed with breath.

THE RUBY'S OPINION

Nigel started toward the stairs, supporting himself on his walking stick, but Joe stopped him, one hand on Nigel's shoulder. "Stay, Enoch. You can barely walk."

"But—"

"I know where it is, remember? I had custody of it while you were unconscious and defenseless."

It was a reproach to Nigel for not trusting him, and, in fact, Nigel felt chastised. Joe could have taken the ruby while Nigel was unconscious. Joe could have let Nigel die, grasping full force on to the field of the carpetship and preventing it from crashing even long after it had landed. But instead, he'd served Nigel with unwonted kindness.

Nigel lowered his head and said, "I'm sorry. I'm so used to it being my responsibility that I—"

"Indeed," Joe said. "I understand."

"But what if the other dragon is up there?" Nigel said. "Waiting? Ready to attack you?"

"No," Lady Jade's soft voice spoke from behind him. "I can sense him if he is that near. That's how I found him, when he was first here. He will not come now. Not until he recovers from the magical blows I inflicted on him."

Joe flashed a devil-may-care grin that made Nigel think that when Joe was much younger, he could not have been all that much different from Ger Southerton, after all. It was the grin of a gambler, of a consummate whip—the sort of grin that seemed to belong to an earlier generation, when society had been freer and men were more daring and less stultified by convention.

Nigel heard Joe's steps up the stairs as he stood at the doorway into the dining room, leaning on his walking stick. Mrs. Perigord and Lady Jade sat at the polished dining room table, and Nigel wondered what Mrs. Perigord made of all this. He'd assumed, what with his having been delirious when brought in, and Joe and his wife spelling each other in looking after him, that she must know at least as much as Joe.

But between looking after a wounded man that her husband told her was an old friend and abetting a girl who was a Chinese dragon—a dragon, furthermore, that she had seen engaged in mortal combat with another dragon in the sky—lay a substantial divide. He could not imagine any woman who would take the challenge so complacently as Mrs. Perigord seemed to be taking it, and if she was truly that sanguine, then Nigel had to assume that Joe had been absolutely right to marry her. For not a hundred noblewomen could have equaled that serenity of mind.

"No, Hettie," Joe's voice sounded, from upstairs. "This is something about which you need not know."

Something answered him—a girl's voice, Nigel guessed, trying to sound both dutiful and curious enough to get an answer.

"It wouldn't help you any," Joe said. And then he was back downstairs.

He motioned Nigel to get into the dining room, and closed both doors. "Hettie," he said, "is far too curious for her own good." He sounded both worried and, Nigel thought, curiously proud of his offspring. "She's always been too curious, even as a babe. Always crawling where she shouldn't go, or making her way into perilous hiding places, from which I and her long-suffering mother had to rescue her—sometimes at considerable expense or trouble to ourselves." He sighed and looked across the table at his wife, who was smiling fondly at him. Nigel wondered what shared memories were in their minds and felt a pang, because he knew it was likely he would never experience this—the joy of fatherhood, the joy of living with a woman he loved.

Carefully, Joe set the jewel on the table. He'd wrapped it in a bit of satin and he presumably had cleaned it of the blood that, if Nigel's memories were true, must have covered it.

Sitting on the table, as the satin fell away from it, it looked like any other ruby. A good cut, medium sparkle. Nothing that would excite the covetousness of half of the world, nor cause Nigel to go, like a hounded man, from land to land and continent to continent, seeking a sanctuary that couldn't be had. Not until the jewels were returned to their proper place.

Squinting, Nigel could see the veil he'd put on the jewel's potency, and the veil that Joe had set on it, too,

when Nigel's magic must have dwindled along with his
life spark. He could rip both veils away from the jewel
with a touch of his hand, but he hesitated.

"The moment the veil is gone," he said, quietly,
"everyone in the world who is looking for it will know
where we are. The moment the veil is gone, every two-
bit soothsayer, every sorcerer with farseeing capabili-
ties, will focus on this place like a beacon. I cannot stay
here once the veil has been removed, even if I put it
back on."

Lady Jade looked up at him. For a moment their
eyes met, and she seemed to understand the responsibility he carried. Nothing was said, but in her strangely
blue eyes there was the reflection of a great burden. "I
will take you wherever you need to go," she said softly.
"Even if the ruby doesn't judge me trustworthy and
doesn't advise you to help me wake the rivers of
China."

He didn't doubt her. There was no room to doubt
that earnest voice, but he wondered where he would
go, weakened and still injured. And yet, it didn't seem
to matter. Jade was already here, and there were Gold
Coats in Cape Town. Sooner or later they'd start inves-
tigating where the dragons might have gone, and why
the dragons might have come here in the first place.

It could be no less than an open secret that Nigel—
the carpetship magician who had so mysteriously saved
everyone—was here. The neighbors would know it and,
likely, the neighborhood merchants, and any friends of
Charlotte Perigord, as well as any friends of Hettie.
There could be no doubt of that.

And Her Majesty's Secret Service knew or had a

pretty good suspicion of who Nigel was, too, else they would not have come importuning Joe for the ruby. It was only a matter of time—and not a very long time—before various people put their heads together, the neighbors talked of the blue dragon perching on the windowsill and someone came to look into the house. And found Nigel. Someone would recognize him—someone who had attended school with him, someone who knew him through his very brief stint in the Secret Service.

Before that happened, Nigel would need to move on. And he would need to do it before these forces had reason to suspect that Joe knew more than he seemed to. Already his friend, for the sake of protecting him, was treading on very thin ice, indeed. After all, he had to know a dragon had perched on his window and flown away with his lace curtain. No one was going to believe he was completely ignorant of that. So Nigel would leave him with a good excuse but, more importantly, Nigel would leave him. Before he got Joe in worse difficulties.

"Very well," he said, as much to himself as to Jade's suggestion. Reaching over, he encompassed the ruby and grasped the magical veils. Then he pulled his hand and the veils away, with a sound like tearing.

Light shone, filling the whole room with unbearable brilliance and sparkling into every face. Even Nigel, who was used to the ruby, had to close his eyes. He could not quite hear the ruby's voice in his mind, but he could sense it. He knew this ruby was Soul of Fire, and that it was both concerned and grieved over the disappearance of the other jewel.

Only, of course, it wasn't as simple as that. The ruby was not human, nor was its personality that easy to read. It was . . . like an old, old creature, like the distilled wisdom of all mankind. It was the same personality Nigel had met when he'd faced the avatar of mankind's magic, but not speaking in words.

He reached for the jewel, almost without meaning to, his hand trying to cup it and soothe its distress, reassure it that he would, indeed, look after it, keep it safe.

His hand met Lady Jade's, which was there just ahead of his. She touched the jewel.

This set off another glow—a strange one that Nigel had never seen. It seemed to him, as he squinted to protect his eyes from the unbridled burst of light, that the red shine entered Jade and shone through her. And though he knew it wasn't true, for a moment he had the sensation that he was watching her heart beat in the midst of the red glow.

"My Lady Jade," he said, softly.

She looked at him through the glow, and their eyes met, and he felt as if the glow of the ruby enveloped and reassured them both. It could not be more clear had it, in fact, spoken in words. It could not be more explicit. It agreed with Jade's plan. That much was clear. It approved of Red Jade. It would go with her wherever it needed to go.

Through the strange bliss, the feeling of being connected to both the ruby and Jade, Nigel heard Joe's voice. "Enoch, my friend. It might not be the best thing to leave it uncloaked that long."

No, it wouldn't be. With an effort, Nigel dragged

himself away. He touched the ruby; his hand was still half enclosing Red Jade's. The ruby flared once, and then the veil fell over it, muffling its brilliance and magic.

"I can't stay," Nigel said, his voice tight. "I must dress, and then we must leave."

Joe looked puzzled. "But you're not nearly well enough to go anywhere."

"And yet I must go," Nigel said. "As far away from you as I can." He enumerated the ways in which he was a danger to this man who had probably saved his life.

Joe frowned. "I don't like it. I have to admit that you are right, and, of course, the last thing I wish is to endanger Charlotte or Hettie." He was holding his wife's hand, on the table, as he spoke. "But all the same, I don't see where you can go that you might heal and be up to the sort of epic journey Lady Jade has described."

Lady Jade looked at Nigel, with an appraising glance. "We must go somewhere in China, where it's open to foreigners, and where, through my connection to the Fox Clan, we can obtain the herbs that will disguise you."

"Hong Kong," Nigel exclaimed, feeling his knees go weak. It was not so much the result of a careful thought process as the result of a process that had gone on beneath the surface of his mind all the while, adding together many things. He looked at Jade, anxiously. "Would you be able to find the herbs you need in Hong Kong?"

"The British free-port island?" Lady Jade asked,

then nodded. "Almost certainly. There are many Chinese there, and I know for a fact there are several were-clans. The Panda Clan came to my father once, with a delegation."

"Oh, good," Nigel said, feeling still weakened, but also that curious relief of a man who glimpses a way out of what he would have sworn was an impossible situation. "And you said you could take me somewhere? I assume you can, that is..." He hesitated, because there was, after all, no way to ask a wellborn lady if she could carry him, or if he could ride on her back.

Jade smiled a little, as though appreciating his difficulties with etiquette. "I can take you with me while I'm in dragon form, yes."

"Oh, good," he said again. And then encompassing Joe and his wife and Lady Jade in a look and noticing that all of them appeared equally baffled, he sighed. "You see, my father has friends in Hong Kong. Distant cousins, in fact. They ... I can go to them and pretend I just found myself on the island, weakened from some fever."

"But I thought," Joe said, somewhat drily, "that it was important that nobody track you."

"It is," Nigel said, with a tremulous smile. "But because I will be traveling by dragon and putting as much distance between myself and Africa as possible, very quickly, this will allow me to stay for a little time with someone I know. By the time word gets back to England and my parents—or even to the ears of the British Secret Service—I will have changed my appearance altogether, and I will be a native amid natives."

"What about the other dragon?" Joe said. "Zhang, Lady Jade called him? What about Zhang and the other ruby? What will you do to recover the other stone? For if I understand it right, you must have both to make sure the universe is anchored, or the magic healed, or whatever it is that the jewels are supposed to do."

Nigel nodded. "Yes, but I have a feeling, if we do what the oracle said, things will more or less work themselves out. And besides—" He frowned at the idea that occurred to him. "I'm fairly sure Zhang will come in search of us."

Lady Jade inclined her head. "Not right away," she said. "He will need to heal from his injuries. I . . . attacked him magically as well as physically."

"Yes," Nigel said. "That much was obvious."

She inclined her head again, in what seemed to be a gesture of acquiescence. "It would be to a powerful magician," she said. "But I don't expect he will give up the quest for this jewel. At least, not unless the British promise him the same payment for one of the jewels as they would have offered him for both."

"And they might," Nigel said. He had been in the Secret Service, even if only very briefly, and he was aware—no one could be better—that sometimes objectives changed, and when a goal proved unattainable, another was substituted. And of course, Her Majesty who—if what he read in the papers was true—was suffering from very ill health and possibly dying, might decide that all she needed was to repeat the feat of Charlemagne and bind the magical power of Europe to herself and her descendants. At that—as a more jaundiced observer of human nature than Charlemagne might have been and also considerably more prudish—she might very well bind all the magic of Europe to herself and her *legitimate* descendants.

It was possible, and if too much time went on, such an end would doubtless come. But until then, he must push himself and try to recover Heart of Light. If not, he would take Soul of Fire back to the shrine. But he knew that with only one jewel, the shrine couldn't hide itself.

And how could he leave the village, the way to which the Secret Service probably knew by now, unprotected, with a jewel like Soul of Fire in it? He might as well give it over to Queen Victoria altogether and accept the destruction of the universe.

He looked at Lady Jade, a princess whose clan had waited for millennia uncounted for the restoration of their line, at Joe and at Charlotte, who had so kindly sheltered him in his need. He thought of his parents back in England, of his ex-wife, Emily, and her new husband, Kitwana, in their mountaintop African village.

If the universe were gone, then those people would go, too, and they were good people who did not deserve that sort of doom. Nigel would not allow it.

He looked at Lady Jade. "Let's leave. As soon as may be."

HALF THE PRIZE

Prime Minister Zhang, Prince of the High Mountain, aspirant to the throne of All Under Heaven, did not bow.

Glaring, he stood in front of the commander of the Special Services here in Cape Town. The man was, to all appearances, a middle-aged colonel—Zhang, who craved power for himself, had long since become acquainted with the insignias of power among the English—but he'd been brought forward when Zhang had given the special words and secret signs that he'd been taught by his British contacts.

The man was rude and didn't offer him a chair. Instead he had taken the only chair in the room, reclining on it haphazardly, with that want of care for appearance that was characteristic of his breed. He looked at Zhang with eyes full of haughty disdain, but Zhang didn't care.

What he cared about was acquiring the other jewel. The Englishmen wanted the other jewel, too, and for the sake of it would endure much from Zhang.

And, Zhang thought, would endure much after

Zhang acquired it—for although he meant to use the Englishmen to help his purpose, he had no intention of handing them the jewels. The English already had too much power, barbarians that they were. In the end, the Mandate of Heaven demanded that the power be kept with the Emperor of All Under Heaven, who would be Zhang.

"I understand," the Englishman said, after giving Zhang an almost contemptuous once-over, "that you have only one of the rubies of power."

Zhang's leg hurt where the concubine's daughter had bit him. His whole body hurt from the flares of her power. It wasn't fair that a creature who was the daughter of a foreign devil should have the ability to defeat him. But he stood proud in the suit that the garrison commander had lent him. The ruby was in a magical belt about his waist, which would survive all the changes in form intact. "Only one," he said. "But I know where to get the other."

Into the commander's ear he poured the tale of the girl who called herself a princess, and the humble home in which she'd taken refuge. "If you hurry," he said, "you might capture her."

But the commander only grunted. "Your kind are notoriously elusive," he said. "I've had reports of a red dragon flying away from Cape Town and out to sea." He shrugged. "It seems as though it is up to you to capture her."

Zhang bit his lip. The problem was, of course, that he knew very well he could not capture the ruby alone. "With your help, I will."

The man smiled nastily. "As an assurance of our help, perhaps you can give us the ruby you now hold?"

Zhang was speechless for a moment. He did not want to give the ruby to the English. For one, he suspected that once they had the ruby, they could track down the other, and he would be expendable. Nor, once they possessed it, would they be willing to give it back. But what excuse could he use?

And then he thought of the perfect reason—what he had heard referred to as the curse of the ruby: that if the jewels were touched by someone tainted with greed, they would burn that person and all around him. Zhang had intended to use his son, Grasshopper, to hold the uncloaked jewels while Zhang channeled their power to himself. He might still do that, but Grasshopper wasn't with him, and fetching him first would delay everything. He intended to make use of some young Britisher infused with idealism and a sense of duty instead. He'd let his superiors select that sprig of virtue, and he'd let the young man get hold of the ruby. And then he'd kidnap him and steal the power. But for now, the curse would serve as an excuse. "The ruby is shielded," he said, "and worse, by the man who held them before. Should he unshield it, it would probably incinerate me. I am taking that risk on your behalf."

"Foolish of him, then," the Britisher said, half-amused, "not to unshield it."

Zhang shrugged. "He can't know it's in hands that crave its power. I might have given it to an innocent to hold."

"As we intend to do," the Englishman said, sounding yet more amused.

"Indeed, but not until the time is right. If you saw a Red Dragon leaving..."

"We did."

"Then you need me," Zhang said. "I know how to track her. I know what she's likely to do. And I know how to ambush her."

He'd dealt with the British before, and he knew what they would endure from a man who could give them what they wanted. They would even endure commerce with a were-dragon, which their own laws forbade.

He stood.

A DASHING OFFICER OF HER MAJESTY

Hettie Perigord was feeling slighted. Or perhaps she was feeling cheated, lied to and ignored. Or perhaps all of the above.

Oh, to begin with, she'd never trusted that new friend of Papa's, the one he'd saved from the crash of the carpetship and installed in Hettie's own room, while forcing Hettie to make do with the guest room down the hall, which was barely larger than a closet.

That was the other thing. Papa had said that the man must be put in the larger room because he was wounded—he would need to be seen by doctors, and people would need to be in and out of his room. The bigger room allowed for greater ease to treat him.

And maybe that was true. Well, at least it was as much true as anything else that Papa or Mama said. Very often they made no sense at all, and Hettie knew she was being given half explanations, as though she were no more than a babe in arms. It was insulting but, in a way, she understood that.

Papa and Mama had tried very hard to have more children, but something had gone wrong when Mama had Hettie, and therefore they must be contented with her. Mama said it was just as well, because Papa traveled so much as first mate for the carpetship line, she'd never be able to keep watch over a passel of brats, particularly if all the brats had been as full of mischief and invention as her Hettie. Only, Hettie didn't think that was quite true, because when Mama said that, she got a sad and distant look in her eyes, as if she were looking at a lovely picture of something that could never be. And Hettie thought that Mama and Papa would have liked to have a dozen children, and since they only had her, they must protect her as if she were an entire dozen.

Only now, she wasn't sure what they were doing was in the name of protecting her. In fact, if anything, they seemed to be going out of their way to endanger her and themselves. And that she couldn't allow, because though she was only seventeen and in many ways she supposed she was spoiled—at least she was the only girl in the neighborhood whose parents had scrimped and saved for years to be able to send her to a private school with the children of wealthy merchants—she did have proper feelings, and she did care for her mama and papa much more than they seemed to care for themselves, absurd creatures that they were.

And when it came to bringing a wounded man into the house, who talked in his sleep—and it was no use at all Papa thinking she did not know what the man said, because she did—and who in his sleep spoke of himself as a lord, and who furthermore called himself Mr. Jones, as if that could be anyone's true name...

Well, it was no use at all thinking that Hettie was going to believe it, because she wasn't.

And then today, with dragons and all, and a completely naked Chinese girl showing up right after the Chinese dragon disappeared, well! Hettie was not a fool. She tossed her head, as she made her way out of the house as quietly as may be.

Hettie had looked through the dining room keyhole and seen a great red glow. There was something about a ruby or some magical jewel or another. She remembered Papa talking to Mama in whispers about a jewel, and she wondered if the man who called himself Mr. Jones had stolen it.

After all, she'd grown up on stories of carpetship magicians, a breed that, until this Mr. Jones, Papa had absolutely no use for. He'd always said they were at the very least petty thieves, and most likely worse than that. He said they were all on the run and most of what they were on the run from was their own bad habits. All of this he'd said throughout most of Hettie's life, only to reverse it now, over this man, as if it had never happened.

And yes, she had heard what the man had done and how he'd saved the carpetship, and Papa's life. But the thing was, even Hettie—who was not nearly as grown up as Papa and not nearly as jaundiced—had seen how often it was true that people might be very brave or very capable of sacrifice in one thing, and yet remain the most black-hearted villains who ever walked the Earth. So how could Papa not think of that, Hettie reflected, as she slipped out the kitchen door and into her parents' carefully planted, well-tended garden. Her mother did most of the work, since Papa traveled so much, but their apple trees were the envy of the neighborhood. And as for their quinces, well, there was simply no one to touch their quality. And their roses, too, bloomed with more color and fragrance than any of their neighbors' flowers. She walked carefully between the rosebushes, taking an odd path to the left, then knitting herself to the wall.

She did not think any of the older people were going to look out of the dining room window, but they might, and if she took the garden path straight to the gate, they might see her. No reason at all that she shouldn't be walking out the back gate, but you never knew when Mama and Papa would decide to go all protective and irrational. She might be going to visit her friend Mary, or her friend Jane, who lived just down the street and who had been her friends since they were all learning to walk. The fact that she wasn't only made it more imperative that no one should see her leave. Because this would be a very bad time for Mama and Papa to get curious.

For almost a week now, she'd managed to keep her meetings with Captain Corridon a secret. He was tall and handsome, with the sort of suntanned pale skin that always seemed to her to bespeak adventure. Except in Papa, where, of course, it just bespoke Papa.

He was the second son of an earl, and so tall. And though Mary said that his red hair clashed with his red uniform, that was just foolishness. Besides, the captain had told Hettie he didn't always wear a uniform. He was—as well as an officer in the army—a secret agent for Her Majesty, entrusted by the queen herself with missions that he couldn't discuss with Hettie, since on them might hang the fate of the world.

In fact, from things he had let drop during their various conversations, she knew he'd been to China and India, knew all of Europe and had visited the Americas, and he knew how to get out of the most harrowing situations. He'd let it drop that he'd once been surrounded by a hundred Zulus on the warpath. He'd never explained how he got out of it, mostly because he'd immediately begged her to forget that he'd said anything at all, since he wasn't supposed to speak of his adventures. But it was clear he had got out of it, because he was now here, in Cape Town.

And though he'd never explained under what circumstances, he'd mentioned hunting the buffalo on the American plains, and he'd said, too, that he'd become a Cherokee chief's son by adoption.

All in all, he was the sort of romantic man that a girl like Hettie could only sigh over. But the best part of all—and probably what caused Mary's untoward comments—was that he liked Hettie and wanted to know her better.

For days now, he'd met her outside her gate, where the garden gave onto the narrow alley between the back wall of their garden and the back wall of Jane's garden.

And it wasn't as if he'd ever said anything improper. He hadn't. He just talked about her, and was delighted to hear all her stories about her father, and what her father had always said about carpetship magicians, and how Hettie could not believe he was now being taken in by this stranger.

Captain Corridon was interested in Hettie herself, and in her life. And it wasn't just because Hettie had used on him that small magic she'd inherited from her father—the glamoury: the ability to make anyone believe anything she said and do her will for a very short period. Mary might say that's what it was until she turned blue, but it wouldn't make it so.

Yes, Hettie had used that glamoury on their minders when they were both very little, and sometimes on their friends, so they could win free of supervision and have some fun. But she had not used it on Captain Corridon. She knew that short-lived glamoury would be a very bad use of magic if what she meant to do was find a husband. Which it was.

She thought he was interested in her, and he just might be the man that Mama had said would one day arrive. Of course, it was also much different from everything that Mama had told her about her and Papa's courtship. Because Captain Corridon was a nobleman, and therefore well above Hettie. While, for all that Mama could go on about what a wonderful match she made, she didn't think marrying a cabin boy on a carpetship was that much of a step up for the daughter of a farmer working as a maid in a noble house.

Mary, who truly indulged in the sin of envy, said that Hettie was reaching far above herself. Hettie flung her head back at the thought as she opened the back garden gate, stepped through it and closed it softly behind her.

She didn't see why, since she had been educated as the daughter of a well-to-do merchant, she should not marry the second son of an earl. Her classmates married lords all the time. She didn't see why she should be any different.

Outside the gate, she looked around the shady lane. He appeared from the end of it, tall, straight, with tanned skin, and dark red hair. "Hettie," he said, extending both hands to her. And then, as though controlling himself with an effort, "I mean, Miss Perigord." He lowered his hands and bowed to her.

She giggled. It was funny that he should be so formal. "Oh, I'm so glad you're here," she said. "Because I had to get out of that house or go insane."

He grinned at her, and didn't scold her for her unfilial sentiments, or some such rot. Instead, with mischief sparkling in his eyes, he said, "And what have your parents been doing, Miss Perigord, to deserve such a condemnation from you?"

It was a relief to tell him everything.

THE UNDERWORLD

Third Lady held the polished copper pot to her husband's lips, and hoped that something would show on the surface. She hoped he still had breath and life within him.

What would she do if she had killed him in her attempt to revive him? She wasn't sure at all—beyond the unpleasantness of being prosecuted as a murderess—that she could go on living without Wen. In fact, she might very well end her life right here, next to him. Let them be discovered when someone else came to this cave, as true lovers who'd left the world together. And let the wheel of reincarnation send them somewhere they could be mere peasants, but peasants who loved each other and were free to enjoy each other's company.

She heard a sob escape her lips, and disciplined herself to take a slow breath. No. Let him be alive. He had to be alive. She wouldn't accept anything else.

Looking at the pan, she was glad to see the faintest dew of water vapor on it. She looked at Wen. Pale he might be, breathless he might seem, but he was still alive.

Which meant his spirit and mind had probably already got free of his body and were hurtling toward the underworld. Which meant she must follow as soon as she possibly could. Else he'd think she had killed or betrayed him. And besides, his spirit might do something foolish, which would allow them to charge his soul with fresh crimes.

Certainly he wouldn't know that he was in the underworld to ransom his soul, nor what he was supposed to do to obtain its freedom.

Third Lady had wasted too much time already. She must hasten to follow.

She took from the recesses of her gown, where she'd hidden her various necessities for this journey, the goods she'd brought along to help her and Wen in the other world. It was an assorted lot—some of it leftovers from various funeral rites over the centuries, which had, somehow, found their way to the records boat and accumulated there.

There were ladies and gentlemen in nice attire—perfect paper dolls meant to follow the deceased in the other world. Though Precious Lotus was not deceased—nor had she any intention of being so—she was going to the underworld, and she saw no reason these servants should not accompany her, if they accompanied the shades of the dead.

There were fifteen or so of each, ladies and gentlemen, some in quite outmoded clothes. She didn't know how long they'd been in the records boat, but she suspected they'd got there in the confusion after some long-lost emperor's death. She was fairly sure the keeper of the records boat would have been very upset had he known that she had made off with the figures under her gown, much less that she was burning them now. Other things she burned—a pair of very good-looking horses, a cart and its puller and—though she was not absolutely sure what good this would be to them—a monkey wearing a very interesting uniform that she couldn't quite identify.

She had ignored all palaces and furniture and anything else that couldn't be moved, but she saw no reason at all they shouldn't ensure that they had some allies in the other world.

After the dolls were utterly consumed in the little cooking fire, she pulled out her roll of paper cash. It was, of course, not the real thing, but paper made to resemble copper coins printed with *100 cash value* each. They even had the hole through the middle, where Precious Lotus had threaded a string, with the help of a needle. As was done for traditional funerals, she'd gathered 999,999 strings of cash. It was the very minimum that deceased were ever sent with, and how could she and Wen expect to get through with less than that? She also burned the various pages of many-colored paper that she'd been assured would convert in the other world to bolts of nine-colored silk.

Last, she burned the contracts, or copies of the contracts, which she'd caused to be drawn so she could— she had told the record-keeper—have copies of certain important things. They included copies of the marriage certificates of Wen's ancestors, whose sons had been the ancestors of both the Imperial line and Zhang's line. Also there were copies of the document detailing the succession of Wen's ancestors, and that Zhang's ancestors had become Prince of the High Mountain—a domain in itself, but not the Imperial throne. Nor had the second son any right to the throne.

She burned these copies of the contracts and then, to establish her credibility and her right to intercede on her lord's behalf, she burned a copy of her own marriage contract, and a copy of the canceled contract that Wen's father had purchased from the singsong troupe. On top of this she burned a copy of something yet more personal—a poem that Wen had written for her shortly after their marriage.

And then, as her fingers trembled, she'd burned effigies of a dragon, a turtle, a bird and a tiger. They'd given her the decree of heaven, she told herself, and the least they could do now was help her fulfill it.

Then she went toward the bed and grasped the porcelain cup filled with now-cool liquid. Before she drank it, she walked around the bed and sat down by Wen's side. Then she swallowed the contents of the cup, rendered repulsive by being cold.

A spasm shook her, before she'd quite finished swallowing. It was a horrible feeling, like being submerged all over in ice and made incapable of breathing. It was in this state, she thought, that Wen had tried to speak to her—and she hoped he'd not thought she was killing him. She hoped he was not angry at her.

She took that thought with her into an odd agony, in which her chest seemed to have turned to stone as unyielding as granite, and in which it seemed her lips were sealed with the kiss of death, her breath stolen, her body made cold.

With the last of her intent and will, she reached for Wen's hand. And, finding it, cold, by her side, she clasped it convulsively.

There was a dark, cold space, as if she went through a narrow tunnel, like when she had led Wen through the stone tunnel in the dark. And then, as suddenly as waking, she was standing by the bed, looking down at herself and Wen, both of whom looked too white, and quite, quite dead.

"Are we dead?" Wen's voice asked softly from the side.

She looked over at him, or at what she assumed was his spirit form. He looked transparent, and she could glimpse the stone behind him through his form. But when she looked down at her own spirit hands, she found them quite solid. She must assume, therefore, that it was the lack of Wen's soul that made him seem less than completely here.

"No," she said. "We are merely sleeping for a time, while we visit the underworld."

He frowned at her. His spirit self looked older and less trusting than his physical self. As though his physical self had remained young—or at least unformed—through his addiction to opium, but his spirit self had aged at the normal rate. Even without the soul to make it more substantial, he seemed more in control than he was in human form.

He frowned while he looked at her up and down. "You lied to me," he said.

She nodded. "I had to. It was the only way I could think of to get you to follow me to the underworld."

"But what good does it do you?" he asked, sounding quite confused. "To take me to the underworld? And how are we to return? And what are we to do there?"

Precious Lotus judged that the time had come to show respect and be formal with her husband, even if they were both in their spirit form. Kneeling on a floor that didn't quite feel as though it were there, she kowtowed to him. "My Lord Wen, True Dragon Emperor of All Under Heaven, your humble servant begs your forgiveness and permission to explain how she did all in your best interests."

His laughter surprised her. She had seen Wen smile, but hadn't heard him laugh in far too long. In fact, since shortly after they were first married. "Precious Lotus," he said, his voice tinged with laughter, "please get up. There is something very strange about your kowtowing to me, and in spirit form yet. I am not angry with you, nor do I suspect you of treason." He frowned a little and for a moment looked very troubled. "You're the last person in my household whom I suspect of treason. If you thought you must take me to the underworld, then there must be a good reason. I'm willing to believe you couldn't tell the truth to my opium-addled body. But I am out of my body now, and ready to listen. Only, please rise, or I'll have to strain to hear you. Your spirit voice is as soft and sweet as your real voice."

Shaken, Third Lady rose. How could she not love a man who would trust her when she had just played such a monumental deception on him?

As quickly as possible, and in spare words, she told

him what she knew of his predicament and why he'd found himself in it. He frowned only at the part where Red Jade was supposed to awaken all the rivers of China while the two of them were meant to recover Wen's soul. "Jade? With a foreign devil? How could you allow it?"

"It was the decree of heaven and the mandate of the Jade Emperor," Precious Lotus said, while she wondered if her husband truly believed she could stop his sister from doing as she very well pleased when she very well pleased. Perhaps he had spent too much time in opium dreams, if he thought that the person had been born—male or female—who could keep Red Jade from doing what she thought was right.

Wen inclined his head. "But she's not one of them," he said.

Third Lady knew better than to say that Jade had quite a bit of the foreign devil in the makeup of her mind. No good would come of it, she thought. And it would only hurt Wen. So instead, she remained quiet and bowed slightly.

His lips tightened. "If that's what she must do, that's what she must do, but I hope the Jade Emperor doesn't mean for her to go and live among her mother's people, for that would never do. She is better than that. She is one of us."

Again Third Lady inclined her head. Like her husband, she was likely to believe that the Chinese were, of course, the best and most advanced people on Earth. She was also likely to believe absolutely that her sister-in-law belonged to them and to the Dragon Boats. But she would never try to interfere with the decree of the oracles. Of course, the oracle had said nothing about where Red Jade would end, or with whom.

"Very well," Wen said. "You brought me here for a reason, so I take it there is a passage to the underworld?"

"There is supposed to be," Third Lady said. "That way." She pointed to a passage that hadn't been visible at all with their physical eyes, but which showed as a fissure in the rock to their spirit eyes.

Wen held out his hand, and she rested hers in it. Surprisingly, for all it looked almost transparent, it felt to her grasp like his physical hand did. He pulled her by it, toward the passage.

They walked together down a dark tunnel in the rock, a tunnel that was probably not physical, with darkness all around them. This time he led her.

At the end of it, they suddenly found themselves in a place filled with light and sound. She blinked her spirit eyes, confused at the scene before her, which seemed to encompass several creatures that were not exactly human, a very large cart pulled by something that was not a donkey—unless donkeys had suddenly become glowing green—and a whole lot of bright red light.

From somewhere near at hand, a voice shouted, "You are arrested, for trespassing in the realm of the dead."

AN HONORABLE ATTEMPT

Adrian Corridon wouldn't have admitted to deceiving Hettie Perigord. If it came to that, he would probably have said he was the deceived one, or at least the one against whom the greatest attempt at deception had been made.

If he hadn't known very well what family Hettie's father came from, if the girl's parentage wasn't written all over her face, which echoed faces all over her father's family's portrait gallery in far-off England, he would never have tumbled that this miss, raised in Cape Town, was anything but what she appeared to be: the daughter of a lower-middle-class family who, for inexplicable reasons, had chosen to save all their money and apply it toward her education.

But he'd recognized Hettie at first sight, because she looked just like her great-aunt, who he'd seen weeks before in London. And while he was willing to believe that her father—who had all the look of the Gilberts, Earls of Marshlake—might be a by-blow, this would be much easier if he did not look exactly like the second son, Joseph, who had disappeared many years ago and who was now, in fact, the surviving heir to the estate.

Having grown up in the region, his own father's estate being adjacent to the Marshlakes', Captain Corridon couldn't help but think of that vast, empty, closed estate, waiting for its heir. And he had to wonder why the heir hadn't come back. If it were, as his own grandmother had assured him many years ago, only that he'd run away with a maid or some such nonsense, he would surely by now have come back to claim his birthright. After all, every expatriate Englishman read news from the home country. Why, there were several newspapers devoted to nothing else. And he would know that there was no one left at home to mind the estate or anyone to refuse him and his lady love, be she ever so humble. More, since the title could be transmitted on the female line, what father would deny that to his only daughter?

Unless he had a very strong reason. And since having his attention forcefully called to the family that went under the name Perigord a week ago, when the farseers within the Secret Service had informed him that the heroic carpetship magician had to be one Nigel Oldhall, one of their own number, disappeared in Africa almost a year ago, Captain Corridon had come to believe that Lord Marshlake, alias Mr. Perigord, must have the strongest of reasons.

He must be working with a secret organization that competed with the queen in her attempts to obtain the rubies that anchored all of the world's magic. That explained, too, not only how someone with Nigel Oldhall's profile—from an old family, bright without being brilliant, with not a bone in his body outfitted for adventure—could have been turned. And how he and Peter Farewell, whom rumor claimed was a dragon but who had just recently returned to his estates and polite society as Lord St. Maur, had managed to avoid Her Majesty's Secret Service all this time.

Corridon was not stupid. He credited individual agency and individual action whenever it seemed possible. But in this case, it had gone well beyond the levels of the plausible. From the intelligence they'd been able to gather, not only had these men managed to lead the Secret Service a merry chase; not only had one of them been turned from being an—unexceptionable—Secret Service man, himself, but they'd had considerable native help so far.

The picture that had formed in his mind was that of a well-funded, well-sprung organization embracing men of all descriptions and motivations. It was far bigger than this chase for the rubies—and this chase for the rubies might be the biggest challenge of his generation. If he uncovered this, he might uncover, at the heart of it, a conspiracy that, for all he knew, had dogged human steps for centuries.

It was more than Captain Corridon, second son of the Earl of Northford and an ambitious man, could resist.

And then there was Hettie. If he'd met her in London, at the home of some fashionable hostess, still Captain Corridon would have noticed her. It was not just that she was pretty. Her beauty as such was the bland and inoffensive look of a well-brought-up miss, and he suspected she had yet to fully grow into her charms. But there was a light in her eyes, a madcap spark that matched his own desire for adventure and fame. He would have responded to that in any case.

Now the young lady, who either was all unaware who she might truly be or was one of the most cunning spies ever trained, was pouring into his ears a fantastical tale. Unless she knew about Nigel Oldhall and the quest for the rubies, indeed, it was an unbelievable tale. That her parents, law-abiding citizens that they were, had agreed to shelter in their house and hide from the search a were-dragon. A Chinese were-dragon that they could not possibly have known until hours ago. That Nigel—if it was him—had released the full power of the ruby just now in their dining room.

Captain Corridon wasn't a trained farseer, and he'd not been trying to scan for the ruby. He'd had a feeling of power nearby, but he couldn't, for the life of him, swear it was the ruby. However, the way Hettie described it, the light bathing the room, was eerily similar to the way the soldiers who'd survived the encounter with the ruby had described it, back in Africa.

"You are very displeased," he said, as a way to keep her from realizing how deep in thought her story had plunged him.

She let out a little exasperated sigh. "Oh, very," she said. "Indeed, how could I not be when my parents are acting quite contrary to everything they've ever told me to do and think?" She bit her lower lip, prettily, in a gesture of vexation.

"Parents," he said, softly, "can be very trying." Was she hoaxing him? Did she know who her father was and, furthermore, was she a member of what must be a vast international conspiracy? And if not, then how could her father leave her thus unprotected? Had he thought that the truth would endanger her?

Corridon had heard from his Chinese contact—a man he neither liked nor trusted, nor should he, considering that he was poisoning his own sovereign with opium in order to advance himself—that he had one of the rubies which he'd obtained from a carpetship magician. That meant the other ruby must still be with the carpetship magician, Nigel Oldhall.

The captain could take Hettie's word for it and call for a raid on the house. Heaven knew he had enough cause for suspicion; none of his superiors would question his decision. But what if this truly was a conspiracy? What if it slipped between his fingers as it had slipped between the fingers of officers here in Africa and in India? What if he was made a fool of, his advancement forever blighted?

One thing he knew for sure, and that was that Lord Marshlake, as much under disguise as he might be, and as deeply involved in a conspiracy as he could be, had only one daughter. And that daughter, from all the information he'd collected in this neighborhood, the lord loved very much.

If Corridon secured the daughter—oh, not quite a kidnapping, but a more delicate affair in which he might compromise her honor but would take care not to—there was a good chance that Marshlake would spill everything he knew and give up all of his accomplices.

A bright future smiled at Captain Corridon, one in which everyone marveled at how he could have cracked such a complex conspiracy that had—possibly—subsisted for millennia. The queen herself, or—if she had died by then, as people kept saying she was likely to do—her son, would reward him amply.

He bit his lip. It might seem dishonorable from the outside, but he was doing it in the service of his country.

"Hettie," he said, putting in his voice that sort of unrestrained passion that very young ladies were likely to confuse with love. "Hettie, listen. Run away with me."

She looked at him, her mouth open, seeming absolutely shocked. For a moment he thought she was going to scream and run away, but instead she stood there, and just started to shake her head.

He reached for her hands and held them, tight, in his own. "I know it must seem like madness to you, but indeed, Hettie, you've driven me mad ever since I met you. I must have you for my wife, and I will have you. It is all I can do to ask you politely, instead of kidnapping you and taking you with me into a forced marriage." She was very young and the idea of a forced marriage would still seem to her more romantic than horrifying. She blushed a little and almost smiled. "But I must have you. My father will never consent, though. You know, he is an earl."

She nodded. She didn't even attempt to make a protest, so he would have to guess her father, indeed, had not told her the truth, and she couldn't know they were equals or nearly so—for there was very little chance that her mother was as highly bred as the Countess of Northford.

"He will never allow me to marry you if we ask his

permission. And it is plain to me that your family is not treating you well. I don't know why, but it is clear."

"Mama and Papa do love me," she said, in a little gasping protest.

"I am sure they do," he said. "But you must admit they've chosen a very odd way to show it."

"Yes," she said, in a low voice.

"So, will you run away with me, Hettie? I can get us a marriage certificate, listing you as of age. I doubt your parents will try to dispute it." His father undoubtedly would. That is, until he realized that through Hettie the title to the estate of Marshlake would descend. He would not be so churlish as to try to do his second son out of a title. None of which signified, as Corridon wouldn't marry Hettie.

He *probably* wouldn't marry Hettie, he added to himself, as he looked into her limpid blue eyes.

She demurred. "This is very sudden," she said. "Why, I hardly know you . . ."

Commotion from the street, outside this alley, called them. "Dragon, dragon!" a voice called. And running, Corridon saw there was indeed a dragon. It was the red one of the two who had fought over this street not so long ago. And on its back sat a man, who looked remarkably like the descriptions of Nigel Oldhall.

"Please, Hettie, please," Captain Corridon said, turning back to see that Hettie, who had followed him, was standing just behind him. "You are my only hope."

THE LORDS OF FENG DU

Precious Lotus, Third Lady of the True Dragon
Emperor, turned around, in confusion, to see three
men marching toward them. Or, at least, they should
be men, but they weren't. They looked from a distance
like soldiers wearing Imperial uniforms of an outdated
design, but up close it became obvious that the uniforms weren't so much worn as were a part of the
person approaching at full speed. "Stop," they were
saying. "Stop in the name of Lord Qin-Quang-Wang,
Lord of the First Court of Feng Du."

There were ten courts of Feng Du, Third Lady
thought, though some legends said six, some seven and
some twelve. But they all agreed that the first court
was the domain of Qin-Quang-Wang. As the guards ran
toward them, she observed that there were three others approaching from the other side of the cavern,
bearing down on Wen. It seemed to her that they were
acting very strangely, since neither Third Lady nor
Wen were in fact moving, but only standing there, confused by these creatures and their peremptory orders.

"The living should not intrude in the courts of Feng

Du," one of the creatures said, when he got close enough, and bowed deeply, as though, somehow, by bowing he could make the verdict palatable. "We regret it, but we will have to arrest you."

"Perhaps we should run?" Wen whispered in Jade's ear, but before either of them could take a step, there were hands grabbing at them. The hands were hard and dry, and felt curiously inhuman, but also very strong, like bands of iron, as they clasped around her arms. Running was impossible. She looked to the side, and saw Wen had arrived at the same conclusion and was sagging in the grasp of his captors.

"You must face the mirror of retribution," one of the guards said. He had the type of voice that sounded like it was being recited in some sort of ritual, and completely divorced from the situation at hand.

"The mirror of retribution is for the dead," Wen said, as the two of them were dragged—without having to move their feet—across the length of the cavern. And the cavern was bewildering. In addition to the first scenes that had greeted Precious Lotus—the strange people that weren't people, and the green donkey pulling a cart of what she very much feared were corpses and therefore refused to look at more closely— it seemed like the cavern unfolded into very different scenes.

It took her only a moment to realize that the cavern was completely formed of mirrors. Mirrors at right angles, and mirrors twisted this way and that, and what they were reflecting wasn't the landscape.

Passing a bank of mirrors that showed what appeared to be a war between two armies, one dressed in red, the other in gray, Third Lady tried, once more, to make their captors see the light. "We are not dead. And as my lord says, the mirror of retribution is for the dead."

One of the guards chuckled, a dry chuckle like the rustling of dried leaves. "You will be dead anyway before you leave the Feng Du."

"No, no," she said. "We can't be dead. This is the True Dragon Emperor, the real Lord of All Under Heaven. He has duties in the world. We were sent here by the Oracle of the Dragon, at the behest of the Jade Emperor, Ruler of Heaven and the Court of the Blessed. It is the decree of heaven."

For a moment, their captors stopped and turned to look at her. Only, their faces were as incapable of forming any expression as they seemed incapable of changing uniforms. "She has invoked the name of the Jade Emperor," one of them said.

The other one, despite completely immobile features, managed to give the impression of rolling his eyes. "What will they think of next?"

"It is true," Wen said. "At least, it is true that I am the Dragon Emperor and that my wife tells me the oracle sent us here. Why else would the living intrude on the world of the dead?"

"Oh, you'd be surprised," one of the guards said, in the conversational tone of a functionary explaining the inanity of life. "Once we had a live monkey in here, and what havoc he generated. All the records were scrambled, and we had people dying out of order and people arriving here years before or after they should have. It took us centuries to clear up his mistakes. He had come, you see, in search of immortality."

"And that was not the worst of it," another guard said. "There was also the time when a man came in here, by magic, somehow, bringing his body with him, thinking that it was the land of the living and he could steal gold. He breathed on the Lord Qin-Quang-Wang.

"He breathed on him?" Precious Lotus asked, puzzled, because it was said as though this was the most heinous of crimes, but she couldn't understand what could be so bad.

The guard bowed, looking curiously two-dimensional as he did so—like a piece of paper or cloth folding. "You must know that the breath of the living is poisonous to the dead."

"But don't get ideas," another guard said. "At least you didn't bring your bodies with you and therefore do not have the breath to poison the dead. I will believe that your crime was not willfully committed. So will His Honor, Lord Qin-Quang-Wang, I am sure. I'm sure you will get off very lightly, with barely more than a warning. Perhaps a century or so of torture, but nothing else."

Precious Lotus glanced toward Wen, but Wen was looking very much like he usually appeared when stupefied with opium. His mouth was slightly open, his eyes vacant. Which meant, she thought, that it was up to her to think of a way out of this mess.

And meanwhile, the guards were dragging them past mirrors. In front of the mirrors, she now noticed, stood people—some dressed as kings and some as beggars. Kings or beggars, they all looked as though thunderstruck—as if some great evil had befallen them, leaving them either stunned or sorrowful. Some were crying into their hands, and others were looking disbelievingly at the mirror.

Beside each of them, and around each of them, were more of the guards. Only, the more Precious Lotus stared at them, the more she was convinced that they were not, in fact, people. They looked, she realized, like the paper dolls burned at funeral ceremonies. Only, from what she'd been given to understand, those paper dolls were supposed to serve the individual deceased.

She had a momentary pang of annoyance, because how stupid could it be if those dolls she'd burned had come to serve as guards and escorts in the underworld, instead of helping her and Wen, as she had hoped?

"I thought," she told the guards escorting them, witheringly, "that you were supposed to serve the whim of those people you were buried with."

This got her a look that caused the head of the figure to turn around almost completely, creases on its neck and uniform showing that it was indeed all of one piece. "We were not buried. Or burned at a funeral," it said. "We are here in service to the gods, as payment for tombs."

Third Lady opened her mouth, then closed it again. She'd never heard of figures being burned as payment to the gods. Nine-colored silk, of course. Paper cash, of course. But never people. But then, Feng Du had accrued over millennia, possibly before people were very aware of it, and it probably included things and customs from the time that was not recorded anywhere.

And it made a certain sense for the guards to be made of paper, if Feng Du got invaded by living humans now and then, and if the living humans could poison the dead with their breath. The paper figures would be immune to such poison.

"Also," another of the figures said, "when those whom some of us were sent to serve move on, through the wheel of rebirth, we are conscripted into the force of Feng Du, for Feng Du must be kept orderly. It is the decree of heaven."

What Precious Lotus couldn't understand was why the decree of heaven didn't allow her own figures, that she'd burned before she'd embarked on this journey, to serve her and Wen. Shouldn't those figures belong to them?

If they didn't, was it because they were living and therefore had no status in this strange land, or was it that their figures had originally been made for someone else, and had now joined that retinue?

The papery figures were dragging them toward a large mirror and Precious Lotus tried to make herself heard yet once more. "I protest," she said. "We are not dead, and we have come here voluntarily, and at the behest of the Jade Emperor, to fulfill a decree of heaven. If I'm going to be punished with death and sent back through rebirth for obeying, what will this do to the filial virtues and the orders to obey authority throughout the worlds of the dead and the living alike?"

The paper creatures hesitated. They moved slightly, as if in a wind. One of them, who wore a golden uniform from which most of the paint had faded, turned to look at her. "But you have no proof," he said. "No documents. Surely you must see that we can't take the word of any living person who comes down here and starts claiming they came on orders. We must have proof."

"I demand to see the Emperor Yu the Great," Wen said then, his voice very loud and full of command. Lotus looked at him, feeling proud. After all, her husband rarely asserted himself, but he had doubtless realized that in this world of the dead, one must speak decisively to get anywhere.

"Yu?" a red-uniform paper-figure asked. "Why? What claim have you on the Great Yu, First Emperor of China?"

"I have the claim of a descendant," Wen said. "Faithfully I have burned offerings to his spirit. I demand that you take me before him. We will be able to explain the situation to him."

Confused as to why her husband was bringing up his most distant recorded ancestor, Precious Lotus jumped in. "We must see Judge Bao at the Office of Speedy Retribution. My husband's soul is being held captive here, with no real cause. It is being detained on a frivolous lawsuit."

"The courts of Feng Du don't make mistakes."

"It is not a mistake," Third Lady said. "It is a frivolous lawsuit brought by an enemy, and it has kept my husband from his full inheritance for years now. I demand justice."

"Me, also," Wen said. "As you can see, I am transparent and not fully myself. And I believe that is due to my soul being held in captivity. The Jade Emperor wishes us to recover it."

"He told us to see Judge Bao."

"And my ancestor, Yu the Great, will vouch for us and look after us."

It wasn't until the paper figures had formed two groups, one on either side of them—though they kept a hold on them through a ridiculously extended set of arms—and were holding a whispered conference about the rights and wrongs of the case, that Third Lady had a chance to turn to her husband. "My lord, far be it from me to question your judgment," she said softly.

"But . . ." he said, a sparkle of mischief in his eyes, as if he knew she would say that.

"But I think that we should try to see Judge Bao as speedily as possible. I cannot understand why you'd want to see Emperor Yu, or what good it will do."

Wen gave her a fugitive smile. "Do you know how old that cave is, in which you performed the ritual to bring us to the underworld?"

She shook her head.

"Well, then," he said. "I should tell you. That cave did not always belong to the Fox Clan. It was first used by Emperor Yu himself, who actually was a powerful sorcerer, as well as a were-dragon. When you gave me the potion, remember there was some time between your giving it to me and your drinking it and following me."

"At first you thought I had killed you," Third Lady said, resignedly.

"No. Why should I think that? I knew you always have my best interests at heart. I was alarmed, it is true, but only because I thought you'd made a mistake. It did not help that you were burning contracts and figures and paper cash and nine-colored silk. I thought you might, after all, have killed me by accident. And then I heard his voice."

"His voice?"

"Emperor Yu's. He said you only meant to bring me to the underworld so that you could ransom my soul. And he said that you were bringing servants and cash with you. Where are they, by the way?"

Third Lady shook her head. "Perhaps they allow the figures to serve only the dead."

"Perhaps, but Emperor Yu didn't seem to think that was the case," Wen said. "And then he told me that we were supposed to come see him as soon as we got to the underworld, and he would do his best to steer us right."

"But can we trust him?" she asked. "I mean, it was a long time ago, and while you might be his descendant, how many generations of father and son, one succeeding the other, are there between you and him? And though there is almost no written history about him, there is the legend of his taming the floods and saving all the people of China, the legend of how his wife, Nu, waited for him for seventeen years after their wedding night, the legend of his engineering feats and his absolute dedication to the people of China. He sounds like a dry stick, to tell the truth."

"It is to be assumed that he was more than a bit of a rogue, since dynasty founders usually are," Wen said, and again the odd sparkle of mischief shone at the back of his eyes. "But all the same, you must admit that no one here has our best interests at heart, and at least Yu is related to me by blood. If he will see me—"

"There is another reason for this," Third Lady said, not even quite sure why she said it, or that she was going to say it till she did. "There is another reason you want to visit him."

"Oh, yes," Wen said, and looked at her, and his mouth pulled a little to the side, in a smile of pure amusement. "You see, he says he's been keeping my palace in order for me, the palace I will again have, when I take over the Dragon Throne. I think it behooves me to inspect it."

FRAGRANT STREAMS
AND GOOD HARBOR

Though Nigel had traveled all over the world, he could not help but feel his heart speed up at the sight of Hong Kong. To be seeing, finally, the city that formed Britain's footprint on the very gateway of China made him almost dizzy. He'd never thought to see this land outside the pages of a book. And to be approaching it from dragon-back—let alone that the dragon was an angelically beautiful and exotic woman—added to the dream quality of it all.

They'd come from Cape Town in a single flight, and no matter how many times Nigel had flown all over the world, this one flight had been a new experience. Oh, more uncomfortable, in a way. In the voluminous coat and pants that Joe had lent him, with a muffler around his neck and head, he'd managed to not actually shiver. Still, it had felt like walking under a snowstorm. But also much, much freer, so that he could see the light on the ocean beneath, and observe all the little boats.

He'd steered Lady Jade away from carpetships as much as possible, knowing the havoc her magical field could wreak on those vehicles, and fully aware that the

Royal Were-Hunters would be coming for them. Not to mention the fact that they were almost certainly being followed by whatever branch of the Secret Service continuing the hunt for the rubies.

So, seeing Hong Kong was a relief, not just because he could now dismount and be warm again, but also because they were at their destination. Hopefully here he could visit his parents' friends and recover enough of his strength to continue the journey, and Jade could find the potion that would so utterly change his aspect that no one would be able to follow them by description.

He, who had thought himself now thoroughly dead to romanticism, he who had seen so many of the evils of colonial will imposed on natives, could not help but feel a swell of pride at this vision of Hong Kong, which only three quarters of a century ago had been a barren island infested by pirates, and which now flourished, its English buildings set amid terraces planted with Asian vegetation. Its port, facing China's shore, allowed an intermingling of modern English boats and native craft. It was thronged with both great ocean liners—still used for most traffic, since carpetships bore only the goods that required timely arrival—and with junks, with their fat hulls, and their sails of matting or coarse cloth stretched on bamboo frames. On some of them, there was a great eye, painted on each side of the bow, a survivor of the ancient Chinese belief that the boat must see to get to the end of the journey.

There were also sampans—low craft that could range from fifteen to fifty feet long, with one end covered over and looking more than anything else like a giant Chinese slipper. In fact, they were often called slipper boats. He wondered if the "barges" that Jade spoke of weren't in fact these slipper boats. They looked nothing like the junks that had attacked the carpetship, but then, if Nigel understood properly, the junks were the highly maneuverable craft that allowed the pirates to attack while their main fleet stayed well out of danger.

He knew from other visits to Chinese provinces that most of the sampans were worked by women and that not only did whole families live in them, but often pigs, chickens and other livestock, also. He'd seen, in a stop at a Chinese port, little children running all over the hull of those craft, balancing well no matter what the boat happened to be doing. He wondered if Lady Jade had once been like that, and let his hand, in its glove, fall upon the scales of her neck.

It had seemed very odd to do this—to climb atop a dragon who happened to be a beautiful young woman. But at the same time, he could find no other way to get out of Cape Town fast enough, and so he must make do as he could.

From the air, Hong Kong didn't look more than four miles wide, with six great hills, and one particularly tall peak towering in the middle. The whole island was so small that Nigel could imagine walking all around it in a day.

He knew, from reading about it, that much of the best land on which the finest buildings now stood had been reclaimed from the sea. Great wharves, shipyards and dry docks had been constructed and harbor fortifications built.

Opposite the island of Hong Kong, across a narrow channel, was the peninsula of Kowloon, which also belonged to the British. There, Nigel could see a great carpetship port at which he had once stopped and which he thought had originally been built by Americans.

As Jade circled, he could see the city, which the British had christened Victoria, though it never got called that—but rather was called Hong Kong, after the harbor and the colony. It lay on a bay on the northern side of the island, and rose in terraces up the slopes of the hills, almost to the top of the tallest peak. Warehouses crowded with the exporting establishments near the docks. John Malmsey, the family friend Nigel hoped to visit, worked in one of those. But the shopping districts of the city—thronged with as many natives in their flat straw hats as with English misses and their chaperones—extended past that. And then, above it, were the residential homes, many of them looking much like miniature palaces.

Flanking the European settlement, there were Chinese quarters with narrow streets and—even from the air—a profusion of natives thronging them. Nigel wanted to go to those quarters and explore them. He wondered if he would get to. He would like to meet with Lady Jade, of course, during the days he stayed in Hong Kong.

And Lady Jade, as though reading his mind, started to steer toward the area of town where the Englishmen lived—without, of course, actually ever going low enough to be seen or noticed. It was very early morning, but who could be sure that no one would look up and see them? So she flew around the less inhabited areas of the isle, bringing him as close as possible to the area in which the Englishmen lived.

As she set down amid the foliage of a small park, and lifted a front paw to serve as a step for him to climb down, Nigel had a moment of panicked doubt. Would John Malmsey still live in Hong Kong? It had been years since he remembered his parents mentioning him.

And how could Nigel contrive to approach him, indeed to stay at his house, without explaining the circumstances of his voyage? He would have to tell him that he was here in the service of Her Majesty. He would have to tell him that was why he was using an alias.

And if, as he assumed, the Chinese magicians that Jade wished to consult needed to see him to adjust the magics to him, how could he contrive to slip out of the Malmsey establishment to visit with a Chinese girl without giving rise to a lot of talk? Some of which, he very much feared, would eventually make its way back to his mother. Or worse, to the Secret Service.

If Jade knew about these magics that changed appearance, wouldn't the wicked minister, Zhang, know as well? And if he did, wouldn't he realize that it was likely that Nigel would have used them? In fact, Nigel remembered, vaguely and not with absolute certainty, that in the distant past, spies disguised by magical means had been sent to China to steal the secret of silk. Those spies, doubtless, had used a similar potion or spell.

He climbed down from the dragon while thinking

this, and no sooner had he stepped off than the dragon seemed to stretch and shrink and spasm. It was the sort of movement that felt as though it should be accompanied by a twang—like the plucking of a cord or the twisting of a bit of metal. But there was no sound beyond a very wet and organic noise of flesh and bone—something like a very large hand slapping another.

Where the dragon had been, there stood Lady Jade—tall and slim and completely naked.

He averted his eyes while handing her the parcel he had kept under his overcoat. This she took, and, after an indefinable time and lots of noise of fabric—and, once, an exclamation as though something didn't fit or didn't tie properly—she said, softly, "You may look now."

When he did, he found she was again in Hettie's muslin dress, looking both incredibly exotic and demure. "Won't you call attention in that attire?" he asked. "In the native quarters?"

She shrugged. "I don't know." The question seemed to amuse her. "You see, I've never been in Hong Kong, but if what I've heard about it is true, then I should not. The two peoples mingle so perfectly here, and in such a way that they will not at all find it strange that I am wearing English clothes. Given that it's fairly modest—" She gave him a sudden anxious look. "It is fairly modest, is it not?"

He looked at the dress, which revealed nothing and covered everything that could possibly be covered. Even if it molded her flesh exquisitely. "Yes," he said. "Very modest."

"Well, then, they will think I'm the maid in some British establishment, or perhaps some charity pupil at one of the schools. I don't think it need signify." She shrugged. "And meanwhile, I will try to locate the Fox Clan establishment, and report to you what I find as soon as I find it."

"I..." Nigel hesitated. "I should be staying with John Malmsey. I'm not absolutely sure where he lives, though he once sent my parents a magical dispatch that showed a tall white house that looked like a palace."

She smiled, a little. "Yes, but in Hong Kong... at least according to what I've seen from the air..."

"Precisely," Nigel said. "I will need to ask someone. But do not worry. I'm sure someone will be able to direct me."

"And quite likely me also," Jade said.

"Yes, but when you need to get back in contact with me... You will need to get back in contact with me, is that correct?"

"Oh, yes," Jade said. "The magics must be adjusted to the person. Besides..." She hesitated. "The Fox Clan is as cautious as you were when... when talking about the ruby. You see, they are the only weres in China that suffer the same reputation as weres in the rest of the world. They are considered untrustworthy and vicious and as likely to betray you as not."

Nigel felt a certain alarm at the idea that they were about to trust people with such a reputation.

Oh, he had learned that not all weres were bad, except perhaps insofar as their position in society made them so. His friend Peter had certainly turned against

everyone because he'd lost his family and his home because of his being a were. If everyone suspected him
his whole life, Nigel might—the idea occurred to him
that it might be much the same with the Fox Clan.

Tentatively, he asked Jade, "Do you . . . agree with
that view of them?"

She shook her head, then shrugged. "I know very
few. My father always said that the Fox Clan were
those of his vassals most likely to change allegiance
when the moment offered or when they thought it
would be to their advantage. On the other hand, I've
always wondered if they did so because that was how
they were expected to behave. You know, if you know
your allies and those you depend on do not trust you,
what can you do but be untrustworthy?" She shook
her head. "On the other hand, I know my sister-in-law,
Third Lady, is never like that. Of all of my brother's
wives, she is the one I would trust with his life. Or
mine. She seems to love him genuinely. And to suffer
for his sake. His condition . . ." She bit her lower lip and
stopped, as if afraid she might say too much. "Well, because of Precious Lotus, I will trust the foxes, and hope
they do not deceive me."

Nigel nodded. It seemed reasonable to him as well,
and he hoped he, too, could trust the foxes, at least in
this one instance.

"Very well," he said. "But how will we meet?"

She bowed to him. "I will find you when I need you.
Your name is Enoch?" she said.

He hesitated. The ruby had vouched for her.
"Nigel," he said. "Nigel Oldhall."

It seemed as though he had passed some test he

wasn't sure of taking. She bowed slightly to him and said, "And you'll be at the home of Mr. John Malmsey? Well, I am not sure that I can find the Fox Clan quickly or easily. I've never, you understand, been away from my family alone. So I will now go in search of them, and when I find them, I will come to you or send you word." She hesitated as if something occurred to her. "Do not worry. If anything should go wrong, I will know, and I will be there. If... if Zhang comes within sight of the island, I will know." She extended her small, warm hands to him. "Trust me."

And Nigel, who for so long had carried the weight of the ruby on his own—Nigel, who fell asleep and woke feeling as though he held the fate of the universe in his hands—did trust her. He held her hands and lightly squeezed them.

Then he turned away from the park and toward the English section of Hong Kong. He wondered if anyone had seen them parting in human form and what a pretty romance they would make of it. It didn't matter. Better see them like that than see them as dragon and human.

He started down English Hong Kong's paved streets, in search of anyone at all of whom he could ask where John Malmsey's residence might be. And he felt, for some reason, very lonely.

A MOST UNREASONABLE
BEHAVIOR

Hettie Perigord thought that her parents knew very well what had happened with that dragon, and where the dragon might have come from. She couldn't believe her staid and conforming parents would behave like that, with such reckless abandon and disregard for their safety—and hers.

"Papa, what was that, and where has the man gone?" she asked as she came into the house and found her father reading his paper by the window of the parlor.

Her father looked up from the paper as though not quite sure what she had said.

"Where has the man gone?" she repeated. "The man who has been lodging here? The carpetship magician? And that very odd Chinese girl for whom you borrowed one of my gowns?"

Mr. Perigord lowered his paper slightly and peered at his wayward daughter with a narrowed eye. "Hettie, leave alone what doesn't concern you," he said. "There are things that are better for a young lady not to enmesh herself in."

Hettie stomped her foot, in a fit of annoyance at this treatment. "I'm not a young girl," she said. "Or at least, I am not *that* young."

"Indeed," her father said, a humorous tone in his voice, as he reached for his meerschaum pipe and started filling it with his favorite tobacco. "You are old enough, my dear, that you should know calling you young is not an insult and you shouldn't resent it."

Hettie, who didn't think of it as an insult so much as of a putting-off maneuver—a way of keeping her away from anything that might be interesting, as well as away from anything that might injure her—stood there and stared at her father. How had she never noticed how fast his hair was receding, and how much he looked like a stranger?

She remembered being very young and looking up at her far-traveling father as though he were, in himself, some sort of magician—a being whose dictates obeyed a far higher command, a being who loved her and protected her like no one else. She had thought, by virtue of being a carpetship first mate, he knew everything and everyone.

In her childhood memory, her father was a giant, whose head touched the clouds and whose feet bestrode the world. And her mother had fostered this idea. While he was gone, and she was alone with Hettie, it was all "Papa says this" and "Papa says that."

It had taken Hettie till the early years of her adolescence, in the excellent day school to which her parents had sent her, to find that the best thing one could be was not first mate on a carpetship. And it had taken her till now to realize her father looked aged and faded. Certainly as nothing to Captain Corridon.

She took a deep breath, "Papa, you realize if you were abetting a dragon, your life and Mama's and mine, too, would be forfeit."

Her father looked over his paper, with a wry expression. "Hettie, my dear, the only dragon I've abetted is your mother's temper, and that I've abetted for the last sixteen years."

"Joseph Perigord," came her mama's voice from the kitchen, where she was preparing dinner. Most of their friends could afford servants, and Hettie knew that they, too, could have had them, except that her parents preferred to save all their money so that they could send her to a good school and give her a good dowry. Something for which she should feel grateful, instead of resentfully guilty because her mother was forever striving to keep the house working and to do this and that, madly, while other mothers could enjoy shopping and parties with their daughters. "Joseph Perigord, I heard what you said!" Her mother's voice tried to sound censuring, but had just that edge of amusement that matched her father's.

"Thank you, my dear. All my wit would be for naught if you did not pay attention to what I say. It is having an attentive audience like you that quite makes my life worthwhile."

Somehow, the fact that both her parents' voices trembled with amusement—the fact that she knew their humor responded to and echoed each other's—only made Hettie more upset. After all, once upon a time she had been the center of their lives. Oh, if she had to admit it to herself, she probably still was. But what did that matter when, in fact, her parents made jokes over and around her, and if she should throw a tantrum they would probably accord it as much respect as they give the tantrums of small children?

"My dear, do you remember I told you of my friend from my youthful days, George Farewell, Lord St. Maur?"

"Yes, I do," her mother called from the kitchen. "Wasn't he the one with the russet hair? The one who stayed in the best bedroom in the northeast wing, and brought with him his own bottles of claret, so that he shouldn't go to the expense of tipping the wine steward?"

"The very same. Do you remember I told you I read his death news in the *Colonial Times*?"

"Yes, my dear."

"Well, now there is the following news: Lately, in New Delhi, Miss Sofie Warington, daughter of Mr. Warington, esquire, of New Delhi, India, was wed to Peter Farewell, Lord St. Maur. The couple is expected to reside in Summercourt."

Mama came from the kitchen, wiping her water-reddened hands with a dish towel. "The daughter of a nabob?" she asked, significantly.

"I presume," Papa said. "Not that I blame him. If George's son wanted to keep that pile that is Summercourt, he would need to lay a great deal for it. George married a great heiress himself, but I think her money came as too little too late. And for the newly created St. Maur to marry a girl from India, with no connections, no real name . . . Well, it stands to reason she, too, must be an heiress."

"Wasn't it George's father who used to spend all his money . . ." she coughed, and looked toward her daughter and added, ". . . on those terribly expensive actors?"

"Indeed," Papa said, mildly, but smiled as though enjoying a very private joke. "Patronage of the arts can be a very expensive endeavor when one takes it . . . er . . . personally."

Hettie had had enough. Through the last few parts of this conversation, something very much like a rage had been growing in her, and now she stomped her foot again. "I think it is abominable the way you talk about people I've never heard of. I think it's abominable the way you keep secrets from me, and the way you treat me as though I were only about two years old, and the way you—"

"Hettie!" Mama said.

And Papa was so surprised that he opened his mouth and let his pipe drop. It shattered on the floor, and Papa set his paper aside, and knelt to retrieve the fragments and the burning tobacco, before it should mar the floor. "And it was just starting to get a good color, too," he said, in the tone he used when something didn't quite go his way.

"I don't care about your pipe," Hettie said. "It is all you care about, your pipe, isn't it? Your pipe and your creature comforts and—"

"Hettie, go to your room," Mama said, in a very displeased tone. "And let me never have the grief of hearing you speak to your father this way again."

Hettie hesitated. She knew that tone in Mama's voice, and she could hear the grief at the back of the anger as well. She knew she had upset and hurt her parents. And yet, she thought, they should not treat her like a child. "Very well," she said, cuttingly. "And when the were hunters come for us, to punish us for abetting a dragon, you may inform them I am in my room."

Mrs. Perigord sighed, and seemed to not notice Hettie's most impressive flounce as she turned to leave the room.

It was not until Hettie was halfway up the narrow stairs that led to the upstairs floor that she heard her mother speak, and her tone was far less angry or cutting than Hettie expected. In fact, her tone was so bafflingly tender that Hettie stopped on the step, listening.

"She's not such a bad girl, Joe," she said.

"Oh, I know that," Papa said. "She is a good girl, and pretty, too. She reminds me of you at that age."

This was answered with a small giggle and then, in a serious tone, "But you know this is a very difficult age, and this is a very difficult situation for her."

"Do you mean having been raised above her station?" Joe said. "Yes, I imagine it would be. But, Charlotte, I couldn't stand the idea that she would marry one of the men hereabouts, craftsmen and workers and...people without future. I had hopes by giving her a better upbringing we could get her married to at least a well-to-do tradesman or lawyer." He sighed. "And we might still."

"I doubt it," Mrs. Perigord said, and sighed. "Oh, don't misunderstand me, my dear. I'm not faulting you—indeed, us, since I agreed with you. But though we've saved what we can for her dowry, surely you see it won't be enough to make people ignore her lack of connections in attaching themselves to her. As your friend's marriage proves."

"My friend's...? Oh, George's son. But...but, Charlotte, you know there is nothing I can do. When hands were washed of me, they were washed very thoroughly."

Hettie frowned at this, trying to imagine what her father might mean, more so as she heard her mother's tart response—one of the few times she had heard her be tart to Papa. "Yes, I do. But I think a lot more money might pass through them before they think themselves quite free of the stain."

"Charlotte! You are not suggesting I go begging to my brother for money?"

"I'm suggesting you do what you have to do for your daughter."

Hettie could not see them, but she could imagine them, facing each other, each of them paler than the other. The only times she'd seen them argue, it had been like that. Things said, and words flung, and those pale faces staring at each other. Perhaps she should be happy that her parents loved each other enough that they could not stand to argue, and that argument against each other only hurt themselves in the process.

What she felt instead was a confusion of resentment, embarrassment and guilt. And hearing her mother say, in a soft voice with just a hint of tears in it, "I'm sorry, Joe. I did not mean it. I just worry. I realize what you gave up for me."

"Indeed," Papa said, and now there was no humor at all behind that word, and there was probably a great deal of paleness, too, and a stiff upper lip, to boot. "I understand, Charlotte." And then, more softly, "Perhaps if we didn't have just the one chick..."

And on that Hettie's feet flew up the rest of the stairs, taking great care to make next to no sound, but wanting to get away from the intimations of that argument below stairs.

She started to go into her room, then realized that none of her things were there still and, what was more, the dragon attack had somehow stripped the window of its lace curtain, which meant it was, by now, probably quite full of mosquitoes.

Instead, she backtracked into the cramped bedroom that had been her nursery when she was really young. Now, with a small bed in it, it served as a guest room on the rare occasions when they entertained guests, which was, normally, when Papa brought a promising underling to spend the night at the house because the young man couldn't find suitable lodging in Cape Town or looked likely to get in trouble if he tried.

When this happened, they did everything but set a guard on Hettie's door. It was clear they believed that she was worth more than her mother—worth more than a carpetship employee for a husband. She had often wondered where they got the idea, and after listening to the conversation right now, she wondered even more.

The narrow bed had been outfitted with her pretty, lacy bedspread, because Papa had said he was sure that the carpetship magician wouldn't care for it, with that edge of joking in his voice that meant he would have found it very strange if the man had.

Perhaps it was too gaudy or too girly, but Hettie didn't mind. Mama had made it herself, and it was lace and flounces all over, the solid bits made of an old satin dress of Mama's, so that they sparkled a pretty cream color. Mama had said that Papa had bought her the dress when they'd first come to live in Cape Town, but she'd found very little occasion to wear it.

It didn't occur to Hettie till now that clearly Mama and Papa had had some money when they'd first gotten married. More money than they had now.

She was piecing together in her mind what they had said, just like Mama had pieced together this bedspread from the bits of the dress she never wore and several different kinds of lace.

Papa had said something about his family having washed their hands of him. Because she knew her own dear papa was neither a gambler nor a drinker, nor anything of the kind, it must be—it could only be—because he had married Mama. In fact, her comment about knowing how much she'd cost him meant only that there must have been some very great objections to Mama on the part of Papa's family.

All of which meant . . . all of which meant that Papa's family must have money. Not lords, Hettie judged. If her father were a nobleman and had enough power to fly a carpetship, he would have taken that post, instead of the less well paid administrative ones he'd taken on his way to becoming carpetship first mate. Which meant, surely, that poor Papa was indeed jealous of carpetship magicians, and it explained how he spoke.

His post, though, required him to read and write

fluently and to have some knowledge of accounting. Were it not for that, he would never have risen as high as he had in the carpetship line. That meant he had to come from a merchant family. Probably a well-to-do merchant family. Which also explained why Papa had chosen to send Hettie to the school he had sent her.

Hettie reached for the center of the bed, where Mrs. Beddlington sat. Mrs. Beddlington was a wax doll, with a realistic face and limbs, a cloth body and an endless collection of gowns, all of which had come packed in an exquisite wooden trunk. Papa had brought it back to Hettie from one of his flights, and had assured Mama, who was alarmed at the expense, that he'd gotten it very cheaply, indeed, in Paris, where his carpetship had stopped on the last trip.

Even back then, Hettie hadn't been so foolish as to believe that the doll had been cheap. Perhaps cheaper than it could be gotten in Cape Town. But nothing that came with that array of gowns could fail to cost a great deal of money.

Hettie had a vague recollection that Mama had sighed, and for a while they'd eaten a lot of bread and soup, and that Mama hadn't bought a new dress for quite a while. But that didn't matter, because Mrs. Beddlington with her gowns and her painted countenance, her hair set in hair by hair so it seemed to be growing out of her scalp, just like real human hair, and her eyes that opened and closed, had been the pride of Hettie's childhood, and the thing that set her apart from her playfellows. Even in school, none of her classmates had anything quite so fine as Mrs. Beddlington.

Some had wax or porcelain dolls, but they were—obviously—of much inferior manufacture.

Now Hettie held Mrs. Beddlington to her chest and looked down at the round blue eyes. If only things could be as simple, again, as they'd been when she was young and all she required was having a doll that she adored.

She remembered once, when some childhood disaster had befallen her, running to her mother, who had held her tightly and consoled her by saying, "May your worst mishap ever be that one, my daughter. And may it always be something I can resolve by showering you with love."

At the time this seemed like a nonsensical thing to say, but now Hettie found herself wishing this very much, indeed.

She reviewed things in her mind. First, her papa had come from a better family, or a better background, and only left it to marry Mama. Very well, perhaps he was madly in love with Mama. In fact, Hettie had no problem at all believing this, as her parents still seemed to be in love, all these many years later.

But then, there was the rest. Papa had said he had married Hettie's mama sixteen years ago, and Hettie was fifteen. She was either the child of their honeymoon or . . . Her mind shied from the idea, but it wasn't so rare that such a thing was involved in these unequal marriages.

And then there was the fact that, for years, Mama had slaved in the kitchen, and Papa had worked himself into the ground, barely stopping in his trips to see his family, so they could keep Hettie in luxuries, and send her to her very expensive school, and accumulate a dowry for her, which, after all, might not be enough to give her any material advantage.

And now Mama would push Papa to go and ask for money from his family. Hettie had no doubt about it. She was quite capable of it, her mama. Normally the most biddable woman in the world, she would do anything—anything—for the sake of Hettie.

Which meant Papa would eventually have to swallow the pride that she'd heard in his voice, and go throw himself at the mercy of the family that had rejected Mama and . . .

She had no idea what the *and* was that followed, and suddenly she didn't care either, because a new and more appalling idea had occurred to her. The dragon and that very strange carpetship magician, with his jewel that was sure to be stolen.

Papa had housed them, hidden them, probably in exchange for the proceeds of their disreputable adventure. That meant he had done it for Hettie.

Well, Hettie would not tolerate that. Not anymore. She was through with having sacrifices made for her. Adrian Corridon had offered for her hand, and though she'd shied away from it and thought it very disreputable indeed—and been afraid of breaking Mama and Papa's hearts—now she realized it was the only thing she could do.

Without thinking too much, almost without stopping to take even a deep breath, she got her wicker suitcase from atop the wardrobe, the one that Mama had given her so many years ago, when Hettie was a very little girl and had gone with Papa on a trip to London, to see the palace where the queen lived.

Each carpetship employee could take only one family member, so it meant that Mama couldn't go, but Hettie had been brave and waited the long days in Papa's cabin, dressing and undressing Mrs. Beddlington. And it had been worth it, to go to tea in the nice big salons with Papa, and eat her toast buttered just so and to see the queen's palace.

Now she opened the wardrobe and picked things to take with her. Two changes of underwear, and a change of dress. She didn't suppose she needed much more than those, since Adrian would, of course, want to buy her new dresses. After some hesitation, she settled Mrs. Beddlington atop the nest of dresses and clothes, and closed the wicker suitcase. Then she opened the window and, following a route she'd only taken before to go play with Jane when she'd been bad and had been sent to her room, she climbed onto the windowsill and from it down to the branch of the apple tree that almost touched it.

When she'd attained the security of a lower branch, she threw her suitcase down onto the soft grass, knowing that with such cushioning Mrs. Bedlington would not be harmed. Then she jumped down herself.

As she took a turn to press herself against the wall of the garden, she cast one look back to the dining room, where Papa was reading his newspaper, and where Mama stood by and looked at him with what Hettie would swear was a fond expression.

Wiping away a tear she couldn't quite admit to, Hettie made her way down the garden, in the fast-growing shadows of the afternoon.

Once she was gone, and married, her parents would live so much better.

THE VOICE OF THE FLOOD

Being dragged through the underworld was not as unpleasant as it might have been, Third Lady realized. After all, as she should have surmised, not every place in Feng Du was uncomfortable, or even dark. No. Some people seemed to live quite pleasantly in Feng Du. Granted, most of those were great heros or renowned characters who occupied some post of responsibility. She thought perhaps the ones who were punished were only tormented because they believed they deserved it before they were allowed to reincarnate.

And as she thought of this, it occurred to her to wonder why Yu the Great was still here. If he was, as family records claimed, the very first Dragon Emperor or, as he called himself, the first king of China, he had lived uncountable millennia ago, long before human memory could have taken hold. That meant, surely, that he would have come through Feng Du and gone away by now, either back to the wheel of rebirth, or to the golden bridge that led to the paradise of deified heros and kings and the presence of the Jade Emperor.

In either case, one thing was for sure, and that was

that he should not be loitering here, in this place that, even when it wasn't devoted to punishment, was a dim reflection of brighter and happier lands.

She followed Wen through the halls of Feng Du, while the paper figures escorted them both. On the way, they saw other paper figures, and other creatures, engaged in various forms of either expiation or incomprehensible work.

Carts were pulled here and there, some of them, seemingly, piled high with what appeared to be all the goods of the world. And here and there, screams broke the gloom.

Precious Lotus noticed, though, that they never left the hall that was filled with and surrounded by mirrors, and that they never strayed far from the people looking into the glass, at scenes of great battles, or lovemaking or—once, glimpsed out of the corner of Third Lady's eyes—a beggar sitting in the middle of the street, hand extended, moaning and sighing, and behaving as though he could barely stand to see any more.

Wen, himself, more alert than he'd been before, was speaking. "So, my ancestor," he said. "Yu the Great, is he in this court of Feng Du?"

"He waits here," one of the paper figures said, in his dry rustly voice, which sounded like leaves—or else like paper—being played upon by the wind. "After the review of his actions, he realized where they would lead, and what path he'd set his dragon-descendants upon. With the ability of a great sage—which he is—he saw at a glance where it would all end up. As such, he chose never to leave here. And when your palace was destroyed and it, too, arrived down here, he chose to guard a semblance of the ancestral palace and do what he could to keep it safe until his descendants could occupy it, rather than to follow the golden bridge to the court of the Jade Emperor, where his status as hero entitles him to be.

"Every year the Jade Emperor insists that Yu the Great come take possession of the place prepared for him in his court. And every year, Yu the Great sends his regrets, saying he can only go when the palace entrusted to his care should be restored to its proper place and the world of the living." The figure made a papery sound, which seemed, for all the world, as though he'd just cleared his throat. "So you see, it is a matter of some chagrin to the Jade Emperor."

"And probably a good reason for him to meddle in the affairs of my house," Wen said, in a whisper, to his wife.

She nodded, in acquiescence, though she suspected there were other reasons as well. In fact, she had started to suppose a lot of things depended on Wen managing to make his position as emperor more than a mystical and symbolic position.

And it had to come to Wen, who had to be Wen—emperor in name only, who could not hold the throne without Red Jade's help.

As they walked, surrounded by the paper guards, Third Lady started hearing the sound of running water, slowly transforming to the sound of many streams at once. They seemed to rush from all around, while the paper guards led Wen and Third Lady around the last set of mirrors and penitents and suddenly, before Third

Lady, there rose the most incongruous of sights in this place of punishment and shadowy presence.

She felt her jaw drop open, as her mind said, in an awed tone, *We didn't get the palace right. Not even a little of it.*

While Jade had made every woman on the barges work on the paper figuration of a sumptuous palace for her father's afterlife, none of it had looked even nearly as sumptuous, as impressive or as magnificent as the building she found herself facing.

It was a construction in white marble, rising terrace on terrace, each terrace cultivated with exotic gardens, each garden filled with strange flowers. Birds sang amid fruit trees. In the distance, over a green meadow, shone a sun that looked like it had been cut out of paper, and yet gave enough warmth for everyone.

Wen had stopped beside Third Lady, staring. And, perhaps because he needed as much support as she did, he extended a hand toward her. All around, amid the gardens, water flowed, in a hundred disciplined rivulets, watering the strange plants, and keeping everything green.

Nearby, a man who appeared to be made of clay, and wearing a detailed armor, knelt, engaged in the homely work of pulling up weeds.

Wen advanced on this creature and bowed to him. "We come to see Yu the Great, my illustrious ancestor, per his invitation."

The creature of clay did not acknowledge him, and went on pulling weeds. "He can't see you," the paper creatures said. "Only we can, because you are alive, and we were designed to patrol against an invasion of the living. But most people and guardians and servants here can't."

He approached the clay statue and spoke in a rustly voice. "We bring the living ones who say that Yu the Great, once king of all under heaven, tamer of the flood, and dragon ruler over all the were-clans, has invited him to visit. Go and ascertain from your master whether the living ones lie."

The clay man looked at the paper man, and no more able to make expressions than the paper man, he managed to convey a look of profound skepticism. He rose slowly from his knees, and Third Lady noticed that the knees didn't so much bend as seemed to develop a lot of cracks, then healed them as fast as they developed, re-forming into another position as he stood.

He then bowed, by the same process, in the direction of the paper man, but giving the impression of bowing to herself and Wen. And then, turning, he made his slow progress through the garden, toward one of the exquisite marble pavilions in this most magnificent of all palaces.

Moments later, laughter was heard. Male laughter and then female laughter. Through the terraced gardens came a magnificent couple. They wore odd clothes, or perhaps the clothes of many generations ago. Both of them were dressed in loose pants and magnificently embroidered jackets made of the finest silk that caught the shimmers and the glow of the paper sun up above.

They walked quickly, but without seeming to hasten, hand in hand, and Third Lady noticed that wherever the man set his foot, a rivulet of water seemed to spring up, if only for a moment.

Where the clay creature had been, the two stopped and bowed in their direction. "Wen, Emperor of All Under Heaven, True Dragon King," Yu said, his voice resonant and deep like the thunder that echoes just before the rain. "I have been awaiting you. This is my wife, Nu Jiao, who waited for me through seventeen years, and then thirteen more after she married me and I did my duty and tamed the great flood." The pretty lady in the jacket bowed to them, and Third Lady thought that it didn't look at all as if she'd be the sort of stoic woman who would endure that separation and absence in good part. And then she caught the lady's merry gaze as she bowed in her direction.

"I would invite you into the palace that is yours, Wen, but you see I cannot, for right now it is my abode, and the presence of future heirs—"

"I understand," Wen said, "and I do not hold it against you, Grandfather."

At the word *grandfather*, Yu's lips trembled, but he said only, "However, my plum trees are in bloom. Let us sit in the shade of them so I can tell you what you need to know to get through your journey in the underworld and return to your world in safety."

As Yu and Nu turned and walked away, Wen and Third Lady followed. Behind them, they heard the rustle of paper, as the paper soldiers prepared to follow.

Yu the Great turned around. The face that had been genial now looked almost scary in its gravity and authority. "Stop," he said. "You, the soldiers, stop. Can a man not have a conversation with his grandson without an escort? I have private business to discuss."

The paper men looked at one another, with every

appearance of distress. "But, revered Lord Yu, tamer of the flood, we must guard these dangers to the world of the dead and keep them confined."

"Are you doubting my word?" Yu said.

The paper creatures looked so confused that Third Lady half expected them to crumple into little balls and roll away. Instead, one of them bobbed several bows, and another one knelt down and kowtowed. "We don't know what you mean, revered lord," a third one spoke.

"If I say that I wish to talk to my grandson, you may assume that I will keep him from being a danger to anyone. He's still my family, owing me obedience and respect. How can you think I'd let a descendent of mine terrorize Feng Du?"

The paper creatures now all fell down and prostrated, while Wen and Third Lady followed Yu and his wife through the deep, soft grass that seemed to be at the height of spring.

Under a plum tree there were some porcelain benches, beautifully painted in delicate colors. On one of these, Yu sat, his lady beside him.

Wen and Third Lady sat on another bench, facing them.

"You have summoned me, Grandfather," Wen said, after waiting a while, to give Yu a chance to speak without being questioned.

"I have summoned you, Grandson," Yu said. "You are my living representative now, the last one of my line. I know that treachery and deceit have caused you to fall prey to a vice that weakens your mind and your body." He frowned slightly. "I confess that I would have been tempted to discard you, to consider you yet another disappointment as so many I've suffered over the millennia. But the truth is that my wife looked at you, and at your third lady, and in your third lady she says she sees the same courage and worthy love she herself had—the love that allowed her to do what was better, not only for myself or her, but for the whole of China. And she said that with your lady's love, you'd be strong enough to do what must be done."

He paused, and when he gave no sign of continuing, Wen said, "And what must be done, Grandfather?"

"Why, you must use the jewels that hold the magic of the whole world."

"The jewels that Lady Jade was sent to get?" Third Lady asked, breathless, unable to hold herself back.

Yu smiled. "The very same. She now has a jewel, and with that one jewel—which is magic enough—she can wake all the dragons in all the rivers in the land. This is important, because when she secures the second jewel, she can then use the two jewels united to summon my armies and the armies of every emperor of China who had a connection with the land."

"The...armies?" This was Wen, a crease on his forehead. "But how, Grandfather, if the mere breath of the living will destroy the dead?"

Yu's gesture encompassed the clay creatures around his garden, hoeing and weeding, clipping and tending the various plants. "These armies, Grandson. I have them, as do many of the other kings and emperors, even some of the interlopers. By being made of the clay of China, and sleeping in the bosom of the Chinese soil for many years, these creatures have come to resonate with the very will and life of China. They will rise when the True Emperor commands them to rise. They will rise and do battle on his behalf, if he can command magic enough. And there is no magic more powerful than the magic in those two jewels."

"They also have the power to heal," Nu said, softly. "And there is much in China that needs to be healed. For too many millennia, foreigners have followed one another on the throne. People with no connection to the true China, whose flesh and blood did not resonate with the land and its people."

"I foresaw this," Yu said. "In many ways you might say we brought this about, Nu and I, though we did not mean it. We established our kingdom from the were-clans, and made them rulers over every echelon of power. We thought being stronger than the nonchanging humans, and also more connected to the land through our animal natures, we'd be the ideal servants for China." He reached over and took his wife's hand in his. "Nu and I were both dragons, of course, children of the nine sons of the dragon. This is why I could control the flood waters." He gestured with his hand to encompass every little rivulet flowing in his garden. "And save the people and their possessions from the flood. And we viewed our power as the way to keep people and the land safe.

"But then others followed us, and the others did not have the same devotion to duty and to the land. Your people, Third Lady, much maligned as some of them are, have also caused a great deal of this. They have an almost childish delight in confounding mere mortals, charming them and twisting them as they please."

Third Lady bowed her head. "I think sometimes," she said, "that being despised by all mortals, and chased out of every legitimate place, has made my people delight in vexing those who cannot outsmart them."

Yu nodded. "And sometimes," he said, "it is the pure spirit of mischief that comes from being a fox-fairy."

She had to smile at that. "Wen calls me that," she said. "But I confess it has been a long time since I did anything out of mischievous pleasure. It is not, it seems, in my destiny, to amuse myself at anyone's expense."

"No," Yu said. "You, Third Lady, have been serious too long. Now that you are in Feng Du, it would serve you well to remember that the underworld runs on rules and laws, on earnest desire and serious behavior, and that in some situations the best of defenses might come from behaving like a fox-fairy." He smiled at her, leaving her bewildered.

"I sent servants," she said. "Like the paper creatures, ahead of me, but none have come. And not the cart I sent ahead. Not even the monkey."

"You sent a monkey ahead of yourself?" Nu said, and looked delighted for no reason that Third Lady could understand. "Very good. You do have the spirit of the fox-fairy in you, after all. Remember, all the creatures you sent ahead of you, every paper you burned, are yours, but they will not come to you, and no one will bring them to you, unless you demand they appear and mean it. Here in Feng Du, guards and servants and functionaries are very simple constructs of wood and paper. Being inferior to humans, they delight in oppressing humans."

Wen, who had been in deep thought throughout all this, looked up and said, "Grandfather, if we can bring the jewels together, and bring the palace out of the Earth, what do you wish me to do? For you cannot mean for me to simply become emperor and then rule as if nothing had changed?"

"No," Yu said, looking grave. "The fact is down here, we can feel the currents of time, like we can feel the currents of water, swirling around us. Bad times are ahead, Grandson, bad times that will require that weres have some power. For centuries now, they have tried to exterminate us a little at a time. The laws of the foreign devils make us illegal. In every corner of the Earth, it seems someone has something against our people. But the darkest times are ahead. By restoring the jewels to the avatar at the beginning of time, a great freeing of magic will result. From this, several weres will be born or manifested who have never been weres before.

"There will be more of us than ever, and considering what our people have done in the past, this will not reassure anyone. They will try to destroy us."

"But you said," Third Lady protested, "that we've been persecuted, and it is true. Now you say we've done something?"

"In the days of the beginning, when all humanity lived by tooth and claw, our people were more powerful, and being more powerful, they became lords. And, as lords, they ruled over all of the Earth. And they treated the normal humans as if they were of no account. However, as powerful as we might be, there are more of them. Everyone throughout Earth rose against us. And we deserved it. We had stepped on their necks long enough. Now..." He opened his hands. "I hope we have learned our lessons. And what I expect of you, Grandson, is that you will create the one empire on Earth where weres and normal humans live in harmony. So that when we are threatened with extinction, and everyone raises a hand against us, we will be able to say that we are not dangerous, nor do we deserve to be exterminated. Only look at China, right under heaven, where weres and normal humans live as brothers and sisters."

With that, he rose, and bowed to Wen and to Third Lady, then Nu bowed to them both. "We wish you a speedy travel through the underworld," Nu said.

"And that you accomplish your mission well," Yu said, "since the Jade Emperor is getting tired of taking no for an answer, and sooner or later he will force me to cross the bridge of gold."

"Do not fear," Nu said. "You have the Jade Emperor's decree on your side, and that Wen should ascend to his throne is, in fact, the will of heaven.

"And don't forget," Nu said, looking at Third Lady, "that you are a fox-fairy and entitled to making your mischief on mortals and dead alike, now and then, provided you never play it on your allies."

"And remember, that though I am not normally allowed to amble the courts of Feng Du at will," Yu said, "which would disrupt the proceedings, I will be able to appear if you summon me as a witness to the Office of Speedy Retribution."

The ancestors stood and watched them depart, and Third Lady, holding Wen's hand for support, walked back to where the creatures of paper waited.

"Now," she said, "take us to see Judge Bao, at the Office of Speedy Retribution."

They looked at her. "No," one of them said. "We have no orders to take you that far."

"You can't make us look in the mirror of remembering," Wen said. "We are not dead."

"No," the paper creatures said. "Please walk with us. We will put you in a cell until we find the appropriate procedure for what to do with you next."

FOX-FAIRIES AND TRICKERY

Jade walked along the narrow roads of the Chinese quarters of Hong Kong. As she had expected, no one gave her more than a casual glance. She was not the only Chinese woman dressed in English attire; though, after looking very closely at some of the others, standing in the doorways of their darkened homes, she wondered if they were perhaps prostitutes.

But other than the women, there was more activity here than she'd ever seen in the few cities in China that she'd visited with her father. Here, there were factories and retail stores. Though it was early in the morning, and the sun just starting to rise, silversmiths resounded with the din of hammers and metal, and restaurants were fragrant with the smell of fresh cooking. Down the street, a vendor was shouting that he had candied ginger.

Jade realized that she felt hungry. Very hungry. Hungrier than she'd been in a long time. And it shouldn't have come as a surprise, except that she hadn't thought of food in so long that now it felt like a new idea. She'd had tea at the Perigord's home, and that was about it since she'd left the Dragon Boats.

The smell of roasting pork over spirit lamps made the water surge in her mouth. She was a fool. She'd come on this errand, spurred by the knowledge that Zhang was there ahead of her, that Zhang was meddling. And she'd come without the magical purse that she normally attached to a bracelet at her wrist. She had, in fact, no cash at all. And she hadn't thought of asking Nigel Oldhall for any.

She should have, she thought, and she frowned. She should have asked him for money. Oh, not as a gift, but as a loan. But having already asked him to trust her with the ruby, and knowing that this expedition was more for her benefit than his own, how could she have demanded money from the man who was protecting her and being so kind as to follow her?

Shaking her head, she told herself that she was the sister of the True Emperor, a lady of the most important court in the world. She would find the Fox Clan, who swore allegiance to her clan. And then she would force them to feed her, as well as to do business with her—to give her the herbs needed to make Nigel look indistinguishable from those Chinese around them. They would want to help her, she told herself, since any help they gave her enhanced the position of Third Lady.

And besides, she told herself, the crown would give them a draft on cash, which would be paid promptly as soon as Wen recovered the throne.

Fortified with these notions, she looked for those signs that the were-clans knew other were-clans kept.

At the edge of an alley, she saw one. It was a silk shop, but the sign over it was a tiger, its mouth closed upon a roll of silk. And the tiger, as Jade knew, was not the generic representation of an animal, but the particular facial shape and look of the leader of the Tiger Clan.

She ducked into the shade-filled shop, where rolls of fabric seemed to occupy every possible surface, as well as propped up against the walls. The place was full of customers and many men were running around attending to the needs of various English misses and various prosperous-looking natives as well. "Miss," a voice called, and she turned to look.

Suddenly the young man was bowing very deeply. "Milady," he said, almost in a whisper, and then, "If you'll follow me."

Jade followed him amid a forest of cloth, a labyrinth of rolls, until they got to the back, where a narrow door opened onto a dark corridor. He took her through it and into a small room. Judging from the cabinet stuffed with scrolls and the low desk covered in paper, this room was used as an office of sorts by the gentleman facing her. "Milady Jade," he said, as soon as they got within.

With a gesture, he lit a magelamp hanging from the ceiling. It was one of those that made use of a paper shade, and this shade was painted with the image of a romping tiger. When lit, it cast tiger-shaped shadows on the wall. But the young man must be used to it—of course—because he didn't spare it even a glance. Instead, he went on his knees and kowtowed repeatedly to her. "Milady Jade," he said. And then, looking up, "I am Fu, of the Tiger Clan. A year ago I was lucky enough to be sent by my people as emissary to your revered late father's court."

Jade nodded to him. "I remember you," she said, and indeed she did. He'd been shyer then, a tiger amid dragons. She hadn't known that he was a prince, much less that he was a draper prince. But then, considering she was a pirate princess, raised on a barge, perhaps she should not consider him too badly. "I am here," she said, "looking for the Fox Clan."

This brought him to sitting on his feet, his knees still on the floor, his face a mask of startled shock. "The Fox Clan, milady? But why?"

"Because I need one of their magical potions," she said. "The one that allows one to take any shape at all. Also..." She paused and frowned. "Because I am terribly hungry, and I left the Dragon Boats without bringing even one string of copper cash."

This brought a grin to the lips of the tiger-youth. Like all in his clan, he had very sharp, very even teeth, two of them prominently sharp, like the teeth of tigers. "We will feed you, Princess," he said. "Indeed, it will be an honor."

A few minutes later, she was sitting before a full plate, with a cup of tea in front of her, sipping it, and eating some delicious noodles with shrimp. "You flinched when I spoke of the Fox Clan," she said. "Is there no Fox Clan in Hong Kong?"

The tiger gave her a half-worried smile. "There are foxes everywhere," he said.

"You act as if they're not loyal to the Dragon Throne," Jade said.

At this, the tiger-man shrugged. "It is not that," he

said. "It is more a question as to which Dragon Throne they're loyal to."

"They're not loyal to the present occupiers?" Jade asked, disbelieving. She knew for a fact at least Third Lady's father was. Else, why would he have married her to Wen? And yet, at the back of her mind something like a needle of discomfort told Jade that, in fact, the Fox Clan were known for hedging their bets and that, having taken one side in a fight, they saw absolutely no reason not to take the other as well, so that whichever side won, they would be protected.

Fu the tiger sighed, as though reading her thoughts. "I know they're not loyal to the present occupiers," he said softly. "That would be too much, I think, for a were-clan, with its link to the land, to be loyal to foreigners who have no link to it and who are, furthermore, not even weres themselves. But you must remember that, during the Opium Wars, the Fox Clan sided with the usurper clan, and even with the English as well."

"And with us, too," Jade said, softly, with a small and rueful smile.

"Doubtless. So it is always dangerous to approach the foxes. Perhaps..." He shrugged. "Is it perhaps something that we can do for you?"

She shook her head. "No, you see..." She sighed deeply and wondered how much the tigers knew. Knowing what the were-clans were like, she very much suspected that the rumors of Zhang's desertion were spread like wildfire all around the nation and maybe even as far as Hong Kong. But she wondered if anyone knew what it meant.

"Ah. You don't wish me to know secrets I might not already know," Fu said. And then, with a smile, "I know that the Prince of the High Mountain has disappeared. It is said that he has been betraying us to the English, which, milady, is a behavior more becoming of a fox than a dragon. Of course, we all know his mother was of the Fox Clan."

Jade, who didn't know any such thing, merely inclined her head. "He has disappeared," she said. "And he was working with the English, though I wish to say that his son, Grasshopper, was not a member of the conspiracy."

"And that you allowed him to keep his full honors and ascend to the post of his father, something that has everyone speaking of your mercy. The thing about mercy, milady, is that it is a double-edged sword."

"How so?" Jade asked.

"Well, on the one hand it earns for you many allies," he said.

"And on the other?" she asked.

"And on the other, your allies might turn on you any minute, because they know they can count on your kindness."

"You're truly trying to warn me," she said, and at the same time, having grown up at court and knowing how the intrigues played in such an environment, she wondered if he was warning her for her own good, or perhaps warning her for *his* benefit. Wen's second lady was of the Tiger Clan. The first one was of the Dragon Clan. Neither of them had much to win if Wen's preference for his third lady held.

"I am trying to warn you, lady. I have heard rumors

from members of the Fox Clan themselves that your brother, the new emperor, is addicted to opium. It is almost assured that he will not be able to hold the throne. And you..." He hesitated. "It is known that your mother was a foreign devil, so I don't think you will be accepted as the holder of the Dragon Throne. At least, not on your own. With the proper husband—"

"I know," Red Jade said impatiently. "Oh, I know. It is said that I should have married Zhang. Half the Dragon Boats seemed to expect it."

"Everyone expected it," Fu said, curtly, "which doesn't mean that all of us hoped for it. No, you have to remember, milady, while the Fox Clan is... what it is, my clan has long been the ruler of several lands."

In astonishment, Jade looked up at this polished youth. He was sitting across from her, dapper in his heavy silk tunic and pants, his hair cut in European fashion. "Are you making me an offer of marriage, Fu?" she asked. Through her mind went some rhyme that her father used to sing to her when she was very young, and of which she remembered hardly anything at all, save that the tigers were ambitious and the foxes treacherous.

Fu bowed slightly. "I think you could do worse, lady."

"My brother's addiction is exaggerated," she said. "He has smoked opium now and then, but he's neither a desperate addict nor likely to make a mistake or die as quickly as all that. He will be emperor for very long, and his children will reign after him." She no longer dared tell this man, who clearly had a vested interest in the politics of succession, that she was trying to recover the throne for her brother—the true throne and the palace of their ancestors. Instead, she looked at him and tried to imitate her father's expression when he was trying to depress the pretensions of a courtier. "He will reign for ten thousand years, and his sons after him. What good could come of marrying me?"

But Fu the tiger only smiled at her, his very even, very sharp teeth glimmering in the magelight. "You forget, milady, that I visited the dragon barges. You did a very good job of hiding your brother's problems from your father. Indeed, your sisterly devotion does you credit. But you must be aware that it's an open secret in the dragon barges. They say he smokes so much that the only reason he's still alive is that his dragon nature allows him to withstand the ravages of the drug upon his system."

He reached for her hand, and almost touched the ring of imperial power, before she managed to pull away. "You wear the Ring of Power. Without you, your brother would never have been able to make the barges fly. Or, indeed, anything. Without your care not to let your father know how far your brother's addiction has gone, you'd now be married to the Prince of the High Mountain or another suitable party, and you would not be alone, out here, in Hong Kong, trying to find a magic cure for your brother's addiction."

Jade noted that the tigers, at least, were misinformed about the nature of her mission, and she decided not to disabuse him. "You are a partisan of the Prince of the High Mountain, then," she said. "You expect me to marry him?"

But the tiger shook his head and flashed his teeth. "You misunderstand me, lady. I know that everyone thought that the Prince of the High Mountain was a good choice, being a dragon, and the highest born dragon after your family. But I also know he's been working with the English and, rumor has it, though it's not proven, he's the one who introduced your brother to the pleasures of opium. I don't think a malicious and disloyal servant should be trusted with the supreme power.

"I also think," he said, and his smile enlarged, "that while the dragons have held the throne for so long, they have yet to restore the real throne to their line. As such, they should perhaps ally with another line who is more resourceful."

"Like the tigers," Jade said, scornfully.

"Like the tigers," the man said, and grinned widely. "Does this mean you accept my offer?"

"Not while I have a say in the matter," she said.

He shrugged. "Well, I did warn you," he said, "that my line is not only ambitious, we are far more resourceful than the dragons."

She looked at him, not understanding.

"There was a drug in the food we gave you," he said, and as she half rose from where she sat upon the cushions, "Oh, nothing dangerous. Not even anything that will prevent your making up your mind on your own. We want this marriage to be legal before the gods and in all the provinces of China. But I talked to my father and he suggested I put a certain drug in your food that will prevent your changing shape. And remember, you are surrounded by members of the Tiger Clan, who can indeed change shape."

He showed her a key that was on a rope at his neck. "I am going to go out and lock the door. You will be given food and blankets, and whatever else you need. But here you will stay until you agree to become my wife."

Jade was so shocked at the idea that anyone who knew what the true Dragon Throne of China was now—no more than a vague and mystical power and connection to the land—should undergo such treachery for its sake, that by the time she'd managed to close her mouth, Fu had left the room and locked the door.

She frowned at the door, and pointed her ring at it. But there were certain things that the Imperial Ring of Power couldn't do and, as it happened, one of them was unlocking doors.

Sitting on her cushion, Jade cradled her head in her hands. What could she do now? She'd told Nigel that she would come for him. What would he think when she didn't appear?

AN ETHICAL DILEMMA

The problem, Captain Corridon thought, was that Hettie was so very beautiful. And stubborn. Both combined to make her bewilderingly enticing and strangely infuriating.

Right then, he was confronting both aspects simultaneously. Hettie Perigord had appeared at his lodgings late that night, carrying a wicker suitcase that, by her own admission, contained two changes of clothing, some clean underwear and a wax doll with realistic hair and closing eyes, which, for some bewildering reason, went by the name of Mrs. Beddlington.

Mrs. Beddlington was apparently possessed of a vast wardrobe which, for reasons quite beyond Captain Corridon's grasp of the situation, had been left at the Perigord home, and about which Hettie—who as far as he could determine had left the home without so much as leaving a note for her father and mother—wished to send her mother a note.

Captain Corridon did not tell Miss Perigord that such a note was impossible. Leading her parents to know she had eloped—as she believed—and eloped of her own free will, would make Captain Corridon's threats far less credible, and less likely to bring about a confession of their part in what must be a gigantic, world-bestriding conspiracy.

Instead, he rang the bell and had his subaltern bring him two pens and several sheets of paper. Some of this paper and one of the pens he pushed in Miss Perigord's direction, and let her pen her own note to her mother, and carefully address it.

While Miss Perigord was thus occupied, Corridon took his own sheet of paper and wrote two notes to his immediate superiors. One of them was for General Boxter, who was in charge of the regular Red Coats. Because the general knew that he only had partial claim on Captain Corridon's considerable ability and reasoning power, this was an easy note to write.

Dear General Boxter, it read, in Captain Corridon's broad and confident hand. *As you know, there are, at times, occasions when I must leave the regiment in order to fulfill my greater duty to Her Majesty the Queen. You will be advised when I shall return.* He folded and sealed the paper, and set it aside while Miss Perigord was still frowning over her sheet of paper, now crossing out a word and writing another.

The next letter was somewhat more difficult, as it must be addressed to Lord Rompworth, the current leader of the Secret Service and Magical Affairs in the government of Her Majesty, Queen Victoria. He frowned over this one a moment, because he must convey enough that Rompworth wouldn't think that Corridon had gone off on a wild-goose chase, but at the same time be sure he didn't say so much that

Rompworth would raise the hare of Corridon's own hunting.

After all, if Corridon was right—and more and more he thought he was, and Hettie's half-sobbed confidences only encouraged him to believe this more—then this might be the most vast of treasonable consipracies, and the man who brought it out into the open would surely earn honors that would dwarf every other honor that any other king had bestowed on a faithful servitor.

Corridon tore himself from a happy vision of himself installed as Adrian Corridon, lord of something or other, in possession of vast domains. For some reason, the image came with an image of Hettie as duchess of something or other and caused him to bite his lower lip in deep thought.

Hettie was devilishly pretty, intelligent and spirited, too. He would not turn up his nose at her and, after all, he knew for an almost absolute fact that her father was an earl. Which meant... Which meant, of course, that she was quite within his sphere, though she might be a little beneath it when he ascended to ducal dignities.

Which was why he must take her with him on that climb, and make her his duchess, he thought as he looked at her beautiful countenance bent over the writing paper.

Adrian Corridon had very few illusions about himself. He knew exactly what he was. He was the second son of a peer, with modest resources and probably not much future except what he could earn by the force of his brain and his decision. He also knew that the reason he was so well suited to the Secret Service and had a great many exploits, in missions all over the world, was that he was possessed of a certain . . . moral flexibility.

Oh, he believed in Mother England, and in the queen. He thought that, by and large, English civilization had improved every place in the world that it had touched, and brought a better life to millions of benighted natives.

There were, of course, some perfectly disgusting episodes in that history—what had happened in India in the aftermath of the were riots; the Chinese Opium Wars, in which England had more or less pushed opium on the natives and told them they did not have the right to close their country to the corruption and destruction brought by the pernicious drug. And there had been others. His mind glossed over minor difficulties with Russia and some rather decided confusion in Africa.

But, when everything was considered, the influence of English culture on the world was to leave the natives more prosperous—Captain Corridon believed—which, being a man in whom the carnal sense was foremost, he identified with leaving them markedly happy.

He also believed that Queen Victoria, for all her strange quirks and almost unbending morality of a decidedly traditional aspect, had been a boon for England. No one wanted to return to the bad old days of the regency, or even to endure the whims of Queen Victoria's uncles.

No, it was all for the best that Victoria sat on the throne of England, and that England stood astride the world. He very much approved of this arrangement. And if getting those demmed jewels for the queen would prevent the revolutions and confusion that had so strongly marred the last century, why, Corridon was all for that, too.

No one in his right mind, no matter how ardent his republican partisanship, could have approved of the horrible excesses of the French Revolution. Let alone all the heads chopped on the guillotine—those of noblemen and prosperous commoners alike. There was a sort of madness that could possess a state, when all of a sudden they thought it was not only right and just to tamper with such things as the names of the days of the week, or even the divisions of the year, but also sought to regulate not only the way in which people lived— which some might argue was a legitimate function of the state—but also the way they thought and felt. And that, Captain Corridon thought, was one step too far, and no good ever could have come of it. Which was why he was quite enthusiastic in his idea that he should get those rubies and give them to the most trustworthy government, run by the most sensible queen in the whole world.

But what he didn't need to do, and his principles would most definitely let him wink on this, was turn Hettie's parents in to the wolf. After all, he thought, it was quite possible that in the end of all this, when the rubies were safely with the sovereign and Nigel Oldhall had been shot as a traitor, and all the various natives and various traitors had been punished, he should wish to marry Hettie Perigord, after all.

So, with this in mind, it would behoove him to protect his future in-laws by not mentioning them in this missive.

Which was why his message to his superior, as finally drafted, read: *Dear Lord Rompworth, as you know, I have for some time now been in pursuit of the rubies that anchor the power of the universe to the eyes of an avatar in deep Africa. It will not come as a surprise to you that these rubies are no longer in Africa—this is widely known in diplomatic circles. Heart of Light, the ruby that remained behind after Charlemagne used Soul of Fire to create power with which to bind the magic of Europe to himself and his descendants, was taken by the agent Nigel Oldhall, who had been sent to Africa by Her Majesty's government and your superior, Lord Widefield.*

We don't know what happened in Africa, but considering that Nigel Oldhall left it in the company of Peter Farewell, whose anarchist past is in little dispute, this leads one to believe that Oldhall was, as the parlance goes, turned. This left us with the unpalatable option of trying to find Farewell in India, where he appeared to be in search of the other ruby—the one that was spent and more or less destroyed, Soul of Fire.

That he found this ruby and somehow restored it will not surprise you, but it might shock you to know— as per my dispatch of a week ago—that the second ruby had been given to Nigel Oldhall, either in Vienna, Austria or in Venice—our contacts were quite shaky on that—and that he then proceeded to take both rubies aboard a carpetship headed for Africa.

Through my contacts, and with a little of instigation on my part, this carpetship was attacked by a man named Zhang—actually, a were-dragon who is part of the broad group of flying junk pirates—a menace that we must eliminate when he is no longer necessary.

I gave Zhang instructions on where to find the rubies and the description of the man who would be carrying them. With native inefficiency, I regret to say, not only did Zhang steal only one of the jewels, but did it in such a way that the entire ship was, in fact, at risk of crashing and losing many innocent lives.

Nigel Oldhall—for I am convinced it was him—held the ship in the air by main force of will. This man, Nigel, was brought to a private home in Cape Town, the home of a citizen who cannot possibly know what Oldhall is. Here, Captain Corridon stopped and chewed on his pen, while he made sure he had been coy enough not to give away anything of importance. Then he took a deep breath and continued. *From this home, I am reliably informed, said Nigel Oldhall has left, headed for Hong Kong, possibly in the company of a were-dragon also a member of the flying junk pirates and, apparently, considered a princess among them.*

I am now doing my duty and following these notorious and dangerous obstacles in the path to the fulfillment of Her Majesty's orders.

I have in my possession an object that gives me a certain power over these desperate criminals. This was, of course, not strictly true. To begin with, no one would call Hettie an object. Second, he didn't exactly have something that gave him power over the people who'd taken the jewels. What he had was someone who had given him power over Joe Perigord, and he was sure this would be enough to leverage Perigord's cooperation and betrayal of all the other conspirators. Corridon chewed his lower lip, and nodded, deciding it would have to do. *I will now leave in pursuit of these said criminals, and will return to you, hopefully soon, in possession of the rubies as well as signed confessions.*

Rereading it, he was proud of the upbeat and confident tone of the ending, and nodded to himself in contented approval. Nothing remained for him now but to make sure that Hettie's letter didn't reach her mother and give Mrs. Perigord quite a wrong idea of what was transpiring.

On this thought, he sealed his own note, and wrote Lord Rompworth's name upon the outside. Then he looked up and asked Hettie, who was slowly and pensively folding her own note, "Quite done, my love?"

When she nodded, he smiled. "Let me take the note, then, and give it to one of my own subalterns, to make sure it reaches your mother in time and that she will take good care of . . . er . . . Mrs. Beddlington's wardrobe."

His intention, of course, once in possession of the folded paper written in Miss Perigord's emotion-shaken hand, was to feed it into the first fire he found burning.

He had to go quite a long while to find it, because, it being quite warm in Cape Town, the only fires currently burning were cooking fires. However, he wasn't willing to risk a subaltern finding the addressed note and deciding to take it to the Perigord's home.

For just a moment, as he came back into the room, he looked at Hettie, who was sitting very still, looking flushed and...well...odd, and wondered if perhaps she had read his letters.

But the wafers he had used to seal the missives remained still quite attached, and Corridon, who had had his share of relationships, was well aware that it was the unbreakable code of British misses not to read letters that weren't meant for them.

Whatever else Hettie Perigord might be—dangerously beautiful or more stubborn than several varieties of mule—one thing he knew for absolute certainty: she was a well-brought-up English miss, and one who would not so easily break the code she'd been taught.

He bowed to her, as he picked up his jacket. "Shall we go?" he said, intending to give his own notes to his subaltern on the way out.

"You have not packed," she said.

"I am used to traveling light," he replied, with a dazzling smile.

She looked as though she would protest, but in the end, she gave him her hand and returned his smile with one of her own. "Very well," she said. "Let us be on our way. Where do you intend to marry me?"

"I believe," he said, "there are some ministries in Hong Kong that will do most admirably. And in those far-off locations, they don't tend to look too closely when one tells them one's bride is of age."

Something like a shadow passed across her face, and he was not at all sure what it meant. But one thing he knew—she put her hand in his arm and walked out of the compound under his escort.

NIGHTMARES

龙

Nigel was sleeping, and he should have been having quite a restful sleep. After all, he was in the broadest bed he'd been in since he'd left his parents' home—a well-appointed, well-cushioned sleeping arrangement, consisting of a carved frame and a heavy mattress, surmounted with soft sheets and quilts.

Though it was a little warm and a little humid, it shouldn't have been warm and humid enough to disturb Nigel's rest. And yet, between the soft, well-pressed linen sheets, Nigel was tormented with unquiet dreams.

In his dream, he was aboard a carpetship. It didn't look like the *Indian Star,* but more like a mishmash of all the carpetships in which he'd flown. On the broad navigation deck, Nigel sat upon the thronelike chair of the flight magician, his magic solidly enveloping him and the ship both, keeping them afloat.

A man bent over him, appearing with the suddenness of dreams, and whispering in Nigel's ear, "Mr. Oldhall, your wife requires your presence."

"Wife?" Nigel said, and turned to look at the man,

wondering how Emily could possibly have made it aboard this carpetship. Hadn't he left her in Africa, remarried—and quite happy, for that matter, in her new life?

In the dream he rose, ready to protest. If Emily was there, she was, in fact, no wife of his. As much as he felt guilty over his haphazard marriage, she couldn't possibly consider herself his wife. They had never consummated their all too short-lived marriage. And she was now living with—and for all he knew, bearing children to—a tribal leader of an old and sacred village in the heart of Africa.

But just as suddenly as he rose, as suddenly as his mind had conjured up the image of this carpetship and its crew, he was in the crew quarters and knocking at a door. He almost called out *Emily,* but a momentary and disconcerting awareness of his body lying on the bed, many miles away from the dreamed space, stopped him. Instead, he knocked again, and the door opened, as though his mere knock had been enough.

In the cabin stood Red Jade Lung, wearing British clothes of a cut and make that Nigel had never seen on her. It was a society's matron attire. A well-tailored dark blue dress with the curious bump in the back unfolded in a cascade of flounces. Nigel was not sure where the awkward fashion had originated, or why females thought it all the crack. In his mind he called it camel's hump, for it seemed just as strange a disruption of a woman's harmonious form. But the dress, at the sides, and in the front, displayed enough of Jade's natural form that he could not help but be charmed, whatever the excrescences of fashion that accrued to it.

A wave of tenderness enveloped him, as though they were indeed married—and for many years now as well—and he extended his hands to her. "My dear," he said.

She extended her hands to him, in turn, with equal warmth, but her face, surrounded by the complex up-swept coiffure of ladies in the social circles that Nigel's mother frequented, remained aloof and, in fact, disturbingly intent. Like the expression he'd seen on her as he unveiled the ruby.

He got a feeling that this dream—and he was fully aware of dreaming—was both more and less than it seemed. It wasn't a dream, as such, and probably it wasn't premonitory.

Though all magicians are subjected to premonitory dreams now and then, the power itself was so little understood and so unpredictable that most civilized countries afforded it little or no credit. And though France and Italy both had graduate programs for it in their universities, and though young foreseers trained at such institutions of learning had risen to positions of prominence the world over, including in such places like at the elbows of English queens and kings, their testimony would not be admissible in a court of law. And no magician over the age of ten gave undue weight to a premonitory dream. The thing was too fluid, the format and the way the images presented themselves too vague, allowing the dreamer to interpret practically anything from the symbols he'd seen.

The dreaming Nigel seemed to be a puppetmaster floating above the scene in which the dreamed Nigel held the hands of his wife, Red Jade, and felt a wave of tenderness for her—together with a sudden concern that something was very wrong. And that made him think about an article he'd recently read in *Magic Users Weekly,* aboard a carpetship on which he'd served.

They spoke of a man in Vienna, named Freud, who was working specifically with farseers and interpreting the symbols that appeared in their dreams, trying to create a stable theory that might allow for routine interpretation. But the dreaming Nigel also knew that he had never met Freud, and suspected that the man's research should, in the end, prove as fruitless as that of the others who had trod that same path.

He forced the dreamed Nigel to lean closer to his dreamed wife, and to whisper in a tone of urgency, "What is it? What is wrong? Why have you come to me and what can I do?"

Had the dream truly been just that, Red Jade— Mrs. Oldhall as she was in this confused scenario— would have been horrified at his seeming repudiation of her and at his treating her like a stranger. Or else, she would have turned into an octopus or something equally unlikely, fulfilling the even deeper and more profoundly unlikely logic of dreams.

Instead, she frowned slightly, like a child trying to remember a lesson, then spoke. "I am imprisoned in the Chinese quarter of the city, in the store of the drapers by this sign." In his mind formed the sign of a tiger, holding something like a scroll in its mouth. "I am in the back room, and there should be access, somehow." In his mind there formed an image of the store—of the two alleys bordering the building, and the road it looked on. "I don't know if you can help me, but I beg you to do what you can. I've been given a potion that makes it impossible for me to change shapes, and the Ring of Power my brother gave me does not seem to be working."

As the dream image stopped speaking, Nigel found himself stark awake in a room bathed by the early-morning sun. His friend, John Malmsey, quite overwhelmed by Nigel's unexpected appearance in his residence, had given him the best bedroom, the one overlooking the harbor. Getting up and stumbling to the window, Nigel took in a vision of a morning sky struck by bands of color between pink and peach, whose hesitant fulgence bathed the ocean in a coppery color.

He'd arrived in Hong Kong almost twenty-four hours before, but he already felt much better. His explanation that he'd been on a small carpetcraft that was attacked by flying junk pirates was not questioned—possibly because everyone in this area believed these attacks to be very frequent. Whether they were or not, Nigel couldn't tell, but he knew from dinnertime conversation the night before that just about everyone believed that any travel around the edges of the Chinese Empire could bring you in contact with the fearsome pirates, and that none of it was safe.

In fact, their depredations on traffic headed to Hong Kong, Macau and Guangzhou had become such that most of the traffic to these cities now took place by carpetship to the Philippines, and from there via boat or ship, as this was safer from pirate attacks—or at least the pirate attacks, not being surrounded by magic, were much easier to counter by normal means.

At any rate, Nigel's injuries were neither strange nor difficult to treat, and a gentleman with white whiskers and a manner much like Nigel's masters at Cambridge had come and given Nigel magical treatment which had finished healing what Jade had simply tried to stop bleeding, and what the people in Cape Town had tried to cure with potions. And when Nigel, curious, had asked the doctor why not use Chinese medicine, he'd been met with an incredulous stare and told that most Chinese medicine tended to focus on that Daoist goal of becoming immortal and, like most such disciplines, neglected the mere correction of physical ills in favor of improving the body immortal.

Nigel, who had met with such pronouncements on native knowledge and beliefs in other continents, hadn't replied. The truth was that, right now, he felt much better than he had in days, perhaps in years. None of which helped him through his very bewildering dream.

Was it true that Red Jade was a prisoner, somewhere in the native city? And if so, how could Nigel save her?

It didn't seem so much a matter for thinking. He realized if Jade was a prisoner he would have to find a way to get her out. And the only way he could determine if his dream message was right was to go out to the native city and try to find a sign with the tiger with the scroll in its teeth. And he'd hope that it was not too common a sign, and that it wouldn't have found its way

into his subconscious via one of those symbols the man
Freud went on about.

He cast off his pajamas and found his day clothes—
purchased just the day before at a native tailor's that
seemed to work at superhuman speed and turn out fitted clothes in a matter of hours. His hostess had told
him how it would be, though Nigel had found himself
unable to believe it until the clothes—several suits,
shirts and a hat—were delivered to his host's home before dinner. He'd also managed to have his hair clipped
by a native barber of his host's recommending, so that
for the first time since he'd left England with Emily, his
hair was exquisitely and carefully cut to mold his head
and display its shape, in lustrous gold and white tones.

With his suit on, he looked, for the first time in a
long time, entirely the gentleman, which might make
him more conspicuous. But, if he was going to have his
appearance disguised by a potion, he doubted it would
make any difference. Besides, in Hong Kong most
Englishmen looked the gentleman's part even when
they were not, in fact, gentlemen.

Taking a teak-and-silver walking stick that he'd purchased the day before, he found his way down the
Malmseys' broad staircase to the front door. Several
Chinese gardeners were already at work in the immaculate gardens, clipping the lawn and doing something
to the roses.

"Going for a stroll before breakfast?" John
Malmsey's voice asked from behind Nigel, and Nigel
turned around to see John coming down the stairs, still
in his dressing gown and smiling broadly at him.

John, Nigel thought, was as close to a disinterested

friend of his parents as he was likely to meet. Though he'd heard of Nigel's disappearance from Nigel's parents, and was relieved and happy to see Nigel again, he had not pressed Nigel for news of Carew, nor had he any suspicion that Nigel had been on a secret mission.

The story of an attack by a native secret order that had killed Emily and left Nigel an amnesiac had seemed to convince him. Nigel had explained that his memory had only come back after suffering severe injuries and a fever in the attack on the small carpetcraft in which he'd been flying. This allowed him to disclaim any knowledge of what he might be doing upon the coast of China, or what it all might mean.

It also allowed him to reassure John that he would write his parents and be back to them as soon as his health allowed. Since John, himself, had told Nigel that it would not be a good idea to engage in a trip so strenuous as the trip back to London would be—since he would most likely have to first take a boat out to the Phillipines, and would only, from there, be able to take a carpetship with any impunity—until he was quite sure of his strength, Nigel was, in fact, safe to stay here for as long as he needed.

After which, he would say he was making his way back to London and his parents' home and, hopefully, it would not take more than a very few days before he could, in fact, do so. Two weeks at most, he told himself, though a nagging voice at the back of his head told him it would very likely be more.

Part of him, too, had no wish at all to go home. He wished he could live, like John Malmsey, an entirely British life at the edge of the exotic. He looked at his parents' friend—a graying gentleman with a happy look about him and a wife at least twenty years his junior—and smiled. "Yes, yes. I have had not a chance to see anything of the land, and you must know that all my life I've longed to have adventures and to see exotic lands."

This got him a surprised expression, followed by an amused smile. "No, really? I would have thought that was Carew's province, but I'm glad of it. Only, don't eat anything in the native quarters. Although here in Hong Kong you're fairly safe from eating rat or dog unawares, their cooking uses spices we do not, and sometimes it has an effect on the European digestive system that is quite unlike anything European food might manage. Even French food."

With that, he waved cheerily at Nigel, who set out in the cool morning sunlight, walking amid manicured lawns tended by natives, slowly edging his way toward the native quarters of town.

He knew that not so long ago, Hong Kong had been a wasteland. Most of the work that had gone into making it the current paradise was doubtlessly native, though the direction was, just as unmistakably, British. In between the two, Hong Kong seemed like a city out of dreams, and a perfect embodiment of what Nigel wished for. Both familiar and foreign. A land where anything at all could happen.

MISS'S REGRETS

龙

What have I done? *Hettie thought, as soon as she had* read the two notes that Captain Corridon had left on the table. *What have I done?*

More important, of course, was what she could do now to remedy her fatal mistake in trusting this man whom she thought might very well prove to be a rake or worse. And then she reproached herself, because he was not, in fact, anything he hadn't told her he was—an agent working on behalf of Her Majesty.

The problem, of course, was with Mama and Papa and what they might have been doing. Hettie was not such a great fool that she couldn't read between the lines of those notes, on which she had so carefully lifted the sealing wafer that it took no more than the warmth of her hands to reseal them again.

Unless she missed her guess, the carpetship flight magician had indeed been a hero, as Papa had said. And perhaps that was why Papa felt obligated to house him. What Hettie could not understand was why Papa had also felt that he must hide that ruby—if the queen wanted it—much less let that man leave the house with the ruby in his possession. She also could not understand what the Chinese dragons had to do with it all.

But it was clear that Captain Corridon had gone out of his way to avoid mentioning her parents, and that this at least meant he was protecting them in some measure. She wondered if he would still not have mentioned them had she not agreed to leave with him. However, it was also quite clear to her, from his saying that he was in possession of something that would allow him to make the conspirators reveal all, that his having obtained, as it were, possession of her, meant that he was hoping to blackmail whoever the conspirators against the queen were and get them to confess all—or at least to give him the ruby.

She looked around the small cramped studio. A part of her, irrationally, wanted to take the notes and her suitcase and run, as fast as she could, out of Captain Corridon's power. But the other part of her was more rational. First, taking the notes would do nothing because Corridon could very well write the notes again. Oh, it might help her prove to Papa where she'd been and what she'd found out, but she rather thought that the moment she mentioned the magical rubies, Papa would believe her.

But worse, given her desire to run back and throw herself in Papa's safe arms, was the certainty that there was nothing she could do that would be more fatal to Mama's and Papa's chances at escaping.

If Captain Corridon was the prime mover of the investigation that might end up with Hettie's parents in jail, or worse, for suspected treason, then Captain

Corridon must not, under any circumstances, be left to his own devices. He must, in fact, have Hettie cleave to him as though she were, in fact, attempting to elope with him.

The other part of this was that Hettie hadn't used her own magical power on him. Glamoury wasn't a very good magical power to have, and particularly when it was as strong as Hettie's; it wasn't considered something suitable for well-brought-up misses to use. But in this case, she would bet she could keep poor Corridon confused enough that he wouldn't know if he was on his feet or on his head until she could find a better plan to keep him away from her parents.

In the same way, she was quite sure, given the time it had taken him to return, that he had not conveyed her note to her parents, which meant she must find a way to do it herself.

In it she would explain—carefully—that she was safe, that she was using her power to stay so, and that she would be home before anything terrible could happen to her.

At that moment, Captain Corridon came into his study, and Hettie smiled at him, trying to make it as fond a smile as she could, while throwing all the power of her glamoury at him.

A PAPER CAGE

龙

"I don't suppose these bars will be any easier to break because they are made out of paper?" Third Lady asked her husband.

Wen, still immaterial and transparent, had been trying without success to bend the bars of the cage. The cage they'd been put in was so clearly a construction made out of colored paper that it seemed infuriating that they could not simply break out of it.

"It is not so easy," Wen said. "You see, first of all, while the cage is made out of paper, it is far more solid and real than a body composed of mind and will and, in my case, no soul." He looked at Third Lady with eyes filled with some form of tragic hurt. "How can you love me, Precious Lotus? Was I already soulless when we met?"

She sighed. "According to the information the oracle gave me, your soul has been held captive and subjected to frivolous lawsuits by Zhang and his relatives since you were maybe twelve. Their suits weren't very strong, and they couldn't have held, if he'd not been careful to get you addicted to opium. He was trying, you see, to..." She floundered, then took a deep breath and got her courage. "He was trying to ensure you did not have descendants. He...thought the opium would eventually kill you and then he would..."

"Inherit," Wen said.

Third Lady nodded. "But then he heard of the Jewels of Power, and I think he was growing impatient and..." She stopped. Wen wasn't listening to her.

"Twelve," Wen said, and the word had a finality, as though he couldn't quite believe the number he'd pronounced. "That long. You'd think one would notice. You'd think one's soul could not simply leave one's body one morning with us never the wiser."

Third Lady shook her head. "I don't think that is how it works, my lord," she said. "I think you quite mistake it. You're not without a soul, as such. In fact, I don't believe it is possible to be alive and function without a soul. I think you have a soul, right enough, only it is held in the underworld and linked to you only through a tether. This means it still animates you, it's just not as...substantial as it should be. And this leaves you incapable of withstanding manipulation...and the temptations of opium. But it doesn't mean I can't see that soul in you, and I can't see, through your weakened form, what you would be should your soul be restored to you." She spread her hands wide. "My lord, the truth is, I fell in love with you the first time I saw you, and I do not even know why. The only explanation I can find is in the legend that the gods link together the souls and bodies of those who are supposed to marry, and that I was linked to you when we were born."

"I wonder," Wen said, heavily, "whether my soul is

held captive nearby and whether it will, in fact, be possible to find it and set it free."

Third Lady, who had been thinking approximately that, frowned. "I'm not sure it would be a good idea, my lord. What I've seen of the underworld appears to run almost too legalistically. I have sent ahead documents and proof against any frivolous lawsuit Zhang might have brought, based on your ancestry and your right to inherit. And besides, Judge Bao is known to be fast and to have very little patience for this sort of lawsuit. And I'm sure if needed we can call Yu the Great to your defense, and with a witness like that, who can fail?"

"If we can ever make it to his court," Wen said as he once more, desultorily, tried to pull at the painted-black bars of their prison, which reacted not at all to his touch. "Those paper guards are still out there, and frankly, they didn't sound to me like they cared at all if we should ever come to judgment or not."

"Well, they probably do not," Third Lady said, and frowned because this was not something that she cared to admit.

"Didn't you tell Yu that you had burned paper figures of our own, to accompany us and serve us?" Wen asked. "In fact, I know that you have. I remember standing around the cave, in immaterial form, as you did so. And I remember watching the figures zoom by me, also in spirit form and animated. Where are they? Didn't Grandfather Yu tell you that all you had to do was call them?"

"I think what he means is that I need to demand them—to demand them loudly and make it clear to

Feng Du's laws and our jailors that I know my rights. The problem with that—"

"Is that we're locked within a paper cage, and that no one is paying any attention at all to what we say," Wen said. "Yes. And those figures out there, our illustrious guards, they don't seem very intelligent."

"If I understand what Yu said," Third Lady said, quietly, "they are not that complex a construction. They are not, in fact, in any way, sentient. Just machines, of a sort, magically animated with certain precepts, and on those precepts they'll live and die."

"But then we are at the mercy of nonintelligent machines," Wen said. "And that means we could spend the rest of eternity locked behind these paper bars." He looked at her. "How long can our bodies subsist without sustenance, in that cave?"

Third Lady's eyes widened. "Well, milord," she said, "I told the lady, your sister—and it is true—that the time down here need have no correlation to the time up there, and that I could contrive to be gone no more than a few hours. While I think this is still true, one needs to get permission for this, by talking to a guardian of the underworld. Judge Bao or another might, in fact, as part of his verdict, be able to send us back to shortly after we left, but . . ."

"But if we're locked in a cell and forgotten, we will never return to the world of the living, and meanwhile our bodies, in their unnatural sleep, will wither and die."

Third Lady nodded once, acknowledging what her husband said. In the back of her mind, something was struggling, trying to find its way to the surface. There had to be a way out of this—a way that would make it possible for them to defeat the bars.

Things came together in her mind, even as Wen said, "Precious Lotus, this will never do. I cannot leave my sister alone and at the mercy of Zhang or his accomplices. For one, now that she knows he is a traitor, he's more likely to kill her than marry her. Not that I'm sure, at all, which one Red Jade would prefer."

Third Lady almost told him to be quiet, because his words interfered with the solution assembling itself in her mind. But she couldn't be quite so disrespectful to the noble husband she loved. So, instead, she merely made a gesture with her hand, as though waving away his objections. "Don't worry," she said. "We will not leave her."

She remembered the figures she had burned—the gentlemen, the ladies and the monkey. The monkey. In the novel *Journey to the West,* a monkey that had achieved sentience and therefore been able to enter Feng Du had in fact wreaked havoc. His exploits were well celebrated. This underworld which ran on laws and regulations—no matter how contradictory those were—had been plunged into chaos.

She should be able to conjure her monkey. He should be able to come even into this prison. Didn't monkeys penetrate the tightest of spaces?

But she had to *demand* his presence. She stood very still and looked up and spoke to what seemed like the vast emptiness of the cell. "Monkey that I sent before me, I command you: come and get us out of this cell."

MORNING IN BRITAIN

It was a brisk morning in Derbyshire, with the sun just coming in over the peaks, when Peter Farewell, Lord St. Maur, joined his young wife in the dining room.

He looked windblown and in quite a good humor, though his clothes were in perfect order, and, in fact, lent his lean, muscular frame quite an air of distinction. Just married, St. Maur was a fine figure of a man, as everyone kept telling Sofie Farewell, nee Warington, Lady St. Maur. And if some ventured to say it was a pity he'd lost his left eye in some unspecified accident in foreign parts, most would agree that the patch that hid the deformity fit his classical profile quite well and lent a certain hint of mystery to his romantically dark and tumbled curls.

Lady St. Maur certainly thought so as she lifted her gaze from her plate of sliced ham to grace her husband with a radiant smile. "Good morning, my dear," she said. And then with a sparkle of humor infecting her voice, "I see you have been for an early-morning excursion."

She was very well aware that the servant in the room, shifting platters on the serving table, preparing to present his master with a choice of viands upon which to break his fast, prevented Peter from answering openly. And it amused her to play this game with her husband, who was a were-dragon and had only recently become reconciled to this aspect of his nature. Peter didn't now change shapes often. Having come back to his ancestral home and settled into the traditional mode of life of his ancestors, he was loath to jeopardize it all and have to take to the wing again, to the four corners of the world, to hide the fact that he'd been born a were—a creature proscribed under English law and facing the death penalty on discovery, for the simple crime of existing.

But Sofie knew for an absolute fact that he'd become a dragon that morning, and gone flying through the calm morning sky. She'd glimpsed him from her window—the only in the house that looked out in the direction of their little wilderness, over which he'd gone disporting.

Peter gave her an amused look, understanding her game very well. "The morning air was particularly fine and very brisk," he said. "And I noted that we need to bring in the hay from the north fields in the home farm, else it will all get ruined when the first rains come."

She smiled fondly at him, because Peter had been getting quite interested in the home farm, in the lives of his tenants and in his buildings and properties. It wasn't how they met, and it wasn't what one might have expected from life with a dangerous were-dragon, who had traveled the world over and had all kinds of

adventures. And yet, Sofie gathered, all of Peter's tenants and farmers were delighted that at last a Farewell
was looking to the administration of the estate and
even buying back many of the lands the previous generations had lost.

Peter answered a discrete question from their attending servant with, "Coffee only, and some dry toast.
I am not very hungry this morning."

"Oh," Sofie said, unable to resist teasing him. "Had
a snack of broiled mutton, did you?"

Peter's eye sparkled a warning. She knew that were
it not for the presence of the servant, he would be calling her *baggage* in that soft, choked voice he used
when he wanted to be particularly tender. "Indeed,
no," he said. "There is nothing worse than mutton in
the morning. You know my digestion could not bear it."

He looked like he would say something else but, at
that moment, one of their footmen, Wilkins, came in,
bearing a letter upon a small silver salver. He stopped
by Peter's seat and bowed and proffered the letter.

Peter took a look at the address and frowned.
Joseph Gilbert. "Joseph Gilbert," he said aloud, in the
tone of voice of a man trying to jog his memory.

"Someone you know?" Sofie asked, alarmed by his
frown.

"No. Or at least..." He frowned harder. "When I
was very young, and while my mother was still alive,
we sometimes had someone to stay who had been one
of my father's friends when he was single. I'm sure that
was the name. Joseph Gilbert. Second son of the Earl
of Marshlake."

"Perhaps this is he," Sofie suggested.

"I...it hardly seems likely. I have some notion, though I cannot tell you how I came by it, that the entire family is gone. The father died, and shortly thereafter the older son died. The younger son, I seem to remember, had disappeared some years before. Not sure what he did, but he must have blotted his copybook very badly, because my father said that the earl would not allow Joseph's name to be pronounced in his presence."

"Well, my dear," Sofie said, softly, not daring to say anything more, "you disappeared from the ancestral estates for some years also, and I'm sure the relationship subsisting between you and your late esteemed father was far from perfect."

Peter looked up, his frown taking a different tone altogether. In that expression, she saw that he understood her meaning. Many were proscribed from English society. It didn't mean they were dead, however much their families might like to pretend so.

"If I may, milord," Wilkins said. "The letter arrived express, via carpetship from Cape Town, in South Africa."

"South Africa!" Peter said, in a tone in which astonishment mingled with alarm. Doubtless the mention of that continent brought remembrance that Nigel Oldhall would now be there, or very soon would be, delivering the rubies to their ancestral homeland.

Peter unfolded the letter, while saying absently, "Thank you, Wilkins. That will be all."

He didn't dismiss the other servant, the one who'd brought him coffee and a plate with dry toast, but the man must have sensed his master's uneasiness, because he coughed once and stepped out as well.

Peter read the letter, once through, it seemed, then frowned at the paper. "The devil," he said, softly, and passed the letter to his wife.

Sofie read what was still a very distinguished hand, even though the paper and pen seemed to be cheap: *Dear Lord St. Maur, you'll forgive me addressing you like this, since I have not seen you from when you were about five or so. And that was a fleeting enough visit, since your father's and my acquaintance had begun to be frayed at the edges. I have recently housed in my home a carpetship flight magician, by the name of Enoch Jones. From his speech while delirious I deduced some things. You might have read in international papers about his heroic actions, which kept the carpetship flying and saved many lives.*

I cared for him while he was recovering, and I happened to see the one artifact he had remaining, of the two he'd sheltered. I also heard your name—and his real name—quite a lot, in that time, while he raved with fever.

I would not dream of bothering you, milord, but now Mr. Jones is gone, as is a Chinese princess he is sheltering and helping. And meanwhile, my daughter, Hettie, has been kidnapped by a member of Her Majesty's Secret Service, who is demanding the objects in question, as well as the denunciation of anyone connected with what he calls an international conspiracy, before he will return Hettie to us.

I wouldn't write, but she is our only child and my Charlotte is beside herself. Humbly, Joseph (Gilbert) Perigord.

"Dear me," Sofie said, feeling puzzled. "What is this? A threat? Blackmail?"

Peter shook his head and sighed. "What it sounds like to me is a man out of his mind with worry for his daughter, one who is grasping at straws."

"Does he know you are—"

"If Mr. Jones was who I think he was and he was raving with fever, what do you think? I'd say undoubtedly he does know."

Sofie found herself biting her lower lip, in confusion. "But...what's to be done?"

Peter swallowed his coffee and got up, unfolding his body from the chair gracefully, like a dancing master. "I think, my dear, I will have to go to Cape Town and ascertain that."

"Are you quite sure?" Sofie asked. "After all, we don't know what they want from you, precisely."

"No, but the very fact that their child is in danger must call for our sympathy and our help."

Sofie rose from the table as well. "I'll go change my dress," she said. "And pack some clothes for both of us."

"Lady St. Maur," he said, his voice attempting to be severe. "Am I to understand you intend to accompany me?"

"Certainly," she said, and allowed her eyes to dance with mischief. "It's been much too long since I've had a good flight."

"But it might be dangerous."

"Precisely. And since when do I allow you to face danger alone?"

RESCUING THE MAIDEN

Nigel found the sign with the tiger easily enough and for a moment stood outside the shop, looking up at the sign, and at the bolts of cloth within the shadowy shop, wondering whether Jade was indeed inside and what he could do to rescue her.

It seemed more and more that his life was defined by people expecting him to do impossible things. Killing lions and rescuing maidens and keeping carpet-ships flying in the face of great odds, until he wondered what would happen next. But it always ended right, somehow, he thought, and sighed.

Here he was, in a Hong Kong street, with the little covered arcades on either side, in case—as John Malmsey had told him—it should piss with rain as, supposedly, it did quite often in these latitudes. On one side of him was a store filled with dark carved furniture. The owners appeared to him to be Indian, though perhaps he mistook the matter. To the other side of the fabric store, past the narrow alley, was some sort of restaurant, from which the smell of ginger and roasted meat came through to tantalize his palate. Farther down the street, a store advertised—in quite large letters, on a street-placed sign—inscrutable prices.

It seemed like not at all the place for a daring rescue. But he remembered Jade in his dream—how preoccupied she'd looked. And he understood that her position—as princess or pirate leader, or whatever it was—would entail certain dangers.

He walked around the building and stood facing the brick wall where, from his dream, he knew a small room lay. And in it would be Jade. They'd given her some potion to prevent her from changing shapes, of course. A dragon would be much harder to confine than a frail young woman. The memory of her in his dream mingled with the memory of her as he'd seen her on the deck of the carpetship—an angel in native attire.

He sighed at the thought of her, in either attire, then put his hand to the brick wall. There was a problem—a very great problem. Certain magics Nigel knew, certain magics he'd learned to use from earliest childhood—tending to the crops by making sure both the soil and the weather were propitious. And making sure that his father's tenants and livestock were healthy.

Other arts he'd learned from tutors and at Cambridge—the things that were expected from a gentleman who might have to serve his country in time of need. He'd learned to charge a powerstick. He'd learned to create minor illusions, which could confuse an enemy. And he'd learned a hundred other incidental things. One of them—apparently a rare talent and therefore not often taught, because few people had the ability to put it in action—was the ability to set fire to things at a distance. But none of these was a magic that could be used to tear bricks down and make them float away one by one.

Something tickled at the back of his mind, as he went again over his meager abilities. At that moment, seeing someone come down the alley, he faced the wall and pretended to be relieving himself against it— something that, judging by the smell just here, was quite often done.

As the people passed by, a Chinese couple chatting animatedly to each other and barely sparing him a look, his mind gave him back one of his abilities in stark and clear vividness: *fire starting*.

He stood up straight and blinked, bewildered, at the wall. It could not possibly be used here. How could it be? Surely, if he started a fire, there was a good chance that Jade would be injured before he could rescue her.

But how else could he save her? The store was full of people, including the one who'd kidnapped her, and doubtless full of natives in the back room as well. The idea that he could go into the store and slip to the back was a forlorn hope as well. How could he? All these people looked alike enough to not be noticed if one of them edged away—except for him. His pale blond hair would glimmer like a light in those shadows. It would call attention to him and to anything he did. Besides, from what he had seen yesterday, any foreigner entering a native shop immediately became a target for obsequious, almost maniacal attendance.

So he could not go in. He could, however, start a fire

in several bolts of silk at once, so that everyone would have to come out of the shop. If he was lucky, one of them would retrieve Jade and carry her with them. Which would bring the problem of rescuing her to the more manageable level of stealing her from amid a crowd of people, rather than the insanely unmanageable one of taking a building apart brick by brick.

Of course, fire-starting—magical or not—was a serious crime throughout most of the empire. But then, denying Her Majesty the rubies she craved was a crime, too. Though perhaps not one that was entered in any law books. Nigel chewed his lower lip as he thought, and then shrugged. If it must be done, as someone or other had said in Shakespeare, it would be best if it was done quickly.

As a last precaution, he checked on the rain clouds and found that they were quite nearby and could be herded in by his weather-controlling facility at a moment's notice. Which would be good, in case the fire either spread or it proved a danger to Jade.

Slowly he walked toward the street again, and stood across from the shop he was targeting. With a good view—through the open door—of the interior, he targeted those silk bolts that were farthest from the room where Jade was being held.

His capacity was a little rusty, but not too much. Once he had the location in mind, he wished impossible heat to various spots at once.

Within seconds, he was gratified to hear a high-pitched, terrified scream, followed by a series of others. The word repeated was always the same, and though in Chinese, Nigel could imagine it meant *fire*. As if to confirm this, he heard the word *fire* repeated a few times. It wasn't long before a crowd came running out of the shop, screaming.

He heard a distant clang that was probably a fire alarm, or the bell of the fire department.

But Nigel had been watching as carefully as he could, and Jade had neither come out nor been brought out. He looked at the store, from which, now, a billow of smoke was emerging.

"Very well," he said to himself, since there was no one else to hear him. "I suppose it must be done."

He plunged into the smoke blindly, going on his memory of where the room in which Jade was kept prisoner lay. On his way through the smoke-filled room, where bales of silk had caught fire, one after the other, he grabbed blindly for the first thing that might help him open the door. It was a yard stick—two inches by two inches and of course a yard long, and from the feel and color of it, made of teak—and Nigel had just realized it was a singularly inappropriate tool, when a creature jumped out at him from the roiling smoke. Without looking—without even thinking—Nigel did what he'd done so many months ago, it seemed like a whole lifetime, in the African savannah. He lifted the yardstick in the direction of the huge body falling toward him, and felt the stick hit and penetrate. He jumped out of the way.

The tiger—as he realized the creature was—fell and writhed, and Nigel would have taken the time to be horrified, except he could hear fists pounding on the wood from behind the locked door, and Jade's voice calling something indistinct.

He couldn't see a key. He couldn't even look for a key. He set his shoulder to the door—got a running start and hit it, once, twice. The door burst inward. Jade ran out coughing. Nigel grabbed for her hand and started leading her toward the back of the building, where there was also an exit. On the way there he stepped over the body of a young man with a yardstick protruding from his chest.

It wasn't till they got to the back alley—after bursting through yet another door—and while Jade was coughing and fighting for breath, that Nigel said, "I'm sorry. I thought . . . I didn't realize . . ." He felt sick all of a sudden, and leaned against the wall. "I didn't realize it was a human being. It sprang at me. I thought . . ."

Jade looked at him, frowning a little. She shook her head. "You mean the were-tiger?" she said. "What else could you do but defend yourself?" She wrapped her fingers around his wrist. "Come. No time to talk. Not here. It's not safe. Come. The Tiger Clan will be after us. Nowhere in Hong Kong is it safe."

She pulled him through a maze of streets. Soon, he saw they were in the British part of the city, in the shopping district by the warehouses. He didn't know if she had meant to go here, or if she had walked at random, and luckily ended up here.

Of course, saying they were in the English part of the city didn't mean that there were no Asians there. On the contrary, a steady procession of women engaged in transporting all kinds of goods—from food to bricks—in baskets suspended from a pole held across their shoulders walked down the middle of the street.

Also in the middle were workers—mostly women—

busy with repairing the street itself. But on both sides of the street, there was a sort of little arcade made of wood, like a covered veranda, no more than a step off the ground. There, the shoppers could take refuge during the quite frequent rainstorms that whipped through the city. And there, English misses and their chaperones mingled with Asian and Indian women, whose attire was wholly English and who clearly came from well-to-do families.

Nigel had only just had the thought that he and Jade wouldn't attract any attention when he realized that they were indeed attracting attention, and that people were staring at them—particularly at Jade's fingers around his wrist, pulling him.

Jade must have realized it at the same time, because she let go, and led him into what seemed at first to be a small park, but was revealed to be just a few trees and grass growing next to one of the warehouses.

"We must talk," she said, looking disturbed—or rather, perturbed, like one who speaks out of a turmoil of mind. "We must leave Hong Kong. I don't know how far this conspiracy reaches, but I doubt we can be safe. I have no way to take you into China now. Not only do you not have any means of disguising yourself, but I do not possess the means of transporting you. What shall we do?"

For a moment, Nigel was as much at a standstill as she was. This entire adventure, he'd done what he had to do, more or less, but now there was nothing he could do. And then his dream came to him, as a premonition, a way forward. "Lady Jade," he said. "What if we go by carpetship and you disguise yourself?"

She looked at him with quite a blank expression, and he sighed. "Look," he said, "I worked as a carpetship flight magician most of the last year. I know that though China is closed to foreigners—and I'm not going to argue it's not justified in many cases, or even that it's not for our protection. Your present rulers endorse xenophobia and encouraged the Boxer Rebellion, but I don't suppose my people's continued attempts to force your empire to import opium have helped."

She shrugged, as if to say that it was all a muddle anyway, and that she wasn't going to discuss it, and he nodded. "But while I realize that most of China is closed to foreigners, I know that I'm allowed to fly into most carpetship ports. I think this is because your native power—"

"Is not concentrated enough for the carpetships," she said. "European power is different, because of what Charlemagne did. That is why you can fly the carpetships, but most Chinese can't. So we have to be dependent on you."

"Though you can fly boats," Nigel said.

"Only the were-clans, and we are officially proscribed throughout the land, though the laws aren't always as ruthlessly enforced as in Europe. As usurpers and foreigners, the current rulers don't want to give us any power. Keeping us in the shadow is a way of protecting themselves."

Nigel nodded. Lately, since he'd come to think about the rules and the laws that had informed his life as less than preordained, he'd wondered often if that was the reason that weres were so strongly forbidden in the West. Because their special powers and par-

ticular magic—not always quantifiable or teachable—
made them more difficult for those in power to catalog
and control.

Jade shrugged. "But you said something about flying on a carpetship."

"Only this," he said, and spread his hands, palms
forward, as if trying to show he was not armed. "That if
you can come aboard a carpetship with me, as my . . .
as my wife or relative—because they allow the flight
magician a relative per voyage—we can fly to any of
the cities in China that have a carpetport. Would flying to any of them help us? Would we find in any of
them the potion that you tried to find here? I assume
you didn't find it."

"I never got to the Fox Clan," Jade said. She
sounded suddenly tired, and wrapped her arms around
herself as though she was cold. "For all I know, they
might be perfectly loyal and willing to help me, but . . .
I never got to them. The Tiger Clan stopped me." She
explained to him, quickly, what seemed to be a byzantine reasoning through which they could claim the
throne by claiming her. "You see why," she said, "it is
most urgent that we use the ruby on the rivers and reclaim the throne and power of my ancestors."

He saw. He also saw that, until then, every hand
would be against them. "But if you cannot go to the
Fox Clan," he said, "how can you get the potion to disguise my appearance? I suppose I could go through
China wrapped in a big cloak, or else—"

But he stopped, because she was looking at him
with a speculative gaze. "There is a big drugstore in
Guangzhou," she said. "It is one of the biggest in

China. And the drugs they sell are concocted by all the clans, as well as by the monks of all the temples. For Guangzhou is a city of temples."

Nigel cocked his head. "I'm sure there is a carpet-ship port there," he said. "I remember seeing the requests for carpetship flight magicians headed there at various ports throughout the world."

She nodded. "There is a foreign section, on the little island of Shameen. There's a carpetship port there, as well as a small city, or village, inhabited by foreigners. We can fly in and no one will know any better than that we came to transact some business. And once we're there, you can wait for me in Shameen while I go to the mainland and get you the necessary drug. And then we can start our journey to the rivers."

"No," Nigel said, and to her surprised look, "Oh, not about the journey, but I don't think I'm going to stay on some stupid island while you journey to the mainland. Something I've learned about these adventures," he said, "is that it's much easier if you have someone at your back."

For just a moment, it looked like she was going to rebel, and it amused him, because the expression in her dark eyes was so little Chinese and so wholly willful British miss. But then she shook her head. "You might be right. If I hadn't been able to touch your mind today..."

He nodded. Then frowned. "Would it compromise you to travel with me as man and wife?"

She looked at him, then shook her head. "No more than this entire adventure will compromise me. I should never have left the Dragon Boats without an escort, and certainly not without my brother's explicit consent. I will have to hope that my daring actions are proven correct in retrospect, by everything coming out all right."

"Is this the Mandate of Heaven which I hear so much about?" Nigel asked. Jade frowned at him, and unable to explain any better, he said, "I mean, that if something comes out all right, then it was meant to happen all along?"

She shook her head. "It's not that simple," she said. "Though that's one way the mandate confirms itself." She looked a little embarrassed. "We had a reading from the oracle, that told us my journey, as well as what Third Lady and my brother are doing, are the Mandate of Heaven. I wish I were equally sure."

SEE FENG DU BY NIGHT

Third Lady waited, her nerves on edge. For a long time, nothing happened, but at long last she heard the distinct shriek of a monkey. If it sounded ever so slightly . . . papery, it wasn't to be wondered at. A rustle from the door, and a monkey dressed in an elaborate uniform pushed through the bars. She heard Wen draw breath.

She wished she could count on his strength to help her get out of this situation—or at least on a man's strength. Wen, impaired by opium, had never been very strong, the whole time she'd known him. But here they were, immaterial even to things made of paper, and there was the fact that Wen was not whole. She must free him. And to free him, she must go to the court of Judge Bao.

The monkey scurried up to her and looked at her with eyes full of mischief. How could she trust such a creature? But then she looked at Wen, who was staring expectantly at her. Well, if Wen could trust a fox-fairy, she could trust a monkey. She leaned down and whispered, not sure what the other paper creatures could hear. "Dear monkey, would you collect the keys and open our cage, so we can escape?"

The monkey looked at her and, though its eyes were immobile, she could swear they danced with mirth. He squeaked and hopped in place. She remembered that most of the destruction the monkey had wreaked in *Journey to the West* had been random. Perhaps monkeys couldn't be commanded. So what had possessed her to bring this one with her? She closed her eyes. But then she heard a rustle and opened them up, in time to see the monkey squeeze through the bars again, headed toward the paper men.

There was . . . a flurry. It was hard to tell exactly what was happening. Papery screams echoed. Suddenly, the monkey was leaping and cartwheeling back, keys in hand, and the men looked like nothing more than twists of paper on the landscape.

The monkey put the key in the lock. It opened with a metallic clang, which made no sense because both lock and key were made of paper. Perhaps in Feng Du, things just sounded like they were supposed to.

She gestured for Wen to run, and was aware—through the corner of her eye—that he was hesitating.

"Run now, Wen," she said, putting all the force of her considerable willpower in her words. And as the monkey bowed to her, it then ran off, in another direction, jangling his ill-acquired paper key ring. Oh, no. She had a feeling bringing a monkey to hell had been a bad idea, indeed.

She ran for the door. Wen was ahead of her—just—as they ran madly through the darkness filled with mirrors.

"Get us out of this confusing place," Wen said, sounding breathless, still running at a full clip.

Rushing beside him, she said, "I am trying."

It wasn't until they found themselves in a deep, dark tunnel, where they could ascertain that no one was pursuing them, that they slowed. In the dark, Wen reached his hand for hers, as though he didn't want to be parted from her at this time.

"Where should we be going?" he asked. "You said the Office of Speedy Retribution, but there seems to be no printed map with helpful instructions."

She flashed a smile at him, not sure he could see it in the darkness. "I have noticed this sad lack myself," she said. "And you know, the accounts of people that have survived a voyage into Feng Du tend to be very clear on the exact details of forms and laws and registries, and—though they do not always agree—on how many courts there are, and what punishments are inflicted in each, but not so clear on the details of the physical terrain. It is possible, of course, that we are seeing an illusion, and that there is no physical terrain of Feng Du."

Wen put his hand out and touched the rocky wall that enclosed them. "I am fairly sure," he said, "that there is indeed a physical terrain of Feng Du. For all I know, it is even carved out of a mountain, as it's said to be."

Third Lady nodded. For all she knew, it was, too. But what preoccupied her more was where to go now. "They are very exact about all the levels of Feng Du, you know, and all the places where one should go when one has committed this crime or that. But they never

explain the other stuff... the people that live here, like
Judge Bao and Yu the Great, and other people who
have settled here as though it were a winter residence.
And they never tell you how to get to the halls to file
paperwork, and this leaves us with a sad impression of
what to do."

"I have an idea," Wen said. "Don't look so surprised. I do have them sometimes."

"I'm sorry, my lord, I—"

"You are not sorry in the least," he said, smiling at
her. And, even in the dark, it was clear that his smile
was both amused and affectionate. "Nor should you
be. The truth is, and you know it as well as I do, that
you have had to do this to save me. You have had to
come here. Your willingness to do so is, I assure you,
perfectly appreciated, and you shall be if not my first
wife, always my favorite one, if we return to the world
of the living. But you must remember that many years
ago I had excellent masters, who taught me everything
about Feng Du and the organization of the universe.

"Now that opium clouds are not addling my thought,
I remember those teachings, and I think, Third Lady,
that the way to the courts must be through the sixth
court, the Hall of Administrative Errors. If my soul is
held in a place here, then it will be there."

"Or perhaps not," she said. "Since no one will know
that your soul being held is an administrative error."

"Perhaps not," he said. "But the fact remains that
the sixth court is presided over by Judge Bao himself, so
that even if he holds the Office of Speedy Retribution in
some other place, this is where we must go to find him.

Of course, we will have to get through three more courts to get there."

She felt herself flinch, and heard Wen sigh. "I realize this is not the news you wish to hear. And I wish I might have saved you from it, but I see no way to do that, just now. We might be able to correct this by going to the Hall of Records."

"But," Third Lady said, "it might be in the Hall of Mirrors, and we might have missed it. Indeed—"

"Indeed, it might," Wen said. "Only this is also the first court and the place where most people arrive. We were arrested right at the entrance, and if you were looking as we walked amid the people watching scenes of their lives in mirrors, everyone was attended by paper guards and sometimes ceramic ones. This means—"

"That it is the best-guarded place in Feng Du," Jade said. "Which must mean that there is no escape through there. I see what you imply. So we must go to the sixth court. But how?"

"This tunnel," Wen said, "seems to be ignored by all the others. Which must mean—"

"That it can only be seen by them if it is revealed, though it is completely visible to us."

Wen nodded. "If I am right, the next court is the Pool of Filth and the Court of Ice, for lustful souls and those who have taken liberties with the lives of others."

"Where Zhang would be," Third Lady said, gleefully.

"Probably, but as far as we know, Minister Zhang is not dead," Wen said. He reached out and grasped her hand. "Let us try to get through these courts as fast as might be." He flashed her a hesitant smile. "Only do not let go of my hand, no matter what. I do not wish to leave you behind."

"Indeed, no, my dear Wen," she said. "You must remember I'm a fox-spirit, and that we're not known for our altruism."

He grinned at her. "I'm starting to wonder if we know as much about fox-spirits as we thought we did."

"I assure you, the basics are true," she said. "Only," she added as the thought struck her, "it all depends on how you use it, of course."

He gave her a curious look, then nodded once, his fingers enveloping hers and holding so tightly that she thought if he had been more material, he would have bruised or crushed her hand. Instead, it just felt like an assured, tight grip. "I think, Third Lady, that is true of all humans. That it is all on how you use your qualities or your defects, for good or bad."

Third Lady looked into his eyes, which were full of grave reflection, visible even in their dim space, and nodded in turn. She was starting to think that though she would not have wished this adventure upon them and very much would have preferred if Wen could have got his throne with no fight and no problems, this was forging Wen into a better leader than he would have been without it.

When Wen started to run, she could do nothing but follow, and the tunnel opened into a vast, cavernous hall, fully as big as the cavern they'd left behind. Here, the cavern was darker—as though the walls themselves were carved out of coal and absorbed all light.

In the midst of it was an unimaginably large pool of reeking blackness. It looked, to Third Lady's eyes, larger than Poyang Lake, which she'd been privileged to see in her travels with her singsong troupe.

The smell was choking, revolting—as though someone had taken all the filth of a hundred farmyards and upon it poured the pestilences of a thousand open graves then topped it all with a million sewers. She noted that Wen, too, had stopped, struggling for breath.

In the pool, there were splashes and screams, and she could see various human forms bobbing up and down while other things—definitely not human—pushed them down again and again and again.

There was a narrow path around the pool, though it glistened, as though covered in filth that had iced over. And, past the pool, she could barely distinguish what looked like a cavern full of stalactites, which she guessed was the Court of Ice.

"Milord," she said, softly, "I think that is the Court of Ice."

"And this is the Pool of Filth," Wen said, wheezing a little at the nauseating smell. And then he started walking the narrow path, carefully, because it was indeed quite slippery. Third Lady's straw-soled shoes had a harder time gripping the path than Wen's more substantial leather-soled boots. She was glad of his hand holding her, and of the sudden, careful touch with which he kept her upright.

They were maneuvering thus, carefully, when a scream broke out from amid the Pool of Filth. At least it would be a scream were it not for the fact that it was uttered in something that was not a human voice, something that sounded like an inharmonic grinding of glass upon glass and stone upon stone. However, even so, it was impossible not to understand what it was saying. *"Living. Catch them."*

Third Lady shrieked and tried to run, but slipped and would have plunged in the cauldron of filth had Wen not grasped her about the waist, thrown her over his shoulder and run with her.

"You cannot carry me," she said.

"I am carrying you," he said, not even having the decency of sounding breathless, as he ran full tilt around the Pool of Filth and into the Court of Ice.

Here, demons—for nothing else could have such bewildering forms—were dipping human souls in water, then hanging them, frozen, from the ceiling. They were multitentacled creatures, with too many heads and eyes. And, in fact, even if Third Lady had time as her husband carried her at a mad clip through the icy landscape, she would not have wished to look too closely at any of them. And yet, the impression she retained, as Wen dodged and careened between them and the icicles, always managing to recover from slips before he fell, was that these creatures were, in fact, careful functionaries, determinedly creating their ice sculptures.

That they did not stir to follow Precious Lotus and Wen—nothing beyond looking up from their work with frowns on their revolting many faces—seemed to bespeak this. Not that it made any difference, because by now Wen and Precious Lotus were being followed by several creatures from the Pool of Filth—giant, sluglike or octopuslike beings, whose appearance was not improved by human faces placed in the most ill-chosen junctures of body and tentacle—as well as by the paper guards who had at last caught up.

Since Wen was holding her facing backwards, Third Lady had a full and glorious view of these monsters, as well as the smell of the creatures, and full enjoyment of their sounds, which were much like the boiling of a stew pot.

"Milord, I don't mean to rush you," she said. "But you must, with all possible speed, find the way to the next court."

"I have found it," Wen said, and as he spoke, he plunged them into another dark and narrow tunnel.

Concerned for her husband, though his breathing didn't sound any faster, and if he still wheezed, it was doubtless the reaction of his living lungs—back in the cave—to the fumes of the Pool of Filth, Third Lady said, "Put me down, milord, so I may run as well. You do not wish to tire yourself out. We have three more courts to go."

He set her down, but grasped her hand tightly once more, and gave her a second to get used to the feeling of her feet beneath her, before he started running again, pulling her behind.

In the next cavern, just as large as the previous, there were people hanging upside down from black ropes tied around their ankles, while many intent demons—seeming as artistic as the ones in the frozen court—carefully and slowly multilated their bodies. At the far end, a giant brazier glowed, where people were being roasted by demons, some of them—Third Lady noticed disquietingly—wearing cook's attire.

"Black Rope Court and the Grill," she shouted, because Wen had stopped for a moment. "Run, milord."

He ran, but staggering, and she had to pass him, still holding his hand, and pull him along to a greater speed, amid artistic devils skinning humans.

"The Black Rope Court," he said, in a tone as if he spoke out of his dreams, "is how drug addicts are punished."

"You will not be a drug addict, milord," she said, sternly, "after we leave here. And besides, remember, souls determine their own punishments in the hall of mirrors. And you're not guilty." But, realizing that this place brought on his worst fears, she held his hand tighter and pulled him faster. Behind her, she could hear the glop of the creatures from the Pool of Filth and the rustling of the paper soldiers, who must have recovered from the twisting given them by the monkey. For some reason, they always seemed to take longer to cross the tunnels than Wen and Third Lady did. Perhaps they, too, couldn't see the tunnels, just like the dead souls couldn't, and had to find them by hurling themselves in the approximate direction in which Third Lady and Wen had disappeared and hope there was a tunnel there. Third Lady was grateful for this. They needed all the advantages they could get to arrive at the sixth court ahead of these creatures.

She noted a tunnel mouth ahead, which the demons just passed by, and she plunged into it, clutching her husband's hand, and did not stop until they were through it. On the other side was a cavern that looked almost exactly like the Pool of Filth cavern, except that there was no freezing court and the pool in the center reeked of blood.

In it, various demons with mallets and knives dismembered screaming souls. "Counterfeits, cheats, tax evaders and unfilial daughters," Third Lady said, hearing her own voice come at her, as if from a distance. Behind her came a glop glop, a rustle, and the tinkle of knives, as some demons from the Black Rope Court joined the others.

Wen picked Third Lady up again, and once more cast her over his shoulder as he ran.

They skirted the pool of blood and found the tunnel easily enough, and plunged into it, to emerge on the other side into...

A place unimaginably hot, filled with boiling cauldrons of oil, in which many souls were being lustily fried. Third Lady didn't remember what this court punished, and there was no point, at any rate, as Wen was carrying her through it too fast to allow her to see. Which given the look of some of the slick, oily demons making sure that every side of the souls were evenly browned, might be a very good thing.

Past the cauldrons was a smaller, quiet area, surrounded by cubbyhole cupboards. In each cubbyhole was a rolled-up scroll. In a large chair sat a creature who looked human, except that he was much taller and better built than any human she had ever seen, and was wearing splendid robes. Where his face should be, there was only light, as though his face were a paper lantern, blindingly lit from within.

He rose from his seat, and Wen checked his step for a moment, then ran past, as the majestic creature yelled, "Who dares defile the fifth court? Are you in the pay of the Monkey King?"

"Yen-Lo-Wang," Wen said, almost out of breath. "The god of death."

"Yes," Third Lady said. "I remember what the Monkey King did to his filing system in *Journey to the West*. He made all monkeys immortal."

"At least for a time," Wen said, and, having found the tunnel, plunged through it, pell-mell.

On the other side there was yet another cavern, this one filled with screaming souls being gnawed by rats and skewered upon various-sized spikes through various parts of their anatomies, all of it kindly watched over by exact and multilimbed demons.

"Liars," Wen said. "Slanderers, deceivers and gossips."

"And sexual sins," Third Lady said. "Which means there must be many a member of the Fox Clan here."

Groans echoed from several throats at her words, and the torturing demons stopped and looked at them. Which was just as well, since the glop glop, sussurating sound of knives and the voice of a very angry personage had caught up with them.

"I demand to know the meaning of this," the angry personage said. "You cannot defile Feng Du for no reason at all."

"It is not for no reason," Third Lady said, turning around as her husband set her, once more, on her feet.

"We are here to see Judge Bao from the Office of Speedy Retribution."

But as she spoke, the demons from his sixth court surrounded them, too.

They were in a circle of supernatural creatures, and there was no escape.

A DAUGHTER'S PRICE

龙

"You must admit," Peter told Sofie, *"it is a much eas-*
ier way to travel, now that I can arrive under my own
identity."

"Indeed," Sofie said, looking back at him and smiling. They had landed—with him in dragon form, of
course—some way from the city last night, after which
he had changed into human form again, and dressed,
and they'd walked into town, where they'd arrived by
the early-morning light. "And it was very good of you to
have purchased our own small traveling rug, which we
can carry, and therefore answer anyone who asks in
what carpetship we arrived."

"And though they think me eccentric," Peter said,
smiling, "no one can dispute that carpetships can be
very disagreeable and are, at the very least, slow."

"Well, likely they think you can't afford the ticket
on one of the better carpetships," Sofie said, as they
walked between the houses of a working-class neighborhood, looking for the address upon the letter Peter
had received.

"Considering the state of our fortune until a few

weeks ago," Peter said, with a grimace, "it is a reasonable assumption. And most people don't know exactly how many improvements I'm making on the estate."

"It is a good thing the estate is so isolated," she said. "Though I don't think you can keep the secret once Summercourt becomes one of the showcases of England."

"Likely not," he said, amused. "But fortunately, my father left things in such a state that it will take many, many years before we are so pleasantly situated. And by then we can easily lie and say we were very lucky with some investments in the exchange." He paused for a moment before a two-floor, whitewashed house. "Ah," he said. "Here it is. Love's Folly. What a name for a house."

"But appropriate, if what you surmised about the owner's history is true," Sofie said, as she glanced around, looking for a bell ring. "I am very desirous of sitting down. The only disadvantage of traveling this way is that we must carry our own valises," she said, as she raised the offending article. "I so badly want to set it down and I do hope they offer us some refreshment." She smiled, teasing him as no other human being would ever dare do. "Some of us are entirely unreasonable in not wishing to take our refreshment off a passing springbok, you know, let alone not having the means of cooking it on the spot."

He grinned at her, knowing she was referring to the dragon's need to hunt after a long flight. He preferred not to think of how he satiated his hunger while in dragon form, though he'd always been careful not to eat a human. He simply said, "I could use a cup of tea as well."

At this moment, he found a metal ring on the wall and pulled it twice. From deep inside, he heard a bell tolling.

After a long while, a man came and opened the door. He was sandy-haired, with a receding hairline and a sun-aged countenance, and for a moment Peter had no idea who he might be, until the man looked up and Peter recognized him to be Joseph Gilbert, who called himself Perigord. The man, in turn, was frowning intently at Peter, before nodding and saying, "Lord St. Maur. You look remarkably like your late mother."

Peter nodded. He knew at least that he didn't look like his father, something for which he'd always counted himself fortunate. He bowed correctly, though feeling somewhat odd that someone who had known him from earliest childhood was calling him Lord St. Maur. "We received your letter, and we came, as you see, with all possible expediency."

If the man knew what means Peter had employed to arrive here so quickly, he chose not to comment on it, and instead bowed back and invited them into the small house, where he installed them in the dining room and a woman who answered to "my dear Charlotte" brought them tea. She showed some signs of crying.

Joseph's repeated looks at Sofie finally brought from Peter the admission that Sofie had insisted on coming and from Joseph a rueful answering smile.

It wasn't until several cups of hot, inky-black tea later that conversation turned to the subject that had brought them here. "Hettie is young," Joseph said, "and we tried to keep her out of these matters as much as we could. I'm starting to think perhaps we did ourselves and her a disservice."

He pushed at Peter two notes, written in an angular hand. Peter perused them rapidly. The first one said, *I have Lady Hester Gilbert. I will not release her until Lord Joseph Gilbert should contact me about his associates in the conspiracy to obtain and keep the two objects Her Majesty desires.*

The second was much the same, but threatened several penalties should Joseph be so foolhardy as to try to recover his daughter or attempt to withhold information.

"You see the position I'm in," he said.

"Yes," Peter said, and hesitated over the names given. "I realize it is none of my business, but I notice this man, this"—he flicked at the paper almost derisively—"Captain Corridon, has referred to you and your daughter by your true surname and title. Does your daughter know it?"

"My title?" Joseph asked, befuddled, running his hand back through his hair. "I am a second son. I have no title. True, I changed my name, but—"

"You don't know, then," Peter said, feeling a certain amount of astonishment. "Good Lord, man, you told me you'd read notice of me in the newspaper, so I assumed you'd received news." He looked at Joseph Gilbert's blank face and sighed. "Your father died something like five years ago."

"Yes, I know. I did read of that," Joseph said. "But my brother Michael ascended."

"Yes, but he, too, died, in a riding accident a little later. For the last five years, the estate has been closed, and deserted—except for those servants needed for maintenance—while they try to find you. I believe something in your father's will forbade them from presuming death for a number of years; otherwise, they'd have done so already."

Joseph sat in silence and after a while put his hand to his head, as if attempting to hold the idea in. "How could I . . . how could I have missed it?"

"You read the foreign papers."

"Indeed . . . Only . . . Two years ago . . . I must have been . . . It must have been when the carpetship crashed in the Americas and we . . . I was . . . out of reach of British papers for months. But then, I am . . . Do you mean to say I am . . . Earl of Marshlake?"

Peter, who had gone through this transition himself all too recently, nodded. "Yes, you are indeed Milord Marshlake, and I daresay the trustees will be very glad to find it out."

A sound of breaking crockery made them look. The new Lady Marshlake, having found out her status, had dropped the teapot to the floor, where it had shattered into pieces and sprayed hot tea far and wide. Stooping automatically to pick up the bits, she looked up and said, "I can't, Joseph. It can't be done. I am no lady."

For a moment, there was a warmly fond look from her husband. "More a lady than many a one that wear the title with great pride," he said. "Don't worry, my darling. I'll be there to see you through." And then, looking at Peter, "But that makes the matter far more important. Because if this man knows what Hettie is . . ." He bit at his lip. "He is the second son of an earl, himself, and our title is transmissible through the female line. Hettie's son would be the Earl of Marshlake after me. And her husband can wear the dignity while administering the estate for the children."

"So you think he could force her to make a runaway marriage," Sofie said.

"I think it's a possibility. Clearly he has no scruples in using an innocent girl," Lord Marshlake said.

"No," Peter said. "What has been attempted to recover her?"

"We . . ." Joseph looked worried. "We found that she left our house on her own, possibly with the idea of eloping with this person. She met him at his barracks, where they spent some time in conversation. After which they took the carpetship to Hong Kong. I've been able to ascertain that through my contacts, even though I found they used assumed names. Reassuringly, they did not travel as husband and wife, but rather as brother and sister—as Adrian and Hester Ryan, with separate, single cabins."

"Do you have any idea why Hong Kong?"

"I'd have to presume because Hettie heard us say . . . other people had gone there. And she was foolish enough to tell this to Captain Corridon."

"Is it possible she is cooperating with him? That he has promised her marriage in return for her help?"

"Anything is possible," Joseph said. "Hettie is fifteen and at that age girls can be more silly than not, even those who have a little more wit than the rest."

"I can't believe, and you won't get me from it," her mother intervened, "that our daughter would lend

herself to threatening her papa and mama like this."
She looked pleadingly at Peter. "Our Hettie is a good
girl."

"Let us pray," Joseph said. "I certainly do."

"Rest assured," Sofie said primly, "my husband and
I will make every endeavor to find her quickly and return her to you unscathed."

"Well, I hope so," Joseph said. "I don't wish to
speak. But it is my daughter, you see. And though I
have gathered that the jewels falling in the wrong
hands could destroy all of the universe..." He
shrugged. "It didn't when Charlemagne got it, did it?
And, if I speak, at least Hettie will be safe." Then he
looked ashamed of what he'd said, and added, "I don't
want to imply that I would want to denounce anyone.
But if I can't save my girl any other way... Well, as
you can see, he gives me an address to make contact
when I'm ready to talk, and a person there will let him
know."

Peter nodded. "You've said quite enough, and I
thank you for your frankness. I will do my best to recover your daughter as soon as humanly possible and I
will keep you apprised of my progress. I hope it doesn't
come to your having to do what we'd all regret."

A MATTER OF THE HEART

龙

There were no passenger carpetships, as such, flying between Hong Kong and Canton—which Red Jade called Guangzhou—partly because all the passengers who might wish to go there would be limited to the small island of Shameen, so it didn't attract any tourist business, and partly because there was no passenger traffic on that coast at all. The fear of the flying junk pirates had done that, and kept the passenger carpetships grounded. In fact, only the cargo that would be of absolutely no use—or at least of no interest—to the pirates flew confidently in the skies between Hong Kong and Canton.

Of course, it had been no problem at all for Nigel to find a job as a carpetship flight magician aboard one of these ships. Though the flights were scarce, the magicians qualified and willing to undertake them were even more so. None of them were willing to risk their lives for very small pay, and the island of Shameen was not a place where anyone in their right mind wanted to go for amusement. Divided between French and English concessions, Nigel understood—from the gentlemen who manned this ship—it was a pleasant enough island to reside in, but nothing extraordinary. All the carpetship personnel stayed at the Victoria Hotel, and, in fact, had reserved rooms.

The ship that Nigel took was called—ironically, he thought—the *Pirate Queen* and was very small, operated by a three-man crew—not counting the flight magician, of course—and transported mail, as well as things the inhabitants had requested. The captain, Gordon, a young man of informal manners, had told Nigel, "You'd think that living in the land from which silk flows, women wouldn't feel a need for cotton muslin, but you'd be quite wrong. It appears that silk is considered too fast and dangerous for the reputations of some of the misses, and so we must take them cotton and linen and who knows what. On almost all our flights, half the cargo is millinery, a lot of it shipped from England and France at exorbitant costs." He'd shrugged. "But what is the use of trying to penetrate the minds of women?" After which he had hastily apologized, because Nigel was, after all, married. "Though you were smart, my friend, in marrying a Chinese. They are raised to be obedient and regard their husbands as their lords and masters."

Nigel had trouble holding his laughter, because he could not imagine Jade thinking of anyone as her lord and master, much less himself.

But he'd done his duty by the carpetship, in the little piloting room that could have fit three times over into the flight room of the *Indian Star*. And in return he'd gotten a small room with a double bed.

There was no question, of course, of his sharing that

bed with Jade, though she had suggested somewhat tentatively that they might share it if fully dressed. Only, Nigel, who had never been able to consummate his first marriage, now felt as if he couldn't trust himself.

He couldn't quite describe it. The enchantment that had been cast over him when he'd first seen her in English attire, sinking into that ridiculously deep curtsey at the Perigords', had deepened and grown. He was almost sad that they hadn't needed to marry, instead of perpetrating this deception on the entire world, and wished he could have thought to convince the girl that she needed to marry him before she dared claim to be his wife.

Only, he'd married a wife, once, for quite the wrong reasons. And he didn't want this woman to marry him for the wrong reasons, too. So he'd given her the bed and he had, himself, slept on the floor.

The journey took only a day and a night, and that because the tiny carpetship, loaded as it was, flew barely above the surface of the water and made—Nigel was sure of it—worse time than a sailboat or junk would have. In fact, the rationality of using the carpetships evaded him, leaving him to guess it was a matter of habit and perhaps of prestige. You sent your letters via carpetship, or sent for your packages from the continent via carpetship when you wanted to be absolutely certain of getting things in the shortest time possible. There was neither discussion nor any thought given to it, otherwise.

Before he went to the flight deck to land the ship, he dressed, using the half-open door of the wardrobe as a shield from his supposed wife's eyes. Also, to prevent him from observing her changing.

"Jade," he said, "how are we to go to Can—Guangzhou, while the foreigners are restricted to the island of Shameen?"

"I've thought of that," she said, amid a flutter and rustle of silks.

Since she was pretending to be his wife, he had insisted on giving her a wardrobe befitting her supposed dignity. Nothing very elaborate, but enough silks and satins and British fashions that no one would presume to question their attachment. If he dared be truthful with himself—something he would much rather not do—he would admit that he had bought her clothes because he had enjoyed it. Because he derived pleasure from dressing her and watching how splendid she looked in her British attire.

They had bought the garments at one of the modistes in Hong Kong, who was skilled at copying patterns from French and British publications, and had a bevy of apprentices as fast with the needle as the ones who made Nigel's suit had been.

When they picked up the dresses, two hours after purchasing them—hours Nigel had spent taking a hurried leave from John Malmsey, while promising to return soon and spend some real time with John and his family—Jade had modeled each gown for Nigel.

Torn between wishing to see her in those much better gowns to which Mrs. Oldhall would be entitled and the pleasure of seeing her outfitted as Mrs. Enoch Jones, Nigel had found himself wishing very much that someone could wave a magic wand and make all this real.

Only, Jade was the princess of a mystical kingdom, and he was ... just Nigel Oldhall, second son of Lord Oldhall. Time would come that he would himself be Lord Oldhall, but if truth be told, his domains were barely larger than those of a village squire, and what were the chances she would aspire to be the lady of such a limited dignity?

Preventing himself from sighing as he buttoned his waistcoat, he heard her say, "I've been thinking about it, and I believe the best way is to take a boat in the night. We'll cloak you and I can use magic, for limited amounts of time, to make you look different than you are. My mother taught me the spell. She learned it as a beautification device, you know?"

"Oh, I can make those spells, too," he said. "They will last only a few minutes, but they will pass."

"Very well," Jade said, from behind the wardrobe door.

Having finished dressing himself, he stood where he was and said, "But if it is that easy to penetrate China, beyond the places where foreigners are allowed—"

"No," Jade said. "If you used such subterfuge to get into a city without a native guide, you would very shortly get caught. And you must understand, though I have no use for the present usurpers ..." She paused, and from the rustling of cloth he presumed some part of her toiletry occupied her. "I do not think that it is just for the protection of their own regime that they keep China closed. There is a very strong strain among the people themselves, which both suspects and fears foreigners. I don't think we can make— I mean, even if Wen should recover the throne, it will take time for the people to trust foreign devils."

"Yes," Nigel said, amused. "I can see that, considering the name we're given."

"I'm sorry, I didn't mean—"

"No. It is amusing, given the names we have for various groups ... I mean, it's only fair that at least one people should consider themselves superior to Europeans."

There was a pause from the other side of the door, and then a half-dismayed question: "You don't think ... That is ... You don't consider the Chinese superior?"

It occurred to Nigel that Jade, too, through all the time of her growing up, had been very isolated, just like her country. And while she might have loved her mother, she'd always seen her mother in a position of outcast and stranger, in the midst of a civilization that the daughter had been raised to believe was superior.

He tried to speak in a way that wouldn't hurt or shock her. The byzantine conditions of her mother's marriage and how that might have affected her daughter was something he didn't wish to think about or explore.

"Lady Jade, I, too, was raised to consider my people superior to all others in the world. In fact, I think this is a normal default position of all humans. That they think of their tribe, their group, their family as the best, or sometimes the only true people. I studied languages, and I can tell you that often the name of the people or the tribe is synonymous for *human*. It seems to be normal to the human mind to think that. But I have since traveled the world, and while I think that some places, some rulers, some tribes do a better job of providing for their citizens, when it comes to people, to . . . persons, one on one . . . I don't think it can be said that any race is superior to the other, or that any has virtues or qualities that make them intrinsically superior or inferior."

"But . . ." Her steps, tentative, approached the wardrobe door, and then she paused, just on the other side of it. "Are you decent?"

"Yes," he said. And before he could close the door and get out of the way, she looked around the door, her eyes wide, her expression so much that of curiosity and interest, mingled, that he wanted to kiss her, or twirl her about in his arms, or something even he, himself, couldn't define.

"But, wouldn't you say that China, being the most ancient civilization of mankind, must therefore be the wisest?"

He frowned at this. "I don't know," he admitted, at last. "There are things in which it seems you've achieved greater wisdom than we have, but . . . By being who you are, and having self-sufficiency upon your own land, you've also . . . not learned from the other peoples around the world. It is like a very intelligent child who is isolated, and therefore can learn only what he makes up in his own mind. Not that," he added, frowning, "it would always be a good thing to rush upon the world with open arms, after a long isolation. I've seen cultures trying to adopt all the worst of Europe and none of the best." He was thinking of the

Hyena Men and their idea that reducing those who had the power would help Africa. "But I think if your brother does win his throne back, he should consider opening up China little by little—cautiously enough to not allow the inexperienced tradesmen and artisans to be exploited, but daring enough that China can learn from the rest of the world. And the rest of the world can learn from China." He blinked at her and felt heat rise to his cheeks, and added, not quite knowing what he said, "I'd like to learn from China."

She seemed to take him utterly at his word, her eyes large and solemn, those black eyes that seemed to hide in their depths that odd almost lapis-lazuli spark. "China has a lot to teach," she said. "In philosophy and law, and in history so long that it can at least teach where the perils are, even where . . . we went wrong."

She was wearing a gown of heavy silk, in a delicate peach color, which emphasized both the almost golden tone of her skin, and the soft blush on her cheeks. Her look, turned to him, was so pleading that he had to say, softly, "I'm sure you can teach me much, Lady Jade."

He closed the wardrobe door carefully, as though it might disturb their thoughts if it were shut too quickly, and offered her his hand. "If you'll come with me," he said, "you can wait by my chair on the flight deck, while I land the ship."

She cast a look at the small trunk with both of their clothes, and sighed. "It will be a pity," she said, in a soft, almost sad tone, "to lose all those pretty gowns. I know I needed some of them for verisimilitude sake, but it seems terrible that you had six of them made, and I only got to wear two."

He offered her his arm, and when she rested her hand on it, very correctly, probably in the way her mother had taught her—the same way she'd apparently been taught her deep curtseys—he patted her slender fingers with his other hand. "But you don't need to lose them," he said. "We shall leave our bags at the Victoria Hotel, and will pay them for storage. I shall say we're visiting friends on the isle and will eventually pick up our luggage or take a room."

"Won't they find it odd that we wish to store our clothes when we are going to be visiting somewhere on the isle?"

The proper answer was that, yes, they would find it odd, but carpetship flight magicians were odd anyway, and no one would give it a second thought—at least not if Nigel paid them well enough. The personnel at the hotel was not, after all, in the business of guarding public morality. And if two of the visitors to the isle chose to wear the same clothes for several weeks, or alternately to go about in a state of nature in whatever little wilderness subsisted around here, it could not possibly be any of hotel personnel's business.

But Nigel could feel behind the tentative question the sort of experience of growing up in a small clan, in a closed society, and of everyone's business being everyone else's. So he explained. "No. Carpetship magicians are odd, and they will think we've made some alternate arrangements. And provided I pay them enough—which I will—they will keep our clothes safe for us."

"But..." Jade said, then sighed—a heavy, doleful sound.

"But?" he asked.

"It seems like such a terrible waste." She blushed a little and looked up at him. Her head was just at the level of his chin, which, his being accounted a tall man, even in his own country, must make her freakishly prepossessing among her people. "You see, I won't wear this sort of gown ever again. Not ... in my brother's court."

"You are then expecting to stay in your brother's court?" And he would have glued his traitorous mouth shut right after he said it, would have called back the words. The look she shot him, all alarm and confusion, made his heart drop. "I don't mean—" he started, and was about to explain he didn't mean to startle her with the vehemence of his affections. Particularly because he wasn't sure they were affections, exactly. Just that she had charmed him and enchanted him, and brought to his life again all the joy and mystery he'd thought vanished from it forever.

But before he could speak, she composed herself and said, soberly, "I suppose Wen might marry me off. I'd not thought of it. You see, I am ... I've been so used to looking after Wen, because of his debilitating addiction, that it never occurred to me ... That is, I never thought he would be able to dispense with me eventually. But of course that is the whole point of this, and of what Third Lady is undertaking. That Wen will, eventually, be able to rule on his own. And he is naturally kind and intelligent, and I believe he will make as good a ruler as our ancestor Yu the Great, but ... with all that ..." She smiled and made a face. "I will have to be brave and get used to not being needed."

Nigel wanted to reassure her. To tell her that she would always be needed. With her beauty, her courage, her intelligence, it wasn't possible for her to simply pass from the lives of others leaving no mark behind. But he had no right to speak. And then, too, in his mind, there was the thought that this was all foolishness. *An infatuation, like a schoolboy's. I thought myself in love with Emily because she was the most exotic female I knew. And now I fancy myself in love with Jade because she's even more exotic. Like a little boy picking unusual sweets from a candy store.*

But people were not sweets, and one couldn't pick them for color and variety. He sighed deeply. "Come, Mrs. Jones," he said. "We will now land this carpetship in the port at Shameen. Not that," he added with a chuckle, "we are such a long way from the ground that landing will be a difficult feat."

WHERE THE ROSE IS NOT WITHOUT THORNS

Hettie had bided her time aboard the carpetship to Hong Kong. For one, she thought, it would be ridiculous to try to escape from Captain Corridon in the midst of the trip. Where could she go, unless she threw herself out of the carpetship while it was flying over Africa or over the ocean?

But now they were a day out from Hong Kong, and she'd sat in her cabin thinking things over and had come to several interesting conclusions. First, however shady Corridon's intentions might be, he did not intend to attempt against her honor. Had he thought to do so, he would have shared a cabin with her. So, on that front she was safe.

Second, Corridon might be threatening her parents—or at least trying to discover if her parents were involved in a conspiracy that might threaten their liberty and their life—but he was, if not in love with Hettie, at least attracted to her. She could not avoid noticing in his eyes the sort of soft adoring look that her mother called mooning over someone, or calf love.

And while she didn't know how true that affection

was, or how lasting, she was not above considering it
useful and flattering, as well as something to be used
against him if at all possible.

The carpetship he'd got them to board, called
Orient's Pride, was not one of the great luxury carpetships, but neither was it shabby. In fact, it looked very
much like the carpetship she'd taken with Papa when
they'd gone to London so many years ago. This reassuring familiarity had kept Hettie feeling secure and
happy in her small cabin in first—but not luxury—
class. She had a room with pale cream walls, a small
but comfortable bed, a desk and a small dresser. All of
it fastened to the wall or the floor, to prevent its moving
about in a storm. Right then, she was sitting on the
bed, with her legs folded under her, holding Mrs.
Beddlington in her arms and trying to think through
her next step.

She didn't believe that Captain Corridon had any
idea that she could use glamoury—at least for a limited
period of time—to make people believe anything she
said. It was a rare enough gift, in fact, that it rarely
manifested. But she could use it . . . She stared unsee-
ingly at the print of a volcano with a plume of smoke
rising from it, which was hung over the desk.

After a while, she rose and set Mrs. Beddlington
down in her suitcase, which she fastened. Then she
walked out the door, looking among her fellow passengers for some who would meet all her criteria. They
must be middle-aged, she thought. And of the sort that
might have children her age. And they must be kindly.

She eavesdropped shamelessly on the conversations
of strangers, until she fastened on a likely couple—a

Mr. and Mrs. William Wood, who lived in Hong Kong and were just returning from leaving their children in London. They'd gone by the Cape to visit Mrs. Wood's brother, which was how they came to be aboard this ship. Their daughter was Hettie's age and had been left with an aunt who was supposed to launch her into British society. They sounded like they already missed her.

Hettie approached them, appearing as innocent and scared as she could, and projected her glamoury at them. "I'm sorry," she said. "You look so kindly. If you'd listen to me..."

She hesitated, staring at the two. Her glamoury or their kindness took effect. They looked at her, and Mrs. Wood clicked her tongue. "Of course, my dear. What is the trouble?"

And Hettie, who had truly not told nearly enough lies in her life, poured into the Woods' unsuspecting ears a story of woe and adventure to chill the blood.

PAPER AND CLAY

"We must see *Judge Bao*," Third Lady said, desperately. "Of the Office of Speedy Retribution." She knelt and kowtowed toward the great personage whom she assumed was Yen-Lo-Wang. "That is all we want."

No one listened to her. The paper creatures, considerably the worse for wear, grabbed at her and Wen. "They are living intruders in Feng Du," they explained, as if this justified anything at all.

"They're in the pay of the Monkey King," Yen-Lo-Wang thundered. Knives clattered and tentacles waved. "I heard there's another monkey loose in Feng Du, and who else would bring it?"

Third Lady could imagine them dragged off to the fate these creatures considered appropriate. She'd meddled in the lives of others—notably in the life of her husband—so she assumed it would be the Pool of Filth for her. And as for Wen, she thought he would end up in the Hell of Addicts. "We are not in the pay of the Monkey King," she said, in a shrill, hysterical voice that shocked even her.

"All we want is my soul," Wen said, "which is being unjustly held for judgment in frivolous lawsuits."

"Which is why we want to see Judge Bao."

The paper creatures were pulling them up. The other demons moved forward. And Third Lady, gone beyond her despair, thought of what Nu had told her. She'd told her to use her fox powers, but she didn't think she could seduce the demons that would operate here. Or if she could, it was more than she wanted to know. No. Here, she thought, she would have to use the thing Yu had told her. That she could call the other creatures of paper that she'd sent ahead of her by flame. And that they would appear if she demanded them. "By the power of fire," she said, "and the power of will and the power of tradition, I demand the guards and attendants, the horses and the cart, the cash and the silk that I burned before coming here!"

Instantly, out of nowhere, they were surrounded by a court of paper creatures—fifteen ladies and fifteen gentlemen, pushing the paper guards and the demons away, and ignoring the illustrious Yen-Lo-Wang, who glared at them.

They pushed to open a path between Wen and Third Lady and the waiting cart with its very good-looking horses. The cart was piled high with cash and nine-colored silk. Third Lady jumped on the seat and took the reins. Wen, looking somewhat dazed, climbed up by her side.

She looked around at their attendants, which had formed a guard on either side of them, and said, "Take us to Judge Bao, in the Office of Speedy Retribution."

The horses started forward, quickly speeding to a

canter, and the attendants followed. And though they were all paper, there was the sound of hooves, and the sound of human footsteps. Behind them followed the other paper creatures, the demons and a very outraged Yen-Lo-Wang, who kept repeating, "They are in the pay of the Monkey King."

They were almost wholly through the sixth hell, when a voice sounded, echoing from every recess of the cavernous depths. "Who disrupts the sixth hell?" it said. "What is the meaning of this?"

In front of them, larger and more ominous than Yen-Lo-Wang, there materialized a creature that took up all the space between cave ceiling and floor. He was a well, if somberly dressed gentleman, with severe, almost ascetic features. He stood in front of them, arms crossed, each of his massive legs as large as all of their bodies put together, each of his feet the size of the cart. "Well?" he said. "I asked a question. What is the meaning of this? And what do you want of me? And why do you disrupt the calm functioning of my sixth hell?"

Terrified, feeling as though her blood had turned to ice in her veins, Third Lady jumped down from the cart. She knelt so that she was very close to the giant foot of the giant creature, and she kowtowed repeatedly. "Judge Bao. We've come in search of you."

The judge stooped. It took a lot of stooping to get from his height to where Third Lady knelt. Then, with an infinitely delicate touch, he put thumb and finger on either side of her waist, and slowly lifted her up.

From behind her, she heard Wen say, "No!" and she

said, "It's fine, milord, it's fine," in desperate accents, even as she felt the terror of being raised past the being's jacket, with all its shiny ribbons, and up to the face, which looked unnaturally large. This close, every pore was exaggerated, each of the nostrils a cavern—and the huge, black, rolling eyes were like two deep pools.

She tried to hold very still and not show her fear. She didn't know if Judge Bao would act like mortal judges and assume that nervousness meant guilt, but neither did she want to trust that he wouldn't. She looked him in the face and, constrained by his fingers around her waist—the only thing keeping her from a precipitous fall to the hard floor below—she bowed. "Judge Bao, my husband's soul has been held in hell for many years, tethered to his body and his spirit by only the slightest of bonds. Because of his lack of a soul, he has fallen a victim to opium addiction. Because of his lack of a soul, he's been fading more and more from life and into the sort of half death that happens in such situations. I know you are the functionary who remedies administrative errors and who repairs gross injustice, and I beg you to correct this injustice and give his soul back to my husband, Wen, the True Dragon Emperor, Ruler of All Under Heaven."

The huge black eye nearest her, so close she could touch it if she extended her hand, surveyed her dispassionately. Then the judge snorted, which she presumed wasn't a hopeful sign.

"You are a fox-spirit," he said. "What is your trick? What deception are you running?"

Third Lady almost rolled her eyes, but she remembered she was in the presence of a supernatural creature who, in fact, had power over her and Wen. It was bad enough to endure this sort of nonsense from humans on Earth, but must she also find it from judges and rulers in the afterworld?

She crossed her arms on her chest and tried to glare back, something made only slightly more difficult by the fact that, this close, she couldn't see both of the judge's eyes at the same time, much less glare at him properly. "I might be a fox-spirit," she said, "but I am running no deception. I am the Third Lady of Wen, True Dragon Emperor, Real Ruler of All Under Heaven. I was chosen for him because my heart was knit with his. I wouldn't be here were it not for my hope of rescuing him."

"It is not the first time," Yen-Lo-Wang said, "that the fox-spirits have tried to attain the throne. We all remember the legend of Queen Eterna, do we not?"

"I don't care if Wen repudiates me when he reaches the throne," Third Lady said. "Do you wish me to promise that I'll be sent back to my father's house, as soon as we return to the world of the living?"

Wen shouted, "No," from below, but no one seemed to listen to him.

The black eye closest to Third Lady blinked. "Do you know what we do to fox-spirits down here?"

"No," Third Lady said. She gritted her teeth and expected at any minute to be tossed into the Pool of Filth or worse. She'd come so far and worked so hard. She'd wanted to see Judge Bao. She'd been so sure that he would be just and understand that Wen's soul must be returned to him.

At the very least, she'd hoped to be given a hearing, able to present her case, to make everyone understand the great injustice that had been done to her husband and how it must be corrected. Instead, she met with this suspicion and conviction that no feeling a were-fox ever had could be authentic.

"We send them back," Judge Bao said. "We don't examine them, we don't sentence them, we don't do anything at all but send them back into the world. So cunning is your kind, and so disruptive to the normal laws of conduct—and so unable to judge its own sins— that you defeat Feng Du itself, and we must send you back, or suffer the same fate that my colleague Yen suffered at the hands of the Monkey King."

Third Lady felt tears prickle behind her eyes. "I'm not disruptive, and I'm not immoral, and I'm not trying to be cunning. All I want is a hearing for my husband. All I want is the chance to prove that his soul is wrongly held in a frivolous lawsuit. Surely you can't tell me that is an immoral purpose, for a wife to fight for her husband's life and health."

The eye regarded her steadily and, goaded beyond endurance, she added, "I didn't want to come to Feng Du either, and you don't need to think that I wished to. I only came because Wen needed help and because no one else cared, and I wasn't willing to let things go the way they had been until he died of it. I came because I am Wen's wife, and it is my duty."

The fingers started downward, carrying her, and she sniffled, sure that he was going to deposit her on the cold floor of the cavern and let the others capture her, but she would be cursed if she would cry or beg for mercy. She'd run as far as she could and she'd done all she could do. If she failed now, let her fail with dignity.

As soon as her feet touched the ground, and the gigantic fingers let go of her, she scurried back to the cart, to sit beside her husband. Wen held her hand in both of his. "It doesn't matter what they do to us, so long as we are together."

She nodded at him, and smiled with tight lips, and tried to look brave. "I am sorry, milord," she said. "I have been a wretched wife to you."

"No," he said. "No, you have not. And if these lords of Feng Du are going to judge you only because of what you were born to be and not of what you are, then I must mock their purported justice and question the laws they uphold." He said it defiantly, with an upward tilt of his jaw, and a glare upward at Judge Bao.

"Silence," Judge Bao thundered. "Do not presume to know what my verdict is before I give it. Do not cast aspersions on the wisdom of this court before you've experienced it."

He bent down again, till his face was level with their cart and he was looking at them both quite close. When he spoke, his breath was like a strong wind. "A fox-spirit who thinks only of cunning and betrayal and power is terrifying enough. But a fox-spirit who truly loves must be the most dangerous thing in all the universes. Just look at what you've done!" A finger the size of Wen's thigh pointed at Third Lady. "You've not only broken into Feng Du, but you've completely disrupted the first five levels, bringing them all into contact, and causing yourself to be pursued by the most ridiculous retinue that has ever followed anyone in these regions." He gestured scathingly toward the demons, then looked up and Third Lady could swear his lips twitched. "And you've upset my colleague Yen."

"We didn't mean to do any of these things," Third Lady said, her voice tight with fear and fury. "We only—"

"Yes, I know. You only came to ransom your husband's soul. And if we don't give in to your demand that I hear your case, who knows what more havoc you'll wreak. One thing is for sure, and that is that you will not allow peace to anyone in this realm until you've had your way."

He clapped his hands. From out of nowhere a troop of attendants emerged, carrying a porcelain stool, which they set down. He sat upon it, and rested his hands on his knees.

"Speak, Third Lady of Wen, True Emperor of All Under Heaven. I am ready to hear your case."

THE PILL OF A THOUSAND EFFICACIES

They'd gotten out of Shameen Island easily enough, Jade thought. It had taken little more than a spell that lasted a few minutes. It had demanded her brazen lies that she was a Chinese employee of the carpetship line, and that she must go back to Guangzhou to visit her ailing father. She said her husband was coming with her, and Nigel had sat there, enveloped in a cloak, actively casting a *do not look at me* magical suggestion.

They'd taken a boat across to Guangzhou and then, early that morning, Jade had taken Nigel to a place she'd only heard about from people who'd been to Guangzhou and back. Most who visited Guangzhou used chairs carried by sweating, half-naked coolies. This was by far the cheapest form of transportation, at least if one preferred not to go about on foot. But like going about on foot, being transported in a chair by humans was not an option that Jade wanted to indulge. Because, like it or not, cloaked or not—and after a while coolies would wonder why Nigel remained cloaked—she and Nigel would need to speak to each other. And because Nigel could not speak Chinese, they would have to—perforce—speak English.

She did not need the whole scheme exposed and the foreign devil in their midst revealed suddenly in the midst of a Chinese street, when she could not change shapes, and when the natives might have been encouraged by hostile forces—she hated to say that her experiences in Hong Kong had made her fear practically everyone, but they had—to think that Nigel was among them for nefarious purposes. So she resorted to a place that she had heard described, which rented ceramic horses, attached to little ceramic carts.

On the way there, she had explained the concept to Nigel, who seemed fascinated. "It is said," she told him, "that they were animated long ago. Warriors and horses fashioned out of clay used to be buried with emperors, you know, with a spell that said they should come alive in times of need. It could be that these horses were once part of some tomb's treasure trove of guardians. Once animated," she'd said, smiling at the idea, "it is possible that they simply could not be put back to sleep. And that someone found a way to convert their magics to good use. On the other hand..." She'd stopped and sighed. "My father used to say that, under our dynasty, people had more access to magic. That we...channeled it?—conducted it?—between China and the people, so more common people were born with magic, and like common people with magic in Europe now, they used spells and magic to make their lives easier."

Nigel had sighed and given her an odd look, half-sad and half-amused. From the depths of his cloak, his odd, pale eyes shone with amusement, while his lips twisted in something like, but not quite, sadness. "The funny thing, my dear Lady Jade," he said, "is that not many months ago, I would have believed that people wanting to use their magic to make everyday life easier were the cause of all our problems."

Jade had given him an appraising look. She didn't like admitting, even to herself, that his odd eyes were looking less odd, and that she liked the way he talked about things—magic and power and what people should do with both—which no one had ever truly discussed with her. No, make that he talked to her as if she were another human being, possessed of just as good a brain as his own. Her mother had talked to her like that, and her father. Wen . . . Well, Wen was something else again, as he'd leaned on her—relied on her—to carry him through. So he'd not viewed her as an equal but as a superior. Or perhaps as a crutch, to help him get through his confused and maimed life.

The thought of Wen made her flinch, then look at Nigel again. He was competent. He appeared to be competent. He'd been all over the world without her. Surely he didn't need her. And he treated her as an equal, something her mother had told her was very rare, even in England. "Why would people using their own power to—" She stopped. "Oh."

"Oh?" he said.

"I just realized it would be like the usurpers . . . all the dynasties since my family. They don't want the people to have magical power, because people with magical power can also use it against their rulers."

Nigel smiled a little from the depths of the cowl. "I

didn't realize that," he said. "I thought just rulers would be exempt from that temptation."

"I hope Wen will be," she said, and meant it. "But I would not wager on it. You see, even the best rulers sometimes feel that they know better than the farmer how to plant rice."

"Yes, I have come to believe that," Nigel said. "We'll have to hope Wen is better when he gets the throne."

Thus talking, companionably, they'd gotten into the streets of downtown Guangzhou, and there they had stopped talking. Nigel had given her the money to rent the horse that he insisted on calling the flowerpot horse.

"You see," she'd said, "that way we can talk and the horse won't know that we're not speaking Chinese. And in a carriage, with the curtains half-drawn, no one will know that you're not Chinese or find the cloak and cowl remarkable."

And so she rented the flowerpot horse, and the tiny carriage that, truth be told, looked rather like a chaise with side curtains. Jade held the reins and controlled the horse, which she'd been told was—and seemed to be—just like flesh horses when it came to obeying commands.

It went when she shouted "Go," and responded to the reins from then on, as she drove it through narrow streets that would be quite inadequate for a normal-sized carriage, much less to those carriages she'd read about and seen engravings of in her mother's book.

As it was, on the little hard bench of the ceramic carriage, she sat rather close to Nigel, feeling the heat of his body through their clothes. It made her wish . . . not so much to be closer to him as for a different life altogether. One in which she was the product of a normal English marriage, having been born to her mother, perhaps, and her mother's long-lost fiancé.

But even if she had been the product of such a marriage, she didn't flatter herself that her life would have had fewer restrictions than her life in China. In fact, it might very well have had more, since, due to her father's indulgence and her brother's incapacitation, she'd been allowed to do things in China that she suspected women weren't allowed to do *anywhere* in the world.

But if she'd been born in England, and brought up as an English miss, then she might have married a man like Nigel Oldhall, who would understand her, and treat her as an equal.

And as a bitter voice of mockery rose within, telling her she might still find a man like Nigel Oldhall in China, once her brother's domain was more than mystical and magical, she almost sighed, because she realized she didn't want a man *like* Nigel Oldhall. She was very much afraid she wanted Nigel Oldhall, the man who had faced down Zhang with the saber, the man who had fought Zhang—in his dragon form—while wielding only a cane. The man who had killed a were-tiger with a yardstick. And who, despite all that, sat next to her, deferential and friendly—not attempting to impress her with his heroic status.

Modest, Jade thought, a quality that was as rare among Englishmen as Chinesemen and, in fact, might be a rarity among all men. She felt her face heat, and couldn't go on with this line of thought. Because to go on would be to admit that she had some interest in this foreign devil. She thought of what her sister-in-law would say. And her brother.

She cleared her throat and started, in her best professorial voice, "Guangzhou is a very interesting city. You know the name means *city of rams*?"

"No," he said. "Is it because of some old cult in this region?"

This surprised her, because she, herself, hadn't thought of that, and she shrugged. "It is said that the city was founded by five fairies, wearing coats of many colors, who came through the air riding on five rams. That is why we call it City of Rams."

He looked at her, suddenly curious. "Are your fairies real? Because ours might be. In fact, the appearances of fairies, and stories of them, and of battles with them, stopped about the time that Charlemagne used the ruby to concentrate and steal all the power from Europe. What that means," he added, "I don't know. It might be that in stealing the power, he stole the very lives of fairies and elves, who might have been creatures made of magic. But it's also possible that, somehow, they . . . went elsewhere. Or always lived between the worlds. And that we simply lost our ability to see them and communicate with them."

She nodded. "Yes. That is more likely. In China, *fairy* is used not just for beings of the spirit, but also for shape-changers. In fact, were-foxes are often called fox-fairies or fox-spirits. I've always wondered if these people who came and founded the city were weregoats. All the more so because the secret of the flying boats has always been a tradition of my people, and controlled by all weres through the power of the True Emperor. Because otherwise," she frowned a little, "I don't understand why rams should fly. Unless they were vassals of the were-emperor and could therefore fly...on boats. Nor do I understand why anyone would expect them to."

"No," Nigel said. "It seems like a very contrived thing, and something everyone would realize was contrived."

"Yes. So I think this city was founded by my people. A different clan, but..." Jade said, and conversation lagged, as though it had quite run out of power.

They were riding up narrow streets from the harbor, turning and twisting in the alleys. They passed three women, harnessed with clothesline to tugging nets of thick rope filled with bricks. They were barefoot, and bent forward, pulling the great loads of bricks. Jade steered quietly around them. They passed a temple where the smell of incense wafted at them from the big incense burner in the front. "You see," she said, as if continuing an interrupted conversation, "Guangzhou is a city of temples. It is said that there is even, in this city, a temple to a man of your people who came here long ago and explored the land. My mother said his name was Marco Polo."

"Not of my people," he said. "Italian." Then probably reading the incomprehension of this in her eyes, he smiled. "From a southern land not like mine at all. Far sunnier and more interesting, in some ways. But not home." He looked at her, and it seemed to her as if he were making an unwanted effort to speak, to find something he could say to her, to continue their conversation. "How do you know so much about this land? I thought you'd not traveled around China."

"I've not traveled much anywhere," she said. "My life has been spent on the Dragon Boats." She realized only after she said it how forlorn and bitter her voice had sounded, but it was too late to call back the words. "But I listened to every story of other lands. I drank in the tales of every emissary, every traveler, everyone at our little court who arrived fresh from the outside." She wondered if she seemed very stupid. It appeared inexplicable to her, this thirst for knowledge of other lands. She was, after all, the sister of the Dragon Emperor, the daughter of the previous one. She should have been contented with her fate. She had been the trusted adviser of her father and the protector of her brother. What more could she want?

But he only nodded. "I used to dream of foreign lands when I was little, too. My brother, you see, was older, and always very healthy. But I was born too early and too small, and I had every childhood illness possible and might have invented a few new ones. So all I did was stay in bed and daydream about foreign lands."

"But you've finally traveled," she said. And then realizing how her complaint would sound, she smiled. "And so have I, I guess."

He didn't answer that, and perhaps it was because she hadn't left him anything to say. Sometimes her damnable pride felt as though she had enclosed herself in a prison from which she could never break out. She reined the horse in, tied it, then put a word of protection on it, so on one else could drive him off, as she waited for Nigel to get out of the carriage—an operation only somewhat complicated by his twice tripping on the cloak and twice more having to make sure the cowl stayed on.

"We are here," she said in a whisper. "Let me speak until I can ascertain if we are safe."

The cart had stopped outside a large establishment that had three doors open across its length. Inside, though there were no windows and the interior seemed deep, many magelights blazed. At the door, there were several apprentice magicians—recognizable by their sky-blue cloaks—calling out to the people to come in and try their various remedies. Above the establishment, a sign flared in paint enhanced by magic, so that the letters appeared to be both solid gold and floating maybe an inch in front of the wood. It read "Drug Hall of Propitious Munificence."

She had heard it was run by the Fox Clan, as was the drug hall of the same name in Hangchow, also known as the City of Heaven, the capital of the province of Chen-kiang. After her experiences with the Tiger Clan, she felt very afraid of approaching the foxes here, but she saw no way around it. Keeping to the side of Nigel, very careful not to step on his cloak, or cause him to trip on it, she walked into the drug hall.

"Lady," one of the apprentices said. "Welcome to our humble drug hall, where you will find cures for everything that ails you. We have the Great Blessing pill, which has ten kinds of different drugs, each with its own curative properties. We have the Double

Mystery pill, very useful for curing skin diseases."
And, in saying so, he looked at Nigel with a somewhat
suspicious eye, as if suspecting the poor man must only
be covered from head to toe because he suffered from
some horrible, disfiguring disease.

She inclined her head. "I am Lady Red Jade," she
said, speaking softly enough that no one else would
hear her, "the only sister of the True Dragon Emperor.
Do you understand me?"

The apprentice's eyes, which had the same sly and
peeking look that Third Lady's eyes could so often display, now narrowed more and he nodded, an expression of awe imposing gravity on a face as triangular and
mobile as that of Jade's sister-in-law. He bowed,
hastily, and cast a look all around.

"I wish to speak to the senior magician or the senior
clan member in this establishment."

"Lady, they are the same."

"Good. Then lead me to him."

"This way, lady." He led her to the back, where a
man, whose white hair looked exactly like fox ears as it
stood away from his head, was talking animatedly with
an elderly lady. The apprentice stepped up to him and
whispered in his ear. The magician, wearing the dark
pants and the yellow jacket of a senior medical magician, widened his eyes as he looked toward her. He
bowed slightly, then gestured hurriedly. Another senior
magician stepped out of the shadows and, after what
looked like a brief introduction, took his place in talking to the portly costumer.

Meanwhile, the elderly magician steered Jade and
Nigel away from the crowd. Then he bowed to her.

"Lady Red Jade, you will not remember me. I was part of the delegation that negotiated your sister-in-law's contract." He looked both curious and alarmed. "Is this about Third Lady?"

Jade had a moment of worry. Did they know that Third Lady was even now in the underworld—or at least so Jade presumed? And if they did know, what did they think of it?

"No," she said. "Or at least, only partly. Third Lady and I consulted an oracle and we were both given missions. My mission involves something with which I need your clan's help."

The man looked at her attentively. Then he said, "This way, please. To a private room, perhaps? Where I can serve you tea and we can talk?"

Jade grabbed for the ample sleeve of his jacket. "In a Tiger Clan silk shop," she said, "I was imprisoned in the back room, and my powers seriously damaged by a concoction they fed me. I will not go into a private room."

He looked at her evaluatingly. "The tigers . . . would this be the same tigers whose silk shop burned to the ground?"

"The very same. So the news spread?"

"The news yes, but not the details." He paused. "I could tell you that we are not playing the same game as those tigers, and that in fact the only reason we know about them is that we'd long suspected they'd allied themselves with the Prince of the High Mountain, Minister Zhang. We thought they were trying an end game around our kind, you see. And our kind hopes that Third Lady..." He looked around fearfully, as if making sure no one heard them. "Surely you can see that with us being the most reviled of the were-clans, we have great hopes for Third Lady. Should the Dragon Emperors be restored, and should she be the mother of the next emperor, it will be the most important thing that ever happened in the history of our clan. It will confirm our honor and power forever."

Jade bowed slightly. "And I could believe what you say, save that, as the tiger said, the Fox Clan—and to be truthful, every other were-clan—always seems to run their game three and four conspiracies deep, trying to ensure that they're on both sides of any dispute. How do I know you don't mean to deliver me to Zhang?"

"Zhang has other allies," the Fox Clan leader said. Then he drummed his fingers on a table loaded with bottles filled with a dubious green liquid. "And yet, Lady Jade, you cannot have come all this way simply to deny conversation with us. And you cannot have wished to come all this way and then stand here, waiting for me to give you an absolute signal of my worthiness." He looked, however, as if he were trying to find a solution to their dilemma. "What if you come with me to my garden, the gate of which will be left open, and your companion..." He cast a curious look at Nigel, his eyes narrowed, in the way magicians did when they were trying to find out if someone had magical power and what the imprint of their magical power might be. "I assume your companion has a magic that I can neither touch nor influence?"

Jade nodded. It wasn't difficult. She, too, had magic

he couldn't touch or influence. Unfortunately, it was not the type of magic that could allow her to change forms and become a dragon. So it was possible, she told herself, that Nigel was no different from her. A Chinese son of a foreign-devil concubine, which she supposed was what they would have to use as an excuse after they disguised his appearance.

"My lady," the fox said, "I suggest that your companion cast a spell to make sure that my garden gate remains open and no one can approach it without his permission. We can then sit in full view of the garden gate, but far enough away that we might have a private conversation." He spread his hands wide. "I beg your pardon, lady, but this is the best insurance I can offer for your fears."

"I am afraid that you are right," she said. "I cannot help but trust you at some point in this ordeal. For should I not trust you, then I cannot take your medicine."

"That is so, milady," the fox-man said, and led her, gently, through a door in the back, into a garden where every single plant seemed to be flowering. In fact, there were more plants and of more different varieties than she'd ever seen together in a single place.

Standing on tiptoe, Jade whispered into Nigel's ear the full story of what the man had said and what she wished Nigel to do to protect them. Nigel nodded once, signifying it would be no problem. She longed for him to be able to speak, but dared not let him speak English words here, amid so many strangers.

The senior magician led them to a set of stools and a table under a small arcade at the end of the garden,

from which they did, indeed, have full view of the gate
and the street beyond. Jade looked toward Nigel, who
gave her a small nod—indicating he had indeed set his
magics in place. If she concentrated, she could see
them barely gleaming around the gate.

"So, Lady Jade," the fox-man said, "I suppose you
have come to me about the affair of the two jewels, the
ones that Minister Zhang wanted but which, if the rumors are true, he failed to secure—or secured only one
of them, which is insufficient for his ambitions. Our Fox
Clan relatives in distant lands had made us aware of
these jewels, and this we made known to Third Lady."

Jade nodded and told him about the oracle's command that she enlist the river dragons to a council of
dragons.

"A council of dragons," the fox-man said, and narrowed his eyes. "I wonder what it all can mean. I've
never heard of such."

"No," Jade said. "The truth is that our dynasty has
been gone for so long, and all the traditions lost, that
I'm sure there is much that none of us remembers.
Besides, from what I understand, the rivers have been
as though in a sleeping death. And in that sleeping
death, they could not help bring about the restoration
of my line. They are the sons of the dragon, the most
immediate descendants of the Great Dragon." She inclined her head. "As I understand it, we must enlist
their help before our clans can rule once more."

He looked at her with curiously bright eyes. "Well,
then, you must mean to enlist the dragon of the Pearl
River, right here in Guangzhou. In fact, I have heard

reports of a dragon, or a dragon power, but never very clear, since I've lived here."

"I will enlist the power of the dragons," she said, and her eyes sparkled bright in challenge. "And even the power of the ram-riding fairies, if I can find them."

He laughed, amused at her sally. "Now, that, my dear Lady Jade, I can no more help you with than you can help yourself, for I've never heard about any ram fairies or Ram Clan. Perhaps there was one, in the distant past, but it is now wholly gone."

"Or perhaps the Fox Clan told people they were the Ram Clan," she said, goading him. "Or fairies arrived upon flying rams."

He looked at her, and his eyes narrowed, his expression suddenly serious. "I've often wondered," he said, "whether they'd not come from the underworld."

"The underworld? You mean, they were dead?"

He shook his head. "No. But if Third Lady brings her case about, she and your illustrious brother will arrive from the underworld to claim their throne. I wonder if the story of the five ram fairies is the remnant of such an event, only reduced so that all that remains of it is a faint echo through which one must divine for the truth."

"What could make you think they came from the underworld?"

"The robes of many colors," he said. "And nine-colored silk. In this world it is but paper, but in the other world it is a splendid many-colored silk, like we've never seen in the world of the living. And you know, the effects of the underworld remain for a little while in this world."

"And the flying rams?"

"They could be anything," he said. "From true rams, perhaps made of clay, to those clay horses that are buried to serve emperors in the underworld, and which, after many millennia of use, might have come to resemble rams." He waved his hand. "You'd say it was nothing. An old man rambling. Or perhaps those pretty words for which foxes are known."

"If you think I'd think that, I wonder that you'd mention it," Jade said, casting an eye at Nigel and wanting to bring the conversation about, as soon as possible, so he could remove that cloak. The poor man must be boiling.

"Well, I mentioned it," the magician said, "because I think the history of China goes back further, much further, than even our people believe. I think that the realm of weres was unimaginably long, before even Yu the Great, and that perhaps there were other losses and restorations."

Jade thought of what Nigel had said about the Chinese civilization being so old, and sighed. Perhaps they were so old that they were far ahead of other people only in the sense that all peoples would follow this endless cycle of rebirth and death and rebirth again. She hoped it was time for another rebirth. She also could see, as Nigel had said, that if this were the case, adopting Western ways and manners without examination would only result in importing the errors of a yet younger culture. She would have to—she supposed—remain by Wen and advise him, after he took the throne.

Perhaps Wen's sojourn through the underworld had

enlightened him and caused him to grow, but she would not and could not believe he could have thought of everything. No human could think of everything. Which perforce must mean that Jade's destiny was to stay in China in her brother's court, and to supplement his thinking and his discoveries with her own, thereby making it more likely that the new dynasty would indeed be a new rebirth.

Since she'd never expected anything else—indeed, never wanted anything else—she was shocked at the wave of grief that washed over her, and she looked down at her hands, flat on her lap.

"But you didn't come to me for my political wisdom, nor even my historical one," the fox-man said. "So perhaps you'll tell me why you did come."

She told him. "I was given a poison by the Tiger Clan, which occluded my power and prevents me from changing shapes. I hope you have an antidote."

"Is that all? You do not need the best pharmacy in the fox world for that."

"It is not all." Raising her head, she said, "The ruby of power already has a holder, and one from which it cannot justly be separated. That holder must go with me when I go to the rivers."

"Ah," the fox-man said, and looked toward Nigel. "I presume that your companion is disfigured beyond the help of the pill of Ten Thousand Efficacies?"

She nodded once, and cast a look about the garden, to make sure that not only were there no servants lurking about but also that no windows overlooked their situation. Then she turned to Nigel. "Mr. Oldhall," she said. "If you'll forgive me..."

Reaching over, she tugged the hood of his cloak down, and for a moment, away from others like him and back in the country where she'd spent her life, she was almost startled by the shining strangeness of his hair. It looked even paler to her now—not just that blond her mother called platinum, but truly light-on-ice pale, as the oracle had said. And his skin looked more marblelike than human—though that marble would have to be very rosy to match the color of his cheeks.

He looked at her and undid the cloak's clasp at his throat, quite casting it aside, to reveal a shirt so soaked in sweat as to have become transparent and display—as though the shirt were no more than rice paper—an expanse of muscular chest. She looked away from it and at the fox-man, who did not look in the slightest shocked.

"You see," she said.

"Indeed I do," he said, and frowned a little, looking at her. "But being a foreign devil is not an illness, so how do you expect me to cure it? It might be an unfortunate condition, but . . . like being born anything else undesirable, such as a were-fox, it is something that cannot be changed and must be endured throughout all of the sufferer's life."

Jade was quite sure he was baiting her. Oh, not trying to get her to incriminate herself, as such, but in the way of foxes, playing the word game until she explicitly told him what she wanted, so that he could be sure she knew what it was he could offer. And also so that he didn't add to the growing legend of Fox Clan deception, she thought, by revealing to her powers she didn't already know he had. She wondered if the tigers were right and the foxes were playing a double game, also.

And perhaps they were, though it seemed unlikely, since they had so much invested in Third Lady—so much of their familial connections and their thoughts, and so much of their own ambitions. Without them, she thought, Jade would never have come here and Third Lady would never be in the underworld.

The corollary would seem to be that this could be a trap, but if you turned the thought around and looked at it another way, you realized that the truth was, by remaining in the Dragon Boats, they would have been open and vulnerable. Wen could not have lasted much longer, and many more people would start to notice his problems now that, bereft of Zhang to run everyday administration, he would have to rely only on Jade. Though it smarted to realize, Jade was unblinkingly aware that many in the Dragon Boats refused to receive orders from women. As did many in the were-clans in the world at large. They would want Wen to give his orders, which Wen could not do. The whole thing could never have lasted more than a week before a revolt killed Wen and installed Zhang on the throne. She was sure Zhang was waiting for just that.

Even with only one ruby, if he were the heir to the Dragon Throne, she was sure the English would lend him their support. It wouldn't be the first time—from what her mother had told her—that they thus manipulated the affairs of other countries, so as to establish one of their vassals in power.

As for the ruby, if Jade had not gone on her quest and interfered with Zhang's plans, he'd surely have come back and gotten the stone from Nigel. Nigel had been valiant. He'd fought very well, and twice he'd repelled Zhang and denied him total victory. But Nigel was wounded and weak, and Zhang hadn't been. And Nigel could not change into a dragon, whereas Zhang could. There would have been no contest, and Zhang, instead of nursing the wounds inflicted by a fellow dragon—which Jade had to presume was what he was doing—would now be in control of the two rubies and ready to claim his reward.

No, if the Fox Clan were playing both sides, they were the worst fools in the history of mankind for having thus created their own opposition. She sighed and said, "Third Lady has told me, long ago, that you have a potion that changes the appearance of a person for some days. And, depending on how the potion is calibrated, it changes it in very specific ways. She says the Fox Clan gave such a potion to the foreign devil Marco Polo, when he came to visit our land, and also that the people who stole the secret of silk from us bought the potion from the fox people, and thus could penetrate China unpunished. And leave again unpunished." She looked at his face, immobile, like the face of a player who will not give anything away to his opponent. "Besides, you must know I heard all the tales growing up, and I know that the foxes have always had a way of changing appearance."

At long last the fox-man nodded, then narrowed his eyes at her. "Would you also," he said, gesturing toward Nigel, "want your companion to understand what we say? Or would it be better for your plans, and perhaps for him, if he doesn't know?"

"Understand what we say?" she asked, in some puzzlement. "How is that possible? Does the Fox Clan, then, have some medicine that teaches language? How amazing that would be, to make all of humanity speak the same language," she finished, ironically, wondering what kind of deception he was trying to play on her.

But he only looked grave. "It is not a teaching pill. Indeed, if those were possible, then my people and I would make a fortune from those who wish to take the civil service examinations. The only way to learn something—a language, a poem or a skill—is to study it and purchase the knowledge with the toil. But this is different. What the pill does, if someone is available who has the ability, is give the one who takes it the ability to—in a limited way—experience the thought of the other. To . . . borrow part of his or her brain. It's a form of the Six Taste pill," he added, as though defending himself from unspoken accusations. "And you'd both have to take it."

"But . . ." Jade said, looking at Nigel and thinking how much easier, indeed, the whole thing would be if he not only looked Chinese but could also speak the language. "How much of my thoughts would he be able to penetrate?"

"None consciously," he said. "Only the words would come to him, as come the words of his mother tongue."

"But there would be more to this link than that, would there not?" she asked, suspicious and all the more hesitant because something in her was exulting and calling for the link, demanding that she accept it. That she let herself be linked to Nigel Oldhall.

The fox-man shrugged. "There have been no credible reports of anything else," he said.

Jade frowned, fairly sure that was fox-speak for the fact that there had been reports otherwise. But, after all, she was supposed to trust him, was she not? She had to or she would never accomplish anything. And the voice within her that had been screaming to her to allow this link was joined by a far more practical side, which pointed out that without it, should they become separated, Nigel would be at the mercy of his surroundings and have less ability than a deaf mute to ask for directions or receive them; to enlist help; to rescue her if needed. Because a deaf mute, at least, knew the society if he'd grown up in it. While Nigel would be wholly lost.

"How far away does the link work?" Jade asked.

"As long as you're both in the world of the living, you will be linked," he said.

"What?" she said. "Forever?"

"Yes, but only where the Chinese language is concerned," the man said.

And while the eternity of the link should have made her decide against it, it perversely made Jade want to do it. Nigel would go back to England and she would stay in her brother's court. They would never see each other again. But if he ever found the need to read or speak in Chinese, then it would be her brain he would be accessing, and their minds would be linked, however ephemeral the tie.

It would be both a guilty link and an innocuous one. And something he need not ever know—or not ever understand fully. She nodded. "Get the pills, then," she said. "The one to change his appearance, and the one to establish the link."

"And the one to get your dragon powers back?" he asked.

"Of course. How hard is it?" she asked.

The fox-man laughed. "Not very. The tiger potion is very clumsy."

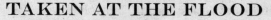

TAKEN AT THE FLOOD

Judge Bao gestured for documents and files, which were all brought to him by creatures that looked like humans made entirely of shadow. It made Third Lady want to smile, imagining them as the perfect functionaries, who spent eternity working in archives until they disappeared completely, save for their shadows. And then she frowned, wondering whether this *was* what happened to perfect functionaries once they died. It might be preferable to the Pool of Filth, but she didn't think she wished for that as an eternal fate, either.

The judge rustled the documents in his lap, looking at one, then at the other, and uttering many deep-thinking ums. Then, looking at Third Lady, he said, "It is highly irregular, you know, to keep the soul of the living here in the underworld. But these lawsuits are very convincing."

"What do they allege?" Third Lady asked. "If I may be permitted to inquire?"

The grave face, looking more human at a distance,

half smiled at her where she stood, some distance in front of his feet, holding Wen's hand.

"That the main dynasty lost all right to the throne by not making any attempt to recover it through all the centuries of dispossession," Judge Bao said. "When a man has a field he does not till or look after, and which is taken over by someone else, that someone has the right to the field, after a time. Or the field reverts to the emperor and may be purchased from him."

"But it is not true," Wen said, frowning a little, "that the Zhang line has any claim to the throne, either. Or at least, not above my family. While I might not have been involved in the running of my own patrimony, my illustrious father ran his, and his illustrious father before that. Zhang's ancestors were no more than ministers. And they, too, made no attempt to recover the throne from the usurpers."

"It says here," the judge shifted papers around, "that the pirate Koxinga—a were-dragon and Zhang's ancestor—made an attempt at unseating the Machu Dynasty from its throne, two centuries ago in Nanking. In his flying boats, he laid siege to the town for twenty days, and only the magic of the city's ancient walls and its ancient inhabitants managed to defeat him."

"Koxinga was an ancestor of Zhang's," Wen said, his voice so steady that it surprised Third Lady. "But so is he mine, on both lines."

The judge looked up and made a gesture. "Bring me the genealogical records of the Dragon Boats," he said, to no one in particular. Several shadows scurried to lay what seemed to be an immense scroll on his lap. He looked at it for a long time before saying, "It is true that he is the ancestor of both your mother and father and Zhang's mother and father. How do you know this? Had you prepared your response?"

"No, Your Excellency. The fact is that there are so many dragons in the world, and in the Dragon Boats, we cannot help being related to one another."

"Um ..." the judge said, and looked through the documents some more. "But this is the oldest lawsuit. There is a more recent one, since your father's death, and in that one the more important testimony brought by Zhang and his ancestors is that your father said you failed to fulfill your duties as the heir and prince, and that Zhang performed them in your stead. As such, he is invoking the privilege of tradition. As Shun named Yu as his successor because he thought him better for the people of China and for his kingdom, so your father, Yi, chooses to name Zhang as his successor, instead of you. How do you defend yourself from this?"

Wen looked too shocked to speak. For a long time he looked up, seeming utterly without words. Third Lady was about to protest for him, when Wen said, "Excellency, are you sure my father said that? Is the testimony sworn? Because, before he died, my father showed me all the papers and the seals and the rings I would need to be an emperor. Surely he would not have done so unless he believed I should be the emperor. What was the good of instructing me, if he preferred for Zhang to reign?"

Judge Bao frowned, then ordered, "Bring me the shade of Yi, True Dragon Emperor and former Emperor of All Under Heaven."

There was a longer wait this time, and Third Lady

wondered what they would do if his father had already been sent to the wheel of rebirth. Would they truly summon him from whatever he had become in his next life, and bring him here to give testimony on behalf of or against his son?

But after a while, her father-in-law appeared, and he looked much as he had in life. He was tall for a Chinese man, which, combined with her foreign-devil genes, probably accounted for Lady Jade's ridiculous height. His features looked like Wen's—the same oval face, and the same regular features. Although, where Wen looked youthful and almost eager to listen to others, Yi had a forbidding expression. He tilted his head, and pursed his lips so that one could not but think that he was very proud and unwilling to listen to anyone else.

"I am Yi," he said. "True Dragon Emperor. Once Emperor of All Under Heaven. Why do you call me forth? Was not my testimony clear?" He did not look at his son, and Third Lady's stomach clenched in worry, because if he wouldn't even look at Wen, it was unlikely he had come to vindicate him.

She knew that, in life, Yi had never been very fond of Wen. This came from not being very fond of Wen's mother. Instead, he'd lost his heart to the strange redheaded concubine he'd stolen from a carpetship.

Third Lady supposed, as far as that went, she could not fault him. Doubtless his first marriage had been arranged by his father. Wen's mother had been a great lady of the Tiger Clan, as were all the first ladies of Dragon Emperors when no marriageable dragon lady was available, from time immemorial. As such, Wen's mother had in a way been born to her position, as much as Wen had been born to his. She was simply the most eligible of the ladies of the Tiger Clan; all the ladies of the Dragon Clan who were of age were probably too nearly related to marry Yi. Besides, the lady had probably been descended from a lot of Dragon Emperors herself, since the daughters tended to marry into the Tiger Clan again if no suitable dragon was available.

It was perhaps not strange that Yi had not fallen in love with his arranged wife. Neither had Wen when it came to that. And if Yi had fallen in love with the foreign concubine, it was just, Third Lady supposed, that he should have preferred it if his concubine had given him a son, and his first lady a daughter. That would, doubtlessly, have fit his notions better. And so far, she could forgive him for being no more than human.

What she couldn't forgive, though, was the way he treated Wen, as though it were Wen's fault that he had been born male and Jade female. And beyond that, the fact that his blinkered affections refused to recognize that even had Jade been male, it would have been almost impossible for her to inherit the throne, since this hypothetical male would still have been the son of a foreign-devil concubine, and all the clans would rebel against that.

But she knew—not through experience, but by being taught by older and wiser women who made it their business to instruct the girls—that when men took a notion into their heads, no matter how unreasonable, it was near impossible to dissuade them or disabuse them. And in Emperor Yi's mind, Wen had stolen the throne from the son he'd never had.

Now he stood, with head thrown back, and a flash of pride in his eyes, and said, "It is the duty of the emperor to choose the most worthy successor to his throne, and this son of mine was never worthy. Even from childhood, he was slow and lagged behind his sister in development. And as a young man, he had no interest in government. I invoked the privilege of Shun, who, choosing the best ruler for his people chose Yu and not his own son, because Yu was the best and the best equipped to rule the people."

"Well, it is your father's privilege as emperor—or late emperor—to choose his successor," Judge Bao said, even though you could tell he was not pleased with having to say it. After all, the purpose of the law was not to please people—or even judges—but to make life more just for the majority of the people. "And the law is the law."

"But consider, sir," Third Lady said. "Lady Jade is dependent on her brother's benevolence to continue living as well. If Wen should die—and Zhang cannot ascend the throne otherwise, in the land of the living— then the Lady Jade's life will be forfeit."

Emperor Yi shook his head. "No, for Zhang has sworn to me, on the tomb of his ancestors, that he will marry Jade and create with her a new line of emperors. He's none too satisfied with that oldest boy of his, the one they call Grasshopper, and certainly they cannot afford to have him inherit such a responsibility as the Dragon Throne." He looked at Wen and Third Lady for the first time. "I had not meant it to be so," he said, in a softer voice. "In fact, the truth is I thought it would be best if Wen lived, and if he ruled, at least for a time, while Jade found herself a husband and got her feet under her. I would prefer Jade has her choice in husbands, which is why I've never chosen one for her. But once I arrived here, I was informed that my successor will regain the physical Dragon Throne—that the Mandate of Heaven, so long against us because of the path my ancestor Qu set us on, has turned once more and that it was inexorably true that my descendent would rule the True Land of All Under Heaven, and not just the were-clans and their magic.

"Wen—or rather, Jade in his stead—would have done well enough to rule the Dragon Boats and to organize the occasional raid against foreign carpetships. But neither of them, and certainly not Wen, could control the vastness of all under heaven. As such, I had to change my mind and give the throne to Zhang, who served at my right hand for many years, and who already knows everything that can be done and should be done to establish a just empire. Thus did Shun choose, and get Yu, the great flood tamer. While Yu bent to the dictates of his heart and the demands of family and chose his son, Qu, who oppressed the non-weres and eventually led us to losing the Mandate of Heaven."

There was a long silence, and then Judge Bao rustled the papers with an air of finality. He looked ready to pronounce a verdict, and Third Lady was very much afraid that she knew what that would be. She reached for her husband's hand again, touching his cold fingers for a moment before he reacted and clasped her hand convulsively.

They didn't speak. They didn't even look at each other, but Third Lady knew that Wen was thinking, just as she was, that they'd come so far and done so much for all of it to flounder like this, on the shores of Yi's old obsession with his son not being worthy enough of him or of his throne.

"Just because Yu made a mistake," she exclaimed in despair, "it is not true that doing the opposite will not be a mistake." She remembered what Yu had said. "I call on the soul of Yu the Great, to help me in my case." When nothing happened, she continued, resigned and steeling herself to fight on alone. "Zhang has imprisoned Wen's soul in this underworld, since Wen was a very young man. And Zhang gave Wen's body opium—which he got from the English traders, probably in exchange for favors when he got the throne—and introduced him to it and encouraged him in taking it, until he was thoroughly addicted. How could he be a proper heir to you, Oh Emperor Yi, if neither his soul nor his mind were fully present? How could he have shown you that he deserved the Dragon Throne, when he could barely think?" She shook her head and, driven by her pain, continued. "It is only because you are not a real father, and never had any care of your only son, that you didn't notice he was addicted to opium, and didn't suspect where it was coming from. Oh, the Lady Jade tried to hide it because she was afraid of what your reaction would be, and what it would do to her brother's chances of ruling. But she didn't hide it so well from anyone else, and everyone else in the Dragon Boats knows the cause of Wen's distress. And knows who is responsible for it. Except you, Emperor Yi."

"You dare talk to me like that, fox-girl? You were no more than a singer and dancer in a singsong troop when I purchased your contract for my son."

"And she's the lady of my heart and always will be," Wen said quietly.

"You speak now in defense of your wife?" Yi said. "You didn't speak in defense of your inheritance. Zhang might not be as worthy as Yu, but at least he would have defended his right to inherit the Dragon Throne."

"Oh, no," a booming voice said from the back. "Never underestimate Zhang." Third Lady started and would have turned, ready to defend herself from some attack from Zhang or his emissaries, but she heard, as an undertone to the words, the sound of running water. And before she could turn, she realized it was Yu's voice. "He might not have had my interest in defending my people and protecting them from the flood, but if making all contrivances possible to inherit the throne makes one worthy to occupy it, then Zhang is very worthy, indeed. Not only did he contrive to imprison the soul of the prince and heir"—he gestured to the papers on Judge Bao's lap—"if Your Excellency will look, you will note that the date at which it was imprisoned was when Prince Wen could be no more than twelve, and therefore not ready to take charge of anything . . . and he also introduced him to opium, which he obtained from British agents, with promises of granting them favors once he ascended to the rule of the Dragon Boats—as Third Lady surmised. As for the opium, as well as for other things necessary for his plans of takeover..." While he spoke, Yu gestured to two of the clay men, who entered carrying what looked like a giant mirror. Third Lady recognized it as one of the mirrors from the first hell, the ones in which one could see one's own life. However, at a wave from Yu, the mirror displayed Zhang meeting with men in English uniforms, in a town that was clearly Hong Kong. It displayed him giving the very young Wen opium. "He also," Yu said, as the scene showed on the screen, "poisoned your drink for years, oh Emperor Yi, so you seemed to suffer from a lingering illness, which eventually killed you, when he chose to up the dosage." He crossed his arms on his chest. "This is the man you compare to me, and to whom you want to entrust all under heaven?"

Yi looked... deflated, and Third Lady felt a sudden sympathy for him, because he looked so much like Wen when he'd been caught at fault and was embarrassed to admit it.

He lowered his head, and when he looked up again, he was frowning, perhaps to hide an expression of contrition. "No," he said. "No, Minister Zhang is not worthy of having the Dragon Throne. I only wish to know if my son is."

"That," Yu said, his voice almost caustic, "none of us can know until we've given the child the power and watched him succeed or fail. There are no guarantees, Emperor Yi."

"Do you then abandon your willing of the throne to Zhang?" Judge Bao asked.

"Yes," Emperor Yi said. "I will it instead to my son, Wen, True Dragon Emperor, Future Ruler of All Under Heaven."

"Very well," Judge Bao said. "Then there is no longer any reason to hold his soul here, waiting further proceedings." He looked toward one of the shadows behind his chair. "Go and let loose the soul of Emperor Wen."

It was the strangest thing. Third Lady was not sure what she'd expected. She supposed she thought the guards would come back escorting Wen's soul. Instead, as the shadows disappeared down a tunnel to the judge's left, there was the sound of a door being opened, and then a sound like the whoosh of wind. For just a moment, she saw Wen's shape rushing through the air as though either blown by wind or pulled by a red cord that seemed to be attached to Wen himself.

Then there was a sound like a slap and suddenly . . .

There was no difference at all. Wen looked exactly the same. Except that he didn't. Where he had been almost transparent in this underworld, he was now solid—his broad shoulders, his narrow waist, his long legs all displaying suddenly to greater advantage. And where his eyes had been calm and patient, they now were infused with a shine and an expression of secret humor, or secret mischief. The Wen that Third Lady had no more than suspected existed beneath the subdued exterior of her husband was now fully present and fully in control.

He looked at her with melting love and breathtaking desire, and for a moment all she could do was look back at him, her breath suspended.

Through this, she heard Yu say, "May I then send them back?"

And suddenly, almost as if out of nowhere, there was water rushing in upon them and carrying them, as if on the crest of a wave.

Halls and caves rushed past them. Third Lady got no more than glimpses of knives and tentacles, of leers and strange machines, and only those glimpses allowed her to believe that these people were, in fact, still part of Feng Du.

Then the wave crashed with a deafening sound, and everything went dark.

She blinked and sat up, and realized she was back in the cave where she and Wen had left their bodies.

Beside her, he groaned, and blinked rapidly, and she realized that he, too, was waking up.

A SOLDIER'S DISTRESS

Captain Corridon would never be able to pinpoint when he'd realized that Hettie had given him the proverbial slip.

He had not been worried when he found she was not in her cabin. She had been very excited about being a passenger in a carpetship. He'd gathered that when she'd traveled before, it had been as a guest of her father's and under strict orders not to bother the paying travelers. And although she could still not mingle on the first-class deck—since Captain Corridon's money hadn't run that high—she had amused herself by walking the second-class deck, talking to anyone who would speak to her, looking down at the vastness of Africa or the deep ocean as they flew over it.

And now, he hoped, she would be watching as they landed in Hong Kong, possibly near the younger people on board. Indulgently, he'd gone around the deck, looking at various groups of girls, and—he'd felt very sure this was Hettie—at a very pretty blond girl surrounded by a group of chattering boys. But it wasn't her.

Hettie was nowhere to be seen. In despair, he'd taken to the top deck, thinking perhaps she'd somehow talked her way up there, or perhaps someone had invited her there. An encounter with a carpetship employee in uniform delayed him, and he had to show papers that proved he was more than what he appeared to be—a militia captain on furlough.

By the time the man had let him through and Captain Corridon had perused the top deck from one end to the other, and not found Hettie, they had landed. The people on the top deck—young couples, elderly travelers—all looked at him as if he were deranged, as he looked in increasingly unlikely places for Hettie Perigord.

Finally, in despair, he'd gone back to their deck, only to find that people were already disembarking, from it as well as from the other decks. But the people who'd left were families with their children. He could still see them on the ground, walking away, going through Customs.

His desperate question to the carpetship employees, "Did you see a young girl disembark alone?" was met with frowns and headshakes, and once with an indignant, "Good heavens, you don't think we'd let her do that!"

And no, he didn't think they'd let her do that. But, as consciousness of his loss dawned, he realized he stood on the verge of ruin. If Hettie was gone, he had nothing—nothing at all—to hold over the Perigords. What was more, he had nothing at all to allow him to unravel what might be the greatest conspiracy in English history.

He was not from a wealthy family, and his own portion as a second son was not large enough to purchase him the advance he desired. He'd been counting on the advancement from unraveling this conspiracy to achieve the level of prominence he aspired to. Eventually, he'd like to be the chief of the Secret Service, the lord of Her Majesty's—or as was far more likely, by then, His Majesty's—information and spying unit.

And he had been counting on that, he realized, with a half-startled laugh, to convince Lord Marshlake to allow him to marry his daughter, Hester. And on this, his breath caught. Because, how strange it was that he'd been counting on his blackmailing of Hettie's parents to secure the needed wherewithal to convince them to let him marry her.

The thing was, for all that, it might very well have worked. After all, though he blackmailed them, he would also be doing his utmost to ensure that they did not suffer for being a part of this conspiracy. In fact, he'd been willing to spend considerable effort and endure considerable risk to prevent them from being in any way importuned. Which meant that when all was said and done, they would have been grateful to him.

And he would have the advancement and the fortune. He would be able to afford to keep a wife in the way that Hettie, daughter of Lord Marshlake, deserved to be kept.

But now Hettie was gone and Lord only knew where. The realization hit him, suddenly, that he did not have any idea where Hettie might be, or what she might be doing, and he felt a sinking in his gut as he sat down on the steps to the upper deck with a loud thud. He felt as if his legs were made of rubber.

Hettie. Where could Hettie have gone? And who knew what dangers she might be risking, what terrible trouble she might be facing? As enterprising and winsome as the young Miss Perigord was, she had never been outside her city, outside her neighborhood, outside the confines of her upbringing. She had no idea what dangers could lurk in the fascinating city of Hong Kong for a young girl of her circumstances who debarked wholly friendless and unprotected.

He held his head in his hands and moaned. He would have to find a locating magician as soon as possible, and he would have to pay him to locate Hettie. She could not be allowed to be out there, running who knew what risks. In his mind, he saw her bound hand and foot and sold into white slavery into the harem of some Chinese potentate, or, worse, into some house of ill-repute. And how could he explain to his superiors that such a slip of a girl had escaped him and left no trace?

"Captain Corridon?" an excessively well-bred voice said, just in front of him.

Adrian removed his hands from in front of his face, and looked up at a very tall man with classical features and the sort of dark curls that foolish romances always talked about but which rarely appeared on real people, much less real men. He would, in fact, have been entirely too handsome to be true were it not for the fact that his left eye was missing and covered with a black leather patch. The other eye was an unusual green color.

Corridon's mouth dropped open as things he'd heard fell into place. "Peter," he said. "Farewell. Lord St. Maur. But...but you are..."

"Very far from home," the man, whom Corridon was almost absolutely sure was a dragon, looked around significantly, as though to show that there were too many people present who might hear them.

But Captain Corridon was not willing to expose Lord St. Maur as a dragon, as he had just realized that here was his solution for Hettie's disappearance. He got up, on trembling legs, and raised his fists in the accepted position of challenge that would have earned him applause in the fashionable boxing scene. "Where is Hettie?" he said. "What have you done with her?"

But he was wholly unprepared for the emotional punch that came with the drawled response. "My dear fellow! I believe that was my line."

DRAGON IN THE FOX CAVE

龙

Third Lady woke and sat up, startled. She didn't know how much time had passed in this world, but it couldn't be long, because the fire in which she had burned the paper figures still blazed. By the light of the fire, she turned and watched her husband.

She was sure he had made groaning sounds and that his eyelids had fluttered. He was now breathing slowly and deeply, his chest rising and falling in an obvious way. Even asleep, he looked healthier than she'd ever seen him. There was color in his cheeks, and his skin seemed more golden than pale. In fact, he looked more like the man she had imagined she was marrying than the bridegroom she'd found on her wedding night.

And this brought a sudden alarm. Wen would want to consummate their marriage, she realized, even as his eyelids fluttered open and he fixed her with those newly intent, almost amused eyes.

Her heart skipped a beat. It wasn't that she didn't wish for him to consummate their union. In fact, through the lonely years of her marriage, she'd wanted nothing more. She'd dreamed of being taken in Wen's arms and of sharing with him those pleasures of which the matron who'd instructed the singsong girls had spoken of so often.

But now, here, in this little cave, in the depths of a mountain, alone with Wen, she didn't know what to do. *It's been too long,* she thought desperately, as her mind tried to summon to itself the images and words she'd been taught about various sexual acts. There had been line drawings, almost too schematic for her virgin brain to make any sense of. And then there were names. She remembered Two Butterflies Sporting on Silk Chrysalis, but since that involved the presence of two girls and one man, she very much hoped it wasn't something that Wen dreamed of.

He took a deep sigh and sat up, offering her both his hands. "My wife," he said softly. "Third Lady. My fox-fairy."

She sighed in return because his voice made every word sweet, but she didn't know what to do, and she had the terrified feeling that he would expect more expertise from her than she had any idea how to show. Because not only was she a were-fox—creatures who were widely believed to be lascivious and utterly devoted to the body and the senses—but she was also a singsong girl, someone who had been taught—at least in theory—the pleasures of the flesh and how to make men feel good. And she wanted to make Wen feel good.

She wanted their time together to be such that she would be the only woman he'd ever want. She wanted her sister-wives, who did not love Wen as she did, to never have visits from him and to either quietly divorce him or to simply enjoy their honors but not Wen. She wanted her ability to be such that Wen would never even consider another woman, not even her sister-wives. She wanted to be branded on his heart and soul.

And he was, earnestly, intently, attempting to undo the ties of her gown.

"Wait," she said, desperately. "Wait!" And she cast about for forgotten teachings in her mind.

He looked like a child denied a treat, as he brought his hands down. There was almost a hint of the old, hesitant Wen, as he said, "You don't . . . You do not wish to attempt . . ." He blushed. "That is, you had said before, and I know it was only an excuse, but—"

"No, no," she said, rapidly, and then realized she might be misunderstood. "I do wish it. Oh, I wish it more than anything! But I want to know . . . That is, in which way can I best please you?"

He blinked at her. "I'm sorry?" he said. "I don't understand."

"In which way can I make you achieve the highest pleasure?" she asked, hearing the slightest edge of hysteria in her voice. "Do you wish to engage in Maiden Boiling Milk?"

He frowned slightly. "Is that where we—"

"I see not," she said, realizing that if he didn't even know the name for the position sketch, it was highly unlikely that he'd long dreamed of that particular pleasure. Thinking desperately, she extracted another image from the long-ago depths of her mind. "Would you then wish for Fluttering Bird on a Branch?"

His hands had returned to the ties on her gown. They had managed to undo the right side, and were now working on the left. "My dear Third Lady," he said, and there was something in his voice that trembled and fluttered.

She realized she was failing him terribly, and, calling to mind the drawing of the Fluttering Bird, realized it would indeed be far too tame for a husband who had waited this long for consummation. "Tiger Lapping From a Milk Stream," she said.

He pulled her overgown over her head, and looked at the little looped string that closed the undergown, like a man examining a mystery. "I have no idea what that means, precisely," he said, "but it sounds entirely too tiring."

She sighed. There had to be something in her teachings that would serve to delight her suddenly hard-to-please lord. "Junk Sails Swelling in a High Wind?" she said, hopefully.

"Altogether too many sails and too vigorous a wind," he said. He pulled her undergown over her head, and smiled wistfully at her body.

He was doubtlessly thinking how beautiful she looked, and yet wondering how she could be as ignorant as she was. His hands caressed her softly, climbing from her waist to her breasts and circling toward her dark nipples, causing them to stand out, eagerly, as though seeking more of his touch. Bewildered by the emotions rising in her, she sighed, and said, "He-Xiangu Grinding Peaches."

He grinned at her, an utterly wanton smile. "Only if

one of us wishes to achieve immortality," he said. "And I'd say that's also too much work."

"But—" she said.

"Well, as the one immortal who is the patron of virgins . . ." Wen said, taking his hands off her body, where they'd been moving restlessly, as if they couldn't quite get enough of the feel of her skin. He pulled off his jacket and pants rapidly, appearing as naked as she was, ". . . I hope He-Xiangu will look kindly upon the both of us at this moment."

"Oh, but then you mean that you never—"

"My dear, I was twelve when my soul was confined to the underworld."

She looked at him, the soft beautiful eyes, the velvety golden skin stretched over just enough muscles to remind her that he was a male. And the rather obvious proof that, despite her clumsiness, he still wanted her, rising proudly at that moment—since she was sitting on the bed and he had stood to undress—directly in front of her eyes.

Wide-eyed, she looked at the proof, then up at his face. He deserved the best. He deserved pleasures reserved for the gods. She wanted to make this true wedding night the best anyone had ever dreamed of. She wanted to belong to him body and soul. She wanted him to belong to her.

Weakly, she suggested, "Rose Petals Atop Bamboo Stalk?"

He smiled. "Maybe later? For now I'd like the more obvious." He sat on the bed by her side and smiled at her.

"More obvious?" she asked. "You mean Phoenix Rising Over Volcano? Or Lizard Feasting on Octopus?"

He took her hands and held them for a moment, his hands very warm. Then, gently, he reached up and pulled at the pin that held her hair. He caressed her hair as it fell—a black cascade—down her back. Then he cupped her face in his hand. "Look at me, Precious Lotus," he said.

She looked. Their eyes met, and their gazes seemed to hold each other as if caught in an invisible net. He brought his face so close to her that she could feel his breath upon her face. "I have spent so much time separated from my soul," he said, "that perhaps the feeling has just become part of me, but I'd swear, my lady . . ."

"Yes?"

"That part of my soul is captive within you."

"Oh," she said, in confusion, feelings warring within her for which she had no name. "I'm sorry. I don't remember any of my training. I must be the worst wife who ever lived. I know that you expect much from foxfairies, but I—"

"Shh," he said. "Shh." And then, slowly, "My love, my wife, my fox-fairy, the only pleasure I want and wish to experience with you right now is Dragon Seeking Refuge in Fox's Cave."

In a sudden panic, Third Lady tried to imagine what he could mean, but her quick mind could not find a schematic drawing that corresponded to such a phrase.

"I don't know what you mean," she said in a hurry. "I never learned that position."

"It doesn't matter," he said, smiling at her, his lips

slightly parted, his eyes dancing with amusement. "I shall teach you."

"But—" she said.

And then he laid her down upon the bed and embraced her. And suddenly she understood.

THE ELDERLY DRAGON
OF PEARL RIVER

The fox apothecary brought out several pills and laid them before Nigel and Jade. And though Nigel could not understand a word of what was being said, he understood enough—particularly when a cup of tea was also placed before him—to know he was supposed to take the pills at his elbow.

One of the pills was bright red, and the other one appeared to be a miniature egg painted with various branches and flowers in delicate golden swirls. He wondered why anyone would take so much trouble painting a pill, then he wondered if the gold was poisonous. And then he stopped wondering, because he realized he truly didn't want to know what was in either of these pills.

Alchemy anywhere in the world was the thing of madmen and fools. Because of its magic properties, the ingredient wasn't potent for its own qualities alone, but for those qualities conferred upon it by the emotions of the alchemist—even when those emotions were shock, horror or revulsion. In fact, no matter what the intent or the end in view, shock, horror and revulsion seemed to be emotions that alchemists or their suppliers often sought to evoke. Perhaps because they were strong emotions that were relatively easy to achieve—as compared to love or hatred or undying devotion.

Only the notorious case of Burke and Hare, who'd robbed cemeteries looking for unhallowed bodies whose parts they could sell to alchemists—and sometimes created less than hallowed bodies whose parts they could sell—had caused the Crown to take an interest and to regulate the ingredients that could be used for public consumption in England.

Nigel was going to assume that Burke and Hare hadn't had a similar effect in China. At any rate, from the things he'd read, the Chinese were far less likely to be squeamish about what went into their pills and medicine than the most sturdy of the English alchemists. Out of the corner of his eye he saw Jade take her pills—a bright green one, and a red one just like his.

Well, then, if Lady Jade could take them, so could he. Otherwise, surely she would think he was too squeamish and too solicitous of his own culture's mode. He lifted the golden pill first, and swallowed it. There was . . . a feeling like a flutter all over his body, and as he reached to pick up the other pill, he realized that his hand, instead of looking its normal pale color was now a gold bordering on the brown.

He heard Jade say "Oh!" and wondered what he looked like, but was afraid to ask. So he took the other pill and swallowed it, quickly. A burst of strange flavor exploded in his mouth and seemed to overwhelm his brain. He closed his eyes, as explosions of light erupted behind his closed lids, and as he opened them again, he found Jade looking at him curiously.

"Do you understand me now?" she asked.

"Yes, of course," he said. And then he realized she had not spoken English. His mouth dropped open. "What...what do you mean?" And then he realized that he wasn't speaking English, either. He had to think, and forcefully, too, to switch to English, as though the mode he was in called for Chinese. "What is it? Is it possible then to learn a language by taking a pill?" In all his years of careful and diligent study of other cultures and languages, it had never occurred to him that such a shortcut existed. He felt slightly duped.

She laughed and shook her head and blushed and answered—in Chinese. "No, they tell me that you can access that part of my brain that knows the language. It will work across any distance, so you can now speak and understand Chinese."

"How convenient," he said, amused, but also somewhat flustered, because he was in part of her mind. Oh, it didn't matter it was only in the language part of her mind—he was touching her. He was touching her in a more intimate way than he'd ever touched another human being.

Looking away, he said, "How long does it last?"

"As long as both of us are alive."

"Oh," he said, and then confused and humble, "It is a great gift. I thank you."

He realized that while they were talking the man who'd been with them had left, and Nigel had a moment of alarm. He was about to ask Jade if she thought there was a problem, when the man came back. He brought with him two sets of clothes and a small hand mirror. The clothes, for both of them, were much like those he had seen Jade wearing the first time he'd met her—loose pants and short, heavily embroidered jackets.

"You don't look right in those clothes now," he told Nigel, and smiled. Then the fox-man looked toward Jade. "And you cannot wear British clothes if you are going farther into China to awaken the rivers."

Jade nodded. The man showed them each to relative privacy behind some bushes. Nigel changed very quickly, afraid something would happen to Jade while he was separated from her. She must have had the same idea, because as soon as he came out from behind his bush, holding a bundle of clothing, she came from behind hers as well.

The old man took the bundles of clothing from them. "I shall send them to the Dragon Boats, shall I?" he asked.

"No," Nigel said. "To the Hotel Victoria. It's where our other luggage is."

This won him raised eyebrows—though he was not absolutely sure what that meant—and then a stiff little bow. "Very well." The man picked up the mirror from the table, and offered it to Nigel.

Nigel examined his reflection and was, at once, both surprised and not. It was not his face as he was used to it, and yet it was still his face. Had he had a Chinese brother, in every detail having Chinese features where Nigel had British ones, he would have looked like that image in the mirror. Nigel's newly black eyes shone with the sort of lapis-lazuli shine that showed now and then in Jade's, but other than that he was an unremarkable Chinese man. A little taller than average, perhaps, with features a little more chiseled. And his hair, which he had cut in Hong Kong, might now be black, but it retained its very short and fashionable cut, so that he looked like a Chinese man who patronized British barbershops. Which he supposed was not that unusual.

The elderly man was bowing before them. "Now go, my lady, my lord, and wake the rivers."

With those words, he led them to the door to the interior of the apothecary, and from there to the street. The flowerpot horse remained tied where they had left it, but this time—unafraid of being seen—they pulled back the curtains of the carriage, so that as they drove they could have a view of Canton.

Jade still drove, since she knew where they were going. And besides, Nigel was far too interested in the passing landscape to be able to think of the reins, much less of this strangely fragile-looking animated piece of pottery.

Though he was fairly sure that Jade had said it was porcelain, the horse did not look like porcelain. The carriage must have been a late addition, because it did, indeed, look like glazed porcelain. White glazed porcelain, painted all over with little blue flowers, looking much like a vase that Nigel's mother used to have in her receiving room. If Nigel remembered correctly, it had been brought back from China by his great-great-grandfather after a brief visit for either trade or war; at a distance of centuries, it was hard to tell. But the horse itself looked like it had been dragged through hell and war. It had no glaze left and it was clear that here and there its flanks and its head and its poor muzzle had been supplemented with clay of various grades and several colors. It could be a horse, and, in fact, Nigel was assuming it was, or it could be a goat or some other misshapen creature.

As the horse trundled along the streets, with various chair carriers and other such little carriages with ceramic horses, more than a fair share of pedestrians got out of the way. An opening appeared in the crowd amid a flowering park, and Nigel glimpsed a building that looked like the classic little pagodas made of cork or ceramic that people brought from China. This one, however, rose seven stories from the ground and ended in a pointy little spire. In front of it was a ceramic beast that looked much like the little horse—as though time and passing fads had changed it so much that it could be a camel or horse, or perhaps a goat.

"It is the Flowery Pagoda," Jade said, seeing him look at it. "It is said that the Buddha statue within is a marvel to behold. Do you wish to see it?"

Nigel shook his head. "Perhaps another time," he said, then realized what he had said and sighed. "I hope that if your brother—that is, when your brother wins his throne back, he'll grant me a pass, so that I can visit China. For now, I want to do what I must do, and return the rubies to their proper place as soon as possible."

Jade shot him a quick look and smiled. "I'm sure my brother will give you a pass to visit China," she said. "We owe you much." She blushed slightly.

Feeling bad, as though he were holding their debt to him over their heads, he said softly, "No, it will all be more than repaid if you allow me to see China. Remember, I used to dream of traveling and never thought it would happen."

She smiled at him—a fugitive expression. They'd now climbed down the hills far enough that they were looking at the lowest street that ran along between the city and the Pearl River. On the river, in barges and boats and improvised rafts of different kinds, appeared to be another city—a floating one, but just as populous. From the look of most of the boats, Nigel wondered if they ever moved. In fact, they were so closely packed together, it seemed if one wanted to move, all the others must, perforce, be dislocated.

Jade drove along the waterfront, passing knots of Chinese businessmen engaged in conversation, and other strolling groups. Nigel was too unacquainted with the culture to identify most of the passersby, but he thought they looked more well-to-do than pedestrians in other districts.

From the boats on the water rose exactly the same noise as if it were another part of the city—turbulent and routine, filled with crying children, with screaming women, with calling men, with the noises of work and leisure.

Jade drove until they were at a narrower point in the river.

"I beg your pardon," she said, "but I did not think we needed witnesses for this event."

She smiled a little. "I have no idea how to do this," she added as she climbed down from the carriage.

"If you are looking for guidance from me, I'm afraid you must be disappointed, for I've never, in my experience, varied though it's been, woken a single river."

She sighed. "We shall have to improvise together, then."

As they approached the river, Nigel reached between the buttons on his shirt, and fished for the little leather bag suspended on a string from his neck. From within, he took the ruby, which, being cloaked, looked rather dull and dingy. He held it carefully in his palm.

"I suppose," he told Jade, "we will have to uncloak it. And your power signature, too."

"I assumed there is no other way," Jade said.

"Well, then, we might as well do it rapidly."

"Wait," she said, and grabbed at his wrist. "You must know first that I expect us to be attacked by Zhang as soon as you decloack that ruby or very shortly after. He will sense the power and will come for it like a bee to honey. And if he sees my power signature with it . . ."

"What do you propose we should do?" Nigel asked.

"You? Nothing. Let me battle with him entirely on my own. Remember, I have dragon powers that more than match his dragon powers. I can defeat him."

"But your powers of transformation have been destroyed," he said. "By whatever it was the Tiger Clan gave you."

"And restored by one of those pills I took."

"Are you sure?"

"Quite sure. I could feel the magic returning."

Nigel nodded. "Then I am going to pull away the

cloaking of the ruby's power now and you decloak your power signature. I trust you to call the dragon. Is the dragon the spirit of the river?"

"Yes," Jade said. "The more ancient dragons had the power to call on rivers and to rule over rivers. They became...fused with the rivers, their bodies and minds and their magic a part of the river's flow. If I understand correctly what the oracle told me, some of them became the rivers themselves, and as unthinking and mindless as if they were just a body of water. From what I understand, if my dynasty is to rule again, we will have to wake them."

Nigel raised the ruby and, with his other hand, performed the minimal gesture necessary to pull away the cloaking of its power. In the next moment, the ruby glowed, its light shining forth and reaching into the river and through the river.

The water of the river, which had been a heavy, dull green—making Nigel think that the river must serve not only as water supply, but also as sewer and rubbish heap to the entire city—now glowed through with red light and became, itself, jewellike. It resembled the fusing of emerald and ruby, shining with a bright, interior light.

Jade seemed to have forgotten how to speak for at least a moment, and then took a deep breath, as though she were drowning. "Spirit of the river, oh ancient dragon, Grandfather and Ancestor, come forth from the depths to listen to the voice of Red Jade, sister of the Dragon Emperor, daughter of the Dragon Emperor. Your humble servant."

For a long, held-breath moment, nothing happened. Then the water of the river surged, and waves formed. From downriver, where the concentration of boats was, they heard wood knocking upon wood.

And then, suddenly, it looked as though the waters of the river rose vertically—a tower of red and green.

Nigel dropped the ruby at his feet, and knelt immediately to pick it up. When he looked up he realized the tower of red and green was actually a glimmering red-and-green dragon, about ten times larger than Jade's dragon form, but having the same mischievous catlike face that all Chinese dragons seemed to possess, and a half-puzzled, half-amused grin.

"What do you wish, oh Granddaughter, that you have woken me from centuries of dreams, and brought a jewel of power from the other side of the world?"

Jade, audibly nervous, cleared her throat. "I wish, oh Grandfather, that you speak for me and for my brother and for my dynasty in the council of dragons, when it meets to confirm my brother Wen as True Emperor of All Under Heaven."

The mischievous cat face grinned. "It will be done, oh Granddaughter."

As it had appeared, it vanished, in a whoosh, leaving waves that denoted it had once more plunged beneath the water.

Nigel, his hand trembling, cloaked the ruby. But there was no one waiting, and they did not see any blue dragons in the sky.

"I wonder why not," Jade said, as they resumed their carriage. "Surely we've left a wide enough trail for anyone to follow. And he knows my power signature."

"Perhaps you wounded him so much that he had to go somewhere to recover?"

"I very much doubt it," Jade replied. "Villains are never that easy to kill."

PLANNING THE STRIKE

"Now," Zhang said. *He sat in a room in Hong Kong* and scanned the mainland with his power. "Now I can feel her power."

But the colonel who had been assigned to him—and Zhang did not like it at all, for it proved that they did not trust him—shook his head.

"My dear sir," he said, in a bored tone. "Don't you realize they are waking the rivers? The river dragons would maul us all if we interfered with her now."

"But then . . ." Zhang said, his hands clenching tight, "how are we to recover the other ruby at all?"

The colonel smiled, a slow, supercilious smile. "Well," he said, "after they wake the rivers, as our students of Magic Tradition tell us, they must go to where the palace of Yu the Great used to stand, so that her brother will be confirmed Emperor."

"Her brother will never survive the underworld."

The colonel looked at his nails, as if they presented a fascinating prospect. "No, of course not. But don't you see? That leaves us free to capture the sister and the British traitor. And then we will reward you." He looked at Zhang. "I think you must find where the palace of Yu was, don't you?"

Zhang nodded. He didn't like being held prisoner, and he didn't like the Englishmen. But his only hope for power lay in finding this palace and ambushing Red Jade.

And then he would deal with the Englishmen as they deserved. He'd let the pure of heart Englishman—he knew the colonel had already assigned one, and he hoped he was pure enough—pick up the ruby, then he'd take the boy far away. And then the Englishmen—and the world—would bow to him.

MAIDEN PERILOUS

龙

"You didn't kidnap her?" St. Maur asked Captain Corridon, who looked at him in astonishment.

"Oh, I did. Or I thought I had. Now I wonder if I did, or if she was playing me all along."

Peter felt sorry for the boy. In his life as an anarchist, he'd spent quite a lot of time chasing and killing Secret Service men. But this one—though Peter had called on a few friends and gathered a dossier for him—wasn't truly a man. He was barely more than a boy. So far, he'd been engaged in simply fetching and carrying messages and papers, and in taking word here and there of this and that. From what Peter was given to understand, he'd performed nobly, but Peter thought he was now out of his depth.

"Where can she have gone?" he asked.

Corridon clutched at his red hair. "I don't know. And I tell you—"

He stopped, as if he'd realized he was about to give away more of his feelings than he intended to.

"And you tell me?"

"I just want her back," Corridon said, miserably. "I

just want to know that she is safe. I brought her here . . . What if she falls in the hands of someone who is unscrupulous and who . . . and who hurts her or sells her to a brothel or . . ."

Peter started to realize that whatever else Corridon was, he was not in this simply as a means of advancing his career. Or, at least, he hadn't taken Hettie from her parents simply as a means of obtaining information from them. No. It was quite clear that, whatever else was happening, Captain Corridon's heart had been touched—and deeply, too—by the Perigord chit.

"You were fairly asking for it, you know?" he said, not sure of which of the perils he spoke: losing Hettie or falling in love with her. "Her parents tell me she's quite a spirited handful. You approached the whole thing very cavalierly, as if she were no more than a young chit with no more knowledge of the world than a baby."

"I know," Corridon moaned. "I was stupid. But . . . but I got a glimpse of this conspiracy, and you'll pardon me, because I would guess you are involved in it." He looked around as if to make sure no one was within sight, then continued. "It has to be a giant conspiracy against the queen, something more complex than was ever assembled."

As Corridon expounded on what he saw as the lineaments of a giant, international, interconnected conspiracy, Peter at first had trouble not laughing. And in the end—and though it was biologically impossible—he found himself saying, with a catch in his voice, "Son, don't you see that it is nothing like that?"

Corridon looked at him, blankly. Peter told him, "It

is nothing but friends and... and people knocked together by necessity or desire to acquire the rubies. They—we—came to realize that the rubies were more than the ambition of any sovereign or any group."

The young man seemed bowled over by this idea. He first frowned at Peter, then his mouth dropped open. "But the queen wants them."

"Well," Peter said, "even the empress on whose empire the sun never sets has to go wanting now and then."

"But..." Corridon said. He swallowed. "I'm Her Majesty's soldier. It is my duty to obtain the rubies for her."

Peter sighed. "I can quite see you imagine it is. However, you will have to decide which is the more important duty—to serve the queen or to make sure the universe doesn't dissolve into its component parts."

Corridon shook his head. "How can I even be sure you're telling the truth?"

"You can't, but I shall make a deal with you. Even now, I'm sure, my colleague is somewhere in China, seeking to recover the jewel he lost. When he's done, he will take it and its twin to the avatar in the heart of Africa. I will endeavor to get you there for that moment, before, with the power of both rubies, the villagers conceal themselves and the rubies from the eyes of the curious forever. I will take you into the cave, where the rubies reside. If you can withstand their shine and their power, which—trust me—can sear into the souls of more hardened men than you, then I will accept that you must take them to the queen. I will even help you. I give you my word on it."

Corridon's eyes searched Peter's face and seemed, at last, satisfied with what they found there. He nodded once. "What do I have to do for this?"

"Well," Peter said, "not denounce me as a were—at least not unless you hear I've taken to feasting on humans. Right now, I'm no danger to anyone but the occasional stray sheep, and my wife punishes me for that by teasing me mercilessly. And do not denounce anyone else, either. Oh, and help me restore Hettie to her parents, where I've convinced my wife to stay for now." He gave Corridon a jaundiced look. "The sad thing is that I think my wife, Sofie, Lady St. Maur, will become quite fond of Hettie and yourself. You both seem to be rogues of the first water."

Corridon looked confused. "But how can I help you restore Hettie to her parents if I do not know where she is?"

"Ah," Peter said. "You see, I have a dragon eye."

"Of cour—"

"No," Peter said, and pulled the object out of his pocket, holding it in his hand, shining deep and green. "The other one. When a dragon sacrifices it, in this way, it becomes the most powerful scrying instrument on Earth. It will show us where Hettie is, right enough."

THE DRAGON EMPEROR RETURNS

They'd slept, and made love, and slept again on and off all evening. In that cave, away from everyone else, Third Lady and Wen had enjoyed their long delayed nuptials. They'd even tried some of the things from those long-ago etchings. Only most of it seemed too formal and too hard to achieve properly, and they'd simply settled for coupling, clumsily and enthusiastically, filled with lust and love for each other.

Third Lady woke in the darkness, aware of being observed by her husband's attentive and tender gaze. The fire, which they'd fed two more times, had now utterly died down. And Wen was looking at her. "I think," he said. "It is time we head back. I do not know how long we stayed in the underworld. I'd guess not long, since the fire here was still burning, but long enough. And any minute now there will be an alarm on the boats, as they realize I am missing. I would hate to think to what madness my absence might tempt them. I'd like to tell you there is absolutely no way they will try to find Zhang, turn to him. But somehow . . ."

"If one branch of the tree disappears, they will look for the other branch," Third Lady said.

"Just so."

They dressed quickly and quietly, by the fairy lights twinkling on the ceiling of the cavern, and cleaned up the place, leaving it as they had found it.

"It could be centuries, you know," Third Lady said, "before anyone needs it again."

"I would hope so," Wen said. "I wouldn't like to think trips to the underworld are all that common."

Later, in the rowboat, crossing the black night, they talked. "We must go to the record boat," Wen said, "and find out for sure where Yu's palace was. Only that will allow us to be there when it rises again."

"We also need to find out where the council of dragons is supposed to take place," Third Lady said.

"Assuredly the record boat will have that, too. The records of the rest of China have been burned several times over, but we still retain all the records we brought from our palace when the first usurpers attacked. And we've only added to it. We will find out."

Third Lady lowered her head. "I hope so. Because I would hate to think that we will never find Lady Jade again."

Wen laughed in that way she was just getting used to. "My tomboy of a sister will find her way back," he said. "And I think I owe her and you the greatest debt of gratitude a man has ever owed two women."

They rowed calmly through the night sky, until they got near the Dragon Boats, when they realized there was some great panic. People were running about, from boat to boat, and from all the boats a lamentation rose. Third Lady recognized it, and her hair stood on end.

It was the lament for a dead emperor—all the women and maidens of the clan ululating in unison.

WAKING THE YANG-TSE

龙

They flew from Canton to the Yang-tse, close to Hangchow, with Nigel straddling the back of Jade's dragon form and clutching a satchel with all her clothes and other necessities—such as soap—which she'd procured in Canton. It still appeared grossly immoral, but there didn't seem to be a faster and less conspicuous way to travel. They'd eaten in Canton, and then flown through the night, largely invisible, mostly over sleeping China.

Here and there, rarely, a cluster of villages broke the darkness with the glow of fires or paper lanterns or magelights. But above all, throughout all, there was darkness and the glistening ribbon of the Yang-tse coming into view as morning approached.

As dawn broke, Nigel could see that the river sat in the middle of a vast delta plain, planted with rice fields. Before they'd embarked on this leg of their journey, Jade—who apparently felt she needed to be his guide—had informed him, in a tight-lipped way, that the cultivation of rice had been introduced to China by Yu the Great, her first recorded ancestor. He didn't so much care about all that, but he wanted to know now which village this one was, or that one, and who operated the boats on the river, and how far away from here her people lived. But he said nothing because he knew that Jade in her dragon form could not answer at all, or only with great difficulty.

They came at last to a part of the river, just outside Hangchow, where it was relatively quiet. A few junks floated far off in the river, and they might go back and report disturbances and dragons, but they would not be so shocked that they would turn against Jade or Nigel.

After they landed, Nigel gave Jade her clothes and turned his back. Seeing her naked was more temptation than a mortal man should have to endure. The desire to hold her in his arms was almost overwhelming, and he thought very highly of himself that he managed to control it.

When she was dressed, she touched him, softly, on the shoulder, and together they approached the Yangtse and held the ruby over the river.

"Elder of the river, Ancestor, Grandfather," Jade began.

Before the words were fully uttered, a huge, red dragon emerged from the river, towering over them, fully overturning one of the junk boats nearby. The glow of the ruby enveloped him as he thundered at them from above, "I know who you are and I know why you're here. I've seen you in my dream."

Jade dropped to her knees and kowtowed, and Nigel thought it wise to do the same. "We meant no harm,"

Jade said. "Indeed, we did not. We are just in search of your vote in the council of dragons."

"You have it," he said, somehow still sounding angry. "We need a true dragon dynasty again. I've been so somnolent, with the energy of the Dragon Throne blocked, that I think I slept away the last six centuries and forgot to change my course twice."

And then he plunged back under the water, as huge waves splashed all around.

Nigel cloaked the ruby again. "I don't know," he said, "if I should feel better that Zhang hasn't found us, or worse."

"Worse," Jade said. "I don't think it is that he hasn't found us, but that he knows his power alone cannot defeat us—not when my dragon power far exceeds his. I think he is trying to find allies who will lend him power. And I think he will meet us wherever the council of dragons is supposed to be. We must make sure to ask that of the elder of the Huang He, or, as you call it, the Yellow River. He will know. And I think that we must be present for the council to work."

"But who or what can Zhang bring to the council that will make such a difference?"

"I don't know," Jade said. "I just know that he will not have given up on achieving my family's throne. His plan of accomplishing it from the underworld has clearly failed. I confess, I am surprised, but it must have failed, because otherwise, how could Wen's power be gone from me? Zhang failed to keep Wen's soul sequestered, which would have killed him eventually, so now he must achieve it in some other way. I wish I could penetrate his mind, but I don't think anyone can who is not wholly born to intrigue."

Nigel sighed. "Well, born to intrigue I am not. But he doesn't seem to be following us, so what would you like to do now?"

"Go to Hangchow," she said. "And find a place to rest and wait until nighttime. Whether Zhang is following us or not, I'd prefer not to leave too obvious a trail by flying during the day."

HOW TO RECOVER MAIDENS NOT IN DISTRESS

Corridon was skeptical at first when the eye of the dragon showed them a middle-class neighborhood, with row upon row of British houses, and battalions of Chinese gardeners looking after the immaculate lawns. But he'd insisted on accompanying Peter to the door.

Upon their knock, the door was opened by a Chinese butler, and when Peter—with his impeccable accent, his impeccable manners and his almost too good looks—informed the butler that he wished to speak to Madame, Corridon heard an echo of Hettie's voice from deep within the house. He would recognize that voice anywhere.

The Earl of St. Maur had told him, gravely, that since Lord Marshlake had married a maid, he might not wish to reclaim his title or to return to polite society. And Corridon had made an appalling discovery. He didn't mind. He didn't at all care, provided first of all that Hettie was returned to her parents, and was safe. Then he could somehow convince her parents— and her—that he was not the worst villain alive and that he wished to court her, earnestly and traditionally.

To that end, Lord St. Maur had offered to help him by speaking to her parents.

Now the lady of the house came to the door. Corridon appraised her easily enough as upper middle class, who, in England, would have a mid-large house and perhaps two or three servants. But here in the reaches of the Orient, she commanded servants almost without count.

She started a little at the sight of the two men. Then she looked directly at Corridon and pursed her lips. Lord St. Maur smiled, but there was nothing that could have prepared Corridon for what Peter said next. "Ah, madame, I understand my little niece has imposed on you most terribly."

"You . . . your niece?" she said, obviously taken aback.

"Yes, Hettie Perigord, as she calls herself, though I beg leave to inform you she's the only daughter of the Earl of Marshlake."

The lady looked at him, speechless, and St. Maur continued. "She is, you see, a very naughty girl. She convinced this boy, a longtime family friend, to elope with her, but then in the carpetship she changed her mind, and she has, you see . . . She has quite cast him off. I don't know under what manner of falsehood she has imposed upon you."

"She said he had kidnapped her," the lady said, her voice tight. "You must forgive me, but how do I know you are . . . I mean . . . how do I know who you are and that you are not in league with him?"

"A very just question, madame," he said. "Permit

me to present you with my card." He extended her a card with his title, style and address. "If you wish to ask at Cooks, with whom I normally travel, or at Lloyds, with whom I bank, I am sure they will be glad to confirm my identity."

"No, but ... Oh, this is very vexing. Hettie, come over here this minute," the lady said.

"I would bet even now she's making her way out the back door," St. Maur said, quite coolly.

The lady issued a few shouted commands, and moments later three servants appeared, escorting a rumpled Hettie between them. "Just as you said," one of the servants reported. "She was trying to escape through the back door."

"And why shouldn't I?" Hettie said, defiantly. "I don't know who his accomplice is, but this man is the most odious man in the world." She pointed at Corridon, her eyes blazing. "He kidnapped me. He tried to marry me by force."

"Oh, Hettie," St. Maur said, his voice filled with the amusement of a relative dealing with a cherished but naughty younger person. "How can you say so? If he wished to marry you by force, he could have done it in Cape Town, or in any of the other places around there. Or even aboard the carpetship. Confess you flew off with him on a romantic fling because you wanted to be on a carpetship without your parents for the first time in your life."

"Madame," Hettie said, turning to her protector. "I beg you to believe I don't even know who the man is who is hectoring me so shamelessly."

"Oh, certainly," St. Maur said. "That's a likely one. You don't know your own uncle. Your father has sent me, Hettie, to claim you and that disreputable doll you call Mrs. Beddlington."

Hetty's eyes showed surprise, and she seemed to be wavering.

St. Maur smiled, crossing his arms on his chest. "Indeed, your long-suffering parents told me to come and get you with all possible speed and that all would be forgiven."

"He told you about Mrs. Beddlington," she said, pointing at Corridon.

"Hardly," St. Maur said. "I know my memory is abominable, but I could never have forgotten that disreputable toy you used to drag to my estate at Summercourt." He smiled at her. "Come, come, Hettie, your father told me to tell you he's forgiven you for causing him to break his pipe, which was just starting to acquire such a nice color, too."

Hettie's expression showed her understanding that St. Maur must, indeed, have been sent by her parents—or at least that's what Corridon saw. "And your mother, while talking to me, in her agitation, dropped her favorite teapot, the one with the red and yellow roses. But they're willing to forgive you all the broken crockery if you will just let me take you home to them."

For a moment, it looked like she would fight, but then he saw the understanding that he knew things Corridon couldn't have told him slowly dawning in her eyes. She had to understand he came from her parents, and if she trusted her parents, she would know St. Maur, therefore, must mean well for her. She nodded once, and then she ran into the house and returned carrying a wicker suitcase. She dropped a curtsey to her bewildered hostess. "Only, forgive me, madame," she said, "for imposing on you so dreadfully. But you see, I had thought better of my adventure, and I thought—"

To Corridon's surprise, the woman laughed. "Ah, child," she said. "We were all young once."

And Corridon thought it was the glow of noble names which burnished the scene, plus Peter Farewell, Earl St. Maur's manners, so polished and suave that made the woman unable to regard any of them as villains.

They left her behind and walked down the street, and then St. Maur said, "We must find a place for me to change."

"Cannot we travel in a carpetship?" Corridon asked, unwilling to think that he would be consorting with someone who was clearly and unavoidably a were-creature, while the creature was in his shifted form. It destroyed all his chances at denying that he knew of St. Maur's condition.

"No, far more expensive, and it would take much longer. And I promised Miss Perigord's parents that I'd get her back to them as soon as humanly possible."

"But what can you mean?" Hettie said. "How else can you get me to my parents but on a carpetship?"

St. Maur sighed, and bowed deeply. "I can get you home on dragon-back," he said.

Corridon didn't know how Hettie would react, and he watched her apprehensively. But the shriek that escaped her was one of pure excitement, and when she spoke, it was in a soft voice. "Dragon-back. What an adventure."

THE BOATS FLY

Third Lady could barely bring the boat down, her hands were shaking so hard. She knew that Wen was safe, but even if the others had noticed they were missing, why would they assume Wen was dead?

Slowly, she brought the boat down alongside the Dragon Boats, and they stepped out side by side. At first no one noticed them, but as they approached the Imperial barge, people turned to look. And stepped back.

"He is a ghost," First Lady screamed, and Third Lady thought that though she was obliged by the rules of society and family and tradition to be respectful of First Lady and call her Elder Sister, she'd always thought the woman was a blithering idiot. Also, now that Third Lady knew that Wen had not consummated his marriage with either of the other two, she was less willing to bow to tradition. Defiantly, she put her arm in Wen's as they walked toward the barge. He shook her hand off his arm, and instead enveloped it in his.

A look over his shoulder, and an impish smile at her, and he turned a forbidding countenance to the rest of the Dragon Boat denizens. "I am not a ghost. What is the meaning of this impertinence?"

First Lady and Second Lady were crying inconsolably in each other's arms. Everyone else was running around like madmen. And through the madness came Grasshopper Zhang, his eyes very wide. "You know what they say," he said. "No ghost can stand being bound." And then in almost whispering voice, "Milord, may I hold your wrists?"

For a moment, Wen hesitated. And for a moment, Third Lady considered that this could be a plot to ambush or kill Wen. But though Grasshopper was a Zhang, she'd seen him grow up during her years on the Dragon Boats, and she didn't think he had it in him to commit treason. Apparently Wen didn't either, because he extended his hands to the boy, who held Wen's wrists in a tight grip for a moment and then let them go. "He's not a ghost," he reported. "I held his wrists tight and he did not try to change shapes, nor did he became a gas or other noxious substance."

"Of course I'm not a ghost," Wen said, his voice sounding equal parts amused and bewildered—a combination the rest of the Dragon Boats had never heard from him, and which was, in fact, enough to stop those closer to them from carrying on in hysterics and pay attention. Calmness spread outward from that center—except for First and Second Ladies, of course.

"First Lady," Wen said, sternly. "Second Lady. Please cease your weeping. It is I, and I am not a ghost." Into the sudden calm that their obedience to his order brought, he said, "Grasshopper, why would anyone think me a ghost?"

"Because the boats stopped flying, milord. We couldn't find you, and then we tried to order the lifeboats to fly, just to see ... and ..."

"Oh," Wen said, and Third Lady understood. All the lifeboats were grounded when the emperor died, until the new one took power and made the barges lift, which allowed the small rowboats to fly again.

"But our rowboat flew," Wen said.

"Which is part of the reason everyone thought you were ghosts, milord," Grasshopper said.

"Oh. No. I think I used my magic without meaning to. You see, my Third Lady, at great peril and through means I shall describe later, restored my health. As my power returned to me, it must have taken it from the ring my sister, Jade, is wearing. So her power is no longer valid to make the boats fly." He shrugged, casually. "It just means I must make the barges fly anew."

He turned to Precious Lotus. "Come with me, Third Lady," he said, giving her his hand again.

She was the only one standing by him as he said the ancient prayer to make the boats fly. And the only one who knew he had held his breath between the concluding words of the prayer and the moment when the barges rose, swiftly and smoothly, into the dark night sky.

From the boats there erupted a cheer, and Wen turned to Third Lady. "My dear," he said, very casually, "if you'd do me the honor of letting me visit your apartments tonight?"

She smiled back. "Gladly. I always sleep much better with you next to me."

Hand in hand they turned, as the barges set gently down again upon the water. Amid the kowtowing courtiers they walked. Before crossing over to the women's barge, Wen stopped and fixed his gaze on Grasshopper's younger brother, who had served as his opium preparer. "Throw the pipe and all that goes with it," he said, "over the side of the barge. It won't be needed again."

THE YELLOW RIVER

The dragon who rose out of the Huang He was the largest of them all. He was also golden, as though he'd been carved of pure metal, and he spoke smoothly and gently, like someone who is so old that he has left all human passions behind.

"I am awake, Daughter," he told Jade. "And I will speak for you in the council of dragons."

Trembling, in front of a creature more magnificent than any she even knew existed, Jade bowed and said, "Where is the council of dragons to be, oh Grandfather?"

He seemed puzzled. "You do not know?" he asked.

"No, Grandfather."

"You must go to the Yangcheng Lake, where the palace of your ancestor Yu once stood. There you must stand and call to us. Then we will appear and bless your brother. And with the unanimous vote of all the dragons, the palace of your ancestor will rise out of the Earth again, and your brother will sit on the throne of his ancestors. You do not need to worry about all the smaller rivers, the tributaries and the lakes. I will wake those dragons with my call. In our dreams, we already agreed that it is time China has a were dynasty again. There will be difficult times ahead—very difficult— and the Mandate of Heaven is that China be made secure."

They thanked him profusely, then turned away from the river, and Jade looked at Nigel, thinking how foolish she was that, even though he looked perfectly handsome as a Chinese man, she longed to see him with his ice-pale hair again, and his blue eyes. What a fool she was. He was not hers. His appearance would revert when he got the antidote pill from a Fox Clan member. But she would never get to see him in that aspect again. And she could not be his.

"I hope . . ." Nigel said, softly. "That is, you told me that your brother would allow me to visit China again. I hope I will be allowed to see you again as well. And to . . . present my regards."

"Of course," Jade said, her smile as brave as it was brittle. But in her secret mind, all she could think was that she would see him again—perhaps—but he would be just a foreigner visiting. And she would probably be married off to some man of her brother's choosing.

HOME IS THE MAIDEN

龙

There had been tears, which of course Peter had ex-
pected. Hettie and her parents had fallen upon one another with glad cries and some weeping.

And then Peter had introduced Corridon and explained both the delusion the young man labored over
and the fact that he begged the right to court their
daughter, properly this time.

It had been touch and go, but Marshlake—who,
during the period of Peter's absence, had decided he
would return to England and reclaim his family's dignity—had ended by laughing and telling the boy that
they'd all made mistakes.

He had been, he later told Peter, swayed by the fact
that not only had Corridon kept strictly separate rooms
from his daughter, but also was even willing to condone
flying on a dragon for the sake of his concern for Hettie.

As for calling on Hettie, Marshlake thought both the
children were much too young. Hettie was too head-
strong and had not even had a London season, and
Corridon was far from established in his career and
not even five-and-twenty yet. But as Corridon was a

neighbor, if he could get himself placed in England and perhaps not in the Secret Service, they would surely see each other now and again. And in two or three years, who knew? They might very well end up together, after all.

After that, it had fallen to Peter to try to convince Lady St. Maur that she wasn't needed on an expedition to the interior of Africa, to the village where the avatar awaited its ruby eyes.

"But I wouldn't miss it for the world," she said, with a grin. "And I'm sure you can transport me and Corridon. Why, it will be no trouble at all. And you wouldn't deny me seeing the avatar, would you? Not if I earnestly desired to see it? I don't believe you could."

Unfortunately, Peter realized he, too, didn't believe he could.

THE LAST GAMBIT

They would never have approached Yangcheng from the air if they'd known what awaited them. Unfortunately, as they saw the expanse of the lake shine from a distance—and, at the same time, a slew of rugs, each of them carrying several English soldiers, rise from the ground to surround them—Nigel regretted the fact he did not have the gift of foretelling.

"Land," one of the soldiers on a nearby rug said, "or we shall use our powersticks, which have been charged against weres."

Jade landed. The English soldiers surrounded them.

"Give us the ruby. Slowly, please," one of them, an officer—though Nigel was too tired and confused to know which—said. "Else we shall have to fire."

And Jade, speaking through a dragon mouth, her words bitten off and deformed by teeth and tongue not designed to pronounce words, said, "You cannot give them the ruby. You cannot let it fall into their hands."

"I must, Jade. Else they will kill us. And then they will still take the ruby." His searching eyes had discerned the crouching shape of another Chinese dragon among them. Zhang. So this was his gambit. And it was just possible that he'd won. If Jade and Nigel were killed, what would stop him from killing Wen—if the emperor was even back from the underworld—and taking over the country? He had delivered to the English that which he'd promised—both of the rubies that held all the power of the universe. He'd now get to rule China for the infinitesimal period it would last, before the rubies were delivered to the queen and the queen tore the universe apart.

And then, like a sound out of a dream, Nigel heard, from above him, the sound of sails flapping in the wind. Everyone looked up simultaneously.

High above but descending fast was an army of barges, and junks, all converging on them.

A BROTHER'S DUTY

龙

"I told you that was Zhang's last gambit," Third Lady said. "I could sense it, even though foretelling is not one of my stronger powers." She was dressed in pants and jacket and stood beside him, holding a saber.

Wen had told her that she could not join the battle, but she was allowed to stand within the Imperial barge and defend it, should that become needed. "But I don't think it will," he said. He was attired in his best jacket and pants, and the few days that had passed since his return had given an even greater glow to his eyes, a healthier color to his skin. In fact, it had amused Third Lady—busy researching the location and protocol for the council of dragons—to watch First Lady and Second Lady trying to get his attention and his favors. They'd seemed quite content to ignore him before.

Wen had told her that, once this was resolved—once he was safely on the throne of China—he would gladly divorce his first two wives and make her his first lady. He would even admit publicly that his first two unions had never been consummated, and he was quite willing to find the two ladies, against whom he bore no malice, decent and honorable husbands.

Third Lady, who also bore them no malice, thought that, doubtless, her father would think that this was a great advance for the Fox Clan. But she did not care. She had what she wanted—Wen's love, and the hope of a child by him sometime in the future.

Now she watched as Wen expertly, using the hand signals propagated from boat to boat, commanded the barges to form a circle, roughly encompassing the British rugs.

"They're trying to rise," Third Lady said.

Wen gestured. The junks, much more numerous than the rugs—much more numerous than the barges, too—came to hover above the barges, effectively forming a ceiling above which the rugs could not lift, even as the barges settled in a ring around the rugs.

"Surrender," the British captain shouted, with more courage than sanity, "or I will order my men to shoot, and we have were-loaded powersticks."

"I understand that," Wen shouted back. He spoke Chinese, as had the British commander. "However, those barges will stop your charges from reaching my men. And your charges are finite, while I have a lot of men. Fire for all you're worth, but afterward, I'll let my dragons attack. Have any of you heard of mercy from a flying junk pirate? Particularly when you've kidnapped the sister of the leader?"

There was a long period of hesitation. One or two powersticks fired, their charges losing themselves harmlessly between the boats. But in the end, there was the sound of powersticks being laid down.

From the middle of the English rugs, Zhang rose. "I will not be denied so easily," he said. "I have not waited for so long for nothing. You must fight me."

But Jade must have changed, because her human voice came from down where Third Lady could not even see her. "Rivers of China, dragons of the rivers, dragon children of the first dragon, come and meet in council now, I ask you."

Suddenly, without word or warning, dragons rose. Only these were bigger dragons than Third Lady had ever seen. Much bigger than Wen. Some of them were bigger than the barges. Red and yellow, green and gold and silver, the dragons gathered around the circle of the barges.

"Oh Emperor Wen," the dragons said in one voice, which made the Earth shake, "we have agreed. The Mandate of Heaven decrees it. You shall sit on the Dragon Throne."

There was a moment of silence, then from below came a voice that spoke Chinese but that, nonetheless, managed to sound incredibly British as it said, "I must have the other ruby now, thank you. No, I don't think you want to hold on to it. You see, I am about to remove the cloak from its power. Remember Charlemagne had his man fetch it from the depths of Africa. He didn't go himself. Those whose heart is tainted by ambition will die if they hold the ruby. The only reason the rubies are in danger at all is that intelligent, evil men can use pure but misguided men to obtain the jewels for them. They can drain the rubies, but they cannot touch them. So why would you wish to touch it?"

THE POWER OF
THE RUBIES

Jade had changed and invoked the dragons, and the dragons had confirmed Wen. While Jade dressed, in the midst of an assembled circle of Britishers and Chinese, putting on her clothes almost casually, Nigel realized her nudity disturbed him more than it bothered her. Or, at least, it disturbed him that she should be naked where other eyes could see her. He had handed her the clothes he'd carried as soon as he could, but she dressed unhurriedly. And Nigel realized perhaps she was keeping the British minds occupied while she waited for the palace to rise.

After a while, he said, "It isn't rising. Why not? They made your brother the emperor."

"I think," Jade said, quietly—so quietly no one but those closest to them would hear her—"that you have to use the rubies."

And then Nigel had demanded that the commander of the British detachment give him the ruby. He was sure he had it, for no one, not even the most casual of Britishers, would allow a native to hold on to such a thing.

He finished with, "I have seen my own brother, Carew Oldhall—" and smiled at the flinch. "I see you know the name—I've seen him, as I said, burned to cinders before my very eyes, as he touched the ruby with his overambitious hands. That was his undoing. And I can do the same to you, easily enough. If you have ambition. If your heart is not pure. If you are not merely acting on orders. How pure is your heart? Can you swear to it?"

He'd taken Soul of Fire from his pocket, and held it in his hand, in plain view, and removed the cloaking from it, so that the light shone full on everyone. He knew that light felt like it could penetrate the hearts of men, and make their vilest desires known to themselves. Such a form of self-knowledge, he'd seen, was the worst punishment. He'd intended to remove the cloaking from the ruby before he handed it over, but he could not be sure that among the Englishmen there wasn't more than one motivated only by a pure sense of duty and honor. On those, the rubies would not work at all, which meant there was a very good chance that he would have lost the rubies. And, quite possibly, his and Jade's lives.

Now he watched as Zhang moaned and tried to crawl away, and the captain faltered and reached for something from his breast pocket. "Take it, take it," he said, and flung it at Nigel with a shaking hand.

Nigel removed its cloak as the ruby fell onto his palm.

Holding a ruby in each hand, the brilliance from them burning the entire area with light, like a twin sunset, he called, "Ancestral palace of the Dragon Emperors, rise!"

There was a quake under their feet. People screamed and jumped out of the way as the ground cracked and trembled, and trees moved, and the lake spilled.

Nigel fell, holding on for dear life to the two rubies, thinking that the Earth would presently swallow him.

When he dared look up again, he knelt, incongruously, in the middle of the manicured grounds of the vastest palace he'd ever seen. There were marble buildings in the center, and small marble pavilions standing amid clumps of trees and flowering bushes. Amid them moved lumbering clay men.

"Thank you, Grandfather Yu," one of the men on the barges, the one Nigel assumed was the emperor because he seemed to give the orders, shouted. And, following the emperor's gaze, Nigel saw a shadowy golden bridge and a couple crossing it, hand in hand.

They turned and waved, then disappeared, seemingly in midair.

Over in a corner, the huge dragons were eating something. Nigel looked at Jade. She shuddered. "Zhang," she said.

"Dragons are cannibals?" he asked, appalled.

"These are not quite dragons," Jade said, softly. "Not like I'm a dragon. They merged with the rivers, see, and became, in a way, river gods. And the rivers eat everything, living and dead alike."

But she turned and hid her face on his shoulder.

Out of the ground, more and more clay men emerged. "What are they?" Nigel asked Jade.

She looked at the clay men and her eyes grew wide. "Soldiers. They're soldiers. All the soldiers who were buried in the tombs of emperors throughout the millennia. Clay soldiers. I should have anticipated this. I think they'll stay with Wen as long as he needs them, so he can secure the country." She gave him a sudden, dazzling smile. "It doesn't matter if you are the anointed one, with the Mandate of Heaven. You still need soldiers."

"Yes," Nigel said. "Yes." He should have felt relieved, because, given the clay-men armies, no one was going to try to steal the rubies from him now. But he felt a little light-headed and lost. He felt, in fact, as though his heart had been taken from his chest. How could he go, leave Jade behind?

Once before, in the African savannah, a woman had become his comrade in arms. But he'd never felt for her what he now felt for Jade. He never felt for anyone what he felt for Jade. It was as though she were a part of him that had accidentally wandered off. To leave her would feel like an amputation.

DUTY

Before Third Lady gave Nigel the pill that would make him look again like the foreign devil he was, she brought him to Wen. After a long conversation the night before—during the celebrations of the recovery of the throne—Third Lady had, with much difficulty, convinced Wen that his sister had lost her heart to this foreign devil.

As troublesome as it was for Wen, and as much as it might make people around him doubt that he really did have the Mandate of Heaven, Wen loved his sister, who had protected him and tried to keep him from harm when he couldn't protect himself.

So he'd told Third Lady to bring him Nigel Oldhall—even the name hurt the tongue to pronounce it—this morning. And now Nigel stood before the golden Dragon Throne, in a magnificent salon. Wen was surrounded by an escort of clay men and two dragon guardsmen, who looked distinctly uncomfortable with their new colleagues.

Nigel Oldhall should have kowtowed, of course, Third Lady thought, but he didn't know it. And all of a sudden she had a sharp doubt whether this could work. But she knew that Wen would try. And she knew that if Jade wanted this man, Jade would make sure it worked. No one could doubt the will of Lady Jade.

Oldhall did bow, and appeared genuinely awed by the magnificence of the salon. "Your Majesty," he said, "I was told you wanted to see me. I hope you don't need the rubies anymore," he said, with a note of weariness in his voice, "since I need to return them to the avatar in Africa."

"I understand," Wen said. "And I do not need them. But I do have a proposal for you."

"I listen, Your Majesty."

"You have done me a great service, and secured my kingdom for me. In fact, your work and heroism were greater than anyone's, save my wife's and my sister's. I propose that, instead of taking the potion to change your appearance, you take another, which will make you look like this permanently. And then marry my sister and stay. I shall make you lord of vast domains."

Third Lady could see that Oldhall was tempted. Desire passed behind his eyes like a storm, and left his face harsh, like a parched desert, his lips white and bloodless like those of a dead man cast to the shore. "I can't," he said. "I wish I could, but I can't. You see, I am the only surviving son of my father's house. Someone must look after my parents in their old age. Bitter as it is, I must go back."

After he had left, Third Lady told her husband, "He is a filial son. Indeed, he has every virtue Lady Jade could hope for in a husband. It is unfortunate their very virtue separates them."

And Wen, looking remote as he did when lost in thought, smiled at her and said, "Not all is lost. Remember when there is a knot, there are two ends to the string."

A ROYAL AUDIENCE

"You called me, Brother?" Jade asked. She'd been summoned to her brother's office, from which he magically directed the armies of clay men who were delivering China to his control.

Wen looked up from the map he'd been studying. Not for the first time, Jade was struck by how different he looked. How intent. How focused.

"I did call you," he said. "I have arranged your marriage."

"You ... you have?" Jade asked, faltering. She'd half expected this from her father on any given day since her adolescence. She'd never expected it from Wen.

"Yes," he said. "It is a marriage with someone I wish to reward for his loyalty, someone to whom I owe a very large favor, and someone, furthermore, who will help me stretch my diplomatic relations in a direction I wish them to go."

"But ..." Jade said. And suddenly, with swelling indignation, "But I don't wish to be married!"

"That hardly matters," Wen said. "You are my sister, and therefore your duty is to the Dragon

Throne. The Dragon Throne wishes you to marry, and you will fulfill your duty."

Jade could do nothing but agree. It had been words like those, or something much like it, that had kept the explanations locked inside her, when she wished to tell Nigel how she felt about him. It had been such words, or some much like them, that had kept her from throwing her arms around him, confessing her love, and asking him to take her back with him to his land. But she was the sister of the Dragon Emperor. And she must obey him. Yet . . .

Her feelings rose within her like bile at the back of the throat, at the thought of marrying anyone but Nigel. "I cannot, Wen. My heart is given, and once given, I cannot stand the thought of marrying anyone else. And him I cannot marry. I will always be your obedient sister and servant, but do not force me to marry."

"If you stay here," Wen said, remote, moving things about on that map of his, "then you must marry whom I tell you to marry. You are my servant, and someone I can dispose of."

"Well, then," Jade said, in sudden rebellion, convinced he would back down once she spoke. "I shall leave. I shall go to my mother's country. I'm sure I have family there. I will throw myself at their feet."

There was a sparkle of humor in Wen's eyes as he looked up, though he made his voice drily official. "If you're going to the foreign-devil land, you might as well follow my command. I wish for you to marry Nigel Oldhall."

"But..." she said, feeling her legs give. "How... You know I... He has left..."

"Only now. I know the carpetship he left in. You can change into a dragon and follow him. Your mind link should allow you to find your way to him, in any case. Just follow your heart."

CAPE TOWN

Cape Town looked harsh and white under the bright sunlight of summer, when Nigel landed, as flight magician in yet another carpetship.

He didn't say his good-byes and didn't wait around for his pay. His pay was unimportant. The carpetship had merely been a way to get him and his rubies back to Cape Town without calling undue attention.

With the carpet he'd brought from the Orient, he disembarked, and as soon as he was far enough away from the carpetship port not to interfere with their flight and landing, he took off, heading toward a destination that had beckoned him all these months.

A few more hours and he would be rid of these rubies, and could resume his interrupted life. Why did this not feel like a triumph?

As he landed atop the flat mountain where the village of the guardians lay, he heard a woman yell, "Nigel!"

Looking over, he saw Emily, who had once been his wife, and who was now the wife of Kitwana, the son of the village chief. She and Kitwana came over, hands extended.

"How well you look, Nigel," Emily said. "So tanned."

"You look wonderful, too," Nigel said, and it was true. Wrapped in a local cloth, with her dark hair unbound, and her blue eyes shining, Emily was one of the most beautiful women he had ever seen. He should have been jealous, sorry that he'd lost her.

He was neither. He felt only the echo of grief, the certainty that he would never meet anyone who would be to him what Emily was to Kitwana, and Kitwana to Emily.

"You'll never guess," Emily said. "Peter and his wife have dropped in on us, just days ago." She proceeded to tell him about some promise or other Peter had made to a young ensign.

The young ensign, a dashing redhead, poured out his story about thinking to recover the rubies for the queen. To Nigel, it was like meeting himself at the beginning of the adventure, and he was amused and saddened at how innocent he had been.

Nigel smiled at Peter and his beautiful, irreverent wife, and said everything that needed to be said. He hoped he was charming, and he hoped he shared their joy. But all he could think was that he would never have the one woman he wanted, the one woman he wished to spend the rest of his life with.

She had her own life, in another court. And doubtless, she would eventually marry at her brother's orders. And he . . . He would eventually marry to produce an heir to his domain. But until then—and even after, he suspected—he'd be alone. Truly alone. Missing part of his soul.

He tried to hand the rubies to Kitwana. "I have returned them," he said. "Now I must go back."

But Kitwana only laughed at him. "No, you must—and you will—return them to the avatar yourself. Come."

THE AVATAR

The cave leading up to the avatar had neither the tests nor the terrors Nigel remembered. Perhaps having lost both of the rubies, the statue had lost some of its power. Or perhaps they'd paid their way in through their effort once and need not do it again.

They simply walked down a subterranean passageway from the floor of the chieftain's hut—down and down, into the Earth.

Where Nigel stood, while the rubies climbed, as though of their own accord, to the eyes of the statue.

"Thank you." The words echoed in their minds, though they were not quite words. At least, Nigel heard them and he could tell from the expression of the others that they did, too. "You have served me well, and all of you have found your soul mates in this. Hold on to your love, all of you—even you, Captain Corridon. The times ahead will try the strongest of men. You and your children must be like beacons of courage and love, lighting up the world, and showing that no land is too distant, no person too different, for human love to conquer."

Nigel felt tears sting his eyes. He thought he'd found his soul mate. But he had lost her, almost immediately. He supposed this was not something one could explain to an immortal avatar.

He watched as red rays of light from the ruby enveloped Peter, who embraced his wife, Sofie, and Emily, in the shelter of Kitwana's arms.

A tear fell from Nigel's eye and rolled down his face.

"Nigel," a woman's voice said softly from behind him.

He spun around. Jade, in one of the gowns he'd bought for her in Hong Kong, was standing shyly at the entrance of the chamber. She'd pulled her hair up, as she'd worn it in his dream, and she was looking at him hesitantly, as if not sure what his reception would be.

"The man upstairs told me to come down," she said. "At least, I think that's what he told me as I dressed. I got my dresses from the Victoria Hotel before I changed into a dragon and caught up with you. That's why I'm late. Oh!"

The "Oh" came as, having torn her eyes from his face for a moment, she seemed to realize that there was a glory of light shining down on them from the ruby eyes of the avatar.

He opened his arms to her, silently. She rushed into them. And the light of the rubies enveloped them in peace and love.

CLEARING THE MIST

*Adrian Corridon stumbled down the mountain, follow-*ing the two couples. He looked at the world through eyes that felt strange, as though misted over. Only, it was the opposite of mist, really.

He wasn't sure what had happened to the other people in the avatar chamber, but to him . . .

First there had been a wind that seemed to strip all the flesh from his bones. Only not the flesh, but those things with which one cloaks one's spirit. Honor, duty, ambition.

Ambition. At the thought of it, he groaned softly. He'd thought . . . He'd thought if he only unraveled this conspiracy, he would be the most famous of the servants of Her Majesty. He would be as highly placed as a man could be who didn't sit on the throne.

Instead, had he succeeded in attaining his ambition, he would have unraveled all the universes. Feeling the power of the rubies, he could not help but know that.

As he couldn't help knowing that everything had changed when they got the rubies back into the avatar's eyes. The worlds that had spread out, in seeming copies of one another, so that each one contained less magic, now all collapsed into one world.

He felt no great difference in himself, and yet he was sure there was a difference the world over.

For almost a thousand years, the anchor of the universe had been missing. Now it was back, and the power configuration would be quite different.

Stumbling down the path, almost at the bottom of the mountain, he looked at the two couples with him, each lost in their own bliss. Both couples included a were. And now, if he understood correctly, weres controlled China. The world that forbade weres was in for a shock. The world, which had been used to a certain amount of magic, was about to get a much greater infusion from all the remnants of the collapsed worlds. Indeed, the world was about to go tumbling, head over heels, into unknown territory.

They'd reached the end of the path, and turned to the dark-haired girl and the chieftain's son waving at them from the top. The other four waved back, and Corridon did, too, to be civil. Then they stepped away from the mountain.

One step, two, and then there was a wind that seemed to wrap the mountain—a wind that was mist and that enveloped it wholly.

And then it spun ... or gave the impression of spinning, like a top, faster and faster and faster.

Where the mountain had been, there was nothing. Only jungle stretching into the distance.

"Well," Lord St. Maur said, "I think we should change and return to Cape Town. I presume you and

Jade will be having something resembling a legal wedding, Nigel?"

Corridon didn't hear what Oldhall said. He was thinking that now that the mountain was hidden, the magic was loose in the world.

And he would have to pick through his loyalties and his fears in the confusing times ahead.

Two things only could he be sure of: one, that it was his duty and privilege to protect Hettie. He would do his best to keep her safe, no matter what turmoil enveloped the world. Two, that he must never again believe what anyone told him about magic; he must examine it himself and make sure of it. And he must never again believe his own fevered dreams. From now on, he must use his mind, unclothed in self-deception or wishful thinking.

"Yes," he said. "Let us get to Cape Town as soon as we can." And he turned to face the future.

WEDDING NIGHT

They'd gotten married three times, which seemed excessive. At least, Jade counted it as three times. First, the avatar had declared them united, which must count for something. Then Kitwana's father had insisted on marrying them in a tribal ceremony, before he and his son used the power of the rubies to hide the village from mortal eyes for as long as they could keep it concealed.

"I don't know the meaning of the thing with the gourd," Jade had said afterward, as they flew back—by rug—to Cape Town.

"I think it's supposed to mean we'll have lots of children," Nigel had said, unwilling to admit he was equally puzzled. "Or perhaps that we'll never go thirsty."

They'd woken up an Anglican minister in Cape Town, and had gotten married in a small chapel, with Peter and Sofie and the Perigords as witnesses. The Perigords, who were leaving that night for England aboard a luxury carpetship, had given them the keys to their home.

"We will be selling it, of course," they said, "but you can use it tonight. Better than a hotel."

And now they stood in the Perigord's best chamber, and Nigel was seized by a horrible fear that it wouldn't work. That it would be like his night with Emily. That his heart would long to possess her, but his body wouldn't rise to the occasion.

Jade had disappeared into one of the other chambers. To change, she'd said. And he'd undressed and put on his dressing gown. And now he stood, smoking, by the window.

The door opened slowly, shyly. He heard Jade's steps. Afraid of what might happen, he forced himself to turn.

She stood by the door in a gown of silk so thin that he could see her body through it—her breasts, the swell of her hips. And she looked like everything a man had ever dreamed of—like home, and haven, and comfort. And like lust incarnate, too.

"Do you like it?" she asked.

He had trouble speaking through the knot in his throat, and his body was not having any trouble rising to the occasion. "I . . . You are the most wondrous beauty I've ever seen," he managed at last.

"Really?" She took a slow step into the room. "Third Lady had a talk with me, before I left, and she told me about all these . . . things one can do. She was a singsong girl," she added, blushing. "They teach them the theory, if not the practice."

She suddenly walked farther into the room. "Let me show you Rose Petals Atop Bamboo Stalk."

His pipe fell to the floor and shattered. They followed it down, ignoring the tobacco and shards. They did not make it to the bed for almost an hour.

And when they did, Nigel said, "I am not nearly as knowledgeable, but your dress looks like peach skin, and I would like to show you Unwrapping the Peach."

He pulled her gown up, and he started kissing her, savoring the taste of her skin, the softness of it.

How strange the world was. He had found his soul mate across the world, and she was perfect and strange and everything at once.

"Sometimes," he said, lifting his lips from her skin, "things happen far better than we could hope for."

Jade looked at him and grinned. "Yes," she said. "Now let me show you Man With Ice Hair Visits Dragon Cave."

"What?" he said.

"This," she said.

Their laughter flew, united, into the night.

COMING HOME

龙

Lord and Lady Oldhall didn't know what to make of it all. The telegram from their son Nigel, who had now been missing for many months, had been, of course, received with great joy.

"Perhaps Carew is alive, too," Lady Oldhall had said, "and will contact us again someday."

"Perhaps," her husband had said. "And he will not be foolish enough to marry some Chinese girl, whether she is the sister of the new emperor or not."

"Yes," Lady Oldhall said. "It sounds so very strange. Just like that, he tells us that Emily is gone, and that he has married a Chinese princess. I don't know what to do. I don't know what I will say to the girl. We must accept it, I guess, but what will people say?"

"Well, it must be faced," Lord Oldhall said. "They landed in London a week ago, and however much shopping they have to do, they will be upon us any moment."

At that moment, the footman appeared. "Mr. and Mrs. Nigel Oldhall," he announced, and bowed out of the way.

Nigel came first, standing in the doorway, looking so tanned and muscular he might have been Carew. But before his fond parents could make this pleasing comparison, he extended his hand and a girl came in.

She was indubitably Chinese, even if tall and very well dressed. But she made a very deep curtsey to them, and as she rose, Lady Oldhall caught something very familiar in her face.

Oh, she was Chinese, there was no doubt about it. But to her expressions, the tilt of her head, her person entire, there was a fond echo of one of Lady Oldhall's oldest friends. "Gussie," she said. "It's Gussie to the life," before she could contain herself. "The same look, the same manner."

"Oh," Nigel said. "I did not tell you, did I? My wife's mother was the former Miss Augusta Bentworth."

"My dear," Lady Oldhall said, and in the smile the girl gave her, she recognized even more of her friend. "Oh, my dear child. It was the fondest wish of your mother and I that our children should unite someday. And now it has come true."

ABOUT THE AUTHOR

Sarah A. Hoyt was born in Portugal more years ago than she's comfortable admitting. She currently lives in Colorado with her husband, teen sons and a clowder of various-size cats. She's never been to China, but she'd like to visit someday. Around four dozen—at last count—of her short stories have been published in magazines such as *Weird Tales, Analog, Asimov's* and *Amazing,* as well as various anthologies. *Ill Met by Moonlight,* the first book of her Shakespearean fantasy trilogy, was a finalist for the Mythopoeic Award. Sarah is also working on a contemporary fantasy series starting with *Draw One in the Dark,* and—as Sarah D'Almeida—is in the midst of a Musketeers' Mystery series starting with *Death of a Musketeer.* Her website is http://sarahahoyt.com/.